Jack Smith

Enjoy Irene

RONG ETCHA

RONG ETCHA

(Just Listen)

Jack M. Smith

Writers Club Press
San Jose New York Lincoln Shanghai

Rong Etcha
(Just Listen)

Writers Club Press
an imprint of iUniverse, Inc.

For information address:
iUniverse, Inc.
5220 S. 16th St., Suite 200
Lincoln, NE 68512
www.iuniverse.com

ISBN: 0-595-23171-3

Printed in the United States of America

Contents

Part III   ILLIUNE'S RETURN

Part IV   THE CALL

PART I

THE SEREPEIN

The Screpein of Nan Madol

CHAPTER 1

The soft, cool, sea-tainted breeze rustled the leaves of the bread-fruit and square-nut trees. Except for the washing of the many shells by the restless water, there was no sound. Palm trees bowed gracefully to one another as they yielded to the pressure of the changing wind. Occasionally a coconut crab would leave his home to search for a meal among the fallen nuts beneath the palms. Mangrove flowers and plumeria perfumed the air. In the open areas, the hybiscus blossoms shone bright and fresh in the green foliage. When the air stilled in the Island's growth, the fragrance of the white ginger added a spicy sweetness, which seemed to filter through all.

One would not need to hunger. Banana plants laden with fruit of all ages of growth crowded in among the papaya and mango trees, which grew in and among the tall graceful palms. No one had worked here for copra. No sign of living man could be seen.

All this flitted through the mind of Illiune as he looked around the small island on which he now stood. He need not fear for lack of food. A protection from the typhoons and squalls was what he felt most necessary, as it was that time of year. It was for this, a place of refuge from tropical storms, that Illiune was searching. He wore only the ragged lava lava, but was not cold. The air was sweet, warm, and moist and would stay that way until the storms came. Illiune feared them. He had reason. A typhoon had thrown the outrigger onto the coral and his father had been lost to the sea. Illiune fought back the tears as his throat tightened. He must not think of it now. He must find shelter.

The Island was not large. One could walk around its shore in, perhaps, an hour. Illiune had nearly circled the small atoll when he found what he was looking for. It was a large square-nut tree, which had an enormous trunk rising out of the coral sand about four feet. It grew outward towards the sea and then curved back toward the inner island. The broad curve of the trunk was nearly twice his height in width and Illiune found he could stand upright within the circle of the trunk. It was what he needed. He could trim and shape the upper limbs so they could be covered with thatch from the pandanus trees, which lined the island on the windward side. From here, too, he could look out beyond the reef where he hoped help would come. Illiune found the large square-nut tree about mid-day. The air was quite warm as he climbed up into his tree house and stretched out full length in the protective circle of the trunk. While lying there, he thought back on the past few days. How strange life had become to him. He was lost, alone and fatherless—a castaway. He recalled clearly the beginning of the tragic fishing trip, the typhoon, the storm squall, the sharks and being saved by the dolphins. He sat upright and looked around hoping it was a dream. It was no dream…it was reality. Illiune would miss his father most. The ache of loneliness and grief was constant.

When Illiune and his father left their village in the outrigger, they hoped to return in the evening with fish enough for themselves and a few to sell. His father was a fisherman. It was his life and as Illiune grew up, he too, learned to love the sea and the thrill of crossing the reef for sailfish, tuna, marlin and skipjack. Whatever the fish, Illiune always felt an excitement that was never satisfied. He seemed happier or experienced most joy when he was fishing on the sea or diving in its water for shells.

They never went unprepared. Extra lines and hooks were acquired by trading fish. Barter was best, as money was so difficult to keep. They took green coconuts for fresh water as well as bananas and papaya. Illiune's grandmother made them small sweet-cakes from breadfruit, sugar cane and coconut milk. In a basket were several round, flat stones which were used to sink their lines to the bottom. The flying fish were kept alive and fresh in a woven basket, which hung over the side of the outrigger. They were well prepared for a day's fishing.

Illiune's father occasionally looked off into the distance and a slight expression of concern caused the boy to look also. At first he saw nothing. Within an hour, however, every breath of breeze died away and off to the south, a cloud of blackness emerged. Their home island could be seen to the northwest and the reef that surrounded it resembled a white line between them and their little village. As the cloud of darkness grew in size, Illiune's father turned the outrigger around and handed the boy a paddle. The sail was of no use in the still air and after taking it down, his father also took a paddle and the boy felt a surge of desperation as the speed of their craft increased.

The cloud continued to grow in size and as it approached them, seemed to lift itself up on a single leg. A deathly calm surrounded Illiune and his father when the great dark cloud by-passed them to the west. The island and reef were consumed in the blackness of the typhoon and when the leg of the giant cloud appeared to have missed them, it suddenly whipped out and bore down on their small outrigger in vengeance.

When the typhoon struck, it was merciless. They were driven out from their home island and because of the darkness caused by the torrential rains, and later by the night itself, Illiune's father had no idea where they were. When the storm broke and the water calmed, the sun shone on a strange world to the two in the boat. They had miraculously survived the typhoon, although their outrigger was severely damaged. The beauty of the sea returned, but only for a short time. In the far distance a gray-blue smudge appeared which Illiune's father identified as an island. A reef outside the island was clearly seen just moments before a destructive squall drove them savagely toward the strange land. Illiune remembered only brief moments during the chilling downpour and lashing winds. The outrigger, weakened by the typhoon, filled with water. They could not bail. Both hands were needed to hold on. When the large wave lifted and smashed them on the coral, Illiune saw his father thrown head-first out of the outrigger.

Illiune remembered no more until he awoke in the water. The poles and lines from the outrigger had tangled around him and kept him from sinking. How long he had been in the sea, he did not know. As the squall came, so it went and calm returned. Illiune was very tired, but not cold. He did not try to swim or untangle himself from the maze of lashings. He was weary and perhaps numbed by what he had experienced. Hanging in the entanglement, he tried to consider where he was and what chance there might be of getting to land safely. He would have visitors from the sea. When they would appear was the question. Thoughts of fear and expectancy filled Illiune with dread.

In time, something caught his eye and a sharp, cold tremor stiffened his spine. He hoped his eyes were playing tricks, but he knew they were not. He half whispered in dread, "Bako!" (Shark). They came in pairs. "Unusual," Illiune thought. He had never been in a situation like this before. His people never deliberately killed sharks. They felt sharks would not harm them if they did not harm the sharks. Illiune had been taught this, but did not believe it. He had reason! He had seen what sharks could do when excited and hungry. His skin felt cold in the warm waters. His legs were like stones. He could only watch, wait and fear.

Illiune recalled in horror the time when he and another boy were playing near an area where the foreign soldiers dumped waste from their kitchen. The splashing and fighting of the sharks as they tore at the refuse fascinated the boys. They crowded close to the edge of the high bank, the boy lost his footing and slipped over. Illiune saw the boiling water and, horrified, watched as the great teeth and jaws crushed the life from the boy and the water became red with blood.

Illiune felt like splashing and kicking and screaming, but knew it would only attract the sharks and quicken his end. They could smell a strange promise of a meal in the water, but would mill around until they found what they were searching for. In the open sea they seldom attacked immediately. Forming a circle around him they moved slowly inward. He felt the first contact when a shark's sandpaper tail rubbed along his thigh. No damage was done, but the sharks became braver, as if the first to touch had signaled the feat to the others. Illiune had heard many times that one who lived by the sea may die by the sea, but now it was a reality. The thought of being torn and eaten by the sharks terrified him. The circle became smaller as the sharks edged in. One rubbed the lower part of his leg and another nibbled at a toe. Illiune screamed and kicked and the circle exploded into a wider ring momentarily. They came back. He was sure his time had come. He wanted to be brave, but facing death like this, to be eaten alive while choking and drowning, filled him with extreme horror. Illiune looked up to the sky and closed his eyes, as the first shark fastened its jaws onto his leg.

He remembered his feeling of complete helplessness and resign when the shark began pulling heavily on his leg. Illiune recalled faintly the flashing, foaming streaks of blue, black and white as he was released from the jaws of death. The water around him became a swirling mass of bodies. He was being pushed forward, backward, round and round in the foaming blue-white water, but still held fast by the outrigger gear, and he was moving. After a time he realized that he was not being pushed to and fro, but in a general direction. It was the turning of the mass that gave him the sensation of changing direction.

The sharks had gone. Surrounding Illiune was a school of dolphins, which seemed to take turns propelling him. Those not involved in pushing, were jumping and diving, creating a constant shield about him. When it was possible to look ahead, Illiune realized the dolphins were pushing him toward an island's reef. While propelling the boy, the dolphins made strange whistling sounds as they surfaced to breathe. At times, Illiune thought they were trying to speak to him. Their voices changed from high shrill wails to low soothing sounds. The boy sensed a strange feeling of comfort and companionship, almost that of being one with the warm blooded, air breathing creatures, which were steadily carrying him to safety. As they moved about him, within inches at times, yet not touching him, Illiune could clearly see their size as about that of himself. They were not large like whales or sharks. They often came up very close to him and looked into his face. When they did this, Illiune saw them not as sea animals, but as humans. Their eyes and face appeared friendly and intelligent. Sometimes, he thought they smiled and their movements were graceful and sure.

Studying the dolphins became a fantasy to Illiune. Somewhere in the depth of recall, a thought fleetingly entered his mind that they were one like him and he was one of them. He was so absorbed in nostalgic recollection that he did not hear the sound of waves breaking over the reef. It was when his feet touched the coral that Illiune aroused to reality. He drew his feet upward with the returning horror of the sharks. As he felt the tightening sensation of fear, he saw the varicolored coral and knew he was over the reef.

CHAPTER 2

Quiet water surrounded Illiune as he found footing in the coral sand inside the barrier. He struggled to free himself from the mass of ropes and poles that had been his security in the savage sea. Unwinding from the remains of the outrigger was not an easy task. Illiune realized his weakness when he tried to walk toward a tiny atoll on the reef. It was a slightly raised area on which two square-nut trees had taken root and were now large enough to offer shelter from the sun and the sea. Several times he stumbled and once fell into the water, which was about knee deep. He felt no pain anywhere, only a pressing sensation of wanting to lie down and sleep.

Illiune knew it was morning when he awoke. He had been sleeping where he fell between the nut trees in the soft white sand. The breeze was blowing inland toward the small island and the sun was in the opposite sky. Illiune felt pangs of hunger, for he had not eaten for two days or longer; he could not remember. Staying on the tiny atoll would not relieve his hunger. Illiune tried to struggle to his feet, when he realized that his leg was swollen and throbbing where the shark had bitten him. He had not noticed the pain while in the water. It was his lower leg, between the knee and foot. The shark teeth had cut like many knife blades and the lacerated area was oozing a watery substance and blood. Fear gripped Illiune as he considered his leg and then looked over the water to the island.

He needed food for strength and medicine for his leg. His hunger was momentarily forgotten as he studied the water of the lagoon in search for the higher coral. Black-tip sharks were often found feeding within the reef. His injured leg would call them and, although they were not so large as the Blue, they seemed to strike more eagerly. Illiune's friends, the dolphins, were gone. He did not know when they left him, but wished for them again.

His eyes, though young in years, were keen with wisdom of the sea. It seemed to Illiune that a ridge of coral sand rose to form a bridge to the island, beginning perhaps two hundred feet from where he was standing. The tide was receding and the currents in the water were encouraging to Illiune. He could work his way along the reef and walk in on the higher sand. When he stepped toward the water on his injured leg, he understood how serious his wound was. The leg would not hold him and he fell sideways on the sand.

In desperation he rolled over and studied the two small trees on the reef. After a time he saw a limb which might serve a crutch, if he could get it down. Crawling over to the square-nut tree. Illiune pulled himself up by the trunk. Stretching on his good leg, he reached the limb and broke it off. He stripped away the small branches and then broke off the tops about six inches above the fork. It made a crude crutch, but not unlike those used by island people. Illiune placed the forked end under his arm on the injured side and began hobbling over the reef to the sand spit. The receding water exposed a long neck of coral sand leading from the reef to the island. This unexpected pathway encouraged Illiune and gave him renewed strength in his struggle to reach the island.

His first thought was food as he approached the land and hobbled up the glimmering white beach and under the foliage of the tropical island growth. The crutch he had made was neither sharp enough nor strong enough to use to open the husk of a coconut. He could see the many palms long before he reached the island. There would be nuts on the ground after the typhoon. He let his eyes search the water's edge for a piece of driftwood that he might use. He found what he needed on the sand, wedged behind the thick roots of a mangrove tree. The stick was about waist high in length and white with washing. One end was pointed by wearing in and among the long, strange, black rocks. Working his way carefully, he picked up the stick and struggled to the bank and set the stick, pointed end up, in the ground. He then leaned it over and wedged it in a cleft of a large tree root. Finding a coconut was no problem. The ground under the trees was littered with nuts of varying size and ripeness. Some had rooted where they lay and some were green and tender. Illiune quickly chose a ripe one and ripped the husk off on the pointed stick. Opening the inner nut required finding a rock on which to break the shell. He picked up his crutch and hobbled over to the bank and slid down onto the soft, damp sand. While deciding where to break the nut, he noticed a piece of rock that had begun to flake off where two lay together. Nearby he found an oblong stone, which could be used as a hammer. Tapping gently at the broken area, Illiune worked carefully. The black rock was hard, very hard. Striking lightly made a ringing in the silent surroundings. After several min-utes of patient tapping, the sliver suddenly dropped into the sand. He eagerly scooped it up and examined it. The end was pointed and one side of the rock was sharp. It could be used for a knife. Illiune inserted the pointed end into the coconut and twisted out the meat from the stem. He drank the sweet milk and then broke the nut open by striking it against a larger rock. He struck it several times as he turned the nut, to loose the meat from within the shell. He increased the strength of the blow and the nut cracked open and the thick, white meat dropped free.

Illiune ate the nutmeat ravenously. It was tender and sweet. By the time he had finished he realized the pain in his leg was becoming more acute and throbbed with each beat of his heart. He knew his wound needed care. Gathering up his crutch and stone knife, he began struggling into the dense growth. He found what he was looking for in an open area not far from the island's edge. It was a young banana plant, leaning outward toward the light. Moving painfully over to the trunk he began cutting at the lower stalk with his crude knife. After working for a short while he was able to break the plant over by pushing above the sliced area. Sitting down beside the stalk, Illiune dug out the soft white pulp and spread it thickly over the injured area of his leg. He covered it well, wrapped it with the green leaves of the banana plant and secured it with vines.

Many hours in the sea and the wound on his leg had drained Illiune of more than strength. The coconut did not quench his thirst and he needed water. The island was too small and low to have a running stream or spring. He would need green coconuts. His injured leg prevented him from climbing a tree even though they could be seen in great numbers. Searching the ground he found three fresh, green nuts torn loose by the wind. Picking one up, he began cutting away the soft, immature husk from one end. When the bright green shell appeared he inserted the point of the knife and cut out a small piece. He lifted the nut and drank the water greedily. It was fresh and cool. It was "Yo, inenen yo", (good, very good). He picked up the second nut and opened it and drank the water. After drinking from the third, he dug out the soft, pale jelly from inside the nut and ate it.

Having found both food and water, Illiune again became drowsy. The throb and pain in his leg told him he should rest. The island floor was soft and the air warm and Illiune was soon fast asleep. He dreamed of strange sounds and those of the dolphins that faded away in time. It was morning again when he awoke. Sitting up, he rubbed his eyes and then slowly stood to his feet. He had forgotten about his injured leg until he was standing. The pain soon let him know of his infirmity, but the constant throbbing had stopped and by putting most of his weight on his good leg, the pain was less severe.

He picked up his crutch and knife and went out to the edge of the island, and struggled down to the coral sand. There was a rippling in the water just off shore and Illiune thought he heard low whistling sounds. As he stopped and listened more intently the sounds ceased. The ripples moved outward toward the reef and a calm settled over the waters of the lagoon. He began hobbling along the water's edge near the bank. Picking his way carefully over the sand and through the strange black rocks, he found a sea urchin under a large piece of dead coral. He scraped it out with his crutch, picked it up and broke it open on a rock. It tasted good and a few moments later he found and ate another. Still working his way slowly in and around the rocks, he saw on a branch of a fallen pandanus tree a blue piece of cloth. The material was like that used for sails. Illiune untangled the piece of cloth from the limb and turned it over and around. It was faded blue and threadbare, but could be used as a lava lava. He was not accustomed to being nearly naked. It was all right when he was a little boy, but a young man of seventeen wore a covering over the lower part of his body. His had been torn to shreds in the sea. Sometimes on the outrigger he would lay his lava lava aside to dive for shells or pearl oysters or fish. Still, he felt awkward without a covering.

Illiune could not explore, as he wanted, because of the pain in his leg. He also needed more food and water. The two urchins only increased his appetite. He again gathered some green coconuts, drank the fresh water, and peeled out the soft jelly-like meat. He would have searched for some bananas or papaya, but his leg forced him to lie down and rest. The warm, sweet breeze sifting through the foliage and whispering softly, soon put him to sleep.

Again he dreamed of strange crying and moaning and the wailing cry of dolphins. They were so loud and real that several times he stirred and almost wakened. When he awoke he knew he had slept through the night again. The air was cool, quite cool, and the breeze was blowing inland from the sea. Hunger brought him to his feet, and he stood with less pain in his leg. He smiled to himself and murmured, "Mwow, mwow," (Good, good). With the cumbersome crutch, Illiune moved slowly through the tropical forest. A short search brought him to a stand of papaya trees, on which several ripe fruits were hanging. They were young trees and the fruit hung low and easy to reach. He ate one ripe papaya and taking another in his hand, he again resumed his exploring. The island was small and soon he was nearly back where he had waded in from the surf. Here he found the large, odd shaped tree, suitable for protection.

CHAPTER 3

*I*lliune worked on his tree house anxiously. A squall might come and they seldom gave warning. The short, warm showers, which occurred almost daily, were no problem; if anything they were welcomed. They gave him the opportunity to bathe. Sometimes he caught some of the fresh water in large, green leaves for drinking. The bone chilling squalls were different. They came with strong winds and often heavy rain, cold and penetrating. With his knife of stone he cut the long leaf fronds from the pandanus tree that had blown down in the storm. He carried several bundles to the square-nut tree. His next excursion was in search of vines to tie the pandanus thatch to the overhead limbs above his "house". The work was not strange to Illiune. He had helped replace several roofs with pandanus fronds. Laid on the supporting structure in several layers, the thatch shed the rain and protected against the savage heat from the tropical sun on clear days. By late afternoon his house was well covered and, although he was exhausted and felt the pain returning to his leg, he went in search of food. He had walked only a few steps when he stopped, turned around and viewed his new home. Another faint smile appeared on his face and he again spoke low but audibly, "Mwow, E Pan Khola Munga," (Good, I am going to eat). Hearing himself speak, he glanced around hurriedly and then smiled. He felt a little foolish for talking to no one.

He found food quickly and without much walking. Many coconuts were scattered on the ground and he also came upon a banana tree with ripe fruit. He recognized the variety and again spoke aloud, "Lacatan, inenen yo". It was one of the better types for eating fresh, even though they were small. He pulled off several bananas and picked up a ripe coconut and turned back toward his "home". He would eat fruit again tonight, but tomorrow he would search for fish or shellfish in the lagoon or on the reef. Before darkness crowded in, Illiune gathered up several armloads of drier leaves beneath the breadfruit and square-nut trees. Sometimes they were friendly to lie in if a squall came.

His bed looked comfortable and inviting when Illiune spread the leaves and lay down. The sweet scented breeze, blowing outward toward the reef was warm and soothing, but sleep did not come easily that night. The moon was bright and the stars twinkled in the blackness overhead. Fish of many kinds made splashes and ripples in the still waters of the lagoon. He could plainly see the white line of the reef in the brightness of the moonlight. Something seemed to draw and hold his attention to the water as he studied the currents intently. He then could hear the crying and wailing of the dolphins far away.

Listening to the whispers of his friends required great effort. Some inner sense seemed to tell Illiune that they were calling to him, they needed him, and they were pleading with him. He considered calling out to them, but as he started to answer, a stronger voice within him whispered, "Rong etcha," (Just listen). The voices of the dolphins seemed to fade away into the pounding of the distant waves on the reef. Illiune quickly arose from his bed and lowered himself to the island floor. The pounding of the surf stopped and it was then that he realized it was the beating of his heart. He ran quickly to the shore and looked out upon the glimmering waters of the lagoon. Straining to listen, he raised his arm as if to wave and then he could see the water churn near the reef and the faint cry of the dolphins as they swam out to sea.

Standing on the wave washed sand, Illiune gazed outward. For a while all was still. Not a sound penetrated the blackness of the island. As he turned toward his tree home, the breeze from the outer reef began to whisper in the palms. The bed of leaves was comforting Illiune, but sleep was slow in coming. Darkness of the island did not frighten him, but he feared he might dream and the dream, he knew, would be strange and terrifying. Never in his young life had he felt so alone or so stirred by his subconscious. These thoughts began tumbling in Illiune's mind when the first soul-tearing moans and screams shattered the stillness of the tropical night!

Paralysis gripped Illiune. This was not a dream! He did not rise up, nor did he move. He was waiting for, yet dreading, and the next outburst of screams. Screams from what? Moments later they pierced the air again and continued for several minutes. The dreadful moaning and screaming then stopped or gave way to high-pitched wailing. This wailing Illiune knew he had heard before. It was the death wailers, like those in his village at a death and burial. He was sure of the wailing sound, but was cold with horror as he realized no people were here—that he was alone. The wailing permeated the island, echoing and drifting and dying. After, perhaps an hour, during which Illiune lay stone still in the leaves, the wailings were joined by moanings for brief a moment, and then all ceased. The island was again enclosed in stillness. He strained to hear the foot beats of the soul spirits coming for him, as they might do in his village. They did not come. Instead he began to hear shrill voices of the dolphins. As they approached the island, their voices increased in volume until Illiune could lay still no longer, but jumped out of the tree house and ran to the shore and far out into the water. He wanted to cry out to the dolphins to take him away from this place of horror, but as he opened his lips to cry out, another voice whispered, "Nununla, rong etcha," (Be quiet, just listen).

He stood motionless, watching and listening. The distant rippling and splashing of water was unnatural. The voices of the dolphins increased in volume as they seemed to strain in motion—and then all was silent. Illiune listened. He waded out further in the friendly water. He wanted to be with the dolphins, where no spirits could get him, but the dolphins were gone. Wading hesitantly back to shore, Illiune felt lost. He had no desire to return to his bed in the tree. The night was far from over, that he knew, but it was dark under the blanket of trees. Illiune feared the island's blackness now, for suddenly, this island which seemed to offer so much toward his keeping and hoping and living, had for the boy this night, become the "Island of the Dead".

Standing at the water's edge gave no release to his fears. He was weighing, in his subconscious, the meaning of it all. He could not escape from his situation immediately. Sharks had attacked him and yet he lived. In the world of emptiness he had all he needed. He was not alone, he had the dolphins. His leg had been seriously torn, but was now nearly well. After considering these many strange happenings, Illiune felt a tiny tremor of shame. Turning quickly, he walked to the shore and climbed back into his home and nestled down in the warm leaves. Before long he was tumbling to sleep.

CHAPTER 4

*I*lliune dreamed of his village life. His mother had died soon after his birth and his grandmother, the mother of his father, cared for him. She was the only mother Illiune ever knew. Many times the other children would ask him about his mother. Illiune grew to resent the questioning. His only real companionship was with his father. His grandmother spent all her time gathering wood or leaves or weaving pretty trays or baskets to sell at the markets. Sometimes, he would help her gather leaves early in the morning, when the air was cool. When the sun came up, the village grew stifling with heat and no one ventured forth to work. They would go into the cooking hut and lie on the boards under the pandanus roof to keep comfortable. Many times Illiune's grandmother baked small sweetcakes for him and his father. Sometimes, she would make breads boiled in coconut oil. Illiune remembered the many things she would do for him and his father, but he knew she expected something in return. His father always allowed her to choose the fish she wanted before anyone else could buy. She received money from his father. Illiune never resented his grandmother. He felt warm toward her, but he often longed for a mother, like other boys had.

When he was older, Illiune spent nearly all his time with his father. During the days of fishing they were together. When the weather was too stormy for fishing, they would go to the hills where they had a piece of land, and cut brush or vines to open new areas for crops. Often they carried young sprouted coconuts or pineapple starts, or papaya seedlings to plant for future use. In all his young life, Illiune never knew hunger or cold and yet he never felt happy. He had no friends in the village. The only comfort he ever experienced was his association with his father and grandmother. His grandmother was too busy or too old to play games like children enjoyed. His father was always near, except those nights when he went away alone to the gatherings where sukow was pounded.

During those nights Illiune felt dejected. When he asked his father where he was going his father just said, "to pound". That was a strange answer. Illiune decided to follow his father one evening. He kept out of sight in the shadows of the trail as his father made his way out from the village. He soon came to a large open gathering house where several men were already sitting around. Before reaching the large, thatch roofed place, Illiune could hear the noise of stones striking against stone and often muffled. As he watched from a distance he saw his father go in and sit down on the floor with the other men. After a while the men near the large rock in the center said something Illiune could not hear, but two men got up and exchanged places with them and began pounding as the two before them had done. Illiune worked his way around until he could see more clearly. The men had a rock in their hands and were beating some roots into a pulp on the large hollow stone. Sometimes someone would add a little water to the pulp. In time another man came in with a piece of green bark skinned off a live tree of some kind. Laying the green bark down with the inside up, the two men who were pounding placed some of the beaten pulp on the bark. Another man came up and two of them wrapped the pulp in the green bark and began to twist it. One of the men who had been pounding came over with a half coconut shell and held it below the pulp-filled bark. As the men twisted the bark, a wet, slimy mixture dripped down into the shell. When it was about half full, the man holding it put it to his mouth and drank a swallow of the liquid. Illiune watched him, fascinated. The man grimaced in distaste, spit several times, and then handed the shell to the next man. Each man in the room took a swallow of the liquid and made an ugly face and spit, just as the first fellow had done. Illiune thought it was quite strange that men would drink something that tasted that bad. He did not understand the effect of sukow. He never knew a woman to drink it. Sometimes, they would go with their husband and just sit quietly all night, until early morning to help their husbands find their way back home. Illiune knew his father came home late in the morning of the next day and sometimes he would sleep until afternoon.

Illiune did not play with the other children in the village. From the time he was old enough to go outside by himself, most children made fun of his hands and feet. His were different from others. His fingers and toes were fastened together by a thin skin. He could do almost everything others did, but when he opened his hands they looked strange. The village children called him "Fish boy" because his hands, when outspread, looked more like fish fins than hands. Even when he was older and could out-swim any others of the village he was still an outcast. Perhaps this was the reason Illiune turned to the sea for companionship. He practiced swimming for hours under all conditions. When he was the best at swimming he would practice diving, not fancy diving like some boys did from a high cliff into a pool, but deep diving over the reef. He would practice holding his breath until he nearly burst and then come up for air and try again. In time he learned to dive for depth and it was while doing this that he found the black coral. Some of his people had remembered when their better divers would gather it. It was regarded highly by visitors on the large boats. He could sell a black coral of three feet in height for thirty American dollars, an enormous sum in his village. No one else could dive for the black coral with Illiune. The other boys would not put forth the effort to become good divers. In time, Illiune's father was one of the most respected men of the village because of the black coral and the money it could be traded for, but Illiune always felt he was an outcast. His ability to swim and dive seemed only to make the other boys jealous and they would often tease him the more. All this did Illiune recall during his first sleep in the tree house nestled down among the leaves.

He was awakened by the sound of the howling wind and drenching rain. Flashes of lightning occasionally illuminated the island. Illiune feared lightning with its thunderous booms. The squall came unexpectedly and went on. The winds ceased. Only the dripping of water from the upper foliage to that below could be heard. When Illiune looked out from his bed he could see the golden-pink rays of the dawn creeping out of the sea to the east. The night was over and with a new day would come light and the end of darkness. The heavy rain seemed to refresh Illiune and as he rose from his bed he murmured, "Mweir, mwow," (Rain, good).

This was the day that he promised himself he would go out to find fish for food. Fruit was good but he needed meat for strength. As Illiune reached the water's edge he sat down and removed the bandage from his leg. He looked carefully at the wounded area and then touched it with his fingers lightly. He was pleased that it did not pain him now. Wading in the water of the lagoon would be good for the lacerated flesh and then he would lie down on the sand and let the sun dry and seal the many small cuts.

Illiune walked along the shore until he found a long, straight stick he could use for a spear. Picking it up he sharpened the small end with his stone knife. It was tedious work as the limb would give before the knife and the blade was not sharp like steel. However, in time Illiune was satisfied and stepped into the water and began walking out toward the reef on the same coral spit he came in on. Thinking about it was strange. It seemed to Illiune so long ago and yet he knew it had been only a few days.

The water was receding as the tide went out, but the coral spit was still about one to two feet underwater. Twice within a few minutes

Illiune saw octopus squirt an orange-brown coloring into the water in front of him and then could see them making a dive for their hole in the bottom of the lagoon. He was not interested in octopus as he had no fire. He liked them boiled, but not raw like some folks. He preferred reef fish or urchins and sometimes would eat raw clams. The many fish around him surprised Illiune. He had never seen so many before and they did not seem to fear him. Reaching an area of coral near the reef he saw many fish about the size of his foot in length. He tried spearing some, but his spear was not sharp enough. He then turned it around and using the larger end as a club, he struck one fish, which was struggling in the coral with half its body exposed. The fish flopped over on its side and began flipping its tail. Illiune picked it up and bit it in the head and it immediately stopped struggling. Holding the fish in his left hand he walked a few steps and killed another. Two would be enough, and then Illiune walked over to the reef and looked out on the broad expanse of sea. The day was clear and calm, but no land showed on the horizon. After looking for some time, Illiune decided to go over to the small nut trees on the reef where he had spent his first night after his trial at sea.

As he approached the trees he saw something protruding out from the foliage. He was startled for a moment and stopped about fifty feet from the trees to look more keenly. Lying partially hidden under the leaves was an outrigger! Illiune could scarcely believe his eyes. He wanted to run to the boat and call out for help, but he was too proud. He knew someone had pulled the boat up under the shade so the sun would not crack the wood. Many people did this. Whoever owned the boat was probably sleeping or fishing somewhere down the reef. Making his way quietly and carefully toward the trees, he kept his eyes moving about. He stopped walking and waited. The outrigger looked to be in good condition. He wondered if the main hull was as sound. Working his way slowly to within ten feet of the boat, Illiune could not see anyone. "Strange", he thought. He could not see any trace of footsteps near the boat, or in the sand.

Walking up closer he noticed the outrigger was much wider and longer than others he had seen. On the bow was a carved head of a young woman. The paddles were tied under the cross braces. "Unusual", Illiune murmured. If one came in with paddles, he would need it free to go out. There was also a long pole tied in the boat which could be used to propel the outrigger in shallow water. Walking around the boat quietly, Illiune looked for someone under the trees. He saw no one. It all seemed puzzling to him. He walked around the trees and let his eyes search the reef. But as before, he saw no one. The more he considered the condition of the outrigger and how it was placed under the foliage of the trees, the more perplexed Illiune became. Whoever came in the boat must have come at full tide or there would be some trace of footprints in the soft sand. Inside the reef there were no waves large enough to wash out tracks, so they could not be seen at all. It was possible that the one, or ones, who came in might have erased their footprints purposely. The more he thought about it, the more uncertain and curious Illiune became. An hour had slipped by when he realized he still had not eaten his fish and that he was nearly famished.

He walked over to the area of the trees and set down in the shade on a large slab of dead coral. Using his rock knife, Illiune ripped the skin of the fish and tore the white meat out and ate it. Reef fish were excellent either raw or cooked. The fish were thick and after eating both, he was satisfied. He turned his attention back to the outrigger. Somehow he was trying to make himself believe that the boat had just drifted over the reef and nestled in under the trees at high tide. He smiled at his own thought, but felt that a boat would be the most useful possession he could have. He could explore the lagoon and outer waters for other islands. It would be necessary to have a boat to get home, wherever that was. All his wishful thinking ended abruptly when he heard a call from out beyond the reef, a shrill, whistling call, which he knew was meant specially for him.

The dolphins were close to the reef and making shrill excited sounds. One would swim in slowly and talk to Illiune and then dive under to be replaced by another. They were trying to tell him something, but Illiune could not grasp the meaning. They changed their positions then and about ten dolphins rose up from the water in unison and lifting their flippers upward, came in toward Illiune with only their tails in the water. Just before striking the reef they made a low straining sound and then disappeared beneath the water. All was still for a time and no dolphins could be seen. Illiune stood transfixed by their unusual antics. He tried, but could not decipher their sounds or movements into any real meaning. As Illiune stood and waited and watched, he recalled the straining sound the dolphins made the night before. He also knew they were somewhere near this place on the reef. The more he thought of it the more he was sure the sounds were identical, but he could make no sense out of it. He wished he could talk to the dolphins. They could make everything clear. They might even show him the way home. Illiune thought a moment and then began wondering why the dolphins seemed to single him out. They saved him from the sea and had never been completely out of touch with him since. What they had just done in their act of unison was, Illiune realized, for him. They were trying to tell him something. At the height of his bewilderment, Illiune looked up and directly in front of him, not over twenty feet away, was a dolphin and in its beak was a large bush of red coral. The dolphin held the coral perfectly still and Illiune could see it was a large piece made up of two main branches. Then slowly turning sideways to the boy, the dolphin whistled softly and another dolphin came up, put its beak over one branch of the coral and they broke it apart. Illiune was fascinated at their actions. He watched carefully as the first dolphin came in and held the coral up and Illiune reached out his hand and took it. When he did the dolphin whistled shrilly as if excited or pleased. It then reared up out of the breakers and swam out toward the deeper area with only its powerful tail in the water.

Illiune stood spellbound with wonder. Why the dolphin had handed him the half coral he could not understand. He looked at it in his hand. He knew it was very valuable. Men on the big boats would pay hundreds of dollars for a piece of red coral this size. Illiune also realized that the dolphin had to dive very deep for it. Red coral grew around a thousand feet below the surface. It seemed useless for Illiune to try to understand what the dolphins were trying to tell him. He did not look out seaward again. The dolphins had gone.

CHAPTER 5

*A*fter his unexplainable visit with the dolphins, Illiune turned toward the sand spit and headed back to the island. He carried the branch of red coral in one hand and the stick in the other. He was so disturbed by recent happenings that his return to the island was accomplished in a trance-like state. Nothing seemed to make sense to Illiune. Unusual and mystifying incidents were continuing to confront the young man. He purposed to return to his tree house where he might ponder the many strange experiences of the past few days. The tide had ebbed and began to change before Illiune started back.

While walking on the reef or wading over the spit, he was so preoccupied by his thinking that he did not notice the school of black tipped sharks that accompanied him toward the island. When he was only thirty feet from the dry sand, one of the small sharks made a darting pass at his leg. Illiune saw the shark as it started in and met its pass with his stick. He did not injure the shark, but the splash caused the shark to turn away. It was then that Illiune saw the others milling. He stopped wading and watching them circle around him. For some unknown reason he had no fear of them. He struck the water with the stick and the sharks scampered out ten to twenty feet. Illiune smiled and continued wading toward the island.

When he reached his house, he carefully placed the red coral in the curve of the square-nut tree. He purposely placed it close to where he would be sleeping. Because it came from the dolphins, it seemed to offer him protection and security.

Although he had intended to rest his leg, Illiune did not feel like lying down. He decided, since it was still mid-morning, to explore the island more thoroughly. Taking his knife and stick he proceeded to walk back into the island depths, watching carefully for whatever he might find. As he continued his way through the dense tropical growth he thought again of the strange moaning and wailing of the previous night. After traveling some distance, Illiune was confronted with a rock wall about ten feet in height. The wall was made of the same strange rocks that lined the shore. Because of the dense growth on either side he could not see where the wall ended. Turning to his right, he followed along the wall to where the wall extended along the edge of the sand for about one hundred feet and then again made a square turn and led back toward the inner part of the island. Illiune walked all the way along the walls. The strange black rocks had been put there long ago because many large trees were growing over them. Without any feeling of fear, Illiune climbed up the wall and walked over it and back and then turned and walked out to the edge of the island, still on top of the large square area.

Something began stirring deep within his recall, something related to the old tales of his ancestors. Before he dared ponder more, he climbed down from the wall and waded out a few feet into the warm water. Looking along the island's edge he could see the strange black rocks continuing on beyond the wall both ways until they disappeared in the water. Illiune began to walk along the line of rocks until he came to the end and there they made a square turn and continued in a line along the back of the land. The line of rocks formed a square enclosing the round island.

The more Illiune searched and discovered, the more his memory kept bubbling. Illiune wondered if he might see land from the back side of the island. He would have given up the exploration and made his way back to his tree house except for the continued persistence of his memory. He looked around and above until he saw a coconut palm that might offer him a better view. He could climb now that his leg was not too painful and Illiune worked his way to the base of the tall tree and began to ascend.

It had been some time since Illiune climbed a tree like this, but he was sure and agile. He made no attempt to look around until he was safely perched among the fronds at the top. His view from there was excellent. He looked first over the island and out along the reef where he had been earlier in the day. He was surprised at how close it seemed now. He could see the square-nut trees and the end of the outrigger. Looking out on the sea he thought of his friends, the dolphins, and wondered if they were there.

He let his eyes move up the reef to the north where it faded into the blue. Allowing his gaze to continue to sweep around, he was sure he could see the outline of an island, or land far to the north, perhaps ten miles. This excited Illiune, and he continued to turn his head so that he could view everything possible. He had almost completed the circle when he saw to the south a small, low atoll on the reef.

Looking carefully, he could see a white cleft in the green foliage of the small island. He surmised that it was surrounded with mangrove except for that spot of bright coral sand. Because he could not see more of the island, he allowed his gaze to drop to the water between the island in the distance and where he now was sitting. There were areas where the water was quite shallow, but he also saw a long line of dark blue forming a strange crescent between the islands. He thought he would like to visit that little atoll, if he had a boat. His mind flashed back to the outrigger on the reef and he smiled to himself for wishing. Before he came down from the tree he twisted off a green nut, cut off the end and drank the cool water. Tucking his knife back into his lava lava he descended the palm and began making his way back toward the tree house.

Illiune was in no hurry as he walked among the varied trees and flowers. He needed time to think and, he thought, something more to think with. His nostalgic recalls did not register a satisfactory answer to his questioning. He realized some things were truths. He had a deep feeling of warmth toward the dolphins. They were more than friends. The island he was on was as close to paradise as one could desire. He had lost his father, but he had been saved by a miracle. These thoughts mingled in Illiune's mind as he worked his way among the tropical growth. Seeing the small island to the south interested Illiune for some reason he could not explain. He resolved within himself that the small atoll would be his first to explore, if he could find a way.

By the time Illiune had returned to his home in the tree, it was evening. The excitement of the day caused him to feel restless and because he was, he walked back into the island and gathered some bananas and papayas. He did not need many, only enough to ease the hunger, which would come later.

Illiune climbed up and into his home and laid down. He was not sleepy or tired. He was perplexed. So many times he thought, "If I could just understand the dolphins." His thinking of the dolphins caused him to turn and look at the piece of red coral. So many unbelievable things had happened to Illiune, he wondered if he were dreaming. He reached over and picked up the half coral. It was an extremely valuable specimen. In all his life he had never received something for nothing. In his village, he was made to work or he did not eat. Some boys were luckier if they had sisters. The sisters did most all the work while the brothers played. But not Illiune, he had no sisters. These simple recollections seemed foolish to Illiune as he recalled them and yet he could not free himself from what his subconscious told him. The dolphins saved him because they needed him. When he thought of this he felt a sudden flash of guilt and shame. After all the dolphins had done for him, was it possible that they had a need of him?

When darkness settled over the island, Illiune was lying in the bed of leaves. The happenings of the day were revolving in his mind. He was warm and comfortable and nearly free from pain. For the first time he was not hungry. The cool breeze from the outer sea stirred in the upper branches of the taller trees. Around him was a warm air, sweet with coconut and plumeria and Illiune dropped into dreamland. The long day filled with strange and exciting experiences caused Illiune to sleep soundly through the moaning wails and cries, which terrified him the night before. During the time of the strange crying, a heavy shower fell which helped to camouflage the horrifying sounds.

The strange voices, which occurred later that night, however, did not escape the ears of Illiune. It was the cry of the dolphins. They seemed so close that he could not believe his ears. He thought he heard them under the tree, but he knew that was impossible. The sounds they made were unlike any he had heard them make before. Illiune could hear the splashing of water above their voices, almost as if they were whispering. He sat still, listening. Just before their noises faded into the night, Illiune again heard that strange straining sound; then all was quiet. Though he laid awake for over an hour, there was not a whisper from the dolphins.

CHAPTER 6

$\mathcal{E}$ arly the next morning, before the sun had caused the sea in the east to take on its usual golden glow, Illiune was climbing down from his house. The morning activities had been planned the day before. He hoped to solve the mystery of the outrigger and have a visit with the dolphins. He also intended to have an early breakfast of fresh reef fish. Hurrying over to the edge of the water, Illiune picked up the stick he used to hit the fish and scare the shark. His knife was already tucked in the overlap of his lava lava. A mist lay over the lagoon; not heavy, but enough that it was difficult to see the reef. Walking out onto the coral spit, Illiune headed toward the area of the square-nut trees. He was most curious about the outrigger. There was no time to look for fish now and the water over the reef was too shallow for shark. It was when he was about fifty yards from the trees that he realized the outrigger was not there. Illiune did not want to believe it had just vanished. A lump suddenly tightened his throat and his eyes became wet with instant grief. He did not know how long he stood there, trying not to believe. He then walked slowly over to the place where the outrigger had been drawn up on the beach. He looked for tracks. There had to be some somewhere. It would have been next to impossible for someone to push the outrigger out without making tracks. Illiune looked in vain. There was no sign of any human and the boat was gone!

Many explanations occurred to him, but nothing could relieve him of a deep loss, even though the outrigger was not his. It had been his hope to escape, to go home. Illiune studied the area carefully. He wondered if perhaps the tide had lifted it off the sand so that it floated away during the night. It could have happened, but the breeze almost always blew toward the reef at night, unless a squall came.

Finally, in futility, he turned around and found his way back to the coral spit. Turning toward the island, Illiune was nearly overcome by grief. He forgot about eating and the dolphins. With a heavy heart and dejected spirit Illiune struggled back with tears flowing freely; tears he could not hold back.

By the time he returned to the island the morning sun was well above the sea in the east. It was that time of morning when the air was cool and fresh and the rays from the sun warmed the earth and gave bright color to all it touched. Had it not been that time of day, he would not have seen the red coral. It was lodged in some mangrove that touched the water when the tide was full. He stopped in surprise and disbelief. Perhaps it was imagination or a defect in his sight, but he was only a few feet from where it lay, bright red in the morning sun. In fear that it was only a mirage, Illiune moved slowly over and reached out and touched the lace top of the coral. Picking it up he stood bewildered, with tear still lingering on his cheeks. He wondered if it were the other half of the coral he had in his tree house. Did the dolphins place it there? He forgot, momentarily, the disappearance of the outrigger in his haste to get to his tree. Because of where he had found the coral lying in the mangrove, Illiune had to turn and walk around the beach a short distance before he found his usual place of walking in and out from his island home. He could not grasp reality for a time. Reaching his house he laid the coral on his bed and climbed up himself. It was then he realized he was not dreaming. He carefully lifted the two coral halves and fitted them together. There was no question, but they were two of the same!

The shock of changing from despondency and sorrow to renewed hope was almost beyond Illiune's understanding. He had heard the dolphins in the night. They seemed to be directly beneath him. He remembered that strange straining sound he had heard before and it came from the dolphins. Curiosity gripped Illiune. He studied the tree house and its location on the island and distance from the water. He noticed something different from earlier observation. He never came directly to his tree house from where it was nearest the shore. He always came in from one side. Illiune also realized that dolphins seldom left the water because of their sensitive skin. In anxious bewilderment he laid the coral on the bed and jumped hurriedly from the house to the ground. He ran over to the sand beach and around the edge of the mangrove to where he had found the second half of red coral. He stood there studying the location of the mangrove in relation to where the tree house was located. The tide was at low ebb and as Illiune walked up and parted the thick branches of the mangrove he gasped in astonishment. Hidden behind the dense foliage directly below his tree house was the outrigger, floating gently in a large pool of blue green water!

Illiune could not utter a sound. He was speechless with surprise and happiness. A strange thought welled up in him for a moment and although he did not understand what love was, his thought for the dolphins was, "E poka poka uk!" (I love you!). Slipping over the black rocks that formed the wall of the pool, Illiune stepped nearer to the outrigger because of the lack of light under the heavy growth. Looking upward he could see through the leaves the lower part of the square-nut tree, which made its large bend in the center and above the pool. Illiune purposed then to cut out the foliage so he could see the pool easily from above. Thinking of how it might be done, he longed for a machete, but of course, he had none. He would need to use his rock knife and mangrove was very hard and tough. Illiune then smiled to himself when he considered his intentions. "People are strange," he thought. He had an outrigger in a secret pool in a perfect location and was planning to change it.

Leaving the outrigger for only a short time was difficult for Illiune. Had it not been for his need of food, he would have stayed longer. However, when he was walking around the island in the sand looking for something, which would relieve his hunger, he was filled with an overflowing of joy. His situation was too mysterious to comprehend. The more he considered this, the more he knew it was all because of the dolphins. It was during this short walk that Illiune heard himself vowing to repay them.

Before the water flowed back into the lagoon, Illiune had gone out and came back with two reef fish. After eating he wanted something more. The events of the morning had whetted his appetite and because of his increased activities, his body required more food. He visited the papaya tree again and before returning to his house he gathered some bananas and coconuts. He considered taking a nap, but knew he could not sleep. Laying the food on a rock at the base of the tree he walked over to the water and around to the entrance to the pool. The tide was full and Illiune could see that the water was high enough to spill into the pool through two passages between the long black rocks. The early morning tide was higher and with some effort he could float the outrigger out of the pool. Remembering the small island south of him gave Illiune an idea. He would gather some food and leave early in the morning to explore the atoll. With that in mind he stepped down from the rocks and waded through the mangrove foliage to the beach. He spent the afternoon gathering more coconuts, green and ripe for food and water, some papayas and bananas. Because of the numerous fish he would have no problem eating well. He carried the food to the edge of the shore and stored it. By the time he had prepared for the morning adventure the sun had fallen behind the island and darkness began to creep in. Illiune crawled into his bed of leaves. His mind was dancing with expectancy of tomorrow's trip, when he drifted into the land of dreams.

That night the noises began with a high-pitched scream which ended in a dreadful wail. Just as the last notes trailed away the low moaning began. Illiune was so terrified the first night he heard them he could only shudder in the bed of leaves. Tonight he did not feel so completely horrified. He listened intently. The moan reminded him of a man who was injured critically in his village. Illiune was very small then, but he did not forget the sound. The man moaned and cried for about two hours and near the end the moans became weaker until he died. Illiune trembled with dread during the crying in the night. He recognized the sound as that of a dying man. In time, perhaps a half-hour, the moanings died away and the wailing began again. He recognized this sound also. It was that of wailers during a funeral. In a short time they, too, faded away and the darkness of the tropical night under the dense foliage seemed heavy with the unknown.

Illiune found himself straining to hear something in the blackness. He was wishing to hear a reassuring voice of a dolphin. When it came, it was so close that it startled him. The dolphin would protect him; it was on guard in the pool below his bed. The night was far from over when the wailing ceased and the blackness was forbidding. Illiune stayed in his bed of leaves and listened to the quiet whisperings of the dolphin. For the third time he wanted to speak to the dolphin, but again the voice came from somewhere that said, "Nununla, rong etcha". Whether it was the whispering breeze or the dolphin, the sounds with the warm, sweet surrounding air lulled Illiune to sleep.

CHAPTER 7

*R*ising with the early dawn was natural for Illiune. As a fisherman's boy, he was expected to wake with the light or tide. Today he purposed to rise with both to float the outrigger out of the pool at the time when the tide was full, and he had planned a long day of exploring. Anxious with excitement and anticipation Illiune dropped to the ground and hurried over to the island's edge and stepped into the warm water. Wading around to the mangrove he could see that the water of the lagoon was about one foot above the rocks. Pulling the lower limbs aside he stepped up over the edge and into the pool where the outrigger was floating free. Grasping the boat by its end, he floated it toward the lagoon. When the limbs of the mangrove caused the motion of the boat to cease, Illiune worked his way over to the lower branches and lifting them with one hand, he pushed the boat with the other. In a few moments it was floating free in the light of the early dawn.

Illiune inspected the boat from stem to stern as carefully as he could. He found it difficult to hide his pleasure. The craft was sound and expertly made. The binding cords were strong and tight and the outrigger secured with tough light poles. There was not a sign of damage to the hull. Again he saw that the outrigger was larger than most, both in length and width. The unusual shape puzzled Illiune. He drew the boat over to the bank where he had stored his provi-

- 39 -

sions. Before putting them in, he picked up a half shell of a coconut and dipped the water from rain and surf out of the hull. Laying the shell in the boat, he lifted the front and pulled it up on the sand. Going over to the island's edge he gathered his coconuts, carried them down to the outrigger and placed them in the bow. He then went to his tree house, gathered his papayas and bananas, tucked his knife into the waist of his lava lava and returned to the boat. He untied the pole, one paddle, and was ready to leave.

Although, already feeling hungry, his desire to get started was greater. He could eat later. Sliding the outrigger off the sand, he stepped into the hull and paddled out into the lagoon and around the island. Remembering the general direction of the small island he had seen from the palm tree, Illiune turned the outrigger parallel to the reef and moved out and away from the shore. He could not see the strange little atoll in the early dawn, but knew it would appear in the brightness of the sun, especially since he was traveling toward it. The water was mirror-like except when it was dimpled or ringed by feeding fish. There was little breeze and Illiune was pleased. Sometimes paddling an outrigger was difficult if a side wind were blowing. He thought of making a sail out of the pandanus leaves when he returned. He would need it to travel home.

The inward feeling of freedom caused an odd happiness within Illiune. While on the island with all its fruit and fish and house, he could not feel free. Sometimes he felt a prisoner because he was used to going out to sea, to be free from the land people. They called him "Fish-boy". He had learned to accept their cruelty and biting tongues but could not let them know how much he disliked the name. His life had been so full of the unexpected the last few days it was difficult to accept. On one hand he was a lost boy on an unknown, weird island of terrible sounds. On the other, he was now was the owner of a fine boat, a good home on an island of plenty and the best friends in the world, the dolphins. Here he was free from ridicule and unhappiness among people, but there was always the desire to return home. Illiune thought that strange, but could not brush the idea from his mind. Even the trip he was now making to the far away little island was in hope of getting some idea of how he might return to the village. Maybe someone lived on the island, if not, he would try exploring to the north the next time. One thing was certain: he was free to search, for he had a boat.

As Illiune moved slowly southward, he began noticing the dark blue of the lagoon and recalled the long crescent of deep water that seemed to connect the two islands. He decided to stay in this crescent or channel for some compelling reason. He would be safe in deeper water if the tide went out. Sometimes it was possible to become caught on the coral in unknown waters. After about an hour of travel the sun had risen in the east and Illiune could see the blue of the far off island. It was early yet. He knew he could spend the night safely, if for some reason he could not get back. With a good boat one could do many things.

The island slowly emerged out of a distance as Illiune continued his steady paddling. He could make out the foliage of the palm trees against the sky and as he approached, he was surprised by its size. It was much larger than it looked and the coral sand that seemed to split the island was almost a hundred feet in length. In another hour Illiune had reached the shore of the atoll and pulled his outrigger up on the sand. It was much nearer the reef than his island. Perhaps it formed part of the barrier on the ocean side. He noticed the area directly behind the long coral sand beach appeared open, as if no trees grew there. "Strange", he thought. Walking slowly up the beach he climbed upon the ridge that seemed to be the top of the bank. Looking over the crest, he was surprised to see a large depression lined with slime and mud, as if the great pond-like place had recently been filled with water, which had evaporated or filtered out through the sand. Illiune was sure the unusual pond of mud was created by the typhoon. It could have torn out the trees with ease and the terrible seas would have filled the hole with water. He could smell the stench of rotting vegetation and dead fish. The only water to be seen was a very small puddle in the center of the mud pond where a top of a mangrove tree was lying, still covered with foliage. Illiune turned from the place in relief. How terrible it would be to be caught in a foul smelling place like that. When turning to leave, he heard the crying whistle of a dolphin.

Looking quickly out on the lagoon he could see a boil of water in the deep crescent behind his outrigger. He stood there for a moment listening, but heard nothing. Again he heard a cry of a dolphin. He had never encountered them inside the reef during the daytime before, but he also realized he did not understand them. He hurried down from the ridge to the outrigger. He listened intently, but could hear nothing. He wondered why he could hear the dolphin from up on the ridge and not down where he had seen it in the water. Dolphins had helped him before many times and Illiune decided they wanted to lead him somewhere again.

He stepped over to the outrigger and pushed it off the beach, into the water. He seated himself in the stern, picked up his paddle and moved out to the dark water of the crescent. He paddled for a few moments, intending to circle the island and perhaps look for the dolphins, but to his surprise he was not moving. The current in the deep water was very strong and he was moving back to where he had beached his outrigger earlier. Illiune had seen many places with strange currents and he hesitated a moment or two, laid the paddle down in the boat and picked up the long pushing pole. Standing up, he proceeded to move out toward the deep water again. The outrigger moved out easily until it came to deep water and then its forward motion ceased. "Very strange", thought Illiune, but he could not use the pole in deep water, and the current forced the boat back. He would have to wait until the tide changed, before the current would allow him to leave the island. He beached the outrigger where he had left it before and pulled it up on the sand. Reaching into the boat he picked up a green coconut, cut off the husk and drank the water.

After his drink, he took a banana and peeled it while walking back up the beach to the ridge. Standing there he studied the currents in the water. He wondered how they could be so strong. When he looked, the water was absolutely quiet. There was no current of any kind. Illiune stood still, looking and pondering. He again heard a cry of a dolphin, but this time it seemed to come from behind him. He was bewildered. There was no question about the voice. What caused Illiune to be unusually astonished was the despairing sound of the cry. Most of the time the voices of the dolphins were soothing and reassuring. Once more he heard the pleading cry and then he was sure the sound came from the mud. He looked over the rotting muck with searching eyes and ears. He could see no movement nor detect any sound. When he was about to give up, his eyes fastened onto the area where the muddy water lay under the mangrove brush. Just as he stopped his movement, he heard again a weak cry and at that momement, saw a ripple in the water.

Illiune was shaken with doubt. He was sure he heard the dolphin cry from the hole of muck, but was it possible? Certainly nothing could be alive in that forbidding slime. Illiune became anxious to know. He raised his head to whistle for an answer, but again something said, "Rong etcha." He kept his eyes glued to the water beneath the foliage. Again he saw a movement of water. He had to go out there to see. If it were a dolphin, his life was indebted to them. If not, it must be one like him, a human. Illiune rushed down to the outrigger and picked out a paddle. It might aid him in the slimy hole. He ran back up to the ridge and dropped into the mud on the far side. At first the footing was not impassable. Although he sank above his ankles, he could keep moving out. It was when he worked down to the bottom of the hole about twenty feet from the mangrove that Illiune was forced to lie down and slide his body over the maggot infested mud, with the aid of the paddle. The stench was almost more than he could endure. He nearly retched when he first began to crawl and when he saw the decayed areas on the dolphin beneath the mangrove, Illiune did vomit and for a moment, he nearly lost consciousness.

The tail end of the dolphin was nearest to Illiune and when he was close enough, he reached out, took hold of its tail and dragged it toward him. His first pull only moved it about halfway from under the mangrove. Working his way backward in the mud, he again grasped the dolphin's tail and pulled it toward him. He continued this action until he was out of the slimy mess of decaying fish and rotting vegetation. The more he looked at the mud-encased dolphin, the more he wondered how it could still show life. As he moved it over the mud the dolphin uttered low crying sounds, which made Illiune think of a small child, sick with pain.

When the muck became thick enough to allow him to get to his hands and knees in a crawling position, the work became easier. It was then that Illiune could look down at the dolphin and the form of the creature seemed unusually strange. It was shaped like a dolphin at its lower end, but its upper portion was different. There seemed to be a neck and head, more like a human, but the sticky mud was thick and he could not see clearly enough to distinguish its features. Looking at the strange-thing nearly caused Illiune to be sick again. There were many places where the skin was torn and the flesh gouged out, revealing rotting tissue. He was careful to keep it from turning over. He knew if it did, it could not breathe. Before long, Illiune was in dryer mud, which allowed him to stand. Rising to his knees, he picked up the strange-thing by sliding one arm under the pectoral area and one under the upper area below the head. Lifting gently, he raised the creature from the muck and holding it close to his body, he stood upright. It did not weigh a great deal, but the footing was poor and Illiune stumbled several times as his feet seemed to stick in the soft, wet slime. He managed to reach the ridge with his burden, carried it down to the water and waded out about knee-deep. He knew if he were to help the poor sick strange-thing, he needed to wash the mud from its body. Kneeling down on one knee, he gently lowered it into the water. Removing his arm from below its lower body, he began to splash fresh seawater over its upper part, while still holding its head out of the water with his left arm behind its neck. Illiune could hear it crying with pain or hunger, or both, as he began to cleanse away the mud. As he washed the foul muck from the creature's lower body, he noticed the color was different from the mud on himself and the upper portions of the creature. It was a blue clay mixed with mud and much more difficult to remove. He wondered why the strange colored patches covered only the lower portions.

Illiune had been sick with the putrid odor of death and decay when he first glimpsed the dolphin-voiced creature. Now he was nearly sick with surprise and disbelief as he continued to wash the mud from its emaciated and deteriorating body. He wondered how it managed to stay alive as long as it had. The more he washed the poor creature, the more he saw the sordid condition of the skin. He had noticed earlier the areas on the lower body where patches of skin hung loose as if something had torn it. The removal of mud from the upper portion of the body also revealed blemishes and pockmarks in the skin, but the shape of body above the mid-section caused Illiune to stare in wonder. That part of the "strange-thing" he saw before him, from the waist up, was of human form!

Illiune was shaken in bewildered amazement. He had heard stories about such creatures, half fish and half-human, but only stories of myths or days of his ancestors. Never had he heard of anyone he knew who had seen an animal or fish of the sea like this. Illiune knew it could breathe air as did he. The more he cleaned it, the more the body resembled a young lady such as one might see in his village. The hair was long and as it drifted, slowly swishing in the clear water, it began to shine like black coral. The head and face were the most human of all. Emaciated as it was, Illiune could see the perfect teeth and the dark eyebrows against its light skin. From the neck down the body was pitted with holes, smaller at the base of the neck but larger near its abdomen.

As Illiune continued washing the "strange-thing", he lowered it more into the water until he was holding only the face above the surface. It would need food. The arms hung nearly lifeless. He wondered how he could leave the creature in order to get something for it to eat. The mud that still adherd to the body would have to remain for a time. He floated the creature to shore and left the body submerged with its head resting face up on the coral sand. Taking his spear stick, he ran quickly out into the surf near the reef to find a fish. He was gone but a few moments and returned with a small one. He took out his knife and peeled the skin off one side. He then cut a strip of white meat and raised the head of the creature so that he could place the meat in its mouth. He knew it must eat. Placing his finger on each side of the jaws, he forced the mouth open and then inserted the strip of meat. It was immediately spit out. Illiune was both discouraged and elated. It did not eat, but it did reveal life. He sat there in the sand holding its head wondering what he might do. Laying the head down once more on the sand, he stepped over to the outrigger and picked up one of the green coconuts. Opening the end, he went back and again picked up the head, held it steady and let the water drip onto the closed lips. In a few moments he saw the lips open a bit. A tongue appeared and licked the lips. Illiune smiled and said softly, "Yo" (good). As he continued to let the water drip, the lips and teeth parted and he let the water-fall into the mouth. He watched carefully for the first sign of a swallow. When it came, Illiune smiled again and whispered, "Menlau," (thank you). He fleetingly wondered why he said it, but was very anxious for this creature to show life and get well. After it had swallowed three times, Illiune put the nut down and picked up the strip of fish. Putting it first near the nose, he then touched it to the lips. The mouth opened immediately and he placed the strip in its mouth. It closed its mouth and began chewing. After swallowing, it opened its mouth again and Illiune was ready with another piece of meat. The creature did not eat even half the fish, but Illiune was satisfied. Later it could eat more.

Because he felt insecure here, Illiune decided to take the creature back to his island. By now, the sun was very warm and Illiune would have to get some green foliage to put over the creature for shade. He realized dolphins could not be in direct sunlight long. If their bodies became dry, they sunburned easily. He determined to place the "strange-thing " in the outrigger and cover it. He would pour water over its body occasionally to keep it damp. Before placing it in the outrigger, he gathered several handfuls of seaweed, laying it in the boat and spread it out. He picked up the "dolphin-like" thing and laid it on the green weeds. Illiune then went up the beach and gathering an armload of mangrove foliage, returned to the boat. He placed the green brush across the outrigger above the creature, forming a shade from the sun. It was time to leave and Illiune pushed the boat off the sand and into the water. Climbing in, he picked up a paddle and moved the outrigger out to the crescent of deep water. The strong current he experienced before seemed to have reversed and Illiune found himself moving rapidly away from the strange island.

Several times during the return trip he stopped paddling and dipped seawater and poured it over the dolphin-like creature in the boat. It seemed to sense being helped or saved, even though it was far from well. Illiune had not heard one whimper or cry from the creature since he had washed it in the water of the lagoon. When he thought of washing it, he realized he had not bathed himself and was still covered with foul-smelling mud. "I will bathe when I get home," he thought and began wondering where and how to keep his sick creature so that it might be safe. He would gather several ripe coconuts and squeeze out oil to rub on the skin of the creature. Fish would be easy to find and perhaps it would eat urchins or clams. It might even eat fruit of some kind. The area directly below his house would make an excellent place to put the Dolphin-thing. It would be nearly impossible for it to escape and nothing could get in to harm it. He could cut the foliage away from below his tree house and watch his patient even while in his bed of leaves or resting in his house. Illi-une was considering how he could better care for his patient when the outrigger slipped quietly into the shade of the island. He was nearly home. He was surprised at how soon he had made the return trip and as the sweet scented air drifted off the island and out to him, he turned the outrigger from the deep crescent and edged around the shore.

CHAPTER 8

$\mathcal{E}$ asing the boat up to the sand beach directly in front of the hidden pool. Illiune stepped out and moved to the bow and pulled it up onto the soft coral. He then went back where he had laid the "dolphin-thing" and after removing the mangrove brush, he lifted his patient from the outrigger and carried it gently up to the rocks which walled the outside of the hidden pool. Sitting down on the rocks, he let the creature down onto his lap and holding it behind the shoulders, he turned toward the pool. As he encountered the foliage of the mangrove tree, he lifted the branches with his free arm and turned his body around and dropped his feet onto the sand inside the pool. He again lifted the creature from his lap and placed it carefully in the water.

Illiune had never taken time to look over the hidden pool before. When he first saw the outrigger floating there he was so surprised, he forgot about inspecting the area. He wished now he had. Holding his patient with it's face out of the water, he walked slowly around the inside of the pool checking its depth and bottom. The walled area was round in shape with a water depth of three feet, except near the edge of the walls. There he found a row of rocks had been placed inside the main wall, which made an excellent place to sit. At the head of the pool, directly below Illiune's tree house there was an area of about six feet in circumference where the rocks were flat and even, under about six inches of water at full tide. He decided he would make a place there to put his patient until it was strong enough to swim safely by itself. He half carried, half floated the creature up to the rock shelf and laid it back away from the water's edge. He did not want to allow it into the water for fear it might drown in its weakened state. Illiune looked around and began selecting mangrove branches, which he broke off to form a barrier between the creature and the pool. When he had a foot high row of branches, he stopped his work and went out for a green coconut. He would try to make it drink more water.

Illiune hurried to the sea-side of the pool and stepped up and over the rock. Not wanting to leave his creature longer than necessary, he ran around the shore for a ways and then back into an area where he knew green coconuts could be found on the ground. He had no difficulty locating some and picking one up in each hand, he turned and ran back to the edge of the pool. Before opening a green nut, he raised the foliage and looked in to see if the creature were still lying behind the barrier. It was, and Illiune took the time to peel off the green husk and open the end of the shell. He turned again and crept under the foliage and waded over to the creature. He sat down on the ledge and worked his left arm under the head and allowed a few drops of fresh water to drop onto its lips. There was no resistance or hesitation. The mouth opened at the first drop of water and Illiune was pleased. He raised the head a little more and put the nut up to the lips. As he tipped the nut, the creature allowed the water to flow into its mouth and Illiune could see it swallow several times. He removed the shell and looked into the face. He saw the eyelids flutter as if they were about to open, but they did not. Illiune was somehow glad they did not because he was studying the face so intently. He could not help, but notice the long dark eye-lashes, the same color as her tresses of wavy coal black hair. Suddenly he felt guilty because of his admiration of this dolphin creature as if it were a human like himself, but of the opposite sex. The face and head of the creature

were free from blemishes like those on the rest of the body. The tiny
specks of decayed tissue began on the neck and increased downward.
Illiune marveled at the clear light skin of the back and upper neck.
There was no color on the cheeks, but the lips were slightly pink.
While sitting there holding the dolphin creature, he wondered how
he could keep it safe during the night. He did not wish to think of
leaving her, but Illiune knew he needed food himself, and rest, and as
an afterthought, a bath. The tide was coming in and it would be at
full within an hour. He need not worry about his "dolphin-girl"
while the water was below the rock bench. He decided he would be
able to leave her for a short time, perhaps a half hour during which
he would wash, eat and bring something back for her.

When Illiune left the pool, he noticed the sun had already
dropped below the horizon in the west. The water was warm as he
waded out to bathe. He was careful to wash himself thoroughly and
then removed his lava lava and cleaned it as best as he could. As he
came in toward the shore, he could see the water was almost to the
top of the rock wall of the pool. He had about enough time to find
water, food for himself and find something for the "dolphin-girl".

Running over to the outrigger, he pulled it higher up on the sand.
He could not afford to lose it if a squall came. When he lifted the
boat he saw the bananas and papayas he had placed there early in the
morning. He knew there was a coconut there also. He would not
have to go out to search for food. It was "mwow," (good) he thought.
He was afraid to leave his "dolphin-girl" for any period of time. Illiune ate a banana and with his knife he opened the papaya and
removed the seeds. Then cutting it into slices, he ate it quickly. To
open the ripe coconut required that he go into the island where the
sharp stick had been placed, that first day. He ran quickly to the
stump, picked up the stick and returned to the tree house. Placing it
point up in the ground, he leaned it against a large root of the square
nut tree. He opened the husk and took out the ripe nut. He opened
the end and drank the milk. Then, tapping it several times on a large

rock, he broke it open and loosened the meat, but left it in the shell. Taking the nut and bananas, he walked to the front of the outrigger and picked up the half of reef fish he had left in the boat. He thought he would try to feed it to his "Dolphin-girl" and if she did not want it, he would eat it. He could get more in the morning.

The low crying sounds caused Illiune to whirl and run back to the entrance of the pool and slide through the mangrove. He splashed carelessly over to where the "Dolphin-girl" lay crying behind the barrier. He laid the food aside and lifted the creature in his arms and holding her gently began swinging slowly from side to side, as if rocking a baby to sleep. He kept saying, softly "Soh, soh, soh, Serepein" (no, no, no, little girl). His actions must have been comforting to her for she stopped whimpering and turned her head against his chest and lay quite still. What had just taken place almost caused Illiune to be embarrassed, but he experienced a feeling that was completely new to him and left him with and excited pleasure. He had been able to help someone who needed him. Illiune knew he could not stand there holding the creature all night. He thought he would hold her in the water for a while and again wash her body with the fresh sea water. Leaning over he eased her gently into the water and began walking slowly around the pool. Because of the deepening shadows he could not see her face, but as he moved her around in the water, he felt she was watching him. After a few minutes of walking, he went back to the place where he had laid the food. He knew she would eat fish, but it was quite dark and difficult to slice. Laying her across his lap, he took a banana and peeled it and held it to her lips. She hesitated for a moment and then opened her mouth and bit off a little and began to chew. In a moment she swallowed. He fed her about half of the small Lacatan and then laid it aside. He did not think she should eat much fruit. He placed his arm behind her shoulders and raised her up and as he did, a bright ray of moonlight momentarily shone full on her face. Illiune caught his breath. As he looked, her eyes flashed open and she seemed to smile. He had never seen anything so lovely and then the moonbeam faded.

In stunned silence, Illiune sat with the creature in his arms. He was confused and happy. He was needed and afraid. He was strong and weak. He sensed all these contrasting emotions within a few seconds. After a few moments of indecision, Illiune ask softly, "Ia edomu, Serepein?" (What is your name, little girl?) There was no answer, but he could feel her move in against him and her breathing was steady and strong. He wished she could talk to him and yet he was glad she could not understand. He could say what he felt if there were no comprehension, but if she knew what he said, he could not speak freely. That is a problem with people, he thought. Again, he spoke softly, "Edei Illiune. Ia Edomu," (My name is Illiune. What is your name?). There was no answer and he did not expect one. He then said very low, "Lipilipil," (it doesn't matter).

There was not much Illiune could do, but to hold her or let her down into the water. He knew the fresh sea-water would wash her injured areas. In the morning he would take her out into the lagoon and let the sun help cleanse the wounds. He would have to remember to keep her damp with water, as she would become sunburned. He would also find fresh fish for her and perhaps a sea urchin. The thought reminded Illiune that he should see if she would eat a little more meat. It would give her strength to open her eyes. He found the reef fish and with his fingers, tore some meat from its side. The full moon allowed enough light to feed her and as Illiune put piece after piece to her lips, she ate them hungrily. He seemed happy and he smiled as he whispered, "Mwunge, mwow, Serepine," (Eat, good, little girl.). When she had eaten the fish he again lowered her into the water and walked around the pool

The moon shone unusually bright and illuminated the hidden pool through the foliage overhead. Illiune could see the sparkling ripples on the water within the secret place. As he was walking slowly with his one arm under her shoulders, he felt her head move suddenly and her body seemed to stiffen and then relax. "Strange," he thought. Moments later he felt her react again as if she had sensed something or heard a sound to which she responded. Illiune floated her over to the lagoon side of the pool and holding her up with one arm he lifted the mangrove branches with the other. He could see a disturbance in the water between the island and the reef. Before he could determine the cause of the ripples and swirls he heard the low excited voices of the dolphins. Never before had their voices sounded so joyful. Always before they whistled shrilly, almost like crying. Illiune was astonished because of the difference. There was no crying of the dolphins now as he listened. They came in very close. How many, Illiune could only guess, but they sent waves and ripples outward to the reef and beyond. The tide was full and they seemed to be passing very near to the hidden pool. Illiune alone did not hear their many sounds. He felt a movement in his arms and when he looked, he saw the flashing black eyes of his Dolphin-girl open wide as she struggled to sit up. He picked her up gently and sat her across one knee with his foot resting on the inner rock shelf. He was amazed that she seemed so alert. She listened with him for a time and then sent out a weak, but definite squeal of joy.

The high-pitched squeal seemed to echo between them and the reef or it was the dolphins replying. She made no more attempts to cry out and seemed content to lay back against Illiune's chest and relax. Whatever it was she said to the dolphins he would never know. Many strange thoughts flashed through Illiune's mind. He was so absorbed in his thinking that he never knew when the dolphins left. The bright moon cast a silver florescence over the lagoon. In the tropical sky the millions of stars shone brilliantly, each winking it own secrets. Before Illiune withdrew from the entrance to the pool, he had resigned himself to reality. His "Dolphin-girl" belonged to the dolphins! There was no feeling of jealousy or hurt within Illiune. He resolved to do all he could to help his " Serepein " regain her health because he owed so much to the dolphins.

The strange sounds of the dead returned that night, but as Illiune held the "Dolphin-girl" in his arms, he did not fear the sounds as before. They did not seem so terrifying. The moanings died away quickly and the wailers did not cry as long. Illiune wondered, for it seemed the dead and dying cries lost something since they had sent tremors of dread to haunt his soul that first night. His Serepein did not seem to hear the sounds of the island. She slept soundly in his arms. He imagined he could feel her strength returning and then accepted the thought as imagination. By the time the many sounds had trailed away, it was near midnight and Illiune found it difficult to stay awake. The breeze coming off the island toward the reef was sweet with coconut and flowers. The water was warm and so was the Serepein. He decided he would lay her behind the barrier when the tide receded a little more. Many things tumbled in his mind and it was the cry of the Serepein that woke him. He had allowed her to slip off his lap and she was floundering in the pool when Illiune found her. He pulled her up to him and held her upright with her head over his shoulders. She stopped crying in a short while, but coughed once or twice. Illiune did not sleep again that night. He was upset with himself. He hoped the dolphins would not hear of his carelessness. During the morning hours he walked in the pool and held his Serepein. He tried laying her behind the barrier once, but she cried and her picked her up again.

It was a long night and dawn came much slower that morning. Illiune determined he would cut away some of the upper foliage to allow more light in. He moved with his Serepein to the reef side of the pool and lifted the mangrove. Pink and gold fingers were reaching skyward far out over the reef. He was pleased. Today he would take her out into his lagoon and let her gaze upon his island. Illiune laughed at himself, aloud. To think his island was the "Island of the Dead". He would prove it could be an Island of Life, when the Serepein, (little girl), was well again. He was happy with his island;

the dolphins seemed satisfied with it too. He lifted his "Dolphin-girl"and raising the foliage, stepped with her out into the morning.

Illiune reminded himself that he should not allow the Serepein to become dry from lack of water on her skin. Her near death on the reef island had injured her severely. He decided he would try applying some oil on her body where the skin had deteriorated. Carrying her to the water's edge he laid her gently down, with her head on the coral sand. As he turned to go back for the coconut he heard her whimper. Stepping over, he picked up her hand and said, "Soh, soh, Serepein," (No, no, little girl). He held her hand firmly and then relaxed his hold, but still held the hand in both of his. It was then that he felt, looked, and saw that her hands were different. They were not really hands at all as he had thought. They were more like fish fins! Illiune heard himself say in astonishment, "Soh, soh, Serepein," (No, no, little girl). Her hands were as his hands; they were the same! For a moment he felt sorry for her. He knew how embarrassing it could be to have fish fin hands. All his life he had suffered because of his deformity. The "Dolphin-girl" had not made a sound while he held her hand and spoke aloud more to himself than to her. When he glanced from the hand to her face, her eyes were open and she was looking at him in wonder. He immediately felt guilty and ashamed and almost pleadingly said, "Makkengie, Serepein," (Excuse me, I'm sorry, little girl). As if she were waiting for an apology, she flashed an innocent smile and he laid her hand down and quickly ran to the pool and returned with the opened coconut.

Illiune could remember watching the ladies and younger girls comb their hair with coconut meat. It made their hair shine. They also used it for soap and a balm for rough, sore skin. Lifting his Serepein 's head, he rested it on his lap and began rubbing her hair with the thick sweet coconut meat. She seemed to enjoy the attention or the sensation for she closed her eyes and relaxed. Illiune had never seen such radiant beauty. He decided her experience had not dulled her hair. He again compared it to black coral, glistening in the early sun. He took more coconut meat and scraped it with his knife, letting the oil drip into the shell. When there was a little oil in the cup he put the knife aside and dipping his fingers, he began rubbing it lightly over the white spots on her neck. He applied oil to the upper part first, to see if it would help heal the blemishes. If it began to improve before her lower body, he could apply some there also. While rubbing oil over her breasts he could see that she was suffering from lack of food. They were flat and lifeless. He knew they should be firm because she was young. Perhaps they had been damaged by the mud or sun. But, Illiune realized, he knew little about the anatomy of girls.

CHAPTER 9

*I*t was time to go out to the reef for fish. This posed a problem for Illiune. Should he take the Serepein or leave her in the pool? It would be difficult to catch fish carrying her and yet he did not want to leave her. Perhaps he might find a safe place for her near the two small trees on the reef. He put the knife in his waistband and carried a coconut to the outrigger and returned. He was gone, but a moment, and when he came back she had turned her head and was watching him. Illiune considered carrying her in his arms and walking out on the exposed coral spit. He could make the trip easier that way, but not did want to keep her out of the water for any length of time. Lifting her from the sand he waded out to where the water was about waist deep. Lowering her into the water he turned her over onto her back and held one hand under her shoulders as they moved slowly toward the reef in the direction of the nut trees. He looked at her occasionally and at times she was looking back at him.

They were halfway to the reef when the first Black-tipped Shark appeared. Illiune reached his idle arm down immediately and lifted her from the water. He felt helpless. He would keep her away from the sharks, unless they came in too large a number. A moment later he saw several circling, some with their top fin and tail above water and some beneath the surface. He tensed as he held her and whispered, "bako!"shark). The "Dolphin-girl" seemed to understand his fear and lifting her head she uttered a series of piercing cries. An answering cry from the sea was almost spontaneous. When the cries of the dolphins registered in Illiune's mind he looked up to see the water at the reef boiling with bodies and many blue-white dolphins leaping high in the air as they jumped the coral ridge and came to rescue them. Illiune stood fascinated as the water around them was turned into a foaming sea of sharks, dolphins and spray. He saw one dolphin burst from the water with a shark balanced on its beak and throw the black tip over twenty feet from where it rose. Seconds after the arrival of the dolphins, the water cleared and calmed, but his friends did not leave them. Almost everywhere Illiune looked he could see them swimming gracefully near. They swam so close at times that Illiune was afraid they might cause him to drop the Serepein. She too, saw them and when she sensed that Illiune was no longer afraid of the sharks, she made a strange cry and the dolphins formed a circle around them and seemed to stop all movement as if waiting for another command from the "Dolphin-girl".

Illiune sensed the strange attraction and communication between the dolphins and the Serepein. He realized he need not fear the sea or anything in the sea as long as they were his friends. There was no doubt in Illiune's mind but that the "Dolphin-girl" was the key to the secret of the strange friendship. They could understand her and seemed to know her very thought. In time he hoped to be able to communicate with them also.

Illiune again lowered her into the water and began wading slowly toward the reef. To his surprise, two dolphins came up beside them and gently took the "Dolphin-girl" between them and bore her on their backs beside Illiune as he waded. They did not try to take her away and they were surer than he and much more graceful. As they were moving she looked at Illiune and smiled and he smiled back. His communication had begun. When the dolphins found the water too shallow for their safety they whistled softly and the "Dolphin-girl" raised her hand to Illiune and he quickly lifted her from the dolphins and they turned toward deeper water.

The problem of finding fish to eat continued to confront Illiune. Looking into the eyes of his Serepein, he tried to explain to her that he must leave her to find fish. She smiled and turned her head and sent out another cry. There was not more than a moment elapsed before he heard an answer from out over the reef. Illiune was more than puzzled, but so many unbelievable things had happened, he was learning to accept reality as a dream. He carried her toward the raised area of the reef and as he reached the shore, he bent over to lay her in the water with her head on the coral. As he leaned down to place her gently on the sand, he was swallowed up in floating blackness.

Illiune did not know how long he lay unconscious. When his revolving mind stopped spinning he slowly lifted his head. The reef, trees, and sky all seemed to be connected in one long movement. When he shook his head and squinted his eyes, the movement halted and he was looking at the two small trees on the reef. It was difficult for Illiune to focus on where he was or how he got there. His memory cleared when he heard a soft whimper beside him. Turning sideways, he looked directly into the coal black eyes of his Serepein, who was watching him with tears on her cheeks. Illiune's first impulse was to touch her cheek, but as his consciousness returned, he thought perhaps he had dropped her or fallen on her. He could see she was hurt or in pain. He began to feel guilty of his weakness. She needed him and he had failed her. He rolled away from her and began to get up and it was then that he understood his apparent weakness. His leg, the one the shark had bitten, was throbbing painfully. A strange fear chilled Illiune as he stood up and looked at the Serepein lying on the sand. He immediately dropped beside her on his knees and took her hands in his. He held them firmly and looked anxiously into her face. He could find nothing to say that could excuse him from neglecting her. He did not know how long he had lain there. He could remember only that he intended to place her near the coral sand so that her head would lie on the beach and her body in the water. At last he mumbled, "Makkengie, Serepein," (Please excuse me, little girl). For a moment there was no reaction from the Dolphin-girl. She only watched him with eyes wet and then she shook her head a little and fluttered her long black lashes as if to rid herself of the tears. Then, as if in response to his statement of guilt, she smiled briefly and he felt her hand tighten on his and then relax. Illiune was thrilled that he had not injured her and he bent his head and touched her cheek with his lips. As he did he whispered, "Menlau, Serepein," (Thank you, little girl). Straightening up he saw her eyes widen for a moment and then the smile flickered on her face again. Illiune did not have to be told she had forgiven him. He knew it, but also knew his problems had increased. Now he not only must care for the Serepein continually but somehow he needed care for his wounds. Because of the constant changing of events the past few days, Illiune had forgotten his leg. He remembered taking the banana poultice off and his intent to wash it and let the sun dry it for a time. He would have smiled when thinking of how events had taken his mind from himself, but this was too serious. How could he leave the Serepein in order to return to the banana plant for more medicine? The tide was beginning to come in again and Illiune realized he should start back to the island immediately. They still had not eaten and he was hungry and the Serepein was hungry also.

Illiune raised himself from the kneeling position and tested his leg with his weight. He could feel the earlier throbbing, but he could hobble on it. His next thought was for the Serepein. He could not carry her the two hundred yards to the coral ridge leading to the island because of weakness and his leg would attract the sharks. He realized that was why they came before when carrying her out. Illiune was unable to make a decision and would not leave the Serepein. When he had exhausted every idea of what he might do, he dropped beside her again and taking her hands in his, he talked to her as if she understood. He told her he needed medicine for his leg, they needed fish for food and that he would need help to take her back to the secret pool. He also told her he needed the dolphins to help him take care of her. She looked at him patiently until he ceased talking and then moved one of his hands behind her head and trilled a cry. In a few moments Illiune could hear the answer of the dolphins. They moved off down the reef and then as their sounds almost died away, he could see then jumping the coral and knew they were coming to help.

When the dolphins came they brought food for Illiune and the Serepein. They came in quite close, but because of the shallow water, he had to wade out a short distance and they held the fish up to him. As he took them he said, "Menlau," (thank you) and the dolphins whistled low and swam out to deeper water and waited. He took the fish and with his knife he cut strips of meat and fed his Serepein. She ate slowly, although Illiune knew she was hungry. After he had fed her half a fish, she refused more. When he realized she was finished he quickly ate the remaining half himself. Then taking up another fish he ripped the skin off and after eating part of the fish he saw her motion to her mouth. He cut another strip and she ate it, but she would only eat one. He again began eating and she motioned again. It was then Illiune realized what she was trying to tell him. They would eat together. The fish were much larger than those Illiune had caught, and two satisfied them. He stood and looked down at his injured leg. Again it was oozing a watery substance and blood. He looked and touched and pondered the leg. The Serepein reached out and placed her hand on the leg and then touched the other. She seemed to inspect the injured leg intently and then motioned for Illiune to raise her head. He sat beside her, lifted her head and laid it in his lap. She turned toward the sea and made another strange trilling sound. There was movement in the water as the dolphins responded to her voice.

The noonday sun began to shine quite warm as they sat on the coral sand and the incoming tide caused the water to rise around them until Illiune's legs were covered and all of the Serepein 's lower body. He put off moving back as long as possible so that his leg could rest. It was when the water rose so that he found himself holding her head up against his chest, did he lifted her away and got upon his knees and moved her up toward the trees.

When the dolphins returned, they brought strange looking seaweed. Each dolphin in turn came in almost to where they were resting on the sand and with a quick flip of its head, threw the weed at the water's edge within easy reach of Illiune. He could not understand their action. Still trying to comprehend why they brought the weeds from the sea, Illiune picked up a handful and inspected it. Holding it caused a sensation of tingling and warmth. He was becoming more perplexed when he felt the hand of Serepein touch his. As he looked at her she motioned for him to put it on his leg. If she had motioned for him to eat it, that would have made sense. He had eaten seaweed many times, not this kind, but another. It seemed strange to Illiune that it was medicine like banana pulp, but to please the Serepein, he wrapped his leg generously with the sea grass. The effect of the weed seemed immediate to Illiune and the tingling and warmth seemed to soothed his wounds as he sat there questioning.

After he had finished wrapping the leg with seaweed, the dolphins came in close again and placed more at the water's edge. "Why?", he wondered. Looking at the Serepein he realized she too needed medication for her body. Illiune gathered some seaweed and laid it on the sand. He then lifted the Dolphin-girl and placed her on the pad so that her back was lying on the weed. Using handfuls of seaweed he wrapped her body carefully, beginning at the extreme lower tail-fins to her midsection. He then placed more on her abdomen and chest area and allowed it to drape down on each side. As the dolphins brought more, he carefully wrapped her arms until they were completely covered. While she was wrapped in the weed, Illiune thought how much she looked like a normal girl covered with grass, except she was much prettier. Illiune smiled at himself for thinking such strange thoughts. Why he had never in his life looked at a girl in the village with any feeling. The seaweed coat he had wrapped her in must have been relaxing to the Serepein because within a matter of minutes she was asleep. With his injured leg lifted across the opposite knee, he too was called into sleep. Just before he closed his eyes in sleep, he looked out to see several dolphins circling slowly and protectingly.

The tropical rain awakened Illiune. He turned his head and opened his mouth and let those drops that would enter. "Water from the sky can be so pure and sweet," he mused. This thinking caused him to open his eyes and look over at the Serepein. She was still sleeping soundly and the rain had kept her from becoming too dry and had dampened the seaweed also. Illiune knew it was late because the air was still, like it is between changing from day to night. The sun was hiding behind the palms on the island. He was thirsty and Serepein would be also, when she wakened. He was worried about staying on the outer reef all night because a squall might come. He did not want his Serepein to get chilled. After surviving the terrible ordeal on the reef island, she should not have to face other hardships. Pondering about his thought, Illiune wondered if he had really been thinking of himself. Without realizing what he did, he rose to his feet and looked over at the island. The waters of the lagoon were mirror-like and the tide was again receding. He was anxious to be going back to the island, but he did not want to disturb his Serepein. While standing there he looked out a few feet from shore and saw a dolphin watching him. It had made no sound. Illiune was wondering why it was so quiet and still when the Serepein whimpered. He looked quickly around and saw her move her arms out sideways as if feeling for something. He thought it was unusual because wrapped in weed as she was, she would not detect much anyway. He watched her touch only the sand and then whimpered again and opened her eyes and looked around and then they closed. When they opened a moment later, she seemed wide-awake. As Illiune moved over toward her, he remembered his injured leg. He stopped and looked and saw it still wrapped in seaweed, but the pain was gone!

"Impossible", Illiune thought, but it was true. The pain was gone and also the throbbing. He moved quickly over to the Serepein and dropped down beside her on his knees. Picking up one hand, still wrapped in seaweed, he spoke to her excitedly, "Menlua, Serepein, neh soh medic!" (Thank you, little girl, leg no hurt!). She smiled at him and then held up her arms and motioned that he remove the seaweed. As Illiune unwound the weeds from her arms and hands he was thrilled with amazement. In place of the sordid pits covering her arms, there was a smooth, soft, light skin with no discoloration as before. Illiune looked and marveled at the renewed look of her arms. He then anxiously lifted the seaweed from her neck and chest area and again the skin looked alive and new. There were still tiny specks where the holes had been, but the festering had ceased and the seaweed seemed to lift away the ulcerated skin as if she had shed her sick covering and as a butterfly, put on that which is beautiful. There was no change in the miracle as Illiune removed the seaweed from her lower body. She was almost a new creature on the outside. He had never seen or known a medicine that worked so well. It was difficult for Illiune to pick her up and carry her to the island. He was so amazed at the change that had taken place, he wanted to look at her only. All during the time that Illiune unwrapped and admired her, the Serepein smiled knowingly. She seemed to understand a miracle had touched her. It was a whistle from the dolphins that returned him to necessity. Illiune gathered the Serepein in his arms and walked slowly out into the water where the dolphins were waiting. As they lifted her from him, he smiled and then a dolphin came up beside him, on his wounded side and Illiune rested his hand on its back as the dolphins and their patients moved toward their home. They traveled straight toward the island as they crossed the lagoon.

The thought of sharks never entered Illiune's mind as they proceeded toward the secret pool.

When they arrived near the shore, Illiune spoke to the "Dolphin-girl" and said, "E pancola peilongo, Ke mwunge," (I am going inland, we eat). Then touching his Serepein and the dolphins, he whispered audibly, "awi," (wait). Then, without looking back, he hurried up and into the foliage and came back in a few moments with two green and two ripe coconuts. The Serepein and dolphins were waiting where he had left them. He waded into the water and toward the mangrove hiding the secret pool. "Kodo," (come), he said and went over to the rock edge of the pool and lifted the mangrove. Holding the branches, he again said, "Kodo," and two dolphins appeared and leaped over the wall into the pool. Illiune dropped the coconuts into the water and then turned and lifted the Serepein gently from their backs and lifting the branch, he placed her on the backs of the waiting dolphins. He turned once more to those in the lagoon and smiled, "Menlau," (thanks you). They whistled softly and rose up on their tails and swam outward from the island. Illiune turned and dropped into the pool and waded over to the rock ledge. The dolphins were waiting there with the Serepein and as Illiune lifted her and placed her on the shelf, the two dolphins swam out and brought the coconuts over and tossed them on the ledge behind the barricade of mangrove.

Light was fast fading in the shadows of the pool and Illiune was troubled with the thought of going to sleep as he had the night before. Something might happen to the Serepein. He had slept some on the reef, but he was still tired and night was only beginning. He slipped over to where the Serepein lay and asked her if she would like some water. She only looked at him with her large black eyes and said nothing. He picked up a green nut and sliced the end and opened the shell. Holding her head up, he let her drink. She was quite thirsty and Illiune was pleased that she drank well. He then thought of the ripe coconuts, but realized he would have to open them out by the shore. Leaving the Serepein with a smile and a touch, he went over to the wall, lifted the branch and stepped out into the evening. He went directly to the stick and peeled the husks off the nuts. He then made his way back to the wall and climbed into the pool. He went over to the ledge and placed one nut on the shelf and opened the end of the other. Holding the Serepein 's head up, he let her taste the sweet milk. She drank only a little, and turned her head away. Illiune drank the rest. He then spoke to her and explained his reason for worry about the coming night. Her eyes seemed to listen to every word. She then trilled a soft cry and the water became alive within the pool. Illiune was surprised at first, but then realized he had not raised the branches for the two dolphins to leave. Moving to the mangrove, he lifted the limb and found, hanging on the brush and heaped on the wall, more of the strange seaweed. He gathered it and carried it over to the ledge. Again Illiune felt relieved because of the presence of the dolphins. They were so close now that he could almost touch them and yet when he moved around the pool, he never made contact. They gave him comfort knowing they were close to help the Serepein. He would have liked to call them over and say, "If I sleep, watch our little Serepein," but of course he did not. They could not understand.

Moving over to the ledge, Illiune spread some of the strange seaweed into a thick mat and placed the "Dolphin-girl" upon it. He then commenced wrapping her lower body as he had before. As he continued to apply the miracle medicine, he wondered just how beautiful this Serepein could be. He smiled at the thought and when he had finished covering her up to her throat, he could barely see the outline of her face in the closing darkness. She was smiling and as he watched and smiled with her, she fell into a deep sleep and would not wake until morning.

Illiune took the green coconut which he had opened earlier and drank the remaining water. He then moved over to the lagoon edge of the pool and lifted the branches, held them in case the dolphins wanted to leave. Speaking to them audibly, he told them they could leave if they would like. He held the branches up for nearly five minutes and then let them down and moved back to the ledge. He felt around for a half shell of a coconut and placed it back against the wall of the pool. He removed the wrapping from his leg and leaning back on the wall he replaced it with fresh seaweed.

Lying down on the ledge between the water and his Serepein, he lay quietly in the warm, sweet air. He did not hear the death wails that night. In his sleep, he dreamed of life, love and hope.

CHAPTER 10

*H*is Serepein was still sleeping when the sound of running water woke Illiune. It was not the rainwater dripping through the foliage, but the sound of trickling water. He had never heard the sound in the pool before and because it was different he wakened immediately. Rising up he first looked at the "Dolphin-girl" who was still sleeping quietly beside him. The sound of running water came from the ledge, far back beyond the foliage overhead. Moving quietly, Illiune stepped over to the protective limbs and lifted them. He was sure the pool he saw was simply a reflection off a wet rock. Moving the branches aside he worked his way to the far edge of the rock ledge and gazed in astonishment. There before him, nearly even with his chest was a round pool of water about three feet in diameter. The water was crystal clear and was trickling into the pool from a rock above. As it overflowed it ran down the rock ledge and into the lower pool. He reached over and dipping his hand into the pool, brought some water to his lips and tasted. It was fresh water. Leaning over, Illiune drank a swallow. He doubted that it could be pure enough to drink. Before long he would know. As he turned, he broke off several overhead branches that had hidden the upper pool. If the water were good, he would not need to bring green coconuts here again. When he had an armful of branches, he returned to the lower pool, stepped down and waded to the lagoon side. He saw that the tide was full because it covered the rocks of the wall. Pushing through the mangrove, he stepped out and laid the branches on the shore. Returning to the wall, he picked up the mangrove screen and held it patiently. Just as he was about to enter and lower the branches, there was a low whistle from inside the hidden pool and two dolphins rose up from the water and jumped over the wall into the lagoon. Illiune watched their wake as they moved toward the outer reef. Turning then, he went back to the Serepein.

Light was filtering through the green covering of tropical growth and in places the bright streaks of sunlight danced on the waters in the pool. As Illiune waded over to the Serepein he was greeted with a smile. He returned the smile and leaning over toward her he said softly, "Menseng mwow, Serepein," (Good morning, little girl). She lifted her hand as though to touch his, but she saw the seaweed wrap and laid it down again. Illiune quickly lifted the hand and squeezed it a little as he said honestly, "Lipilipil," (It doesn't matter).

With the promise of another beautiful day, Illiune was impatient to be doing. He wanted to inspect the upper pool and the source of water, but his Serepein would always be his first consideration as long as he had her. The thought of what he was thinking was sobering to Illiune. He did not want to lose her. During the little time since he found her, he had become almost one with her. Whether it was eating, sleeping or being, they had been almost inseparable. To change his thoughts to something brighter Illiune reached over with his free hand and picked up a green coconut and held it before her. She smiled and he released her hand and prepared the drink. She drank readily. When she finished, she lay back, but the brightness of her eyes told Illiune she expected something more.

Picking up her arm he began to unwrap the seaweed from her hand. She quickly withdrew her hand and Illiune was puzzled. He said aloud, "I do not know what it is Serepein; perhaps you can tell me." She watched him for a moment longer and then moved her arm toward the entrance of the pool. Illiune could not mistake her intent.

He slipped his arms under her and lifted her from the ledge. Wading over to the mangrove screen, he sat down, placed her on his lap and then lifting the foliage he turned toward the reef. As they faced into the dazzling sunlight, she uttered a bell-like treble and nestled her head against his chest. He had never heard her speak like that before, but for the first time he knew that she was speaking to him. It was a wonderful sound and made him feel strange, excited and uncomfortable. He would have sat there until she spoke again, but she did not and he carried her over to the edge of the surf and kneeling down laid her gently in the clear, warm water with her head on the coral sand.

There was no pain in Illiune's leg this morning. He would take off the seaweed later, but decided to remove the miracle medicine from the Serepein first. He began talking audibly to himself, yet addressing the "Dolphin-girl" as he lifted one of her arms and began removing the seaweed. "I will see how beautiful you are this morning, Serepein, but I think you are quite pretty now. Do you know that you have the prettiest face I have ever seen? If you become more lovely than you are, I think I will fall in love with you." Illiune almost wished he had not made the last statement aloud. It was possible someone might hear and tell the Serepein. By this time he had removed the wrapping and the change in her arm startled him. The skin from her shoulder to the elbow was satin smooth and the color of ivory. The lower arm looked translucent with blue, gold and silver. His fascination was so intense he could only look and wonder, until the Serepein touched his hand and looked at him in question. The touch and questioning eyes returned Illiune to reality and he began removing the covering from her other arm. He rather knew what he would see when the arm was free of seaweed, but when the last strand was lifted, Illiune could not help, but draw his breath in quickly with profound awareness. The magic seaweed had turned the Serepein into an enchanting beauty.

Illiune removed the mat of weed from Serepein's breasts and abdomen. Again he was amazed at the change. There were no signs of ugly ulcerated areas anywhere to be seen. The magic poultice had lifted all the old skin with its imperfection away and left only the iridescent colors of blue, gold and silver. It was similar in hue to that of her lower arms, but less translucent. The Serepein's eyes expressed her knowing of the mind of Illiune. She smiled at him and when he was about to speak she put her hand to his lips and whether she knew what she was doing or not, he remained quiet. Illiune continued to remove the seaweed until she was completely free from the wrap. One more time Illiune was spellbound by brilliant beauty. In all his days of fishing he had never seen any fish that possessed the startling sheen that the Serepein displayed from her abdomen downward. The rays of the sun reflected from her body as they would from a mirror. The brilliant blue and silver scales were tiny and delicate. Around her waist the miniature scales formed a band of gold resembling a wide belt that separated the shining blue from the lustrous silver. Her breasts were much more firm and rounded and the silver scales made a lacework, which enhanced the contour of her body. Except where the silver threads crept upward over her breasts, the Serepein's skin was the color of ivory but soft, warm and smooth. As Illiune considered and drank of her beauty he could not help say audibly to himself, "Serepein, surely you are a Prinsess. A more beautiful Serepein has never been." Thinking of the working and results of the strange seaweed, Illiune considered his leg and how the pain had been removed. The Serepein had been wounded also and he knew she was in pain because of her whimpering. A sudden thought struck Illiune. Could his leg show the gold and silver of scales because of the magic poultice? He stood up quickly and stepped back from the Serepein and removed the wrapping from his leg. There was no sign of pain or injury, but when he rubbed his hand over his skin, it felt like sandpaper. This disturbed Illiune. He would rather have shiny scales like the Serepein than skin like a shark. The very thought caused him a feeling of dread. He then decided his leg would be smooth later.

Forgetting himself for the time, Illiune spoke aloud to the Serepein, although he did not think she would understand. "We will go out to let the dolphins see how pretty you are. I know they will not believe it. No one could see and believe. It is only magic that makes you appear so beautiful." She watched him speak and then, as he stooped to move her to deeper water, she pushed his hand aside and motioned to her hair and then toward land. For a moment Illiune stood perplexed. She ran her hand over her hair as if she were combing it. Illiune laughed. He turned and ran up onto the island and into the tropical growth. In a few minutes he returned with two ripe coconuts. He peeled off the husks and tapped them to loosen the meat from the shell. Stepping over to a long black rock he broke the shells open and took out several large pieces of nutmeat. He also put some in his mouth and began chewing as he turned and walked out to drop down beside his Serepein. She smiled and opened her mouth. He held the smaller piece to her lips and put it between her teeth. She surprised him by biting off some nutmeat and began chewing also. He then sat down and placed her head in his lap. When he thought she was comfortable he began rubbing her hair with the white meat of the coconut. The beauty of her long tresses surprised him. The oil caused the hair to shine in the sunlight. When Illiune had oiled her hair well, it cascaded down her back in thick waves of blue-black. He stopped and sat quiet, waiting. She rubbed her face and neck and smiled again at Illiune. He took another piece of coconut meat and with awkward hands, he worked it gently over her face, shoulder, neck and upper breast. He knew coconut oil was good for the hair and skin. Most all women and girls in his village rubbed it into their hair and on their body. Sometimes they made perfumed oil by adding flower scent to it. Thinking of this, Illiune lifted her head and rose up and eased her head back on the coral. Running up on the bank he went over to a hibiscus and picked two bright red flowers. Returning to the Serepein he knelt down and pulling a thread from his lava lava he tied the flowers in her hair, one on each side. Her eyes flashed a questioning look, but his smile must have reassured her. Illiune then lifted her and carried her out to deeper water and let her down, still holding his hand under her shoulders. He wondered if she would get strong enough to swim. She seemed quite well and her injuries had disappeared. Perhaps she was afraid to try, he thought. Maybe he would have to teach her. Illiune was thinking about this and as he did he reached back and lifted her lower portion up and then let it down as he thought she must do while swimming. She made no effort to try herself. Illiune wondered again if she would ever learn to swim. She would be entirely helpless in the sea. Perhaps the dolphins would carry her. But would they always be with her? Many questions flooded his mind as he walked her out to the reef.

Illiune never thought about sharks on the way. How could he find the dolphins? He wondered if she could call them again. They were quite hungry by now and he was still not able to leave the "Dolphin-girl" alone for long. He would also like to wrap the Serepein in the seaweed once more. He wondered if she would reveal more beauty. They were almost halfway to the square-nut trees when they heard the cry. The Serepein trilled a response and the water around them was soon alive with friendly and excited dolphins. Illiune was so anxious for them to see their Prinsess that he began talking to them. "Look at the Serepein. Is she not beautiful? Your magic weed has made her into a creature of loveliness. Come close and see how soft and clear her skin is. See the shiny beauty of her tail. Do you think she could be a Prinsess? I can never thank you enough for your magic and kindness. I will need help to feed her and care for her because I am only a boy and she is so helpless. Could you help her learn to swim? I can hold her up, but I cannot teach her because she cannot understand me." All this Illiune said as the friendly dolphins came and circled them and made low whistling sounds. Two dolphins seem to rise up below her and lifted her away from Illiune and moved her slowly beside him as he waded chest deep toward the reef.

The Serepein made one low cry and several dolphins raced away, making waves in the water of the lagoon. By the time they had reached the area where the water was only waist deep, the dolphins carrying the Serepein stopped and moved slightly away from Illiune. This puzzled him, but he was not especially displeased. She was smiling at him and he secretly knew she was teasing him. While watching her and the dolphins, it seemed to Illiune that they were anxious to do whatever she desired of them. He also knew that the communication between her and the dolphins was nearly perfect. "Much more than between people," he thought. "People never seemed to understand each other at all times. They do not always try to help each other like the dolphins did the Serepein and himself. Being a dolphin might not be too bad," he murmured. "They are strong and graceful, free and helpful. No, being a dolphin might not be bad at all."

A low whistle caused Illiune to turn and there behind him was a dolphin with a reef fish in his beak. Illiune took the fish from the dolphin and said, "Menlau," (Thank you). Taking his knife, he broke the skin and peeled it off the sides of the fish. Holding a strip of meat up toward the Serepein, he said, "Innenen yo", (Very good). She smiled, but made no attempt to come to Illiune. He ate the meat and tore another piece and ate it also. "Perhaps she is not hungry", he thought, "but she has not eaten this morning. It is possible that our Serepein is not feeling well?" He tore off another piece and held it out to her. She did not respond. She continued to smile at him, in an odd way. Trying another approach, he said, "Please come and eat, Serepein. I do not wish to eat alone and I know you are hungry. If you do not eat you will not stay beautiful". The Serepein then twisted her head slightly and made the same bell-like treble that seemed personal to Illiune. She whistled low to the dolphins and they carried her over to Illiune and as they held her, he fed her. They ate three fair size fish, each taking a bite and then the other. Illiune was puzzled by her actions. She must have been pretending she wasn't hungry. He wondered if all girls wanted to be entreated like the Serepein.

After they had eaten, Illiune turned to the Serepein and said, "I would like to go outside the reef and swim with the dolphins. Would you like to go, little girl?" She smiled and again made a bell-like treble. He lifted her from the dolphins and waded over to the coral reef. Standing there with the lovely "Dolphin-girl", Illiune momentarily felt as though he were one with the dolphins and the Serepein. These few days he had shared with her and her friends were perhaps the most pleasant of his life. For the first time he had no fear of man or beast. His only concern was meeting the needs of the Serepein. He did not understand her actions at times and he was afraid for her; afraid something might happen and he would lose her. To think of not having her was a distressing thought to Illiune, but somehow he knew that when she was completely well and able to swim, the day of separation would come. For a moment he wished he had not asked the dolphins to teach her to swim. If she could not care for herself in the water perhaps she would always need him. He wondered what the people of his village would say if he took her back with him and said, "I have found a little "Dolphin-girl" which cannot care for herself. Is she not a lovely creature? Would you help me care for her, grandmother? If she ever learns to swim, we can let her go, but now she is so helpless, I cannot leave her." Somehow, Illiune knew that it would be impossible. Boys of the village would throw rocks and sticks at her and make fun of her because they would be jealous. The girls would be jealous too, because the Serepein was so much prettier than they. No, he knew he could never take her back to his village. Again Illiune was brought to reality by the playful antics of the dolphins in the deep water beyond the reef.

Wading out on the bright varicolored coral, Illiune stood in chest-deep water holding his Serepein. Sometimes he felt guilty about looking at her because he realized he was struck by her beauty and could not help himself. When she caught him looking at her, she would flash her dark eyes and twist her head just a little and smile. The hibiscus flowers were still in her hair. He said to himself that he would make her a "lei" and a "mar mar" when she was well enough to care for herself. He needed a few minutes of free time to gather flowers. His thinking was interrupted by some dolphins, which came up gracefully and lifted the Serepein from him. "Please be careful friends. She cannot swim and is far from well. You see, she is quite helpless."

When the Serepein was about twenty feet away from him, Illiune dove into the water and swam out-ward beyond her and came up far out beyond the dolphins. In a matter of moments, the sea around him was filled with the clowning creatures. They jumped, whirled, splashed and whistled as they frolicked around Illiune and his Serepein. He was at that time intensely happy. He dove and played with the dolphins for about an hour. All the while the Serepein was carried slowly and gracefully on the backs of two dolphins, which occasionally changed places with others, as if each wanted a turn. At times Illiune would swim over near the Serepein and smile at her and touch her cheek and say, "When you learn to swim, little girl, we will come here every day."

Illiune remembered the Serepein should not be exposed to the sun too long and swam over and motioned for her to come back with him. She smiled, but would not go in toward the shore. Again he tried by saying, "You must come in now, Serepein, or you will suffer greatly from the hot sun. Perhaps we will come out tomorrow." She would not yield. When he swam over to her and tried to take her from the dolphins, she whistled shrilly and two dolphins came up beside Illiune forming a block so he could not touch her. Illiune was becoming worried, but realized he could not take the Serepein unless she was willing. In desperation he called to her and said, "Please, little girl, will you come with me to the reef so we can rest beneath the square-nut trees? I know you are having a wonderful time with your dolphin friends, but I am afraid you might have pain later. You know

I am almost in love with you and if you have pain, I will be pained too." When he had finished speaking, the Serepein whistled low and the dolphins carried her back to the reef and waited for Illiune to take her from their backs. Illiune was again perplexed. He could not understand her and was troubled because of it. However, when he lifted and carried her into the shade of the nut trees, he forgot being impatient. He did not want her to become dry by being out of the water too long and he did not want to lay her on the dry sand. In pondering, he said to the Serepein, "It would be more comfortable for you if your dolphin friends would bring some seaweed for a bed. I am afraid your skin might be injured. We cannot allow that to happen because you have just become the most beautiful Prinsess in the world." Illiune thought more but did not say it. His Serepein was listening. She seemed to enjoy the attention and his talk of her beauty. She whistled low and it was only a matter of moments when the dolphins appeared with the seaweed. They brought more than enough, as if they enjoyed it. Perhaps they saw the change it made in their Serepein. Illiune placed her in the water while he fixed a bed of seaweed and then laid her on the weeds under the shade of the trees. While she was lying there he covered her lower body with more seaweed. Then Illiune gathered leaves from the trees and lifting her head he formed a pillow for her. All the time he was working to make her comfortable, she watched him with those black flashing eyes and a half smile on her lips.

After seeing that the Serepein was comfortable, Illiune sat down and stroked her hair and ran his fingers lightly over her face, neck and shoulders. In a short time her steady, deep breathing told Illiune she was sleeping. He lifted himself carefully and walked out on the coral. This was the first time since being cast ashore that he had been able to inspect the reef. Walking rapidly, he moved toward the place where he had washed in. He wanted to look at the ropes and poles that had protected him and kept him afloat. The pile of lashings was still lying on the reef. Not knowing what to expect, Illiune began sorting and untwisting the poles and ropes. He was surprised that the ropes held together as well as they had. They were made from coconut fronds and braided. He salvaged two fairly long pieces and then, with astonishment, he noticed that the mast and sail were half hidden under the pile of weed and sticks. Illiune worked hurriedly and before long was able to lift the sail and mast free from the debris. Excitement flooded him as he was thinking of putting the sail on his outrigger. Gathering the ropes and sail, he walked back up the reef where the "Dolphin-girl" was sleeping. Laying the objects on the beach under the trees he determined to return with the outrigger to carry his treasures back to the island.

The Serepein was still sleeping when he returned. Even though she was lying in the shade, the brightness of the day allowed Illiune to look at her intently. He had never actually studied her features in bright daylight before because she, too, was awake and Illiune felt uncomfortable. He did not go too close for fear of waking her. Studying the perfections of her features and the contrasting colors of ivory, blue, gold and silver with that of her jet black hair, Illiune whispered half aloud, "No, Serepein, I will not learn to love you. I cannot because I love you already. Did you hear me, Serepein? E poko poko uk", (I love you). Illiune felt foolish for speaking aloud especially saying such a thing. He had no right or reason to say he loved the Serepein. He should only love another human, a girl of his own kind. Illiune felt awkward with embarrassment, but when he thought over what he had said and how it caused him to feel, he only smiled to himself and again repeated, "E poko poko uk."

While the Serepein slept on, Illiune walked along the reef in the opposite direction from which he had been. Watching the reef sweep out and around he wondered if his home island was north or south. Thinking of home he admitted to himself he might have to travel east or west. He would do some sailing in his outrigger some day and perhaps find his way back. Why he wished to go home, he did not know. His grandmother might like to see him and he would like to see her also. She would be especially happy to see the red coral. She could sell it for many dollars and she would even make Illiune some sweet cakes. The boys and girls would not welcome him in his village. That he knew. He was puzzled by the thought that came back to him so often, "He would like to go home." Happiness was here with the dolphins and his Serepein, on his island.

Walking back to the trees he looked again at the Serepein. She was still in dreamland and Illiune lay down quietly near her and watched the clouds high overhead as they brought the promise of a warm rain. Many recollections flooded his mind as he lay there. In time, a story began emerging from his memory that caused Illiune to struggle to comprehend. It was about his ancient ancestors who had built a beautiful palace on a low, canal-laced land. The buildings and walls were built of long black rocks, which had been dragged from high up on a mountain and loaded on large rafts and floated to the place of building. It was a beautiful city that one could only reach at full tide. It was a palace for the Kings. Many miles south of the palace was an island that had been selected for a burial place for the Kings when they were called in death. The island was an especially beautiful place, which had specially prepared for the royalty. Every type of fruit, flower and tree of the tropical area were planted there. The island was protected from evil by many long, black rocks, which were lined up in a square just outside the island. Much work was done there to make the burial island a paradise. Special pools were built for both sea and fresh water. The place of entombment was on the northeast side of the island where the Kings, in death, could watch over their people and always greet the new day from their bier. The few people who had visited the island years later told of the mourning of death and wailing of sorrow. Because of this, the island was taboo. No one would go there. Many people doubted the strange sounds of the dying Kings, but the old man of the village said it was so. Perhaps that was why no one believed. People said he was "likum" (liar) and funny in the head because his tales were so strange. He would visit with Illiune's father when Illiune was very young and tell of the time when the people of the sea, his ancestors, were in some ways related to the dolphins. He would tell of the Queen of the sea people, who ruled over all the warm-blooded creature of the sea and his ancestors. Were not his forefathers people of the sea? But people said he was crazy, "likum".

Illiune was awakened by a low trebled cry. He woke with a start and when he tried to clear his head, he felt a warm hand on his. The Serepein was patting his arm as a mother does in a soothing a baby. Illiune thought he must have been quite troubled in his sleep. Again he was embarrassed. He could not let the "Dolphin-girl" know he was troubled. Because he was shaken by the revelation in the dream and because she had wakened him, he did not know what to do. Not knowing, he leaned over and touched her cheek with his lips.

The tide was low and he decided they should go in. She could not get away from him now and he said, "Eh pan cola palio," (We will go over there), and motioned to the island. She looked at him as if to resist, but he removed the seaweed from her and picked her up and carried her down to the water and waded across the lagoon to their secret pool. Illiune noticed something different as he made his way through the water. The Serepein put her arm up and around his neck. She had never done that before. "Strange", Illiune thought, "She must think I will drop her."

CHAPTER 11

By the time they had crossed the lagoon a warm rain had begun to fall. It was the kind of rain that Illiune enjoyed. There was little wind, if any, and the air was always sweeter when the rain stopped. He had many things in mind he wanted to do. He needed fresh fruit and coconuts. The outrigger sail and ropes were on the reef and he planned to bring them to the island. He also wanted to inspect the fresh water pool above the ledge. When he thought of the pools he recalled his dream on the reef. The old man "Likum" had talked of the pools of Paradise Island, built of long black rocks. The dream would haunt Illiune for some time. Whether it was what he knew that caused the dream or whether the dream was actually a revelation of truth he did not know, but he was sure the island he was on was a paradise and the rock walls were here also, and the pools.

Illiune had placed the Serepein on the seaweed bed after soaking it well with fresh water. He used the half shell of the coconut as a dipper. While she lay on the shelf, Illiune was busy breaking off branches around the upper pool and overhead so that the secret area would be much larger. He also wanted more light to shine in. When he worked his way back to the fresh water pool, he leaned over and took a drink. The water was sweet and refreshing and Illiune thought the Serepein might like a drink also. Stepping over, he picked up the half coconut shell and returned to the pool where he rinsed it out well. He then filled it with water and carried it over to the Serepein. Lifting her head he held the cup as she drank. She smiled and he eased her head down. Illiune did not know how long it would be before he could leave her alone. She seemed well enough, but she could not swim. This posed a double problem for Illiune. He could not leave her long in the water for fear she might drown and he could not leave her long out of the water. Still he was responsible elsewhere and for her food and water. Dolphins brought fish for them, but Illiune had to feed her. His Serepein was as helpless as she was beautiful. With all his problems, Illiune was never sorry he found her. Having the Dolphin-girl to care for was good. It kept him busy.

Because they had not eaten fresh fruit for some time, Illiune decided he should gather some papayas and bananas. Maybe he could find some mangoes also. Speaking to the Serepein, he asked, "Would you like some fresh fruit, little girl? I will gather some if you think you will be safe here. I will not be away, but a short while. What do you say Serepein?" She did not seem to understand what Illiune said. "Of course," Illiune thought, "she cannot know what I am saying. She seems to be safe enough just now. When I return with fruit she will know where I have been." Reaching over and touching her cheek he said, "Kaselahia, Serepein", (Goodbye, little girl). Getting up, he waded across the pool and lifted the mangrove branches to step out. Her cry stopped him and he turned and hurried back. Her cry was one of pain or hurt. Illiune sat down on the ledge beside her and asked, "What is it, little girl? Would you like to go with me?" She smiled when he asked and Illiune slipped his arms under her and leaving the pool, he carried her over to the outrigger. The recent rain left and inch or two of water in the boat and Illiune laid the Serepein in the bottom so her head rested on a cross brace. Shoving the boat off the sand, he stepped in and lifting the paddle, he slowly moved along the edge of the island watching for fruit.

There was a warm breeze blowing in from the reef, but not strong enough to ripple the water within the lagoon. Sweet perfumed air drifted around the edge of the island. Occasionally, Illiune would turn his head from the island to the front of the outrigger and the Serepein would flash him a smile. When he did not respond to her actions, she pretended to avoid him. After a time, Illiune wished again that they could communicate better. He would tell her he was watching the progress of the boat and also for fruit. Studying her strange behavior provided no answers to Illiune. A banana plant with ripe fruit, leaning outward from the island, gave release to his thoughts as he turned the outrigger in and stepped out. Pulling the boat up on the sand he said, "See the ripe bananas, Serepein? I will pick them and you may eat as many as you like. They are sweet like you." Moving over to the banana plant Illiune cut off several bananas. He walked back to the dugout and placed them near the Serepein. Picking a ripe fruit, he peeled it and smiling at the dolphin girl, he held it up to her. She bit off a little and chewed it timidly. While she was chewing, Illiune broke off a piece and ate it. In a few moments she was her smiling, happy Serepein again and they enjoyed the fruit together. Illiune wondered why he seemed to mis-understand her. He thought it could prove difficult if, when he was attempting to do something to help her, she were not willing or unhappy.

Shoving the outrigger out from the sand, Illiune stepped in and continued to circle the island, still watching for fruit. As they glided quietly around the end of the atoll opposite from the reef, Illiune looked south and in the distance he could see the small, blue island with the cleft in the center. Since the day he had found the Serepein there, his life had changed greatly. He remembered why he went to the island. It was in hope of finding some clue to where he was or where his home might be. He recalled the mud-filled hole where the Serepein lay sick and decaying. His whole being revolted at the thought. Glancing at the Dolphin-girl he found it nearly impossible to believe such a lovely creature could have looked as she did when he found her. This must be a place of much magic, Illiune thought. The sight of papaya trees with ripe fruit in a small clearing among the coconut palms interrupted his thinking. He beached the outrigger and walked up toward the trees. Hearing a treble from the Serepein he turned and she was holding up a hand as if beckoning for him. He hurried back and as he leaned over, she raised both arms as if wanting him to pick her up. In wonder, he lifted her carefully from the boat and she motioned to the papaya tree. As he started climbing the bank he felt her put one arm around his neck. When they were near to the tree Illiune said, "I will have to put you down now Serepein, so I can pick some fruit." She tightened her arm around his neck and pointed at the tree with her other. He considered her motions dubiously and then stepped over close to the tree. She reached out and picked a fruit. Dropping it onto her abdomen she picked another. When they had four, Illiune turned around and walked back to the outrigger. He was quite pleased with her ability and she was watching him with a satisfied smile on her face. He wondered what else she could do. Perhaps, before long she could take care of herself. As he placed her back in the outrigger he said, "Every day you seem to do something new to surprise me, little girl. I wonder what it will be next?" When he had pushed the boat out again and resumed their slow journey around the island, he again began talking aloud to himself. "When you learn to swim, we will swim together every day. Your dolphin friends may join us if they like. We will dive for pearl oysters and coral and when we have enough to make me as rich as a King we will have more in common. You will be the Queen of the dolphins and I will be their King. Of course, I will not be as handsome as you are beautiful, but we can pretend…Can we not? I must tell you honestly, Serepein, you and the dolphins have made me very happy. No other boy in our village is as lucky as I." Illiune smiled at himself and the Dolphin-girl and at what he had just said. Again he mused, "I speak too freely at times, Serepein. I realize that you and I could not be married because we are so different. But I know that love is more than between people. People really do not understand love like it is here. I know the dolphins love you and I love you. Life is good here and I think I would enjoy living here. Of course, it would be better if my father were here too and maybe my mother, so father would be happy. I know my father loved my mother very much, from things he would say. She must have been very beautiful, Serepein, perhaps like you. Some day when you are well and able to swim I must go back to my home to let grandmother know I am alive and well. She should know about father too. He must have proper wailing. Grandmother will need some money and food. I am sure she is very poor now. What money she has left after buying a few articles, she spends playing strange games with other older women. She is not very lucky at games." If the island had been larger Illiune would have talked on, but he soon found himself busy easing the outrigger into the shore.

CHAPTER 12

That evening Illiune and the Serepein ate bananas and papayas, while sitting in the warm seawater looking out toward the reef. The breeze had changed and the perfumed air of the island drifted around them and on out to the east. Sometimes Illiune thought the sun came up bright and warm because of the sweet air of the islands that moved eastward to greet the sun before it appeared. Before the cover of darkness enveloped the secret pool, Illiune had opened another coconut and worked the oil into her hair and over her arms, face and shoulders. She seemed contented to lay with her lower body in the water and her shoulders and upper part resting on Illiune's lap. That night he had placed the outrigger so that he could lean back against it and made sitting more comfortable. The tide was almost full when they heard the dolphins. They came in quite close and made low whistling sounds. The Serepein tensed several times and then lay back, but Illiune knew she did not relax. As the whistling continued the Dolphin-girl raised up by herself and answered the dolphins with a low cry. The action surprised Illiune because she had never raised herself upright before. As the dolphins continued their calling, she looked at Illiune and motioned outward toward the water. Curiously, he got up and lifting her carefully, he waded out to the dolphins. Before he let her down into the water, he murmured, "You seem so strange now, Serepein. I cannot keep you from going,

but please promise you will come back. I am not ready to lose you."
He spoke to her more seriously than ever before because he sensed a
deep and far away calling of that which he could not comprehend.
She uttered a low treble cry and lifted her hand to his cheek and
smiled at him and he let her down into the water and felt her move
away on the back of the dolphins. In a few moments she was swallowed up in the vastness of the waters and the darkness of the
evening. He stood still waiting and listening. "Surely," he thought,
"the dolphins will bring her back because she is not well. They are
very wise creature and would never hurt anyone unless forced to.
They are subject to our Serepein and I believe I am also. I must do
what I can to make her well because she must go with them to fulfill
some decree of the sea, of which I can sense but not understand."

Before turning to go to the secret pool, Illiune spoke aloud,
"Please, Serepein, have our dolphin friends gather some fish for us
and also some more magic weed. We need the fish for strength and
the seaweed for healing one more time." He had hardly finished
speaking when there appeared a whirl in the water not more than six
feet away and he heard a low whistle as several waves appeared in the
moonlit waters of the lagoon. He knew then that the dolphins were
as protective of him as they were of her and it comforted him. No
harm would befall the Dolphin-girl and they were caring for him so
he might continue to care for her. The situation was beyond his
imagination. There was no relaying of his message by the Dolphin-
girl and yet the dolphins seemed to hear him and responded to him.
He would know later for sure, if they came with fish and seaweed.
The ability of the dolphins and Dolphin-girl to communicate by
sound was understandable, but he imagined the dolphins could also
understand his speech or read his thoughts. He even imagined the
Dolphin-girl understood what he was thinking sometimes. When he
considered this idea he felt hot with embarrassment and yet he realized it was as impossible to stop thinking as to stop dreaming.

When the dolphins came, they waited until Illiune raised the mangrove covering and then laid the seaweed on the rock wall. They brought much Illiune thought, maybe more than what was needed, but he could place some in the outrigger when they went out to the reef in the morning. While he held up the foliage several dolphins rose up and jumped over the wall and in a few moments returned and leaping over, swam excitedly out to sea. Illiune was trying not to worry about the Serepein, but in vain. He spent some time gathering the seaweed and carried it back to the ledge. It took several trips and he could feel the magic in the miracle weed as he held it and allowed it to string down upon his wrists and lower arms. Illiune wondered how deep the dolphins dove for such weed. It could help humans too, if they could find it. He then thought there might be some secrets of the sea that humans would never understand.

Before he had carried the seaweed to the ledge he sat down on the wall and treated his leg one more time as he waited for his Dolphin-girl. He wrapped it with a thick covering of weed and then sat still, waiting anxiously for the return of the Serepein. While listening intently, the tropical night seemed to explode with the sound of dying. Illiune tensed with dread and the same fear he experienced during his first days on the island. He was not thinking of himself this time, he felt something had happened to the Serepein. The moaning sounds did not continue long and the wailing was weaker. As they faded out the tropical darkness seemed blacker and heavier than it had for many nights. When Illiune could sit no longer, he slipped off the wall and waded out away from the black shadows of the tropical growth. The stars were visible only far to the north. A cloud hid the moon and Illiune feared it could mean the coming of a squall. When he could contain himself no longer he cried out pleadingly, "Oh, please Serepein, if you can hear me, please come back. I fear for you and I fear a storm is coming. You have been gone far too long. Tell your dolphin friends I need you, Serepein, and remember, E poka poka uk" (I love you). When he ceased speaking out he heard a ripple in the water and then a low treble cry and as he knelt down, his Serepein swam into his arms.

CHAPTER 13

Carrying the Dolphin-girl, Illiune felt his way to the rock wall and lifting the foliage he sat down with her on his lap. Turning inward, he carried her to the ledge and laid her on the seaweed bed he had prepared. The blackness of the night prevented any sight of form or movement. Illiune felt along the wall beneath the fresh water pool until he found the half coconut shell. He filled it with fresh water and carried it back to where the Dolphin-girl was lying. Speaking softly, he said, "You are probably thirsty now, Serepein. Here is some fresh water for you. I am happy that you are getting stronger. I think you are healthier now too, because you are weighing a little more each day. It is good that you are putting on more flesh. You were very slender when I found you. You learned to swim today also. The dolphins must be good teachers. Tomorrow we will swim with them beyond the reef, if you would care to." Illiune spoke softly and reassuringly to the Serepein, as he held the shell to her lips. She drank all the water and he laid her head down on the foliage pillow and filled the cup once more. This time she drank only a few swallows. He placed the cup on the edge of the pool and returned to the Serepein. Again speaking softly, he asked, "Would you like to be wrapped in seaweed again tonight, little girl? I think you should because your arms are not at all as well as they might be. This may be the last opportunity I will have to put the magic weed on you and I want you to be completely healed." She did not answer, but reached up and placed her hand on his cheek for a few moments. When she removed her hand, he began wrapping her with the seaweed from the lower end upward. He held her body up with his left arm and placed the weed with the right until she was completely wrapped to her hips. He then lowered her and covered her abdomen and breast with a thick layer, tucking it around and under her back. His final work was wrapping her arms and he had just completed covering her when the squall struck.

Illiune first thought was the outrigger. He hurried out of the pool and waded around the shore where the boat had been pulled up on the sand. The cold rain was beating down, but the wind had not reached the height of its fury. Illiune worked his way to the front of the outrigger and straining with effort, he dragged it further up and away from the water. He knew the waves of the lagoon could get violent if the winds were severe. When the craft was secured, he returned to the Serepein. By this time, He encountered very strong winds and the shelter of the secret pool was a warm welcome. Wading across, he spoke to the Serepein. "It is but a rain squall little girl. Do not fear, for I am here to watch over you." The howling wind and pelting rain prevented him from hearing any response from the Serepein. Because of the warmth of the magic weed, he was sure the rain did not chill her and he laid down beside her quite close with his arm around her in case she feared the squall. The thick foliage overhead took much chill from the cascading torrents and fearful as he was of the squalls, Illiune soon went to sleep beside the Dolphin-girl.

Morning came with a freshness in the perfumed air of the island. The heavy rain had washed the tropical greenery and the remnants of the downpour were dripping steadily to the forest floor. Illiune could hear the stream of fresh water cascading from the little pool at the back of the ledge. He lay quite still after waking for fear of disturbing the Dolphin-girl. She needed sleep. It would help her get strong. He looked into her face, lying quite close to his. He marveled at the beauty of this creature, half-human and half dolphin. There could be no living girl from his island that possessed such flawless skin and beautiful hair and eyes. Illiune imagined he saw her more as a lovely girl every day. "Strange," he thought, "but when she is unveiled this morning I will know for sure." She was still breathing evenly and he knew she was sleeping. He reminded himself that he would be more careful of his thinking because she seemed to understand. Illiune again realized that it would be impossible not to think. Moving as carefully as he could, he eased away from her and stood up. The morning promised to be radiant as the peeping rays of the sun filtered through the leaves. Illiune lifted the mangrove and stepped out. The coolness in the air contrasted with the water in the lagoon. He noticed how warm the water was as he went around to look at the outrigger. Everything was safe and Illiune went up the bank and over to his tree house. He smiled at himself when he thought how important it had been to him during his early days on the island. He could hardly remember when he last laid in the inviting leaves of his bed. The red coral was where he had placed it. He wondered if the Serepein would like to see his tree house. As he moved toward the outrigger he said aloud, "I will ask her when she is awake." As he approached the boat he saw that the bananas and papayas were still hanging where he had tied them. "We will have breakfast and then go out to the reef", he mused.

She was awake when he came back to the ledge and gazed down on her. She looked at him with questioning eyes and pointed to his injured leg. He raised it a bit and she smiled and then motioned for him to take her out of the pool. He understood readily enough, but thinking she might like some fresh water, he went over and filled the cup and returned to her side. He lifted her head and she drank and then again motioned to the outside. He picked her up and carried her over to the wall, raised the mangrove and lifted her out into a glorious morning. He thought of lowering her into the water, but she was still shrouded in the magic weed. He carried her to the coral sand at the edge of the water and let her down gently. Talking to her quietly, he said, "I will release you from your magic wrappings Serepein. If you are more lovely this morning, I will not believe it." She looked at him with an odd smile on her face and then trebled a lilting cry, almost inaudible and laid back as he began to remove the seaweed. Illiune's mind seemed to run in a maze of questions as the weed was taken off and he laid it in the front of the outrigger. He did not stop occasionally as before to admire her new beauty. When he had removed all the seaweed he then stepped back and let the light of the morning sun display the magic work. He had intended to look first at her arms to see if the translucent quality had turned to ivory or silver. That was his intentions, but when he finished, the Serepein raised up into a sitting position, with her hands braced on each side and smiled up at Illiune, knowing he could not help but admire her. He was sure it was the sunlight after the rain. She could not have changed so much more. The colors were deeper and brighter and there was no sign of loose skin or malnutrition. She was perfectly proportioned and her breasts were round and laced with silver which tenacled upward from her belt of gold. The arms were graceful and smooth and the silver lace came up from the wrists to the elbow. She would not require the seaweed medicine again. She was healed completely and he knew why the dolphins admired her and loved her. She said not a word as he considered her beauty. Suddenly he felt embarrassed for looking and to break the spell, asked, "Would you like a flower in your hair this morning?" She smiled and flashed her eyes and he turned and went into the trees of the island and returned with a ripe coconut. He husked it and broke it open and took out the meat. Then he walked back and picked two fresh hibiscus. Returning to the Serepein he knelt behind and began combing the oil of coconut into her hair. Illiune enjoyed pampering the Dolphin-girl. He tried to conceal it by entertaining the excuse that she was the only one he had ever been able to do things for. He smiled at his own deceptiveness. He knew he pampered her because she was not only beautiful, but there was an unexplainable attachment between the two and he was thinking, "I am in love with her and I cannot help myself, but it is all right because I know she must leave me." He stopped himself hurriedly, remembering she knew what he thought. It was too late because when he hesitated, she turned and trebled that soft little cry and looked at him sweetly.

He placed the flowers in her hair and tied them fast with another thread from his lava lava. Going up to the beach he brought back two papayas and several bananas. Slicing the fruit took a moment and they ate breakfast happily. Illiune knew it couldn't be now, but some day he would like to spend all his time in such idyllic idleness. When the fruit was eaten, he pulled the outrigger into the water and lowered the Serepein in the bow on the mat of the seaweed. He had placed some foliage against the front brace so she could sit up and look about. "The Serepein looks happy this morning," Illiune thought, "But she seemed different also. Perhaps the dolphins can help me know what has happened."

They moved rapidly out to the reef and beached the outrigger at the base of the square-nut trees. He stepped out and dragged the boat up a little on the sand. Coming back he lifted the Serepein from the boat and carried her over the reef. She put her arm around his neck and they stood quietly on the reef, enjoying being together and almost trying not to look ahead. After a time, he walked out into the edge of the open sea and paused in water about waist deep, so that the lower body of the Dolphin-girl was submerged. She seemed to know he expected the dolphins, but she also knew that being alone with her was a greater happiness. He realized the reverie was over and that he must share her with her friends, for they came unseen until they were milling about them and whistling low. Remembering the night before when she swam into his arms, he said, "Your dolphin friends are here for you, Serepein. Will you promise to come back to me if I let you go with them?" In answer, she raised her head and touched his lips with hers and then with a squeal of delight she rolled quickly out of his arms and dove into the sea.

The immediate and unexpected independence revealed by the Dolphin-girl unnerved Illiune. He wanted her well from the first time he saw her, but there was the sting of hurt because she did not need him as before. He did then what he always did when he was made an outsider at home. He dove into the inviting waters and swam out and deep. His ability to swim was good medicine for Illiune. In twisting and turning in the warm clear water, he reveled in the comfort of the sea. He wondered if he dove deep enough he might find some pretty shell that the Serepein would like. Surfacing for a moment, he filled his lungs with fresh air several times and then dove. The water was exceptionally clear as he went down. Before he reached a depth of eighty feet the coral sand bottom lay before him and he stopped his descent and swam along, watching. The pearl oysters were in an area of sand and easily seen. Illiune picked up four shells and rose quickly to the surface. The dive had winded him. He realized he had not dived deeply for some time and he was not properly conditioned. He purposed to practice more as he knew he could sell pearls if the shells contained them. He carried the four shells to the reef and opened them. Only one contained a pearl, but it was large and of excellent color. "That is good", Illiune mused, "one in four is very good." He placed the pearl on the highest coral growth and as he turned back to the sea he noticed he had not removed the seaweed from his leg. "It might have caused me to tire," Illiune thought. Sitting down on a sandy area he unwound the magic poultice and stretched his leg out in the sunlight. He recoiled in disbelief! His leg below his knee looked identical to the Serepein's arm. Blue shining scales covered his foot. From his ankle upward about three inches, the scales were gold in hue and above that were the same silver lace that was on the breasts of the Serepein. The sunlight revealed more to Illiune. As he reached down and touched his leg he saw for the first time that his hands and wrists and lower arms were also scaled like the Dolphin-girl's. He looked in utter bewilderment. Now he was beyond a doubt, "Fish-boy". Why?, questioned Illiune, but as quickly as he was surprised, he knew. It was the magic seaweed; that which made the Serepein so beautiful. Now he was like her, but he was not beautiful. He sitting there looking and not believing when he heard a low treble cry; the Dolphin-girl was calling him.

When he looked up she was not more than twenty feet from him in a deep pool outside the reef. She held up a hand as if waving and smiled at him. Her radiant beauty made him forget himself and he rose and went over to the pool and slipped into the water beside his Serepein. She knew and understood and drew him near and touched his lips with hers one more time. They then turned and hand-in-hand dove into the depths within the circle of waiting dolphins.

Throughout the day, the entire dolphin family reveled in ecstasy and excited pleasure as if being alive was enchanted bliss. The day was one Illiune would never forget. When they dove for pearl oysters he and the Serepein were hand-in-hand. It was a game to the dolphins. By the afternoon they had deposited many pearl oysters on the reef. Illiune was surprised at her swiftness and agility. She was quite at home in the water and could swim and play as gracefully as the dolphins. Sometimes she would circle Illiune as they were diving, but she was always near. He knew she was happy because she wore a constant smile. As the day turned into evening, Illiune was weary and he swam to the reef and waited for the Serepein. This might be a time of trial to see if the Dolphin-girl would go with him willingly or not. In a few moments she swam up and looking at him, smiled and uttered that low trebled cry. He spoke to her, explaining why he came to the reef.

"Serepein, we have been swimming all day and I have enjoyed it very much. I am not able to swim as easily as you or the dolphins and I now must rest. While I am resting from our play, I will put the ropes and sail on the outrigger and break open the shells to look for pearls. If you would like to swim with your dolphin friends for yet a while, you may do so. Please do not stay too long, for I will miss you and worry. Tomorrow we will return if you would care to." Illiune then reached down and touched her cheeks and she turned and disappeared into the sea. After she had gone, Illiune wondered if she thought he wanted her to go. He never asked if she would like to stay with him. Still considering his awkwardness at speech, he walked up to the pile of pearl oysters and began opening them with his knife. There were many oysters. The dolphins dove quite deep and Illiune wondered if they knew what he was looking for. The ones they gathered for him were much larger than those he had found. Illiune had experienced so many strange surprises since he was cast into the sea, he wondered if he would become accustomed to them. He did not think so. Already he had forgotten his scaled hands. At first, he remembered, he was nearly terrified for fear of being teased. "How odd," he thought, "I will hold up my hands and head for anyone to see. If I look a little like the Serepein. I am proud of it."

When he opened the second shell and ran his fingers through the flesh, he knew his sense of touch had failed him. The pearl he was holding was larger then any he had ever seen. It alone would be worth enough to keep a family for a year. Laying the large pearl on the high coral with his first one, he continued his work. Having found the one large pearl he doubted if he would be surprised again. He was wrong. The fourth oyster produced another large pearl. When he had finished opening the shells, he had twenty-seven medium to extra large pearls of excellent quality. He knew he was rich, but except to marvel at the size and number of pearls, he did not feel any different. He was much richer when in the company of the Serepein and her dolphins. Illiune carried the pearls over and placed them in the bottom of the outrigger. He gathered the ropes and sail and carried them to the boat also. By the time he had completed his task, the sun had long dropped behind the island and it would be dark in an hour. The tide was nearly full and there was no need to slide the outrigger through the sand. The water was deep enough that by pulling a little it was floating free in the lagoon. He was ready to go and he turned to the sea and called to his Serepein. "It is time for us to go in now, little girl. If you can hear me, please come to me. We will spend the night in the secret pool and return here in the morning." Speaking more quietly, he almost whispered, "Please hurry, Serepein, I too, love you." The water over the reef was quiet. Waiting for a sound from the dolphins Illiune heard a ripple behind him. When he turned, the Dolphin-girl was waving at him from inside the reef. Again, Illiune found it difficult to believe. He wondered if she, as the dolphins, jumped the barrier, and if not, there must be a passage not too far away.

Walking over the reef and out to the Dolphin-girl he took her hands in his and leaning over asked, "Would you like to swim to the pool? I will follow in the outrigger." She held on to his hands and he lifted her from the water and carried her to the boat. When he bent forward to lay her on the pad of weeds, she would not remove her arm from around his neck. Looking down at her he asked, "What is it, Serepein? Do you not want to go in to our pool?" She was smiling at him and raised her head and pressed her lips on his and then laid back in the outrigger and placed her arms across her lap. Surprise again flooded over Illiune. She had never done before, as she just did. "Her lips were so warm", he thought. He wondered if all girls had warm lips. Even if they did he knew they could never be so lovely. Pushing the boat out he stepped in and moved across the calm water of the lagoon.

Illiune could see the island in the glow of the setting sun and beached the outrigger at its usual place. He stepped out and moving to the front of the canoe, pulled it up a few feet onto the sand. He moved back and lifted the Dolphin-girl in his arms and carried her around to the wall. As he was about to put her on his lap to free one hand, she reached out and raised the foliage and he stepped over and into the secret pool. By now it was dark and Illiune moved cautiously toward the ledge, lest he trip or somehow injure the Serepein. Before he released her he wondered how many more times he would lay her down to sleep on the rock ledge. "Perhaps this may be the last time," he thought, and the idea chilled him. He put her on the weed pad and filled the shell cup with water for her. He drank also and as he did not feel hungry, he doubted if she would be. They both had a tiring day and it was not long before the Dolphin-girl was sleeping. When he heard the even breathing he lay down beside her and put his arm around her waist. "Perhaps if she wakes," he thought, "she will know I am close and will not be afraid." Lying there in their hidden pool in this magic world, he could not help but feel a deep pleasure. Even though he sensed this brief happiness would soon end, for the moment he was a prince.

CHAPTER 14

Night seemed to have passed almost instantly for Illiune, as the breeze whispering in the tropical growth overhead awakened him. It was difficult for him to get his eyes focused. He blinked them several times and then understood. He was lying on his side and his face was almost touching the Serepein's. She was wide-awake and smiling at him as usual. He raised up quickly and said, "I am sorry if I crowded you, little girl. I only meant to be close so you would not be afraid." She continued to smile, but there was something in her eyes that told Illiune she knew he was not being entirely honest, and he was not. Rising up he went over to the fresh water pool and filled the cup for her. She drank and he also. Going back to the pool he returned with a full cup of fresh water. He let it trickle slowly on her cheeks and shoulders and then wiped away the water with his hands. She watched him in silence and when the cup was empty she motioned toward the lagoon.

They ate papayas and bananas for breakfast and she again had Illiune work the coconut oil into her tresses. When he had finished, he sat her beside the outrigger and went up and picked two more hibiscus for her hair. "Tomorrow," he said, "I will make you a lei fit for a Queen and also a mar mar. Your dolphin friends will know you are a Prinsess." Lifting her gently, he picked her up and sat her in the outrigger. Sliding the boat into the water, he paddled slowly out to the square-nut trees. Illiune was not in a hurry to reach the reef. The dazzling beauty of the Serepein was pleasant to enjoy. If they were with the dolphins, she would be almost as one of them. "This is no way to think," mused Illiune. "They have first claim on her. They have been more than kind to let me help them a little." The outrigger grated to a stop on the inner reef, but Illiune sat quite still looking at the Dolphin-girl. "Today we will swim with your dolphin friends again, Serepein. And tomorrow we will swim with them together. After that we will see. There is a voice, strange and far away that speaks to me that we must part. If it is not true I will be happy with you, but if it proves true, we may not see each other again for many days. Maybe never. But whatever comes, you know I love you and always will. So for what time is left, let us be happy with your friends." These things Illiune told her almost in a whisper, but the tears in her eyes let him know she understood.

As he lifted her from the outrigger he returned the kiss she had given him the day before. It thrilled him, although he could not help but feel the tears as he laid his face against her for a moment. Turning with her, he walked over the reef and into the waves of the welcoming sea.

They swam joyously together for an hour, oblivious to anything or any thought. Today again Illiune felt awkward when he watched the graceful movements of the lovely Prinsess. Even while far below the surface her colors of blue, gold and silver were rich and brilliant. He looked at his hands and marveled. They too, shone bright and colorful in the filtered depths. Illiune vowed that he would never be ashamed of anything again. He had lived a lifetime in a few days, as a poor dying boy and a rich prince. The reverie below the sea was interrupted by the circling dolphins that swam in great circles, protecting them. When Illiune realized what they were doing, he swam over to them and led them back. The dolphins put on a display of beauty and speed and grace for their Serepein and Illiune. In ecstasy, they leaped and dove and laughed like happy children at play.

The dolphin's family and Illiune worked their way along the reef until they were opposite the sand spit which led to the island. The dolphins then persuaded him to dive with them. It did not take much encouragement as they seemed excited. He turned and went down in the blue water, down, down and as they approached the hundred-foot level he saw a beautiful black coral just below him. He had never seen one so large. He turned toward it and broke it loose at the base and returned to the surface. He swam over to the reef and stepped out of the water to admire the near perfect specimen. He was still looking at the black shiny coral when a low whistle caused him to turn and see a dolphin approaching with a pink coral just as large. Walking over he took it from the dolphin, reached over rubbed its back and smiled a thank you. The response was traumatic. Before long there were several dolphins with coral. It seemed to Illiune they were all trying to outdo the other. When four large, pink, coral lay on the reef, Illiune spoke to them. "No more coral now, friends. It is more than I can use. I thank you very much for what you have brought me already." They whistled their understanding and returned to play in the blue water.

Cavorting with the dolphins caused Illiune to forget the Serepein altogether. When he remembered her he felt ashamed. Yesterday they were nearly inseparable, today they swam together but an hour. Surfacing, he whistled shrilly and a dolphin came to his side. "Please take me to our Prinsess," Illiune stammered. The dolphin turned and swam slowly northward along the reef. The dolphin moved easily with little effort and yet Illiune found it difficult to keep up. After an hour, the dolphin turned toward the reef and as Illiune followed, he saw the dolphin Prinsess in a deep sheltered pool ringed with bright varicolored coral. She was waiting for him. When he swam up beside her, she put her arms around him and gave him a quick hug. That was all and then the dolphins brought them their dinner.

They ate their meal of white meated fish while sitting in the coral pool. When they finished, Illiune spoke to her again as he had the day before saying: "I have some things I must do, little girl. You may stay with me or you may swim with our dolphin friends. They brought me some beautiful pink coral from deep water, much deeper than I can go. They are strong and graceful and kind, somewhat like you, Serepein. I must also see if the sail will fit well on my outrigger. I sense a strangeness in the sea that makes me worry for you. However, I cannot be selfish. You are free to choose now that you are well. I only ask for one more day with you. That could be forever or it may be just tomorrow. Your friends are waiting now. What will you do?" There Serepein did not smile as usual. They both knew he was being honest and what he said was not easy. Large tears again appeared in her eyes and found their way over her cheeks to drop onto her breast. Illiune wished he had not said what he had. Remembering that she could understand his thoughts gave him the freedom to speak audibly again. "Do not fear that I do not love you, Serepein. I always will and I purpose to return to our magic island when this inner voice tells me it is time. When I am released from my duty to my grandmother and my father I will be free to come back to you. This must be so Serepein because my dreams tell me the decree of the sea will be fulfilled. We both must endure loneliness so that we can be together another day. My hands and feet tell me we belong to each other in some world of magic that is so strange to me."

After speaking those words, Illiune took the Serepein in his arms and held her to him. "When the time of our separation is completed, we will have each other, always. This I have been told in my dreams." She did not resist his embrace. He knew she also had revelation of the great secrets and that their bliss and idyllic days were numbered. He released her and looking into her face said, "Let us enjoy our time together, whatever it may be. When the time comes, it must come." She kissed him, turned and whistled into the blue water. Illiune stood motionless for some time. What had just taken place left him sick with a misty vision, which formed tears in his eyes. When he turned, he was crying openly and unashamed.

CHAPTER 15

The sail needed only a little work to make to make it seaworthy. He would gather the pandanus fronds when he returned to the island. They would be ready for use in a few days. He could pound them and split them with ease. Loading the pieces of pink coral with the one black, was no problem. Illiune tied them onto the carrier with the ropes he had salvaged. His urge to begin the journey home was becoming stronger each day. The revelations in his dreams told him he must sail north for at least three days and then west. Whenever he could forget his Dolphin-girl the work went well and the tasks light. When he thought of losing her, every action was painful and he felt heartsick.

Evening came with a full tide and the Dolphin-girl was waiting when he called. He lifted her with care and placed her on the mat in the outrigger. That evening they sat outside the pool for a while and he combed her hair with coconut. After her hair and upper body had been smoothed with oil, he walked up and over to a plumeria bush and picked off a cluster of sweet scented blossoms. Going back to the Serepein he worked them into her hair and secured them with a thread. For over an hour they sat watching the moon and stars. He was leaning against the outrigger and she was lying back on his chest. They did not speak, but there was communication. When Illiune sensed that she was drifting into dreamland, he gathered her up and carried her to the secret pool and the bed of seaweed. After they drank from the fresh water pond, they were both sleeping in moments. The magic of Mystery Island was at work.

Morning came with refreshing rain that continued for about an hour. Before the skies had cleared, the tropical flowers were competing in fragrance. Illiune awoke before the Serepein and lay quietly pondering what he would do that day. He would gather some pandanus leaves for drying. They needed more fruit, which meant paddling around the island. Coconuts must be gathered for oil for the Serepein. With these tasks in mind Illiune knew his day would be full. He also planned to make a lei for the Dolphin-girl and perhaps a mar mar. The dolphins would be waiting for them beyond the reef. He looked at the Serepein beside him and then realized he should not have. With all the work to be done he could not spend any time gazing wistfully into the face of the Dolphin-girl, but it was too late. He could not believe how enchanting her face had become to him. For the first time Illiune sensed that he allowed the idea a place in his thoughts. He passed off the selfish wish by realizing if she were fully human, he could never win her love. She would be far too beautiful and could choose anyone she desired for her husband. "No, it is better this way," he thought. "Time will give us the answer, but for now we are together and we should not waste away our days by wishing that which is not."

He was smiling to himself when she startled him by opening her eyes and returning his enchanted gaze. He felt a bit awkward because she caught him looking at her. Reaching over, he touched her cheek and said, "Menseng mwow, Serepein," (Good morning, little girl). With that, he rose and went to the fresh water pool and came back with a drink for her. She took the cup from him and drank slowly and daintily and then returned the cup with a smile. Illiune went back to the pool and drank and then rinsed his face and hands in fresh water. Filling the shell cup he returned to the Serepein and dipping his fingers in the water, washed her face, hands and shoulders.

Thinking audibly, he said, "What will we have for breakfast, Serepein, fruit or fish? We do not have either unless we find it." She motioned for him to help her into the pool and as he did, she slipped free and into the water. The surface of the secret pool boiled with movement and in a few moments she rose to the surface with two large reef fish, one in each hand, with a happy smile on her face. Illiune was surprised, but he remembered the night the dolphins came with the magic weed. Some brought fish and he knew then that they had put them in the pool. He shook his head slowly as he took the fish from the Serepein and prepared them for breakfast. They sat on the rock wall as they ate and watched outward toward the reef. The sun rose to spy on them as they welcomed the day. Illiune looked at his Serepein to ask, "Would you like to go with me in our outrigger to find fruit? When we return, we will visit the dolphins." Her answer was a motion toward her hair, a combing motion and Illiune smiled in acknowledgment. He stepped off the wall, lifted her and carried her to the back of the outrigger and kneeled as he eased her into the foot deep water. Rising quickly, he went into the island's growth and returned with ripe coconuts. She turned and watched him open the husk and break the shell. Returning, he sat down and laid her head on his knees and began working the oil into her hair. When the tresses looked like black coral, shining, he took more coconut meat and worked it gently over her face, neck, arms and breast. It was a regular morning chore with the coconut, but he enjoyed it. It was an exciting way to begin the day. She reminded him of another morning duty also after the oil bath. Reaching up, she smiled and touched her hair near her temple and her slave boy rose up and returned with both plumeria and hibiscus. Working carefully, he tied white plumeria blossoms with one bright red hibiscus flower on each side. He rose up, stepped back and looked at his lovely Serepein. There was nothing to say that he had not said before, but she smiled because she understood.

Illiune spent a few moments removing the coral and sail from the outrigger and then continued along the shore. By the time they had made the circle of the island they had much fruit. Between stops, the Serepein would let her hands play in the water. When she thought he was not watching she would splash water at him and then look quickly away as if pretending she had not done it. Illiune did not mind. He seemed to enjoy any excuse to look at her. He wondered how one so grand and lovely as a lady could play childish tricks and when he wondered, she would only twist her head quickly and utter that low treble. By the time they returned to the launching place they could hear the dolphins near the reef.

Several days passed as moments, it seemed to Illiune. They would awake, bathe, breakfast and then he put oil on her hair and upper body. Sometimes they would go directly out to the reef and spend the day. Other times they would travel together in the outrigger. At night they would return to the secret pool and the magic of mystery. The sail had been patched with strips of green-dry, pounded pandanus that Illiune wove into the original one from his father's outrigger. He was bothered more each day with the thought that he must return to his village and see about his grandmother and have wailing done properly for his father. Usually he was reminded of this in a dream. His nights were beginning to become dreadful for some reason he could not understand. Illiune lay close to the Dolphin-girl and she would sleep soundly while his dreams became weird and mysterious. He dreamed his father was alive and searching for him, while he was staying on this enchanted island. Sometimes he was speaking with "Likum" and the old man would tell him of the ancient people of the sea, the magnificent palaces and the Island of the Dead. At other times he was a dolphin and lived in an enchanted castle under an island on the reef. Interspersed with these varied thoughts was the dreadful mourning cries of the dead Kings coming for him. There were other times when he dreamed he was married to the Serepein and he was enchanted with the thought. When he dreamed this dream he always woke up feeling unhappy or distressed. Many times during the latter days Illiune had been awakened by the Serepein. She would pat his arm with her hand until he opened his eyes and she knew he was awake. There were many times when she woke him with tears in her eyes and he feared what he might have dreamed. Illiune took consolation in the realization that their days together were idyllic.

The Serepein was completely well. The outrigger was ready for a journey and there was the growing sensation that told him the time was drawing near. Illiune learned to fear the idea. He was young, but had experienced enough in life to know the unknown can be harsh and cruel. The busy days with the Serepein and the dolphins made all worthwhile. The day they swam far north of the island, Illiune was never to forget. How far they traveled, he did not remember until later, but the day was bright and warm and the water calm. He and the Serepein swam together as usual and the dolphins played around them. When they were hungry, they were fed by the dolphins. When they tired, they were carried by dolphins. When they were dreaming together, they were protected by dolphins. Illiune could never understand why they were so friendly or protective.

Early in the afternoon the Dolphin-girl swam toward the reef and paused near a channel that led into the lagoon. It was easily wide enough for an outrigger and very deep. When Illiune came up beside her, she took his hand in one of hers and pointed toward the channel. He noticed there was high sand on each side of the opening on the reef and some small trees were beginning to grow. Leading him by the hand she swam up near the reef and motioned for him to wait. Illiune obeyed her command. The Serepein disappeared in the clear blue water. Waiting was not easy for Illiune. Many thoughts flashed through his mind. Was she gone forever? Could she leave so naturally? Would he see her again…ever? His questioning was interrupted by a low whistle and he turned to see a dolphin waiting for Illiune to take the large red coral it had brought. "Menlau" was all that Illiune could say and the smiling dolphin seemed satisfied. Three more dolphins came in with red coral and although Illiune knew it was worth many dollars he said, "Please do not bring more, my friends. I thank you very much for your thoughtfulness, but it is all I could possibly carry away." The dolphins were listening quietly and when he finished speaking, he waded out and gave each one a friendly rub and they whistled into the blue. Illiune carried the coral to the higher sand and turned and walked back to the place where the Serepein left him. It was perhaps an hour later when she returned amid a crowd of happy dolphins. She came up to Illiune and in her hand was an odd looking shell, such as he had never seen. The Serepein held it out as though it were a secret that only she and the dolphins knew. He turned the shell over slowly and noticed it had a row of natural holes along one edge. The shell was conical in shape, but rough with pearl-like points. In the sunlight it was bright with blue, gold and silver. It was a personal gift from the Serepein and it held some mystery that he knew not of. All the time he inspected the shell she smiled and the dolphins smiled with her.

The dolphins led the Serepein and Illiune back toward the outrigger. They never tired, but continued their antics of joy as if that was their only purpose in life. So many times Illiune wondered at the dolphins. They seemed to enjoy helping, protecting and guiding and always with a smile. He had never seen them angry with one another. They were not cruel. Illiune knew if they were like humans, they would abuse the Dolphin-girl because she was different. He remembered how he was treated by the other children of his village. Many times he desired to run away to the sea forever and never return to suffer at human hands and mouths. This was a sobering revelation to Illiune because now that he was away from them and free, he was preparing to return, if he could find the way. "Life is so confusing," he thought, "What could be its purpose?" Sometimes Illiune sensed an overwhelming desire to forget his village and make his home with the dolphins. Since the Serepein had been well, life was nearly perfect. His days with her and the dolphins had been filled with happiness that few people could imagine. Illiune realized he had experienced one of the strangest relationships that a human had ever encountered. All these mental reflections occupied his mind as he and the Serepein swam south.

Almost every day brought a new and strange excitement to Illiune. As the Dolphin-girl became more strong and beautiful she seemed to find some new secret to show him. Sometimes it was a physical change such as learning to pick fruit or drink from a cup. Sometimes it was a feminine subility such as the oil bath and flowers in the hair or making Illiune plead with her. There were also those times when she touched him or looked at him or kissed him that thrilled Illiune. He knew she often seemed human in desire for attention and love. Illiune considered all these riches of young life and a fear seemed to drown the joy, the fear that his feeling for the Serepein and hers for him was becoming deeper than he could explain or cared to explain. It was something that came from the depths of being and it was a secret of the universe. He said aloud as if to change his thought, "If the time is tomorrow, then let it be. She may be strong, but my heart will break. Perhaps the shell will be a comfort." That did help change his line of thought and because they had arrived at the two square-nut trees, he gathered her in his arms and carried her over the reef to the outrigger.

They moved across the lagoon with the dolphins following. The tide was full and some jumped into the secret pool. Illiune could hear them splashing and whistling. He did not take her to the pool. The day was far from spent and he decided they might spend an hour or two in the water near the tree house. They could eat there and the dolphins could stay yet a while. The Serepein seemed secretly happy and as they sat side-by side, she took the shell and put it to her lips and pretended to blow. She then gave it to Illiune and he put it to his lips and blew. At first it made no sound, but in time he could detect a shrill whistle, almost like a dolphin far away. She smiled excitedly and then took the shell and dipped it into the water and handed it to him. He tried blowing again, but when he could make no sound she reached up and tipped the shell and when he blew again it sent out a low treble, exactly the sound the Serepein made when talking to him. Illiune nearly dropped the shell in surprise. He knew the secret of the shell. It could call the dolphins and the Serepein. He made another vow. He would never be without the shell. It was his connecting link with the dolphins and the Serepein, his hope and happiness.

Illiune arose and walked to the front of the outrigger. Picking up the ropes, he chose the smaller one and returned to the Serepein and sat down. By untwisting the coconut rope he formed several smaller sized cords about a foot in length. Taking up the shell he passed the small cords through the line of holes in the shiny ridge. The ends of the small lines were then woven and twisted back into the original rope. Illiune had put splices in lines before and when he was finished the shell was fastened securely on the end of the rope. Unraveling the main rope, Illiune cut off about three feet so that he could loop it over his shoulders or neck. When it was tied just above the shell, he placed the loop over his neck and the shell hung secure and close. While Illiune worked on the special gift, the Serepein watched in silence. When he had finished his work, she smiled and whistled. The dolphins swam out to the reef and into the outer sea. She then motioned for him to blow on the shell. He raised it to his lips and blew a shrill call and immediately the reef exploded with incoming dolphins. Within a matter of minutes the dolphin family was milling around them waiting to be commanded.

While Illiune was pondering his new power and ability to call the dolphins, the Serepein whistled again and the dolphins made waves outward toward the reef. When they had gone, the Dolphin-girl motioned for Illiune to go up on the shore. She made him understand by motioning that she wanted oil on her face and shoulders. He rose up, waded to the beach and stepped out onto the sand. She stopped him there with a low treble call and as he turned to her, she held up her hand for him to stop. He stood still, puzzled. She then motioned for him to blow the shell. He raised it to his lips and blew another shrill whistle and watched out toward the reef for the return of the dolphins. There was no response. He put the shell to his lips and blew again, much louder. He waited several minutes and then, when he began feeling dejected because he was wrong about his abilty to call the dolphins, the Serepein motioned him to return to her. He waded out slowly and she raised her hand and pulled him down beside her in the water. When he was sitting, she reached up and put the shell to his lips again with that irresistible smile. Had it been anyone but the Serepein he would have refused. He had just whistled twice with no response. Raising the shell to his lips he knew he was a slave to her command, as were the dolphins and as they thrilled to obey, he too, was warmed in compliance. Again he sounded the shrill whistle and before he could release the shell, the water was foaming with responding dolphins. As they were arriving and circling the Serepein smiled at Illiune and motioned to the water. She pointed to the land and outrigger and then the shell and shaking her head "no" she pointed at the dolphins. Still half-smiling she touched the water and the shell and his lips and again pointed toward the dolphins and looked at him as she flashed her eyes at him. A slow smile spread over Illiune's face in comprehension. She had shown him that he must be in the water when he blew the call. He surmised that it was not the whistle, which he heard that the dolphins detected, but a vibration in the water. When he fully understood the importance of this knowledge, he leaned over and embraced the Serepein and holding her close for those few seconds he whispered, "E poko poko uk", (I love you). Upon a command from the girl the dolphins raced seaward and in a short while they returned with fish and they ate together in the placid waters of the lagoon in the land of magic.

CHAPTER 16

*T*ropical stars gleamed eagerly for attention that night. Even the lunar glow could not detract from their brilliance. They sent myriads of silver ribbons dancing through the palms and undergrowth of the enchanted island. There was no death moaning during the night that Illiune could hear. While waiting for the dreaded sound he wondered why the Serepein did not fear it. She must be able to hear it, but perhaps there was a reason she did not react in any way. Even the voices of the wailers seemed much lighter. The flower scented breeze wound whispering through the island growth, over the secret pool and on across the lagoon to meet the sun far out to sea.

After their supper with the dolphins, Illiune and the Serepein had returned to the pool. The spirits of both were light and gay in the dazzling splendor of the island's magic. After their usual drink of fresh water from the upper pool they lay on the shelf looking happily at one another. He knew she could understand his thoughts and now he did not mind. In the morning he would keep his promise and make her a lei and a mar mar fit for a Queen. Before drifting off to sleep their lips met once, warm and exciting and then he placed his arm around her waist and they fell into the magic of dreamland. If the dolphins were in the pool on guard, they too, would have sensed the ecstasy of love.

He awoke early as planned, very early. Slipping with care off the ledge, he waded quietly out to the lagoon and went up to the plumeria tree. Unraveling a long thread from the lava lava he began picking the fragrant blossoms and strung them on the string. He made it long enough to double and when finished, he placed it on his bed of leaves in the tree house. Returning to the plumerias, he made a mar mar from white blossoms, working a bright red hibiscus flower into the center and wove more plumeria around it. When finished, he looked at it with satisfaction. It was good work and resembled a tiara of flowers in the front. He placed it beside the lei on his bed and then returned to the Serepein in the pool. He did not know if she were sleeping. Lifting the coconut shell, he walked up to the fresh water pool and dipped a cup and drank. He washed his face and hands and then returned to the Dolphin-girl with more water. He sat down beside her and reached down and picked up her hand and squeezed it a little. She was turned toward him and opened her eyes and looked at him with a strange expression, almost of dread, as if Illiune thought, she would rather not wake up. He knew how she might feel. He too realized that this was only a dream and he did not want to wake. She closed her eyes for a moment and he felt the pressure of her hand increase and then she opened her eyes wide and smiled. "She must be trying to hide something from me", he thought and then remembered the lei and mar mar. He lifted her head and she drank the water. She was willing to be carried out of the pool and when he sat her down in the warm, clear water of the lagoon, she smiled as always.

When the hair dressing was over and Illiune had rubbed her with oil from the waist upward, he went up to the tree house and returned with the flowered gifts. He doubled the lei and placed it around her neck and then put the mar mar on her head. Illiune saw before him the most beautiful Prinsess in the world. Her flashing eyes and smile of knowing added to the beauty of the girl. He knelt beside her and gathering both hands in his he said.

"I do not know what the future will bring us, but I know if I ever loved it is you, now. We both realize our present love can never be complete and we cannot remain together as we now are. Someday soon I must go to my people, but I will return here to you and our dolphin friends. If I cannot find you, I know they will lead me to you. I tell you these truths because my love for you is too strong to continue as we now are and too strong to die. Is it not the same with you, my Serepein?" Before he had ceased speaking, she was crying, openly. She could not speak, but she moved her head in acknowledgement and he knew. There were tears in the eyes of Illiune also, but he was not ashamed. When he tried to say some words of comfort to her, she put her fingers on his lips and her eyes said, "Rong Etcha".

How long they sat together in love and heartbreak Illiune could not remember. It was the cry of their friends that stirred them. As he leaned back from her he saw how beautiful she was, even in sorrow. He leaned forward one more time and touched his lips to her brow. That was all. Lifting her gently, he waded reefward with his dolphin Prinsess. Their journey to the reef was slow, but steady. He wondered if the dolphins would know their secrets. If they did, Illiune would not care. He knew nothing in the world could be so special to him as his Serepein and her friends. He was an outcast among his own and had found a new life of hope with the warm-blooded creatures of the sea. He marvelled at the thought. He would visit his grandmother and see she was not in need. The death of his father should be told and then he would visit the old man "Likum", (Liar). After that he would return to his happy life…on the Island of the Dead.

Illiune presented the charming Prinsess of the dolphins to her subjects, bedecked in the lei and mar mar. They received her with joy, but they seemed to realize the spirit of carefree happiness was missing. Their morning frolic was more somber than usual, even though he and the Serepein swam hand in hand in the tunnel of dolphins. Illiune found it impossible to keep his eyes from the lovely creature beside him. When the dolphins brought them fish, they could not eat. She, he knew, felt as he and Illiune was too heartsick to think of eating. He feasted on the beauty of the "Dolphin-girl" and was partially satisfied. In recent days he had looked upon precious pearls and exquisite coral, but they could not compare with the beauty of the Serepein. He knew she was fully well now and there was not a blemish on her anywhere. Even while swimming, as well as other times, he thought he must be dreaming. How could he, an outcast and malformed human, love and be loved by the Prinsess of the sea? This question returned to Illiune many times. Both he and the Serepein pretended they were thoroughly enjoying their play, but truth in love was stronger than pretense. When the sun was directly overhead, the two turned toward the reef and swam into the small, protected coral pool on the reef's edge. There was not much to say. Both knew that destiny had called. He took her hands in his and spoke ever so gently.

"I must go in now, my Serepein. There is much I must do. You may swim with your friends if you like or you may come in with me. The tide is low. If you stay out I will look for you when the tide is full." All the time he spoke, she looked at him with her enchanting eyes. She did not smile as usual, but when he finished, she put her arms around him and gave him a lingering, warm kiss and he returned it eagerly and pressed her to him. When the embrace ended she turned and slipped into the waters of her home.

Illiune stood there, still. He raised an arm hesitantly and then lowered it. Turning away he wandered carelessly up and over the reef and headed for his island through the mist. He must keep busy. It would be better. The outrigger was waiting when he reached the island and Illiune straightway began fitting the sail for a long journey. By evening the mast and sail needed no more work. To pass time he wandered back onto the island and returned with some bananas and papayas. Laying the fruit on the carrier of the outrigger Illiune decided he should also get more ripe coconuts for the Serepein's hair and skin. By the time he had brought them to the boat the tide had reached its high mark and looking out seaward, he saw nothing that resembled the Serepein. Standing there gazing out with a longing in his heart he thought of blowing for her on his shell. "No", he mused, "This not the time." The longer he watched and waited, the more misty the reef became. When he gave up his watch, he dropped to his knees on the sand and wept.

The night was unbearably long and several times Illiune walked to the wall from the ledge and listened and waited in vain. Although the moon was bright and the reef and lagoon appeared radiant in the glow, it could not lighten his gloom. The lump in his throat seemed to choke him at times and by morning his eyes were red with weeping. Rising early, he sat about preparing for the return trip home. He could not eat, but did gather extra fruit and nuts, both green and ripe, for his journey. He would not spend another night on the island. Never once did he consider staying and waiting for the Serepein's return. Although in his heart he felt he would meet her again, he realized that the time was not now. He hurried his work, trying not to think about her. The red and pink and black coral he loaded carefully and tied it down. He would pick up the other red coral at the passage in the lagoon. When ready, he stood up tall and walked slowly around and into the secret pool. Wading over to the ledge he climbed up and drank deeply of the fresh water. Moving back, he lowered himself into the water and moving over to where the Dolphin-girl had lain so many nights, he bowed himself and pretended to kiss her goodbye. Rising up quickly, he felt his way from the pool and around to the outrigger.

Without looking back once, Illiune travelled north inside the reef until he saw ahead the red coral, marking the entrance to the sea. His only break in the long journey was when he stopped to tie on the four pieces of red coral. While there, he held tightly to the shell and remembered the embrace of his Serepein. He climbed into the outrigger, passed through the channel, and set sail north. The wind held steady and fair all day and well into the next night. Illiune had sailed enough with his father that he knew his course was straight. He could tell by the feel of the sea and the stars and the sun. The wind eased somewhat during the night, but to Illiune's amazement his speed did not slacken, but rather increased. Again he could tell by the feel of the sea. Several times during the night he felt himself drifting into sleep. He did not want to dream and fought against sleep…in vain. When he woke in the morning, the sail was full and he was on course.

Hunger stirred him and he opened a ripe coconut and after drinking the sweet milk, ate several pieces of the thick meat. He could not have hoped for better weather. The breeze was steady and the sea rolled with long gentle swells. By the time the sun rose high enough to be uncomfortable, clouds appeared and a warm rain fell over Illiune and the sea. By afternoon he had eaten some bananas and a papaya and drank the water from a green coconut. Before the sun dropped behind the friendly sea he was again nodding in sleep. His last thought before he gave in to drowsiness was that he would like a fish for breakfast. Twice during the night he woke to check his course and slept on. He dreamed he heard voices of his dolphin friends, so real he nearly answered in his sleep. When morning came, he was awakened by a boil of water near his outrigger and a large fish dropped into his boat. "Strange," Illiune thought. He had never known of a large reef fish to jump into an outrigger so far from land. For a moment he looked around, thinking of the dolphins, but all was calm on the sea. Before eating, he checked his course again and saw that he was still moving north. Illiune was amazed at the ability of his outrigger to maintain course through the night. He would always be indebted to the dolphins for such a fine craft. After eating the fish and drinking the water from a green nut, Illiune sat back and relaxed. He was filled by breakfast and with all going well, he allowed is mind to drift off in meditation.

The tales of the old man had haunted Illiune for many days. Now that he had left the magic place he knew that it was the Island of Paradise and burial place of the Kings. He would never forget the horror he experienced during his first days there. He did not fear these sounds now. His strange association with the dolphins and the Dolphin-girl seemed to soften the cryings. It was almost as if the dead Kings and wailers were praying for her. Illiune would remember the island as the Magic Island of the Dead. He must visit the old man again and listen more intently to the weird stories, which he told for truth. Illiune would let him see his hands and feet without shame. The Serepein had hands like his. When he had spoken long with old "Likum" he might know more of the magic of the sea and his ancestors. The old man could have a share of the wealth from the pearls and coral. It meant little to Illiune. Any wealth it might bring among people would only cause trouble. Jealousy, malice, and greed would rob them of the joy of being wealthy. He would see that his grandmother would never need again. Wailers for his father must be found and paid. He would also give a gift to the King. It was a custom. Illiune would then return to the Island of Magic and look for the Prinsess, but he would never tell the village people of the island. If he told of living on the Island of the Dead, he would be stoned because of disrespect for the ancestors.

Illiune mused on concerning his return to his people. He would stand tall and upright in his outrigger and drive it straight to the beach near the center of the village. Many people would come to see this strange sight. He smiled as he thought of the village dogs and what an uproar they would make until they were driven away by spectators. When his boat stopped, Illiune would drop the paddle and hold up his hand in greeting and say, "Kashelalia, Mine Ko," (Greetings to all you people). He would stand very still in the outrigger, which was loaded with great wealth in exquisite coral and hidden pearls while all the people would gaze at him unbelieving. He would then say, "I am Fish-boy". Tell the great King I have brought him a gift." The people would only stare and then one man would disappear and soon return with the King. He would try to suppress his surprise when Illiune said he could choose a gift befitting a King. A feast would be made on orders of the King, not for the return of the "Fish-boy", but because of the wealth he brought. Illiune also knew he could choose any girl in the village for his wife, but he would not. There would be no open ridicule by the village boys; that would come later from pathways and darkness. Illiune would ask some willing people to carry his coral to his grandmother's hut for storing and they would jump forward anxiously to please the rich young man and touch the valuable coral. He would reach into the fold of his lava lava and take out a large pearl and present it to the wife of the King. She will smile and bow and say, "Menlau", (Thank you). He would then take out an ordinary pearl and give it to the small boy near him and say, "This is for you if you will tell old "Likum" I am home and desire to see him." The boy will open his eyes wide and blink and run pell-mell into the maze of huts.

Illiune smiled at himself and his foolish thoughts. He had no feeling of wealth or show or desire for place. All the wealth he owned, a fortune, meant nothing to him. He intended that once his grandmother was provided for and he had visited old "Likum" and gave him some wealth also, that he would be ready and anxious to return to the magic island. As Illiune thought of the return voyage he looked down at the brilliant shell hanging at his chest. He touched it tenderly and sat bowed in wonder. He was aroused by a boil in the water near him and looking up he could see the outline of a reef. He heard a whistle, low and clear and looking out to the sea, he saw the dolphins. Illiune rose quickly and raised his arm and the dolphins whistled and disappeared. The "Fish-Boy" turned toward the entrance of the lagoon and sailed in. After he had passed the great rock marking the entrance to the harbor he took down the sail and rolled it around the mast. Then sitting down, he used only the paddle to carry him into the village.

PART II

THE SEARCH

CHAPTER 17

*T*he vicious, wind maddened waves drove Eliakim and his son toward the unknown reef. They could not maneuver their outrigger. The violence of the sea during the typhoon had so damaged the boat it was split and filled with water. They had managed to hang on, but were unable to control the action or direction of its movements. The outrigger poles and carrier were broken loose and formed a tangle of poles and ropes that somehow held fast to the side of the main boat.

Eliakim's hope was to reach the reef, which he had seen in the distance before the black squall dropped upon them. His son, Illiune, was holding fast to a brace in the bow and at times Eliakim could see the muscles of the boy's back bulge with effort as the sea tossed their outrigger as if it were a dry coconut. Their hope to reach the safety of the reef ended as they were dropped from the crest of a monstrous wave and struck a hidden coral growth, which protruded from the trough between the mountains of water.

The impact threw Eliakim out of the boat and into the foam-filled trough. He struggled desperately to get back to the outrigger and find his son. What had been a weakened boat was now a maze of wreckage. He saw his boy a short distance away, caught in some floating debris, where he had landed when thrown from the catapulting outrigger. Eliakim fought his way through the protesting sea to his son. The boy was unconscious, but tangled in the poles and lashings. Eliakim caught up the trailing ropes and secured Illiune as much as possible to the wreckage. He noticed the mast and sail were part of the support to which he had tied his son. It would aid in floatation and provide a stabilizing effect to keep the mass from spinning. Eliakim knew it would not support his weight also and he took a firm hold onto the smashed hull. The floating section holding his boy broke loose and father and son were violently separated as another mountainous wave built up and broke over them. He saw his son no more.

Eliakim prayed desperately as countless, pitiless waves bore him skyward and them pitched him into the trough of the angry sea. He dared not relax his grip. How long the squall continued he did not know, but it was growing dark, very dark. He felt his body pounding against something sharp and unyielding and realized he was in shallow water. The storm had passed on, and when he could focus his vision he saw that he was on a reef. The piece of outrigger he had clung to increased his buoyancy and allowed his body to be raked back and forth over the coral. His lava lava had been ripped and torn, exposing more area to be cut and bruised. When he was able to think clearly, he released himself from the remains of the outrigger. This allowed him to find footing on the coral. Looking along the reef he saw a raised area where the waves only washed occasionally. Moving toward the exposed coral, he felt the pain from the pounding his body absorbed in the raging sea. A blazing sun in a blue sky reclaimed its place above the sea and the waves lost their sharp crests. By the time Eliakim stepped up on the dry coral reef the changing sea revealed little sign of the destructive force, it had displayed a short while before. Eliakim's one thought was for the safety and reunion with his boy. He strained his eyes searching the sea and reef. There was nothing. The wind and waves were from the south and he realized Illiune, in his mass of poles and lashings, must have been driven further north. However, the possibility of the boy coming in near his present location kept Eliakim from leaving the tiny sand atoll. Looking south along the reef gave him no encouragement. He could see a narrow passage through the coral about twenty feet across. This also added to his inclination to move northward. With the cuts and bruises on his body, it would be dangerous to cross a deep channel because of sharks. They frequented such areas and sometimes dozens of hungry "bakos" waited there for a meal.

Eliakim knew by the position of the sun that it was mid afternoon. He realized it would be necessary to find a higher area on which to spend the night. Traveling along the coral in darkness without a light would be dangerous. After searching the sea again for a sign of his boy, Eliakim turned northward and began picking his way along the reef. He had only his knife. All else had been lost with the outrigger. Even his lava lava was nearly gone, torn into shreds by the water or reef or both. His knife was securely fastened in its sheath, which was tied to his leg above the knee. He did not think about food. He would have liked some water, but there was none. His son was his main concern and he drove all other thoughts from his mind as he made his way searchingly over the sharp coral.

Because he stopped often to look out on the water for something floating, Eliakim did not travel hurriedly. Although he realized the day was close to ending, he could not think of himself. His boy, Illiune, was all he had in the world. If there were any chance to find him, Eliakim would try. The typhoon had dislodged much foliage that drifted both inside and outside the reef. Many times Eliakim strained his eyes to see his boy's head above the debris, but was always disappointed. When the sun began dropping behind the western horizon, he became alarmed. He had to find a dry area to spend the night. There remained about one hour of fair light, and Eliakim, for the first time that day, allowed a place of refuge from the sea to become the object of his searching.

Just before blackness settled around him, he found a spot on the reef, which offered some protection from the elements. Two large pinnacles of coral about fifteen feet apart stood on a raised area. On the lagoon side the wind and waves had piled up a mound of coral sand which sloped toward the lagoon. With little difficulty Eliakim flattened the sand so that he had a place to sleep. If the weather remained calm, he would have a welcome rest from the sea. When he lay down, it was with an aching heart. He had not so much as looked at his bruised and lacerated body, because of his searching for Illiune. In the morning he would retrace his steps for a half mile or more to be sure he had not missed his boy in the evening shadows.

Eliakim did not feel like sleeping, but he knew there was nothing he could do toward finding Illiune at night. He stretched out on the coral sand bed and listened to the pounding surf. The air was warm and in time he was sleeping. He experienced a fitful sleep. Perhaps because he was so bruised and torn, but also because of his deep grief for his son. When he rose from the sand in the morning the sea was much quieter. The golden pink sunrise promised a clear day and Eliakim was grateful. With luck he would find his boy.

CHAPTER 18

The tide was out when he left his bed and started his backtrack south along the reef. Because of the brightness of the morning and the absence of water on the reef, he made better time than the evening before. He looked in vain for some sign of the outrigger and his boy. If Illiune were on the reef he would find him. It would just be a matter of time. This thought fed Eliakim's hopes. Reaching the area of the narrow channel he stood and looked searchingly south along the reef. A blue haze in the distance revealed the presence of an island. Eliakim could not tell how large an island it was, but again decided he should turn back north.

He was becoming very thirsty and there was no sign of rain. With the thought of thirst become a craving for food. He could not remember when he had last eaten. There were many fish about in small pockets on the reef. He would find a limb or stick and use it to kill some for food. There were several coconuts floating along the reef where he had traveled that morning. They would ease the hunger and furnish something to quench his thirst. It was not a simple task to move north again. He thought he might miss Illiune if he came in from the south, but he realized the boy should have been washed in sometime during the night. With reluctance and anticipation Eliakim began working north again. Before much time had elapsed he found a ripe coconut which he managed to husk with his knife. After drinking the milk he broke the shell on the coral and ate the white meat. The food was, "yo", (good). Within two hours he was back where he had spent the night, and pausing only a moment for a look from the higher coral pinnacle, resumed his trek north.

Far to the west he could see a large land mass, but was incapable of swimming that far in his present condition. He also knew his son could not be on that far away land. If Illiune were on shore it would be the reef on which he was searching. By mid-day he had found a limb from a mangrove tree that had washed free of foliage on the coral. It was useful as a walking stick and also to kill the fish. Before the sun touched the western sea Eliakim had traveled about four miles along the crest of coral which formed the reef. Sometimes he could walk on coral or sand free of water, especially when the tide was low. Other times he waded in water up to his hips when the tide was full. At noon the water was higher than any other time. When another day had passed without a sign of Illiune, Eliakim became sick at heart. He realized that the longer his boy was in the water, the less chance he had of survival. Many things could happen in an angry sea. There would be the need for fresh water. One could survive several days without food, but not without water. Although he tried not to think about it, he knew there were many "bako", (sharks) which would be feeding after the storm. There were times when fishermen were thrown into the sea near reefs and before they could reach the safety of the shallow water they were attacked by large barracuda. Eliakim shuddered when thinking of these vicious fish. They were much more violent than the shark. They struck instantly with the long, sharp teeth. Eliakim took hope in the realization that his son was wise concerning the sea and its dangers. He had taught him well. Eliakim's pressing problem at the time was in finding a place to spend the night.

It was quite late when the mass on the reef emerged from out of the dusk. Eliakim did not stop to look at the yet unidentifiable object. He needed to find a resting place where he could sleep without fear of being washed away by the waves when the tide was high. He knew that in his condition he could not stand up all night. Hunger and thirst were causing him much suffering. His torn and lacerated body was swollen and feverish. No, he knew he must lie down for the night. It was "mwow", (good) that he had found the walking stick. The reef is not an easy place to walk even in the daytime, and Eliakim used it to feel the deep areas and high growths. He moved slowly, very slowly. Not only because of the precarious footing, but also his weakened condition would not permit greater exertion.

Darkness was closing in when Eliakim reached the remains of a ship that had wrecked on the reef many years before. The rusty bow of the freighter was wedged upright high on the coral between two large ridges. Eliakim found no resting area near the wrecked ship. He walked around the bow, looking for a sand drift, but there was none. By moving up very close to the rusted hulk he found a large hole in the port side about four feet long and large enough to crawl through. He dropped to his knees and worked his way into the bow and was surprised to find coral sand built up within the wreck. The sand sloped gradually upward and by crawling toward the narrow prow he found a level area. On his "bed" he lay down and almost immediately was asleep. He did not hear the tropical rain that fell at midnight. His eyes were closed to the silver moon and winking stars. He slept the sleep of a man completely overcome by fatigue and fever. When he opened his eyes, the sun was sending out its golden arms to pull itself into the sky. Eliakim awakened weak and in need of water and food. Although he slept all through the night he did not feel refreshed. When he rose unsteadily to his feet, flashes of colored light raced before his eyes, and he dropped quickly to his knees. He staggered down to the hole in the ship's hull and crawled out into the early morning.

Had it not been for his weakened condition he would have worked south along the reef, in case he had overlooked something in the evening dusk. Standing as steadily as possible, he scanned the reef he had traversed the day before. He saw nothing. His grief for his son was almost greater than the will to live. He had to find strength himself if he were to help his boy. With that thought in mind he hobbled slowly around the bow of the old wreck and moved north. As the sun rose, the coolness of the night gave way to the warmth of the tropical day. Eliakim was again reminded of his weakness, when after traveling only about a hundred yards, he felt exhausted. Fear gripped him, not for himself, but for his son. It was necessary to stay strong. Watching the reef more carefully he found a pocket in the coral which was full of water. It was a small pool, but contained several edible fish about six to ten inches in length. Lifting his stick he struck the water with all the strength he could muster. Water splashed upward and outward and when it settled he saw two fish lying on their sides, stunned. He knelt down and lifted them from the small pool. With his knife he ripped the skin off one side and cut the white meat. The two fish were only enough to whet his hunger. When they had been eaten, he struck the water again. He missed. Striking again he managed to kill one more fish which he ate, chewing with care and purpose to work the moisture from the meat. "There will be larger fish", he thought, and he picked up his stick and moved on.

Traversing the reef was not easy for Eliakim. Some obstacles, which would have gone unnoticed under normal conditions, proved exhausting. If he could not find water before evening, he knew this would be his last day. One could not live more than three or four days in the tropical sun without it. This would be four or five days for Eliakim, during which he only had the milk from the coconut. He allowed his eyes to sweep back and forth across the reef as he stumbled on. During one of those sweeps he saw a green coconut floating in the quiet water inside the reef. He found a reserved energy and hurried over toward the promise of a cool drink of life-prolonging water. Before covering half the distance he found himself floundering in the deep water inside the reef. He struggled up on the coral and looked out to the green nut. It could not be reached unless he was able to swim out to it and bring it back. Desperation overcame Eliakim. Even though he was weak and sick, he felt he had to have that drink. He dropped his stick and was about to dive into the dark water when he saw the fins and tails of the sharks searching for the food they had detected. Eliakim did not fear sharks, but had never dove or swam in shark infested water while bleeding from an injury. Looking down at his body he could see the small tracks of red seeping from his fevered places where the coral had scraped off the skin. His tumble in the deep water had caused the sharks to appear in expectant excitement. They were not large. They were the smaller Black-Tipped variety, but he realized he could not retrieve the nut without being attacked by them. Within the mind of Eliakim the fear of death seemed greater than the wish for life. He smiled at himself when he considered the irony in his choice. The smile increased and in a few moments Eliakim was sitting on the reef laughing hysterically.

The lapping of the waves on his body awoke him and he realized he had been sleeping. He could not understand why he had been sleeping on the reef during the mid-day. The dream was so real he could almost see the green coconut and the sharks, but when he looked there was nothing resembling them in the water of the lagoon. Eliakim became resigned to the thought that he may not see tomorrow. Stumbling along the endless reef his eyes took in less and less as he grew weaker and weaker. Because of habit or desire for life he stopped and looked far along the reef toward what he surmised was an atoll or small island. What he saw was still unclear, but realized it offered hope and with renewed vigor he made his way, three legged, toward the island that might offer life.

Several times he fell on the uneven coral, but struggling to his feet, moved on. He did not know when the squall came, but feeling the cold rain he stopped and opened his mouth to drink in what he could. Holding his hands up he turned his face into the rain and wind and tried to steer more water into his craving body. Whether he received much water that way he did not know, but somehow felt refreshed in spirit if not physically. When the rain reached its peak he desired that it continue. He thought it strange that he was wishing for more of what he most often feared. When the rain ceased, he stood still for a few minutes and in a short time the moon and stars illuminated the waters and the reef. He then resumed his struggle toward the island of refuge. He was still working north when the first sign of dawn spread around him. Many times he had fallen and sometimes did not rise until his knees and hands became too painful to allow him to crawl. As the fiery glow from the east brought the new day, Eliakim stopped long enough to search out the island ahead. Disappointment flooded over him as he saw only the blue-gray lump on the end of the ribbon-like reef. He shook his head to clear his vision and it seemed to bring the island nearer; near enough that he could see the restless palm tree fronds silhouetted against the distant sky.

CHAPTER 19

The vision of hope stirred Eliakim to watch for fish on the reef. It was necessary to find food before the heat from the sun beat down upon him. When he found them, he was staggering in weakness. They were large reef fish. Some were swimming with their back above the water. He was weak, but careful when he approached the first and nearest fish. He struck, and the fish turned over on its side and laid shivering in death. Dropping to his knees he seized the fish with both hands and lifting it to his mouth, bit into it and ripped out a mouthful of quivering flesh. Eliakim was ravenous. He tore at the fish with his bloodied hands and in minutes was looking for another. There were many fish and he was hungry. After eating four he felt the pain in his stomach subside. Still he clubbed several more of the larger reef fish. These he cut the white flesh from and squeezed the juice into his mouth. He had to have water, and knew the liquid from the saltwater fish could substitute for fresh water if necessary. Eliakim spent the better part of an hour squeezing the liquid of the fish flesh into his mouth. He thirst was not quenched, but he was strengthened. Before leaving this area of many fish, he killed two more to take with him. He would need them later.

Clouds hid the sun for a while in the morning and a warm tropical rain fell for about a half an hour. During the rain Eliakim again tried to steer the precious drops into his mouth. After the rain the sun became nearly unbearable to the sick man struggling along the coral trail to safety. He stopped about noon, long enough to eat the two reef fish. They helped, but he was still desperately thirsty.

When he came upon the green coconut, he nearly stumbled over it. It lay on the center of the reef, tossed there by the waves. Eliakim reached for his knife as he dropped to his knees and grabbed up the nut. With raw and clumsy hands he worked the knife into the green, immature husk. Before he had cut to the inner nut his hands were bleeding freely and the nut was wet with blood. Eliakim worked frantically until he saw the bright green spot of the water reservoir. He checked his action, realizing that he could lose the nourishing liquid if he were too hurried. Turning the nut up on end he held it between his trembling knees while he cut a small hole where the bright green spot appeared. The inner shell was soft and yielded to the knife. A small hole was made and Eliakim picked up the nut with both hands and brought it to his lips. He was shaking so with anticipation he feared he might drop it and lose the precious water. Spilling the water from the nut into his mouth he gulped feverishly. He drank too fast and began coughing. "Soh, soh", (no, no), he told himself. Overcoming his emotions for a moment, he drank slowly the rest of the liquid in the nut. When there was no more he continued holding it to his upturned lips, relishing every draining drip and the thought of water. When no more would drain out he lowered the nut and placed it again between his knees. He picked up the knife and began opening the husk more until half the inner shell was exposed. He then cut through the green shell and scraped the thin white copra out with his knife and ate it. Eliakim spent nearly an hour in drinking and eating from the green nut. Ordinarily he would have opened it and drank the water in minutes, but the thought of leaving any of the delicious, life-saving nourishment prevented him from moving. For the time his whole thought was on the contents of the nut. He was aroused to reality when he saw the fresh red blood from his hands making trails up to his elbows while holding the nut up to his lips. When he saw the blood and discovered its source he rose to his feet and held his hands out, palms up, and inspected them. He did not remember how they had become so torn. If he could not reach an island by nightfall, he might not be able to use his hands. Dropping to his knees again he gathered up his knife and walking stick and continued to struggle north on the reef. Occasionally he would deliberately put his hands into the salt water to keep them from becoming dry and cracked. Staggering along the coral he felt the effects of the water he had consumed. His mind became more clear and within an hour he could walk a straight line, with the aid of a stick. His vision improved too, and when he stopped to look toward the island, it loomed up before him like a giant wave of the sea.

Shaking his head in disbelief, he looked more carefully and he could see the white sand at the water's edge and the different types of trees. Again he shook his head and with the back of his hands he rubbed his eyes. He wondered if he were dreaming. If that proved to be an island he might get some relief for his fevered body. Most of all he needed more water. Assured that his vision was real, be began to run. When he did, he fell heavily on the coral reef. The fall stunned him momentarily and when he raised his head he could again see the island, an island of refuge. Gathering himself cautiously to his feet he used the walking stick, and stumbled on. Before he reached the white sand of the shore the sun had dropped below the edge of the sky in the west. The distance was not great, but his strength was gone. Many times he stumbled and fell. He tried crawling, but his knees and hands were swollen and bleeding and the pain was excruciating. When he did reach the area of the island growth, He stumbled one more time and fell face downward amid the tropical foliage.

CHAPTER 20

*D*arkness dropped over the island and Eliakim lay as a man dead. He returned to the world in the morning. Cold rain poured down upon him as the squall raced in from the sea. With pain he rolled over and reached up his hands for water. The soothing liquid washed his feverish sores and swollen body. Within an hour, the rain and wind moved on and the sun reclaimed its place in the sky. Eliakim strained to his feet. Every muscle ached in resentment when he moved. It was the desire to live that drove him to hobble inland in search of water and food. After about thirty painful steps Eliakim came upon an open area where several coconuts, both green and ripe lay close on the ground. Because of the stiffness in his joints he could not kneel down. Turning to one side he fell to the ground and then rolled over onto his seat with his legs out-stretched in front of him. Almost before he had sat down he reached for the nearest green fruit. He spread his legs and placed the nut between them just above the knees. With clumsy, swollen hands he took his knife from the sheath and began cutting away the soft, green husk. The work was slow and awkward. He could not hold the knife tightly and he dropped it three times before he could see the bright, green spot of the inner nut. Eliakim cut a hole in the soft, green shell and laid his knife down. With shaking hands he lifted the nut from between his legs and drank the life-giving nectar. When the water was completely drained, he reached out and picked up another. Eliakim consumed the water from three nuts before his thirst slackened. By working painfully he managed to open two of the green ones and ate the whitish, jelly-like substance from the inside of the shell. He would have liked the meat from a ripe nut, but he did not have the strength in his hands to sharpen a stick or cut the husk with his knife.

The typhoon that had caused Eliakim and his son to become lost and had broken their outrigger, now proved beneficial to Eliakim. The driving winds had torn off numerous coconuts that could easily be found. Fronds from the palm and pandanus lay on the ground along the water's edge. From where Eliakim sat he could see several banana plants lying broken and tangled within thirty feet of him. Reaching out for his walking stick he gathered himself up from the ground and hobbled toward the broken trees. Medicine for his wounds was needed, now. If he waited longer the fever and infection would cause him to die painfully. He had watched many people die because of wounds that were not cared for. Stumbling over to the banana plants he chose the youngest and began digging out the soft pulp from the heart. Even though his knife was sharp, the work was slow because his hands were swollen and tender. When the young plant was forced over the trunk was split lengthwise. This made the work easier for Eliakim. He could get a large amount of pulp, and much was required.

He needed small vines to tie the poultice onto his knees and other areas of his body. They were not easily found. After searching until exhausted he had only a few, but they would have to do. Struggling back to the banana plants he eased himself down with the help of his walking stick. He placed the pulp on his knees first. The coral had cut them deep and ragged. Because he had much medicine he applied it generously. When the wounds were covered he wrapped the knees with green strips of leaves and tied them on with vines. His hands proved a problem. Eliakim decided to make a bed of the banana pulp and lay in it with his lacerated areas on the medicine.

This he did, and spread more on his thighs and chest. Gathering a handful of pulp in each hand, he lay back to rest. The water had eased his thirst. Exhausted, Eliakim faded into unconsciousness.

Sometimes he was aware of warmth, then coolness, lightness and darkness, pain and release, always with the feeling that reality was just beyond. He did not know how long he rotated with the repetition of these sensations. It was the driving need for food and water that aroused Eliakim. Sometimes he drank only water and then slept again. Other times he struggled through the tropical growth of the island in search of fruit. Not many people visited here and he had no difficulty finding bananas and papaya. However, the pain he endured in hobbling through the thick foliage was excruciating. He wanted fish, but was not able to walk safely on the uneven coral. After the fourth day of lying on the bed of pulp, Eliakim could feel the fever subsiding and the redness of infection was less. He struggled with helplessness and discouragement. Whenever he thought of his son he was overcome with grief. While lying sick with wounds he had little hope of finding Illiune alive, but as he gradually became stronger his hope increased. Anxiety became enemy for a time. He often had a desire to return to the search, but was not well enough. Eliakim found some comfort in knowing his boy was wise in many ways. Illiune had no equal among all his people in strength and ability to swim. If he had reached land, any land, Eliakim felt he would survive.

How many days were spent in convalescing, Eliakim could not recall. When he was able to grasp the knife and walking stick without drawing blood, he went in search of fish. The most pain was in his legs, and he could not bend a knee. His excursion for fish was painful and trying. He could barely walk and the uneven coral presented a continual obstacle. He groped, rather than walked. Because of limitations in movement he had to depend on patience. He managed in time to find and kill two fair size reef fish. They did not satisfy his hunger, but he was pleased with his returning ability. Because of weariness Eliakim turned from the reef and struggled back to the island. Reaching the shade of the island growth was tiring, but being hungry still, he decided to sharpen his walking stick so that it could be used to open the husks of ripe coconuts. They were plentiful. The typhoon had shaken many, both green and ripe, from the palms. One could survive on coconuts because of their rich meat and the green ones contained pure water. Sharpening the stick was a painful ordeal for Eliakim. His hands were still tender and any pressure resulted in pain. Determination resulted in forming a point, which would pierce the tough fiber of the coconut husk. Placing the stick on the ground with the pointed end up he leaned it against an upturned root. Using the stick to tear off the outer covering, Eliakim opened the end of the nut and drank the milk, "Yo", he said aloud, "Innenen yo" (good, very good).

CHAPTER 21

$\mathcal{E}$ liakim had lost track of time. He could not remember how long he was on the reef, nor did he know how long he had been on the island, He surmised it had been more than two weeks, but he was not sure. His fevered body and grief stricken mind caused him to dream many strange things. He could not separate reality from the subconscious. One vision that seemed especially real was accompanied by the shrill voices of dolphins. He imagined he awoke and, because of the unusual cries, made his way to the edge of the island and looked out over the reef. There in the bright moonlight was an outrigger moving slowly south. The sounds of the dolphins came from the water near the boat. Eliakim seemed to remember calling out to the boat, but there was no response. He studied the outrigger in amazement. It was moving south and yet the breeze was toward the north. Still more perplexing was that there was no one in the boat. He was puzzled by the vision and yet he knew the boat could not move against the wind without someone paddling. Thinking of this caused him to believe he was often delirious. There were times when he could not sleep and times when he could not clear his vision. He understood how a sick body could weaken one's mind. He was encouraged by his physical improvement, but his dreams continued, or were they dreams?

Several nights he dreamed about his son and of former days. Eliakim also dreamed of his wife. At times she was still alive and young and beautiful. Other times he had visions of her in the days when he found her and learned to love her. Whether it was in dreams, or reality, when he recalled the days they spent together and how she had been taken from him, he was sick with grief. Many times he shed tears for her, and was not ashamed. Eliakim often blamed himself for his wife's death. If he had not taken her to his village she might still be alive and happy. The people of his island did not accept her, especially the women. They made fun of her openly and often threw sticks at her to show their contempt. Eliakim knew it was because of her strange hands and feet that were webbed, and she could not speak. She made only a few low treble sounds which Eliakim alone understood. He had built a woven pandanas fence around his home except where it faced the lagoon. A small fresh water stream ran beside their hut and she did not need to leave their home for water. All the other provisions Eliakim gathered. If she were not happy with him, he never knew, because she almost always smiled in his presence. Never had she been angry with the women of the village. She did not let their rude treatment cause her anguish. Eliakim wished many times he were more like her. She had learned to do many of the tasks required of a wife, and even though her hands often bled, she worked willingly.

Eliakim knew the village women resented her for other reasons. She was by far lovelier than any other. She had no scars and blemishes on her as did others. Her skin was the color of ivory, smooth and light. Her hair was long and wavy and shining black. She was quite slender compared to the village women and nearly as tall as Eliakim. She could swim faster and dive much deeper than her husband. She always accompanied him when he went fishing. She caught fish in her hands as easily as Eliakim could with a spear. Sometimes she would gather pearl oysters and other times she would surprise him with black coral. He did not resent her ability. She could tell by his look that he was proud of her. She also knew he loved her. She went with him in the outrigger until a few weeks before the birth of Illiune. When she made him understand why she must not go, he did not leave her. They had more than enough supplies to keep them. And so it was Eliakim was with her when the baby was born.

The birth of the baby was strange to Eliakim. When asked if he could get some older lady to be with her, she shook her head, "Soh", (no). Perhaps it was because of their treatment of her, but Eliakim knew she did not want to burden anyone. He started once to get his mother, but she called him back. She seemed satisfied to have him near her and share the pain. She was strong and the time did not take many hours. When the baby came she took care of it herself. Eliakim wondered how she knew. She had never assisted anyone in the village. She had heated water and sharpened a sliver of bamboo to sever the cord. When the ordeal was finished and the baby was taking food at her breast Eliakim reached over and touched it. He knew it was a boy because he had seen when she was tying him. With awkward tenderness he took a tiny hand in his and lifted it gently. His wife was smiling and even though she was exhausted her eyes revealed the same love and happiness so common to her. When Eliakim opened the little hand his eyes or expression must have revealed his shock. The boy's tiny hands were webbed like those of his wife! He did not think of his wife's hands, because he loved her, but he knew the humility she had suffered among people because of the difference. His immediate thought was that his son too, would suffer unfairly because of the fin-like hands. However it was, his wife saw the disbelieving look in his eyes and tears spilled down her cheeks. She knew the reason for his reaction, and she felt herself to blame. Eliakim could never understand how the pain cut so deeply. From that day on she began to weaken. Even though something other than feelings could have been the cause, Eliakim felt responsible. Because of him she had suffered much. Many times during her few remaining days he wanted to take her back where they had met, but she only held his hand and shook her head, "Soh" (no).

Illiune was exactly one month old when his mother left them. From that time on his grandmother cared for him. Because of the boy, the grandmother grew lonely. Other people shunned her because of the boy of the "Fish Woman". Eliakim endured his grief by going out fishing each day. When he returned, he sold his catch and purchased whatever his mother needed for the little boy. Eliakim spent many days of anguish. It would have been so easy to hate his son because he lost his wife. He knew some others who did. Yet every feature of his son was that of his mother. His skin was light and he was much longer than most babies. His eyes were exceptionally dark and he was usually smiling. Eliakim could not help but love his son. Even though he knew of the unfair treatment he would experience at the hands of other children, he carried him proudly around the village.

Eliakim would visit "Loud Likum", (Old Liar), every day when he was not fishing. They would visit for hours about the secrets of the old days and customs and ancestors. Illiune was too young to understand the conversations, but knew his father spoke differently with the "Old Liar" than with anyone else. Sometimes he saw tears in his father's eyes, but did not know why.

When the boy was older, Eliakim took him fishing in the outrigger. He taught the boy about sailing and directions. He let the boy steer and explained the use of stars and sun while at sea. The boy learned to eat raw fish and clams and urchins. When Eliakim began showing his boy how to dive and swim, he was amazed at his son. Within a year the boy could dive deeper and swim faster than his father. Eliakim remembered the boy was ten years of age when the games were held in the village. His son surpassed all others in water contests, even though he was yet a little boy in years. Eliakim marveled that his son was so tall, much taller than most boys, and with his height was strength. Alone, the boys of the village would not harass him, but when there were several they teased Illiune. And yet, through it all, the boy did not show a desire to fight back or learn to hate. Not only did he resemble his mother in looks, but Eliakim knew his son had a disposition like her. In a short time Eliakim learned to love his son with an intense devotion. In him Eliakim had both his wife and their child. Nothing else in all the world mattered. It was this overpowering love that drove his father to continue his search for the boy. He vowed never to cease looking until he found him alive or proof that he was lost.

CHAPTER 22

$\mathcal{A}$ s he became stronger, Eliakim planned to resume his search. His boy was not on this island. If he had washed ashore he would have walked this way. The more he considered possibilities the stronger became the thought that Illiune might have regained consciousness and untangled himself from the maze of ropes and poles. If so, he would have swum directly into the reef, as he was as much at home in the sea as he was on land. Eliakim wondered why he had not considered this before. If his boy had reached the reef across the channel he would have traveled toward the small island to the south. Eliakim also believed that if his son reached the reef or island he would be alive. Even though the new reasoning encouraged him, he knew that he should not rush off unprepared. After considering the possibilities he determined to build a raft on which to travel along the reef inside the lagoon. With this he could pole or paddle his way and stop to search wherever he so desired. With excitement stirring within him, Eliakim took his walking stick and set out to search the island for suitable material for a raft.

Debris, caused by the recent typhoon, made traveling almost impossible through the tropical forest of the inner island. Because of this, Eliakim waded along the coral sand at the edge of the water. Some places he encountered mangrove trees with their maze of impassable roots. When approaching these, he found it easier to go around them if the water allowed. If it were too deep he made his way slowly through the growth on the island above the mangrove. The trip around the small island was difficult for Eliakim. Before having gone half way, he was tired and his legs were cramping from abuse and pain. He rested often, but he realized in order to gain back his strength he must keep going. With this thought as a stimulant he kept moving, slowly moving. After nearly circling the island he came to a coral-bottomed channel leading into the interior. The water was crystal clear and nearly twenty feet in depth. The water was placid and every leaf and limb reflected in the mirrored scene. Eliakim thought it strange that the luxurious growth had not closed in over the entrance. As the banks were clean, he waded slowly into the channel and along the edge until it opened up into a small pond about thirty feet across. At the edges of the pool were many tall bamboo trees that had been broken by the typhoon and lay in pieces in and around the pool. Eliakim smiled in anticipation. Here was material for a raft. He only needed to place the poles in the enclosed waters and tie them with vines. Anticipation turned into excitement, and as he strained his tired legs to circle the pool, his excitement turned to dismay. The solid coral bottom had turned into a thick blue clay that tugged at his legs and made each step slow and painful. He reached down and gathered some blue mud on his hand and looked at it in curiosity. He had seen many areas where mud was thick and black, as in the mangrove swamps, but never blue on a coral reef island. As his eyes swept over and around the area he could see that it had been a beautiful place before the typhoon. The blue clay made the water bright blue almost to the narrow channel. When he attempted to shake the clay from his hand, it did not fall off. When he rubbed his other hand over the clay, both became sticky with the strange material. He reached out his hands into the water and began washing. Eliakim decided that it was the most difficult substance he had ever seen. Nothing was so stubborn. He washed for about a half an hour before the clay was off his hands. He was not afraid of ill effects. He was only amazed because of its ability to adhere.

Trying to forget the clay he looked again at the bamboo trees. Many had been uprooted and when they were hurled to the ground they had broken in varying lengths. Some were splintered and some were completely ruined. Eliakim knew it would be a trying task to untangle that mess and build a raft, but with observation came determination. He moved out deeper into the water until there was little weight on his feet. By doing this he was able to walk through or over the blue clay with ease. He worked his way to the opposite side of the pool and then struggled back. The clay would present a problem, but there were many pieces of bamboo for a raft. Reaching the bank where he had begun his observation, Eliakim turned and retraced his steps haltingly, to where he had first stepped onto the island.

Eliakim spent his last night on his bed of banana pulp. After locating the bamboo near the strange pool he decided to find a place there to sleep. Walking around the island each day would be a waste of time. The recent typhoon had torn off coconuts everywhere. They would be plentiful across the island also. Eliakim made his plans as he lay on the bed of healing pulp in the warm, sweet air of the island. He had never noticed the fragrance before. That night, before dropping to sleep, he could hear the faint rustle of the leaves as the soft breeze wound its way seaward. The peaceful sound, the spicy air, and his luck in finding material for his raft, allowed Eliakim to fall away into slumber in a pleasant atmosphere, the first since his ordeal at sea.

He was up with the early glow of dawn and after drinking water from a green coconut he began his walk around the island. His legs seemed to resent each step, but by forcing himself on they slowly limbered to the task. The trip around to the bamboo pool seemed much longer than he anticipated. Perhaps it was because of his desire to start selecting the logs for his raft. Eliakim did not understand how he could be so weak. Stopping to rest he became hungry and knew he should eat. This would be a good time to go out to the reef for fish. Taking his walking stick he worked his way around to the reef and out on the coral. The tide favored him and he soon had two fair size fish. He carried them back to the island, sat down in the shade and ate. With renewed energy he returned to the bamboo stand and began working at his task. He did not hurry at the work. When he found a suitable pole he moved it out and laid it in the water of the pool. Those that were too long took much more effort. With his knife he cut a groove around the smaller end and then broke it by placing it between two palm trees and pulling sideways. Some snapped easily. Some did not. After two hours of steady work Eliakim was forced to rest. Resting was not easy, but necessary. Sitting at the edge of the pool he counted his small collection of bamboo poles. Shaking his head he stood up and resumed his labor.

While working among the fallen poles he noticed several that lay broken clean at the ends, but were split in places lengthwise. The more he walked over them and worked around them the more he felt they could be useful. In time he thought of the blue clay and stopped his work. He took one clean broken bamboo about twelve feet long and dragged it to the bank near the water's edge. Turning it so the cracks were facing upward, Eliakim dipped his hand into the water and brought out a handful of the strange blue clay. He smeared it onto the bamboo where it was split. The material was quite workable and he covered every area where a split had occurred. Eliakim then placed it across the several floating logs in the water with the clay in the sun. When he had finished the task, he washed the clay from his hands. While washing he was again amazed at the sticky texture of the unusual substance. In time he cleaned his hands and, being thirsty, walked back into the island and gathered two green nuts. He opened one and drank the water. The other he laid down near the bank. By evening there were many more poles lying near the shore or in the water. Eliakim reasoned that by tomorrow evening there might be enough to begin tying them together. With the thought of tying, he realized the need to find some vines. Before searching for suitable ones, Eliakim went over to inspect the pole on which he had applied the blue clay. When he felt of the clay, he was astonished. It was smooth and hard and even with his knife he could not scrape it off. If it would not become too soft in the water it would work as a sealant. With the thought in mind, he pulled the length of bamboo off the other poles and placed it in the water with the clay downward. He would look at it in the morning.

Eliakim had not found many vines by the banana plants, but realized there could be some on the island elsewhere. He began walking slowly in and around the lush growth. By the time darkness was, but a half hour away he had not found one suitable vine. "Strange", he thought, as he turned and began walking back to the stand of bamboo. Finding a place to sleep was no problem. Eliakim gathered several armfuls of small limbs from the tops of the bamboo trees and laid them under a leaning pandanus. If it rained, he would keep dry. The large fronds shed water very well. Before going to sleep, he again heard the breeze in the foliage and noticed the sweet air of the warm surroundings. Sleep did not come as he expected. Even though tired, he was filled with an anxious excitement of his coming journey, the journey in search of his son. The foremost problem at the present was in finding material for tying. If he could not find vines he would have to make ropes from coconut fronds. He was braiding the ropes in his mind when sleep carried him away.

With the morning came a soft tropical rain. Eliakim lay in his bed of bamboo leaves and though anxious to be up and working, he remained quiet. As the odor of fresh rain drifted around him he said audibly, "Mweir, mwow", (rain, good). He would work on the raft poles during the first few hours because the rain would make the air cooler. After the clouds passed on he arose stiffly and went in search of food. Luck was with him this morning. He found both papayas and bananas, ripe and delicious. He returned to his bamboo pool with fruit for lunch and another coconut for water. Eliakim began to feel a confidence he had not possessed since his vigil at sea. "Perhaps", he thought, "it is because I am getting well from my wounds." He felt much stronger. After returning from his early walk he realized his legs were much better. During the morning he worked steadily. By mid-day he stopped to rest from labor, but instead of sitting or lying down, he ate some fruit, drank some water, and then walked back in the thick growth to search for vines. He returned disappointed, realizing he would have to make rope from coconut fronds and it would take several more days. On his way back he had watched for young palms. They were easier to make rope from, as older palms had tougher fiber. If necessary he could weave rope from the fronds of the pandanus. He was not concerned about making rope, but discouraged that there were no vines.

By the forth day Eliakim had sufficient poles for his raft. During breaks from wrestling bamboo, he had taken coconut fronds and worked them until the fibers were separated. These he laid on the ground near the shore. The next few days were spent in twisting and braiding the strings into ropes. Ropes made this way were better than vines, but it took time. When he had enough rope he was glad that he had woven them from palm. He next task was to tie the poles together to form a raft. Eliakim was adept at tying a weaving and when the work was completed, he was pleased. The raft was large enough that he could carry fruit and coconuts for water. If necessary he could sleep on the raft. It was about twenty feet in length and six feet in width. The day after he was finished with building he spent making a paddle and pushing pole. Had he not been so anxious to begin his journey he would have woven a sail. "Maybe later", he thought. His last preparation consisted of gathering fruit and water. He spent his last day on the island placing both green and ripe coconuts on the front of the raft, with bananas and papayas. As he worked, he often considered the poles that he had sealed with the blue clay. Once dry, they did not absorb water again. Eliakim would remember this island. The strange clay would be valuable for trading and patching outriggers. After setting out on his journey south, Eliakim wondered how long he had been there. He guessed it might have been about two months since he washed up on the reef. "A long time", he thought, "a very long time." He had never been separated from his boy for more than one day before.

CHAPTER 23

The lagoon was calm the first day out. There was no breeze and Eliakim pushed his raft along with the pole. The tide was full and he could travel near or over the reef most of the time. When he was forced into deeper water he used the long handled paddle he had made. His first stop was at the place where the old ship had run aground. Eliakim only faintly remembered the night he spent here. He saw no tracks other than his own, and he returned to his raft and moved on. He watched carefully every projection which showed above the water over the reef. He did not intend to miss anything on this trip. By evening of the first day he reached the two raised areas where he had spent the first night. He admitted to himself that he had not expected to find any sign of his boy here. Eliakim hoped his son had come in to the reef farther south. He had pulled his raft upon the coral and then lay down to sleep in the sand. He slept soundly and awakened late the next morning. After breakfast of fruit and water he continued his journey. At mid-day he saw an outrigger with a sail that showed signs of patchwork. "Perhaps a poor fisherman," Eliakim mused. He could see a man with a blue lava lava sitting tall in the back of the outrigger. There was something loaded on the carrier, but Eliakim could not see what it was. Because of the pounding surf, he knew it would be useless to hail the man. He would not hear. Eliakim took courage in knowing that there were people here and he might find someone who could tell him about his son.

Within an hour after he had seen the outrigger, Eliakim came to the raised area where the channel cut the reef. If anyone had traversed the atoll, there would be tracks in the soft sand. Before he had beached the raft Eliakim's heart seemed to rise up into his throat. There were fresh tracks in the sand! Tracks made less than a few hours ago. Jumping off the raft he ran over and inspected them carefully. He could only make out fresh tracks at first. Then, as he stepped back he saw his own footprint—that it was different. The person who made those tracks earlier had a strange foot or thong. Eliakim could make out the heel and toes, but they showed no separation between the toes as his did. His heart again began to hammer in his chest and throat and he felt like crying out in joy. His boy would make print like that…barefoot. But Eliakim did not cry out. He was too afraid of disappointment, and yet he knew somehow that he must continue his search. This was the first encouraging sign he had encountered. With renewed anxiety he stepped back on the raft and paddled south again.

Late that evening Eliakim could see a small shadow on the reef about half mile ahead. Because of curiosity and anticipation he increased his speed. By the time he reached the shadow he saw that it was formed by two small square-nut trees which had rooted on the reef in a raised area. This would be a good place to spend the night and Eliakim pulled the raft up on the sand and after eating some fruit and drinking water, he crawled under the trees and fell asleep.

Awaking with the early dawn, Eliakim left his soft coral bed before the sun climbed above the sea in the east. The air was sweet with the scent of coconut and flowers. He did not need to look to know there was an island near. Soft was the breeze that wafted out seaward carrying the tantalizing aroma to greet the golden sunrise. Eliakim stood silent and motionless. For a moment, a feeling of strange joy to be alive flooded his thoughts. Just as suddenly, he lost the feeling to the reality of why he was here. As he began considering what he should do in searching, an odd sense of mystery remained to haunt him. Eliakim wondered if it could be the perfume of the breeze. Perhaps there was magic here. He had lived long enough in the tropical islands of the vast sea to know that there were many mysteries which people could experience only if they believed in magic. Old Likum, "the crazy man", people called him, knew the secrets of the old people of the sea, and their ancestors. Of all the folks in his village, only he and Old Likum understood. Some day Eliakim would tell his son, Illiune, about those mysteries. This thought brought Eliakim out of his trance and as he turned he saw the rays of the sun slowly forming a beautiful island in the mist of the lagoon. Drawing in his breath, he watched spellbound as the island took shape and color where the piercing fingers of gold penetrated the fog and Eliakim knew he was viewing the magic unveiling of an island.

Driving himself to action he began looking around the area of the two trees. There were tracks here, but older than those he saw yesterday. Near the water's high point he could see where an outrigger had been pulled up. Marks on the higher sand revealed where something like a pole had been dragged. Recent rains made the signs difficult to read, but he went over every inch of sand with care. When his eyes followed the marks of the outrigger to the water's edge Eliakim saw unusual seaweed where it was matted beneath the front of his raft. Walking hesitantly toward the weed he picked some up and looked at it with astonished eyes. Only once before had he seen seaweed like this. It was when he had been cut deeply on his foot and could not stop the infection. His wife had gone into the sea and returned with much weed which she wrapped around his foot. Within two days his wound was healed. This was magic healing grass, but how did it get here? Eliakim moved the raft and grounded it away from the weed. "Whoever had placed it there must have been very ill", he thought; there was so much. He reached down and lifted a handful and experienced the odd tingling sensation he had felt that time long ago.

Amazement overcame Eliakim. No man of his village had ever found weed like this. It had power to heal wounds, great power. Here was a bed of healing power. Eliakim gathered it carefully and placed it on the raft. If he became injured, it would make the wound well. His surprise in finding the magic weed drew Eliakim to search the ground more carefully. He found a flower from a hibiscus, old and faded. It must have floated in with the high water, he thought. When he picked it up he saw that it was tied securely with a blue thread. Examining the flower gave him no lead, but as he looked at the thread he was reminded momentarily of the man in the outrigger. "It could have been from his lava lava", he mused, but because of the remote possibility, he laid the flower back on the sand near the trunk of one of the square-nut trees.

Hunger called Eliakim to the raft where he picked up a green coconut and opened it. He drank the water and then ate a papaya and two bananas. From where he was near the trees he could see the reef to the south projecting from the water. He leaned down and picked up his walking stick and headed down the reef, slowly. Because the fish were large and numerous he easily killed two and laid them on a high mound of coral. They would be good later. He had not walked over fifty yards when he came upon a maze of broken outrigger poles and lashings lying on the dry coral. Eliakim did not have to inspect them to realize they were from his smashed boat. He knew his ties and twisted cords. Frantically he tore at the debris looking for the mast and sail. They were not there. Neither were there any ropes. Eliakim knew one of two things had happened. Either his boy had washed in and freed himself; or the storm had torn them apart. That would account for the missing mast and sail and ropes. He was instantly both heartsick and elated. He dared not raise his hope too high, and yet he would not allow himself to think Illiune was dead.

CHAPTER 24

*A*s his strength returned, his vow to continue his search became a driving force. There was no one on the reef. Perhaps he would find him on the island. Hurrying back toward the raft, he stopped only to pick up his fish and then went on. Just as he pushed out from the sand, the sun dipped behind a cloud and a heavy, warm rain began falling. Ignoring the downpour, Eliakim pushed his raft straight toward the near island. Before he was within fifty feet of the shore he could see where an outrigger had been beached. Pointing his raft toward the place he soon found himself looking into a crude shelter built within the curved trunk of a giant square-nut tree. There was no sign of a fire. Whoever made the shelter must have eaten raw meat and fruit. Eliakim also noticed the pandanus fronds were still green. They had been placed there a short time before. Climbing up into the bend of the tree he sat quietly, contemplating. While he was wondering, the rain stopped and only the dripping of water from the overhead foliage could be heard. The bed of leaves did not show much use. Eliakim thought whoever built the tree house have used it sparingly. While he pondered and questioned his eyes fell upon a small piece of red coral at the end of the bed near the tree trunk. He stepped over and picked it up. With his knife he cut at the broken end and knew it was taken from the sea recently. It had not yet begun to harden.

While studying the coral, the dripping rain ceased and in its place Eliakim could hear a trickle of water. Curiosity overcame him and he moved over to where the sound was directly below. With his knife he cut away the branches and was looking into a small pool of water. So strange, he thought, and continued cutting branches until he could see a rock ledge, Eliakim was struck by disbelief. Before his eyes lay a large, clear water pool, surrounded by strange rocks. He leaned over the small pool and using his hand as a cup he tasted the water. It was fresh and good. "Unbelievable", he thought, and yet it was there. Someone must have built it long ago and before he could wonder more, he recalled the stories of "Loud Likum" (Old Liar), and he knew he was standing on the forbidden Island...the Island of the Dead!

An unexplainable fear overpowered Eliakim as he looked and saw and realized where he was. This island was a "taboo" island. Although he had never been here before Eliakim had heard of the island of moaning and wailing—the burial place of the Kings. Old Likum had told him of the ordeal that one must suffer if they spent the night here. Old Likum had been washed ashore here one time after a storm and he knew. Maybe that is why the bed of leaves shows little use, he thought. Perhaps the spirits of the ancestral Kings had carried the people or person away. He caught his breath with the thought. Perhaps his son was the one. Dropping down to the ledge on his knees Eliakim found half a coconut shell and to his surprise, a pile of mangrove limbs that had been placed on the rock bench recently. The penetrating light also revealed something else to Eliakim. Behind the barrier of limbs lay a pad of the strange magic sea plant and when he lifted some in his hand he could feel its odd sensations. The more he looked and discovered, the more fearful he became. He knew from the tales of Old Likum that the Island of the Dead Kings had been made into a paradise for the Spirits and Eliakim began to feel a horror that he was intruding on this forbidden place. If his son had been here, fear would have driven him on or the old Kings' Spirits had taken him. Without waiting a moment longer, Eliakim scrambled out of the pool and onto the raft. He was lucky to be alive! As the water between the raft and the shore increased Eliakim's fear of the unknown subsided, but because of the possibility that his son might be somewhere on the island, he felt he should make an effort to contact him. Perhaps if he circled the island and whistled intermittently he might hear an answer. He had gone but a little distance, when he saw some banana plants that had recently been stripped of fruit. Time after time he paused and whistled and listened. The only audible sound was that of the soft lap of the water as it washed against the black log-like rocks and the distant lashing of waves on the reef.

Eliakim's heart became heavy, and as the raft moved slowly around the shore he noticed an area with a white coral beach on which was a pile of pandanus fronds and leaves. He turned the raft and approached the place. Someone had been here quite recently because the cut leaves were still green and fresh. They were much greener than those on the tree house. Those had become wilted. Even in the shade, while these lying partially in the sun had not changed. He could see the narrow strips that had been made for weaving and his mind pictured the outrigger with the patched sail. Remembering the scene with the tall man in the blue lava lava, Eliakim smiled within himself and his heart's tempo increased. He thought audibly, "My son is not here. That outrigger was heavily loaded. Illiune was heading home. Yet, how could he build an outrigger in such a short time? Or is it possible that I was sick much longer than I thought?" Closing his eyes, he could hear the lapping of the small waves, and when his head began to droop, he could hear the crying and whistling of the dolphins. His head jerked erect and his eyes opened wide. There were no dolphins and no whistling, just the lapping. "When did I see dolphins last?" he asked himself. "Was it a dream? They were pushing an empty outrigger and it had no sail." Reality or a dream, he asked himself. He began laughing aloud. "My son is now a man! He has stolen an outrigger from the dolphins and patched up our old sail. I am wasting my time here. I must hurry after him." Eliakim then stopped his ranting and thought, "No, I am mad!" He realized that his ability to reason was becoming frayed, and yet he could not help but question. If it had been Illiune, why did he take fruit and fronds from this island? He surely robbed the dead Kings, and he would suffer. With the thought of the punishment his son would experience he was once more engulfed in grief. He wished for a sail to help propel his raft, but dared not step foot back on the island. He was fortunate to be off the Paradise Isle of Dead Kings and he must be far from here before night. Turning his raft south he began paddling along the dark waters of a strange, deep crescent in the lagoon.

CHAPTER 25

Occasionally, while moving slowly south along the reef, Eliakim would turn and gaze back at the island of terror. Old Likum had told him about that special burial ground for the ancient Kings who ruled during the time of the great civilization of the palace people. Eliakim knew other people considered the old man crazy, but not he. Likum did not persecute Eliakim's wife. If any feeling was portrayed it was in awe. The old man always treated Eliakim's wife as if she were a Queen. During the years of their marriage, Old Likum would do anything possible to make life easier for both her and Eliakim. After her death they became closer friends, if it were possible. There were times when the old man would come to the house of Eliakim when the boy was sleeping and they would visit for hours about the strange days of old. Sometimes Eliakim would take his son to the home of the old man and they would visit there. The boy did not understand the tales, but he remembered the visits very well. There were times as he grew older that he recalled words or ideas he had heard during these conversations, and he would ask his father about them. Sometimes Eliakim would answer, but if it were about Illiune's mother or the ancestors, the subject was changed.

He watched the reef as he moved southward. When he saw anything that looked unusual, the raft would turn in and he would inspect more closely. The tide was in full at mid-day and few areas revealed projected coral. During the trip he ate some fruit and one fish, but he did not feel hungry. He ate for strength, because he needed strength to search. In the distance an island began to take shape, and because he was moving toward it, he could observe the trees and contour of the beach from far out. It would be late evening before he arrived. He could see that it lay close upon the reef; "Perhaps part of the reef", he mused.

Just as the sun was lowering itself over the western sea, Eliakim turned to look one more time at the dreaded island he had left. His surprise of disbelief caused him to throw up his hand as if to protect his eyes. From where he looked he could see the area where the island was as a bright, golden ball of fire. Fascinated, Eliakim watched awestruck. As the sun sank lower, the lagoon sent up a heavy mist and it slowly dissolved the island. When the last arm of the sun's glow was drawn below the sea, the island had completely vanished. Eliakim blinked his eyes in wonder. He looked again, holding his hands cupped along his eyes for shields. No, it was not there. His knees felt weak and his heart was pounding. The Island of the Dead came and went with the magic of the unknown. He did not need to wonder now what would have happened to him if he had spent the night there. When he considered it, he shook with fear.

Before complete darkness closed in on Eliakim he had come upon a large point of coral inside the reef. Moving over to the projection he tied his raft. He did not intend to go onto the strange atoll at night. He was still chilled with the sight of the vanishing of the mysterious island. No, he would spend the night here where he would be safe. In the morning he would go in search. Stretching out upon the raft he was soon dreaming. His was not a resting sleep because of his dream, but he could not shake it from his subconscious mind.

Eliakim blamed himself for his son's malformity. When the boy was very small, a foreign doctor came to his village. He had heard of Illiune and when he looked at the boy's hands and feet he told Eliakim he could make the boy like other children. Making the decision was not easy for Eliakim. He knew the boy would suffer ridicule because of his strange difference. Often he had thought of taking the boy and leaving their village, but no matter where they lived, he knew the boy would be rejected by others. The doctor advised Eliakim to make his choice regarding the operation within a month as at that time the hospital ship would arrive to treat medical problems in the village. This gave Eliakim more time and relieved his anxiety, but it only prolonged the final decision. He recalled in bitter grief the day Illiune was born. The day he lifted the tiny hand and allowed his wife to see the look of disbelief in his eyes. He believed that her failure to give him complete happiness through a normal child was that which caused her to give up the desire to live. Eliakim had never before revealed any sign of being unhappy with her. Their love was pure and equal, warm and complete. It was the look in his eyes when he looked at the little hand that broke her heart. Eliakim blamed himself for his wife's death and whenever he recalled the tragedy he wept bitter tears. Their little boy was so much like her in many ways he felt he could still love her in their son. In desperation he turned to the old man Loud Likum, (Old Likum), for advice.

The night he visited with the old man he left the little boy with his grandmother. After talking with Likum he would make up his mind. There had been an unusual awareness revealed by the old man concerning Eliakim's wife. She was more to him than just the wife of a friend. Eliakim knew there was a strange knowledge shared by the two, which was a mystery to him. He did not resent their shared secrets. There were things perhaps he would never know.

The old man lived on a point of land where a small stream ran into a slough. It wound its way around through the mangroves and emptied into the open waters of the lagoon. His home was only a small hut made of mangrove framing with a thatched roof of pandanus. All his earthy possessions were few. He slept and ate in the open hut. Sometimes he would cook taro or yams or fish over the fire, but as often he ate fruit and fish raw. He did not worry that anyone would rob him. He had nothing worth stealing, and most people feared him because of his weird stories. When Eliakim appeared at Loud Likum's hut that evening he was greeted warmly. The old man could tell by Eliakim's features that he was worried or puzzled. He seated himself beside the old man and looked out over the water of the lagoon. The night was peaceful and warm. The breeze blew outward, down the small stream, along the slough, and over the placid water toward the reef. Every flower and fruit gave of itself in making the zephyrs sweet. After a full half hour had passed without a word, the old man spoke up softly.

"You are much troubled tonight, my friend. You have come to open your heart, but it must be very grievous to you. You can pretend I am not here. That which you wish to tell me I will hear, and forget all else. It is easier for two to bear a burden, than one only." Eliakim heard the old man out and sat silent yet a while. In time he told Likum of his problem. After he began speaking, as if talking to himself, the grief was slowly released. Eliakim kept nothing back. His feeling were revealed to the old man, haltingly at times, but completely. When he finished he sat quietly again, waiting for a response.

Old Likum considered with wisdom, and in a kind, but broken voice, spoke. "Remember, friend, the power of the Spirits cannot be disregarded. What they will…no man should seek to change. Did they not give you a wife more beautiful than any other? Was she not loved by you? I know, friend, that she meant the world to you. As the Spirits made her, she was. As the Spirits made your boy, he is. Did your wife not surpass you in the sea? I say the Spirits know best. If you go to the land beyond, your son will be able to care for himself because of his gift from the Spirits. I believe that the foreign doctor can change your boy. They also have power. Would you change his face because your wife was rejected by others? Now I will tell you, my friend, the strange powers of the Spirits could have planned all this for reasons we know not of. If I were to choose, the boy would stay as he is. If you choose otherwise, I will honor your judgment. We will remain friends."

Eliakim sat quietly when the old man finished speaking. Slowly, a warmth began to drive the chill of dread from his heart. In time he arose and walked away, leaving Old Likum sitting alone and still.

The steps of Eliakim increased in tempo and length as he neared his mother's hut. He spoke to her from the doorway before entering. She was waiting for him because she raised up from her mat quickly. He said only, "I have come for my son. We will return home now." Leaning down he gathered up the little boy, tucked him into the crook of his arm and walked to his hut in the bright moonlight. When the doctor returned, Eliakim met him on the beach with the boy. The doctor smiled a greeting and said, "So you have decided on the operation." Eliakim bowed to the doctor and then answered, "No, I want him as he is." The doctor looked surprised and then advised, "We will be back again sometime, perhaps then?" Eliakim only turned and stepped into the growth of the tropical forest.

CHAPTER 26

*E*arly dawn greeted Eliakim when he awoke. There was little sound near the raft. The water inside the lagoon was like a glass, smooth and mirrored. Occasionally a fish would dimple the surface, but caused no noise to disturb the stillness. Eliakim could hear the waves of the open sea when they ended their journey on the reef. No birds greeted the day with song, and the breeze had ceased blowing seaward and was resting before its return to the island. Awake he was, but not rested. He rose to his knees and released the raft from the coral projection. Lifting the paddle he moved slowly toward the beach.

The raft eased in against the coral and Eliakim stepped off and pulled it up on the higher sand. He could not go far on the island because the tide was low and he did not want the raft to float away. He would return within the hour and pull it in again. While considering this he decided he would look for some vines on this island. They could be used to secure his raft to the shore. As he turned toward the shoreline he saw some small clots of blue clay lying on the coral. He reached down quickly and picked up a piece. Squeezing it in his fingers he imagined it was the same as the clay in the bamboo pool. When he tried washing it from his fingers he knew for sure it was the same. It seemed more like glue than clay. Eliakim was puzzled. He wondered how it came to be here in small traces. Perhaps there was more on the island. Turning toward the bank again he walked slowly up the beach toward the break in the mangroves. He was interested in finding out why there seemed to be a large hole in the center of the island.

Before he had reached the shoreline he discovered tracks in the sand. They were quite old, but they had been made after the typhoon. Following them caused Eliakim to wonder more. The tracks led up on the ridge of sand and over into a forbidding, and foul smelling hole. Not only did the mud and debris look revolting, but also it reeked of rotten vegetation and fish. Eliakim could see millions of flies hovering over the decaying mass. Whoever walked into or out of that odious muck must be from the island. He did not intend to paddle away. Perhaps he should circle the atoll and search the reef side. With this idea in mind he moved his raft slowly around the shore to the south side of the island. While working his way over the mirrored water he was thinking that it was good that the breeze did not carry the foul smell down to his raft during the night. After watching the magic island disappear he would have been frightened. The Spirits of the islands had much power. Eliakim could see only destruction on the small island. There could be little fruit here other than coconuts. All else seemed to have been ripped off by the screaming winds. Occasionally Eliakim would cease paddling and whistle. He did not want to allow any excuse for missing his son, if he were on the island. When Eliakim arrived at the back side of the atoll he saw that it was actually part of the reef. He could not circle the island and there was no place to cross the barrier. Eliakim had no desire to travel on the outside of the reef because of the danger of the squalls. In rough water the raft would be nearly impossible to control. Moving in toward the shore he eased the raft up on the sand. Stepping into the water he waded to the front of the craft and pulled it higher on the beach. He then turned and went into the wind-whipped growth of the island.

Coconuts were strewn everywhere on the ground. He found no fresh fruit. What fruit he did see was smashed and decaying. Continuing his search of the island he came to the area of the mud depression. He spent no time looking at the devastation wrought by the typhoon. He had seen enough from the opposite side. Turning from the scene he walked back into the wind whipped growth and to his surprise he found himself entangled in a thick growth of long, tough vines which were twisted together by the typhoon. When Eliakim became caught, he backed out and looked more carefully at the maze. They reminded him of a fisherman's net. Removing his knife he set to work salvaging what vines he could. After an hour of cutting and coiling, Eliakim returned to his raft with a large pile of small, tough ropes. Before pushing out he gathered several green and ripe nuts for later use. He then opened two ripe ones for milk and food, and a green one for water. After breakfast he pushed out and turned his raft northward. Eliakim had intended to continue south for several days, but he knew the further south he went the less encouraging were the signs. Since that day he saw the tall man in the outrigger with the patched sail, he heard an inner voice telling him he should return home. Had he not identified the Island of the Dead he would not have known where he was. He knew now. He was many long miles south of his village. With an outrigger he might journey to his village in one week, but with a raft he would spend more days and it would require constant paddling or poling. Eliakim had no intention of giving up looking for his son, but he could not forget the man in the blue lava lava and the fresh tracks on the channel bar. When he reached his village he would find an outrigger and continue the search, if Illiune had not returned. There must have been a physical reaction to Eliakim's plans giving him renewed strength. Before the sun had touched the western sea, he was approaching the island of terror. In the warm afternoon sunlight it resembled any other island except that it was completely surrounded by beautiful white sand. Most islands were closed in with mangrove and one sometimes had difficulty finding a place to beach an outrigger. Eliakim was surprised to see how little damage was done by the typhoon here. The island he had just returned from and the one on which he had built his raft were both devastated. "It is the power of the Spirits," Eliakim thought, and he moved outward...away from the mysterious island.

CHAPTER 27

Sunset found Eliakim on the reef where the tangled poles and cords from his old outrigger lay on the coral. He picked up the remains of the boat and studied them with care. He found nothing encouraging. The fact that the mast and sail were missing, gave him the only hope that Illiune was safe. Thinking of the patched sail Eliakim remembered the pandanus tree and the recent work there. The most puzzling feature was that whoever worked here had defied the Spirits. If it were his son, he would be punished. Eliakim shuddered at the thought. He was standing near a higher ridge of coral when a ray of sunlight revealed a shiny spot on a ledge near the top. Looking closely he saw a round, shiny, bead-like object. He reached down and lifted out a large perfectly shaped pearl. Again he was astonished. How did it get washed out of an oyster and on the shore? Eliakim was sure someone placed it there. Walking over, he inspected the outer edge of the reef and found several large pearl oyster shells. He thought of his son. Eliakim knew of no one who could dive as deep as Illiune and he also knew these shells came from the deeper water. Almost everything that Eliakim discovered caused him to be more convinced that his son was alive. Just the word "alive" thrilled the father. Nothing in the world could mean so much to him as that of finding or knowing his boy was safe. Eliakim stood straight and smiled. In the morning he would start north to his village and his son. When he realized the daylight had passed he walked back to the two square nut trees. After tying his raft with a vine he stretched out on the warm coral sand to sleep. He did not feel either hunger or thirst, and he relaxed in the cool spicy-scented breeze coming from the magic island.

Hunger woke Eliakim in the morning. Shaking his head to clear away sleep he looked out upon a sunless sky which threatened a squall. The tide was about half out, and he took his walking stick and moved south on the reef, looking for fish. There were many and in a short time he was back near the raft. He had eaten well of fish and fruit when the squall came in. Chilling rain was lashing the trees over his head and the wind howled in the branches of the small trees. Eliakim expected them to rip out of the soft sand at any moment, but they did not. They held well and afforded some protection. During the squall he watched the raft, that it remained tied. The rain and wind ceased as suddenly as they came and Eliakim watched the black squall race toward the Island of Death. The cloud completely hid the island as it engulfed it. Fascinated, Eliakim wondered which would be stronger in the contest of the elements. Had he guessed, he would have been right. The island emerged shimmering in a golden glow of dazzling sunlight; the squall was retreating westward. Three hours of steady paddling brought Eliakim to the channel in the reef. After dragging the raft high on the sand, he walked to the raised area where he had seen the fresh tracks. Rain had faded them, but they were the only recent signs he had seen. He was sure the strange tracks were made by the tall man in the outrigger. Walking curiously around, Eliakim saw something familiar lying partially covered with sand. He reached down and took up a small piece of red coral about six inched in length and half inch in thickness. He inspected it dubiously and then went over to the raft and picked up the small piece of red coral he found on the bed of leaves on the island of terror. Holding them close together he could see that they were from different coral. The coral, the magic seaweed, and the pearl caused Eliakim to ponder in amazement. He had never known anyone among his people who could dive deep enough for red coral. He had found pearls in shells when he was younger, but he knew of no one who dived for them now. When he considered the better divers he knew, the only one in his village who would be able to dive for pearls was Illiune, his son. The more Eliakim puzzled over his discoveries, the more anxious he was to be moving on. Stepping aboard the raft he began the tedious paddling which moved him slowly northward.

By late afternoon he approached the raised area where he had spent the first night on the reef after his near death in the sea. He remembered, too, he had slept late here on his first trip south and he did not see the outrigger until it was too far away to be hailed. Eliakim resolved he would not sleep that late again. Because of the oncoming darkness he would spend the night here. With his stick he followed his previous footsteps along the reef until he found a shallow area where the fish were feeding among the small tenacles of coral. He watched until they came near with their backs above the water and he stuck them with the stick. Getting fish here was easy. He wondered why there were not more fish along the reef near his village. He was only wondering to pass time. There were few fish there because they had been hunted for many years. When he was young, the fish were plentiful, but too often they were killed for sport or greed. Eliakim did not waste fish. When he went fishing he traveled far, but always returned to the village while they were still fresh. Very few people in his village would go fishing now. He and Loud Likum were the only two who were successful fishermen. Sometimes he worried about his people. They depended too much on foreign goods and food. His people were becoming lazy. No more did they have large rice paddies or sugar cane fields. Few gathered copra. Even though his people were cruel to his wife and boy, he did not hate them. No, he only felt sorry for them. In the old days they went to sea for fish and pearls. They went to the hills for fruit and breadfruit and coconuts. Now they depended on the foreigners. They did not teach the young to fish or work. They depended on foreigners to teach their children in foreign schools. When they finished school they did not have work. They began to play games of the foreigners and even went to their buildings where they had pictures where people moved and lived on large white sails.

The old days were gone, and his people were becoming weak and passive. Eliakim still enjoyed the games during the New Year Celebration. Then the men and boys had contests of strength and speed on land and water. He never missed the games when he was young. He spent many days and hours strengthening himself for the contests. He won many, especially those at sea. Now he only watched. Those who competed were fat or easily winded. Many, too many, smoked like the foreigners and some drank strong drink which made them act very strange. Some beat their wives or children or fought other men. The strong foreign drink made them mad. Eliakim had become quite wealthy by selling fish and coral to the foreigners, but he often wished they had not come to his village. When darkness settled around him, Eliakim was still thinking of his people and their problems, but when he relaxed in the warm sand he dropped into sleep, a peaceful sleep, undisturbed by dreams.

When Eliakim opened his eyes early, he was looking out toward the calm blue water of the outer sea. He lay on his side with his head pillowed on his arm. A movement close to his hand caused him to look down where there were several hermit crabs crawling, looking for a place of refuge. He slowly cupped his hand and immediately two little crabs crawled under his palm and stopped to rest in the hidden cave. Eliakim smiled for a moment and then moved his hand and arm and rose to his feet. "It is good to see the beauty of life", he thought, and then stretched and turned toward the new day.

Again Eliakim ate fish and fruit before beginning his journey. He had only begun to move north when the sun climbed over the edge of the world and made the dark water shine like gold. This was the best time of the day for most people of the islands. The air was refreshing and not too warm. Work seemed easier in the morning. His raft made light rippling sounds as he moved steadily along the coral barrier. Eliakim marveled that his mental outlook had improved with the healing of his body. Many days passed when he had little desire to live. His torn body was fevered and his loss of the boy grieved him nearly beyond endurance. He would have been satisfied to enter into that long sleep had it not been for that hope of reunion with Illiune. Now he was well, physically, and each day he seemed to grow stronger. His search was still his first duty, but he was now capable of better planning. When he reached the island of refuge he would make a sail and a lava lava. There was material from the pandanus trees. He had much rope, and he could find a mast among the bamboo trees at the blue clay pool. His next few days would be busy, but the time lost would be made up if he could make the wind help him. He passed the wrecked freighter at noon. There was no need to stop. If anyone were there they would have made some kind of tracks. Those that he could see were old and close together. He recognized them as ones he had made when he was sick and weak. Eliakim never knew how he found the strength to walk to the island. Many days passed while he was ill, days that he could not recall. By the time he arrived at the island the day was nearly over. The sun had disappeared and the shades of dusk were closing over the lagoon. Eliakim managed to circle around to the inlet of the bamboo pool and maneuvered his raft to the shore. Within a few minutes he was sleeping on his old bed of bamboo leaves.

PART III

ILLIUNE'S RETURN

CHAPTER 28

The sun was lowering itself gently beyond the village when Illiune approached the shore. He had planned beforehand where he would beach the outrigger and how he would greet the villagers, but when he was nearing the island, he turned slightly to his left and as he drew within fifty feet of the sand he turned his craft to the right and paddled parallel to the shore. The tide was full and high, and for this reason Illiune decided he would maneuver his outrigger into the entrance of the inlet leading to Old Likum's home. There would be no need to ask anyone to help him carry his coral to his grand-mother's. His approach did not go unnoticed. The village dogs warned everyone that a strange craft was nearing. The first villagers to appear on the shore were the smaller children. Within minutes, however, older people seemed to emerge from everywhere until the beach was lined with curious onlookers. Illiune paddled slowly, pur-posely. He sat straight and tall in his blue lava lava with the shiny shell around his neck. Although he did not know it at the time, he was not recognized by anyone. Most of the people could see only the great load of valuable coral. Few had ever seen pink coral and when they saw the red also, they were amazed. Illiune did not desire to appear important. His only purpose in moving abreast of the shore close in was because his experience of the past weeks had taught him that, although he was the "Fish Boy", he was now pleased that he was different. He wanted the people of the village, his people, to realize he was not ashamed of his malformity and he could stand tall and equal with any. As his outrigger moved on he could hear the villagers speaking excitedly about the strange boat, and the red coral, and the great man. He smiled to himself when he heard the references to him as a "great man". "If they knew who I am they would be taunting me", he mused. He smiled to think they did not recognize him. Thick mangrove prevented the villagers to continue walking abreast of him, and in a short time he was alone on the lagoon. He continued his steady rhythm in paddling and when he drew near the passage he turned the outrigger and disappeared into the jungle of mangrove.

Loud Likum was sitting motionless on the point of land where the dancing waters of the tropical stream entered the lagoon. Neither he nor Illiune spoke until the outrigger touched onto the bank. Likum lifted his hand and held the bow of the craft and although the heart of Illiune was bursting with joy to see the old man, he tried to conceal it. Laying the paddle down with care, Illiune bowed respectfully to Loud Likum and said, "Kaselehlia mein", (hello sir). The old man looked stunned. He seemed speechless for a time and then with a halting voice he asked, "Is that you, Illiune?" Illiune raised his arms and held them outward with his palms outstretched. Old Likum saw and a smile of happiness spread over his wrinkled face as he spoke. "Come, my boy. Let us talk." Illiune came forward and stepped out onto the shore. He lifted a coil of rope, which was tied to the cross-member at the bow, and looped it over a stake in the ground. There was little conversation until Illiune walked up and sat down beside the old man. Likum was old, but wise. He did not have to be told that Illiune had gone away a boy and came back a man. Illiune realized the old man wanted to ask him about his father, but would not. After a time of silence, Illiune began. He related what happened during the typhoon and the squall. He spoke slowly, sometimes barely audible. In time he poured out all grief of loss exactly as he remembered it, but he never spoke of the dolphins, the dolphin girl, or the

Island of Magic. When finished he said, "We must pay someone to mourn for father. If the coral does not bring enough to keep you and grandmother, I have many pearls. They mean nothing to me. I do not intend to stay in the village for many days. All these have been given to me. I trust you will keep all I say to yourself. You are my only friend in the village. The coral must be kept safe, and you will make a good keeper. One of us must stay with it until we find a foreign buyer. Tomorrow I will go visit grandmother." Illiune ceased speaking and a quietness settled over the scene. The only words the old man uttered came later when he spoke low. "I think you have much to tell me. That will come in time. For now it is good to know that two men make better watchers than one. We will have visitors soon. Greed is a sickness." They came singly and in pairs, nearly all the able bodied men of the village. Behind them were younger men about the age of Illiune, and they could see women looking out from behind the trees. Old Likum had just spoken when they began to appear. They said not a word. They were waiting for Old Likum to welcome them. Illiune saw their eyes on the loaded outrigger and knew why they were here, but he waited also for the old man to speak. Slowly Likum pulled himself up from his seat and turned to the visitors.

"Kaselehlia, mein ko." (Hello, all of you). I welcome you to my humble home, but it is not to see me you are here. I would have you meet one of your own, one who went away a poor rejected boy and returned a rich man. If he speaks to you it will be his choice." Likum returned to his seat beside Illiune. The introduction had been made and now Illiune knew it was his turned to speak. Before rising he considered carefully what he would say. He did not intend to offend them. He would honor Likum by his speech and make it as short as possible. He rose slowly and stepped out toward the waiting group. There was no smile on his face and for the first time, no fear. As he was about to speak a thought fleetingly entered his mind that these were only humans, so unlike the friendly dolphins. Illiune stood well above the tallest in the crowd. The experience of the past weeks seemed to make his voice strong and controlled. His words were steady and clear when he spoke.

"My friends, it is good to see you and your interest in my return. I am honored. Never before have I been welcome in my village. Much has happened since my father and I went away. It is the wish of the great spirit that my father will not return. He was claimed by the sea, and I was spared to bring you word. The coral you see on the outrigger is for my grandmother and Likum. It was given to me by our great friends of the seas because the spirits so desired. Tell the King, Eliakim's son, "Fish boy", will visit him tomorrow with a gift". When he spoke the words, "Fish boy", he held up his hands, palms outstretched, almost touching those near him. They drew back in dread. There was something strange about the man with the fish-fin hands. Without a word they turned and melted into the forest. There was little conversation between Illiune and Likum that evening. Several times when Illiune thought of asking a question or telling Likum more of his experience, that mysterious voice seemed to say, "Nununle, rong etcha", (Be quiet, just listen). The words were the same as those he had heard many times before. When complete darkness closed around them, Likum moved the coals around in the fire bed and added more wood. When the flames lit up the small area he removed the green leaves near the small blaze and lifted out a baked fish and a pot of steamed rice. He walked out from his hut and returned in a few minutes with some large green leaves. He handed a leaf to Illiune and said a few words, "You must eat now".

Illiune did not eat as the old man expected. The food tasted strange. He had not eaten cooked food for many weeks; besides, he was not hungry. He was thinking how different his homecoming had been from what he had imagined on his return. "It is so very strange", He mused. "Even living among your own is a new experience each day." He smiled at his thoughts and at that time Likum pointed to a mat rolled up beside the wall. Illiune bowed to the old man and gathered up the mat and was about to step out into the darkness when old Likum said, "No, Illiune, you must not leave the safety of the fire tonight. There may be strange animals in the darkness." Illiune stopped and turned back into the hut and rolled out the mat on the floor near that of the old man. He smiled at the talk of Likum. There were no animals on the island. There was nothing to harm a person in any way, unless it was—. A chill swept through him when he considered the danger of having something others coveted. When his mind weighed the truth he knew the problem with people was that they allowed the wrong desires to control them. The dolphins seemed to enjoy doing good for the joy of doing. Illiune had never understood humans and he realized that his brief association with the dolphins had given him greater pleasure than he had experienced in years of association with his people. An eerie uneasiness crept over him as he drifted away into sleep.

CHAPTER 29

*I*lliune dreamed that he was on the magic island. He was lying on the ledge beside the dolphin girl. They laughed and ate and he talked to her of those feelings he wished to conceal, but could not. They swam with the dolphins and gathered pearl oysters and coral. They brought riches up and then dropped them into the deep waters. It was a game and they did not value them. Illiune was smiling with happiness when he heard the strange sound of fire burning. Old Likum was caught looking at him intently. The old man did not pretend he was not watching and he spoke softly, "Your other world must be a very beautiful place, to speak of it so freely. The spirits tell me you have had an experience with destiny that few can understand. Your secret is forgotten already. I do not remember well. Come, let us eat. There is much to do today."

Illiune was momentarily embarrassed by the honesty and frankness of the old man. "He is like a dolphin in spirit", Illiune thought. "He is always so honest and friendly." The more he considered the comparison, the more he was sure, and he wondered if Laud Likum could become dangerous if pushed too far. "Perhaps", he mused, "the dolphins, too could be violent if necessary." He then recalled the actions of the dolphins when he had been attacked by the sharks.

After they had finished eating, the old man spoke to Illiune in warning. "You must visit your grandmother this morning. No doubt she has heard you are here, and there will be many there who pretend to be her friends. Speak with care of her son, your father. If you would take the advice of an old man, it would be better if you do not ask for a wailing. We can not be sure he is in the next land. Let us wait yet a while. Your grandmother is quite old and perhaps bad news would be too strong. I know you are able to speak soothingly." Illiune did not reply to the words of Likum. He knew his advice was good. Rising to his feet he bowed to the old man and said, "Menlau, e pan cola", (Thank you, I will go).

Illiune walked slowly through the tropical forest until he came to the path leading to his grandmother's hut. He was dressed as he came in from the sea. He wore only the faded blue lava lava and around his neck hung the strange, shiny, blue-gold shell. He held the shell in his left hand as he walked. It gave him a warm feeling and his heart seemed to beat stronger when he touched his gift from the Dolphin-girl.

She was expecting him. He walked up and said smiling, "Hello, grandmother. It is good to see you." She raised to her feet from her sitting position, with much effort. A smile creased her broad face as she said admonishingly, "You have been gone too long, my son. Why did you not tell me you would be gone many weeks? Do you not think I worry for you? See all these sweet cakes which need to be eaten. You would rather play in the boat than eat your grand-mother's food. You are a bad boy. Come, sit down. You have some-thing to tell me and I have much to hear." His grandmother was smiling at him, but he knew she was wondering about his father. "I left father on an island far away grandmother. There was not room on the outrigger to carry us both home with a load of coral. Father wants you to live in wealth your remaining days. After I sell the coral to the foreigners on the ship, you will have much money. When you are quite comfortable I must return to find father and bring him home. Look, grandmother, father wanted me to give this to you so you would know he is safe." With a quick pull of his lava lava at the

waist he removed a large pearl and held it out to her. She saw the
pearl and as she reached out her hand she stopped and gasped, "Your
hands! Your hands! They are scaly like fish!" Illiune stood straight
and tall and unmovable. "They are my hands, grandmother. Those
that I received from my mother and my father. They serve me well. I
would not want it any other way." He continued to hold out the pearl
and she took it from him with trembling fingers. She was careful not
to touch him, and a pain pierced his heart. She clutched the pearl
tightly in her dimpled old hands and Illiune knew it would be other
hands by night. She looked at him strangely and said, "There is no
need to wait for a ship to sell coral. A man has come to our village
from far away. He has much money and he buys goods from all who
will sell to him. Perhaps you should take some coral to him. He is
very shrewd and knows good from bad." Illiune let her finish speaking and then said quietly, "Perhaps I will do that, grandmother, but
now I must go visit our King. He is expecting me." With these words
he turned and walked away, with the pain still in his heart. He was
nearly back to the home of Likum when he remembered he did not
eat a sweet cake. She had made them especially for him that morning. He knew that, but felt he would have become sick if he had eaten
one.

Likum was waiting. He had moved the outrigger up sideways to
the shore and had removed the coral with care and tied it to the poles
which formed braces for the thatched roof. The old man was looking
with great interest at the outrigger when Illiune returned. When the
young man said nothing, Likum sensed the meeting had not been as
warm as it might have been. "Would you care to open your burdened
heart to a willing, but forgetful listener, my friend? While you release
your feelings I will continue to admire your outrigger. I have not
seen one like this for many years. I am full of questions, but I speak
too freely." Illiune was amazed at the ability of the old man to sense
feelings. "He has strange power also", thought Illiune, "He is much

like the Serepein in knowing one's mind. I do not need to speak. He already knows.

With the old man there could be few secrets, and as Laud Likum admired the lines of the outrigger, Illiune spoke, "Grandmother was waiting to see me. Others were there also, but they stayed back. I spoke only to her. I told her I came back alone and left father on an island, because the load was much too heavy for both to come home. I wanted her to believe I had a gift for her from father and I gave her one of these." Illiune turned down his waistband and took out another pearl. Walking over to the old man, he held out his hands and arms. Likum took the pearl very slowly. In doing so he took one of Illiune's hands and held it while he removed the pearl. He seemed to have more interest in the hands as the sun shining on them sent out gold-blue and silver rays of reflection. Finally the old man spoke evenly and truthfully to Illiune. "You have hands and arms and feet like your mother. She was the most beautiful of all women. In all the islands there was no one who could compare to her in grace, or beauty, or kindness. She was superior to anyone in swimming or diving. I would feel fortunate to have those hands. Some day you will understand more than I can tell you now. We will speak of these great mysteries in time. This is a pearl of great price. Here, you must sell it for your grandmother." Illiune stood wordless for some time. There seemed to be a great weight lifted from him. He knew it was because of what Likum told him, and Likum did not make up stories. When he could speak, Illiune said, "This pearl is for you as are many more I have to give you if you will have them. The coral also is to be used to make you comfortable in your remaining years."

The old man seemed reluctant to take the pearl, but realized that it actually held very little value to Illiune. "There is a trader in the village who will buy your pearls and coral. He does well because he does not pay what articles are worth. He is not a good man. You may visit him, but it could be bad for you if you refuse to sell at his price. I tell you now, a pearl of this size and quality should bring eighty dollars at the least. The trader will sell it to ship people for perhaps two hundred. Your red coral is unmatched in beauty. Each piece should bring to you two hundred dollars and the pink, one hundred and fifty. Black coral is easier to find, but this one should bring about fifty. The trader will not offer this price. I only warn you to be wary. I do not wish for you to be harmed." Illiune heard the old man out patiently and then rose up and taking a piece of red coral he walked out through the stands of sugar cane and papaya trees forming a border for the path, and entered the shade of the rain forest. Before he came to the path leading to the village center he removed another large pearl from his waist and held it in his hand.

The path led to the center of the village where the King lived in his large house. He knew the King would be home. He would be expecting Illiune and would not leave and miss the opportunity of receiving a valuable gift. The greeting was as it should be when addressing royality. Illiune bowed respectfully and said, "Kaselehlie mein, (Hello sir). The King spoke kindly and called for his wife to bring a cool drink for the good man. When the Queen came with the drink, Illiune bowed low and said, "Menlau", (Thank you). He spoke to her while holding the pearl in the cup of his hand and continued, "I would be honored if you would accept this small pearl as a gift to the royal lady." Her eyes opened wide as she saw the large pearl and she smiled when she took it from him. He was careful to keep his hand turned upward to keep the bright scales from frightening her. He was successful. He stepped back and spoke to the King, "Would you honor me by walking with me to the hut of the trader? I would know the value of this small coral. If it is not valuable enough for a King, I will bring a larger one." His plan worked. The King stood up and together they walked through the village to the shop of the trader. Illiune did not like the man before he spoke. The trader's eyes saw neither the King nor Illiune. They were glued to the coral. "Greedy eyes", Illiune thought, "greedy and cruel and deceitful."

CHAPTER 30

*W*ith the King in his presence as his friend, Illiune spoke to the trader. "What would you pay for this coral, friend?" asked Illiune. The trader reached out quickly for it, but Illiune pulled it back. "You may look at it only while you answer. Until then you will not touch it. One must dive very deep for a coral such as this. I would bring larger ones, but they are not easily carried." The trader looked at the tall man with a surprise on his face. He had never heard a villager speak like this before. He had to be wise in speaking to this stranger. If he had much coral and could get more by diving the trader might get rich quickly. "I would say seventy dollars. Now may I touch it?" Illiune drew back again and spoke to the trader with words for the King. "You are not fair about prices. You would cheat even our great King. He is too wise to sell for such a small price. The King knows this is worth at least two hundred dollars. I say now to our King, if he does not pay a fair price he should be beaten and thrown to the "Bakos", (Sharks). This coral was a gift from me to our King. You insult us both by your small offer. I say now, what is the coral worth?" The sun was shining down on the village and the air was humid. Illiune realized it was unusually warm, but he also knew the beads of perspiration running down the whiskey redden face of the trader were caused by more than the weather. Illiune held the red coral up close to the eyes of the greedy man. He was caught in a trap and could not escape. Illiune knew the trader wanted his goods. He was also aware that the King was honored to be in the company of such a wealthy man. The King would have destroyed the trader then if Illiune had so desired. Finally the trader stammered, "I offer you two hundred." As he spoke he reached out for the coral, but Illiune stepped away. "You do not hear well, my friend. This small coral is a gift from me to our King. I wished only for him to know what a fair price would be. Our King is wise and he knows that when the ship comes in this coral would bring five hundred dollars. How you deal with the King is not my affair, but I have much coral and the King will come with me to trade. We will always have fair trade while we have a great King." With the visit over, Illiune turned, gave the coral to the King, and ask, "Would you walk with me to your home sir?"

Illiune realized the King would sell the coral to the trader at the earliest possible time. That was his business. Illiune had accomplished what he had set out to do. When they approached the King's house Illiune murmured, "If I had someone to help, I would take all my coral to the trader. I know our King would demand a fair price." The King spoke to his wife who again brought a cool drink. It was a custom to sit with the King until he excused the visitor. Before long several men appeared and stood patiently, waiting to do the King's bidding. The King spoke to Illiune so that the waiting men could hear. "I thank you for honoring me with your visit. These men will go with you and obey your every command until your need of them is finished. I ask that you would honor us at a feast given for your safe return. The feast will be three days from now." With that the King turned, and with his gift, walked into his house.

Illiune turned and headed down the path that led out of the village and through the forest to the hut of Likum, and behind him the strong, curious men followed. When they approached the old man's hut, Illiune stopped the men, and leaving them at the edge of the clearing, he walked on down to the house. Likum was sitting between the hut and the outrigger in the shade of the breadfruit trees. Illiune spoke to him and explained what he had in mind. They would go sell all the coral and what pearls Likum would suggest and put most of the money in the money house for safekeeping. The King would know where the money was and several men would know also. Illiune did not want to endanger the old man by giving him a great amount of ready wealth. Likum agreed reluctantly and Illiune walked out and motioned for the men to come. There were seven of them and Illiune saw that each carried a piece of coral. He did not need to tell them to be careful. They handled the beautiful coral as if it were a baby. Never in their lives had they touched anything so valuable. Few had ever seen coral of that size. Illiune asked Likum to walk ahead and he would follow in time. Likum asked no question, but started up the path to the forest with the men following. Illiune took time to take out eight average sized pearls. These he placed inside his waist where he could reach them quickly without exposing the others. They walked from the hut in single file and did not stop until they approached the King's house. The King needed no special invitation to accompany Illiune to the house of the trader. Before they were half way, there were many villagers following along, admiring the riches and the tall, muscular, handsome stranger with the unusual shell and shining hands. Illiune's plan was working well. He had one more task to do. When the procession was in front of the money house. Illiune asked them to stop. In the company of the King, he entered the building and asked to speak to the head man. When the man introduced himself, Illiune explained his visit. He wanted to do some business with the "Officio", (official). The man looked a bit curious at the tall stranger and suggested they go into a room to talk. Illiune told him the King wished to oversee a trade and desired that he accompany them. Again Illiune used a bit of trickery, but the man could not refuse.

The procession moved down to the hut of the trader and again, at the command of Illiune, they stopped. He raised a hand and held it. All noise ceased. He spoke loud enough for all to hear. "You are very fortunate people to have a great King who is wise and will look after your interests. Whenever you have something to trade or sell here with this gentleman, your King will see that you are treated fairly. All this coral you see is to be sold to the trader at whatever price the King asks. If a question of value comes between the trader and the King, Likum will be the judge of a fair price. The money from this coral will be placed in the money house. Likum will be allowed enough to live comfortably and the King will see that an equal amount is given to my grandmother. Neither will ever be allowed a great sum for fear of being robbed." All was said that was necessary.

As the King bartered with the trader Illiune pretended not to hear, but the trader dared not question the King's price. Much more money was marked for their account than they expected. The trader paid dearly for the coral, but Illiune knew he would still make a profit. When the men who aided Illiune were free of their duty, Illiune called them to him. He gave each man a pearl and said, "If you would sell it, do it now while your good King is here to see that you get its worth. The men spoke to the King and he in turn dealt for each. He marveled in his duty of importance. When all was done the men bowed to Illiune and turned and smiled off toward their homes. Illiune had one more dealing with the trader. With Likum and the King standing near, he spoke to the red-faced foreigner. "I have found an average size pearl. It is not large, but of exceptional color." Holding it out toward the trader he asked, "What price would you pay for this?" Instinctively the trader reached out for the pearl, but Illiune pulled his hand back. "You do not learn easily, friend. When you offer a fair price, you may touch the pearl." The trader again began perspiring unnaturally as Illiune held the pearl before him. "I cannot offer a price until I see it," he croaked nervously. Illiune laid the pearl on the counter and purposely withdrew his hand. Immediately the greedy hand snaked out for the pearl and closed over it. The act was natural for the trader, but Illiune expected it, and before the hand lifted from the counter it was enclosed in a webbed vise of shiny scales. Illiune's hand terrified the trader and he screamed to be released. Illiune turned to the King and said, "Sir, would you remind the trader that he is not to touch anything until a fair price is offered?" The King came over to the trader and spoke with authority. "You are not to touch any article of trade until a fair price is offered." When the King had so instructed, Illiune released his hold and stepped back. "What is a fair price for the pearl, friend, or shall we ask the King?" That pearl will bring one hundred dollars when the ship comes in." Illiune was purposely telling the King the value of the pearl, as he had the coral. Once the King knew the true value he would be sure it was paid. Because he was being left out, and because he wanted, at all costs, to be a friend of Illiune, the King spoke up. "The pearl is worth fifty dollars." He then turned to leave as the trader whispered low, "No! that is too much. Look, here is a pearl I bought today for twenty dollars. I will not pay fifty for a small one!" Illiune recognized the pearl instantly. It was the large one he had received from the dolphins and given to his grandmother. For the first time in his life Illiune felt a hot rage building up within him. His first impulse was to destroy the man, but he controlled himself long enough to speak again to the King. "Would you allow this man to rob your old widows, oh King? He has stolen from your people today. If you do not force him to amend the wrong, they will lose faith in you. I know you are an honest King. Come, ask the man what he has done."

Again with a flourish of importance the King returned to the counter of the trader's hut. "What is it that I should see young man?" With difficulty in controlling his anger Illiune spoke between clenched teeth. "Show the King the great pearl you bought from a woman of the village today for twenty dollars." The trader lifted a trembling hand and stepped beck as he opened his fingers to reveal a large glistening pearl. The King looked unbelieving at the article in the trader's hand and then with a sucking noise in his throat he lifted his right hand, and in it was a razor sharp machete. The trader's face lost its redness and within seconds he was cringing in terror. Illiune thought the King was an excellent pretender, but he did not understand. Holding the machete back in his right hand, the King reached over and grabbed the horrified trader by the front of his shirt and jerked him halfway over the counter. Then with a voice cold with heat, the King uttered two words, "Let's talk!" Illiune had faced death himself and had seen people die, but he could not find pity for this greedy man. If the man said one wrong word his head would be split instantly. He was trying to talk, but fear prevented anything but a gurgling sound. The King's face changed from chalk to red as the blood began returning. He managed somehow to ask the trader the question he knew would condemn him. "Did you rob the Queen ?" The man could not answer, but he began shaking his head and finally blurted out, "No! No!" When the King heard his reply he slowly relaxed his grip on the man and trying to regain his composure somewhat he whispered hoarsely, "You talk now, or you die!" There was only a thread holding the life in the man. He dared not to talk, and yet he knew his words would bring death. In a few moments the King raised his machete and moved to strike. As he did the trader burst into a babble, almost impossible to understand. "An old widow brought it. She needed money for food. I did not want the pearl. It is of no value. I only felt sorry for her. I paid her twenty dollars for it. I will give it back!" The King had regained control of himself again and put out his hand and ask to see the pearl. The trader handed it to him with a trembling hand. Slowly the King turned the pearl around in his hand and then spoke to Likum. "Come here, old friend. Tell me the value of this pearl to the buyers on the ship." Likum came over and bowed to the King. He lifted the pearl carefully between his thumb and forefinger and held it up to the light. He then rolled the pearl in the palm of his hand. Looking directly into the eyes of the King he said, "This pearl is of great size and beauty. I have seen many pearls. This came from water very deep, deeper than men can dive today. The value of this pearl is beyond comprehension. In a market where pearls are traded, it would be worth at least five hundred dollars."

The King looked into Likum's eyes steadily and the old man returned the gaze. Then Illiune saw the knuckles on the King's hand turn white when he gripped the machete anew. "You would rob an old widow of this priceless pearl and say it is of no value? I say you will pay three hundred more dollars for this pearl. You will also pay the tall man here fifty dollars for his pearl. Now hear this: You will never buy in this village again without my presence. I will set the price and if you want the article you will pay what I say. Likum will judge a question of value only, as he has done here. He is rich now and has nothing to gain or lose. My people need your business, but they will never be cheated again!" With that the King stood back and instructed the trader to produce three hundred and fifty dollars for the pearls. With feverish hands the man complied, and as they turned to go, the people of the village were standing silent, watching. When he saw them, the King lifted his head and they opened a path for him. He had served his people well.

CHAPTER 31

L eaving the King after being excused, Illiune and Likum turned down the path leading out of the village. They were followed by scores of youngsters who babbled along in hope of a gift. They were disappointed, but covered well their feelings by speaking knowingly of the tall, handsome man. Likum was leading when the trail lost itself in the tropical forest. Before the green enveloped Illiune he noticed a movement behind a banana plant. Curiosity caused him to stop and step back for a closer look. Standing directly behind the tree was a girl, and without requiring closer observation, Illiune could see she was old enough to be eligible in marriage. Her rounded curves contrasted with the straight trunk of the tree and he could see a bright hybiscus blossom in her hair where the unmarried girls wear them. Because she was watching him, he could see her face clearly. It was a lovely face, outlined by dark wavy hair. The eyes were large and smiling and when she knew he had looked well, she laughed silently revealing small white teeth, and disappeared into lush growth. Illiune was surprised…surprised that the girl had the nerve to stand in the shadows alone, so near the "Fish boy" and Likum. He was surprised too, at her beauty, and it bothered Illiune that he could not get her out of his thoughts as he neared the old man's house.

Illiune had no idea that Likum was aware of the girl, but when they were sitting down to eat the old man's brow rose up and down and a smile added to his many wrinkles when he said, "Rare are the banana plants that possess such curves and grow hybiscus." Illiune hung his head and tried to forget the incident. There were still some things that old man did not know. He did not know that Illiune had given his heart to one more lovely than any, but the encounter caused him much uneasiness.

After eating, Likum turned to the boy and said huskily, "You are unusually kind to me Illiune. I am rich now because of you. You are also a strange man, one of power and strength. Your grandmother is also rich because you made her so. The King has new strength and power because of your words. The villagers are yours to command, but I know you do not want power or wealth. You have a mystery about you that gives me great joy, but we will speak of that later. Today was a great day for our village. Even I, Laud Likum, have gained respect and place through your words. Although I thank you, I have no desire for power. When the King comes for information I will give it to him because of you. Now hear this, my young friend. You have made an enemy today who will be a danger to you. If the banana plant continues to have curves, you will have another enemy. Young love is difficult to comprehend. She is being trailed by Dagus, the village bully."

A vivid picture of his cousin, his father's sister's son, appeared when the name was mentioned. He was the leader of the tormentors who had teased Illiune unmercifully as far back as he could remember. Dagus was not only the local bully, but a thief and a coward. He never teased Illiune unless backed by two or more village boys. Illiune would not forget Dagus.

Speaking to the old man Illiune asked, "Would you care to go with me to the home of my father? It will be for a visit only. I am not yet prepared to return there to live. If you will allow me, I will stay with you for a few days more. If I decide to leave soon, all will be well. If I decide to stay, I will go to the home of my father. Any burden can get heavy in time." The old man heard him out and answered, "You will never be a burden to me, Illiune. Rather you are a giver of new hope. I will accompany you as you visit your home, but will tarry at the proper place until you bid me come in." With that the two stepped away from the hut and made their way through a seldom-used trail.

The path to Eliakim's home was a winding way leading to a sheltered cove in the valley nearest to Likum's. The trail led to a bubbling mountain stream which tumbled from the high ridge to the valley floor and on out into the blue waters of the lagoon. It was not a long trail, but it gave privacy to Eliakim. When Illiune and his old friend reached the pool of fresh water, formed by the blocking of the mountain stream, Likum sat down and Illiune continued walking toward the thatched roof house hidden behind the woven pandanus fence. His father had built it to provide privacy for his wife, Illiune's mother. Now that she was gone he kept the fence to recall memories.

Likum sat quietly, contemplating. The only sound was the soft murmur of the small stream as it entered the pool and trickled out toward the sea. A sharp cry of desperation caused his head to jerk erect and he could see a figure lurching toward him. The man had a knife in one hand and the instant before Likum was bowled over into the pool, he saw in horror, blood dripping from the blade. In disbelief and dread the old man floundered out of the pool and made his way to the hut. Illiune was lying on his back on a mat in a circle of fresh blood. Before the old man could speak, Illiune said with effort, "It is nothing but a scratch old friend. Do not fear. There is no pain now. A sharp blade does it's work well." Likum dropped to his knees beside the young man and lifted Illiune's hands away from the wound on his upper leg. The bright blood was bubbling out steadily. When the old man looked and saw and knew, he said, "You are lucky, Illiune. Surely the spirits are with you. An artery has not been severed, but the cut is deep and you will lose much blood." Likum stood up and unwound his lava lava. He ripped it in strips and then folding one strip into a pad he bound the leg snugly and in a few minutes he could tell the bleeding had begun to subside. "I will go for help, my young friend. You must lay quietly while I am gone." Illiune spoke to the old man weakly. "In the bow of my outrigger you will find some seaweed. It is a magic weed. Please bring it to me, old friend." The old man needed no explanation. He rose and hurried for help.

Likum was old and limited. He realized if he hurried home he might not get back in time. He decided to go directly into the village for help. This he did although the day was far gone and darkness was setting in. He reached the open trail leading to the village and met one of the men who had carried coral for Illiune. Wasting no time in greeting Likum cried out. "Go quickly to the King and tell him the tall man has been dangerously injured. Tell him he is at the home of Eliakim, by the sea. He will need an outrigger. He will need fast strong men like you!" The man turned and ran and disappeared into the yard of the King's house. Before Likum could catch his breath, the King and the men came running up the path. When the King was standing by the old man he said, "Speak, friend." Likum told him only that Illiune had been stabbed by a man and was bleeding profusely. He told him he should have two men take Illiune's outrigger around to Eliakim's hut. There was no time to say more as the old man saw several men spring to help the strange man of power.

CHAPTER 32

*I*lliune lay helpless, waiting for Likum to return with the magic weed. He did not try to rise to his feet. He knew he had lost much blood and he realized blood meant life. His mind drifted back to the times when he cared little whether he lived or died. Now he had much to live for. The memory of the Serepein stirred in him the will to live. When he was well he could go back to the island of magic. Perhaps the spirits or the dolphins would help him find his dolphin girl. He would have dreamed on, but a strange voice was speaking to him, "You will be well soon, great friend. Many hands are here to assist you. If you are well enough, you may instruct us in what you desire. Your outrigger will be here in a little time. Would you care for a drink of water?" Illiune asked them to raise his head, which they did with sure and steady hands. One held a half shell of water to his lips and he drank. He knew he must drink water. It would help to make new blood.

The King came into the hut and looked down at Illiune. Dropping to his knees he asked, "Do you know what happened friend, that you have been wounded?" When Illiune was slow to reply the King looked about and the said, "I see you fought well, there is little left of your home." His statement startled Illiune and he let his eyes scan the room. Again that strange hot rage built up within him. The feeling surprised Illiune, but he could not control it. The King watched the features of Illiune and ask, "Do you know who wounded you, friend? If he is one from our village he will pay with his life. You have brought good to us. We should give you better than a wound." For the moment Illiune was unable to answer. The King and his men thought it was because of the wound, but the feeling of rage and helplessness prevented him from speaking. Once he placed his hands by his sides and tried to lift himself to see more of the damage his father's home had received. The men held him down and spoke reassuringly to him. For a while there was subdued talking, and then Illiune heard a footstep and then silence. No one spoke, not even the King. Likum had come and the men moved to give him room. He knelt by the side of the young man and asked, "How is it, friend?" Illiune could not speak, he had never felt so weak and helpless and filled with anger. He tried several times to answer the old man, but checked himself because he knew he would speak in tears or sob shamefully. Likum was nearly overcome with grief. He thought the life was ebbing away and there was nothing he could do.

The old man had just turned to the King when he heard the splash of paddles. Leaping to his feet he cried, "Come!", and several men followed him to the beach. Reaching into the bow of the outrigger he lifted out several handfuls of seaweed and placed it in the hands of the men. "Take it quickly to the wounded man," Likum ordered, "It is his only chance for life." They were waiting beside Illiune when Likum returned. He took a knife and cut the binding off the leg. Leaving the pad in place he covered the area of the wound generously with the weed and then said aloud to any man, "I will need a lava lava." Almost before he finished speaking someone handed one down and Likum wrapped the seaweed close to the leg and tied the legs together at the ankles and knees with strips from the long cloth. Looking up to the men he said low, "Our friend must be taken to my house as quickly as you can get him there. The outrigger will be easier. Who will go?" He needed not ask twice. The men worked quietly and there was no sound except when Illiune was raised from the mat.

The thick blood lifted the mat, and when it was pulled away there came a sound of indrawn breaths.

After Illiune had been placed on the outrigger, Likum turned and saw the King waiting. "He has been wounded very deep, oh King, He had no chance to defend himself. What you see in this, his home, was done by the one who wounded him. The man was searching for pearls and coral. Illiune and I came to see his home after being gone for many weeks. I was waiting at the pool until he bid me come. The thief heard him coming and drove the knife in as our friend entered." The King heard him out and then asked, "Did you see the thief?" Likum did not have a ready answer. If he told the King who it was, the new blood spilled would be that of Illiune's father's people. "I honor your question, oh King. I saw the thief. He ran at me and knocked me into the pool. Yes, I know him well, but I do not believe the sick man would wish me to tell. He would see to his own problems." Likum waited and when the King spoke there was much truth in what he said. "We have not been good to this man for many years. We will feel dishonored if we cannot revenge his attack." Old Likum knew the King could demand the name, and because of this, he answered,

"If the great one becomes well, he will avenge his own. I will tell you, oh King, the medicine that is now on his leg is a secret healing gift of the great spirits. In time I will show you, but this you should know: If this man dies because of the wound, the spirits will cause much suffering among your people. I have been called "Likum" because of what I have tried to tell our people these many years. I know you are wise and just because the wounded man spoke the words. You cannot be any other kind of King now. You will have honor and respect among your people, which you have never had before, because the great man said it would be. Is it not so? Yes, it is true! Now I tell you one last thing. This strange man is not only of your people, but of the old people of the past. This secret only you and I know. Keep it and remember it, and you will live many days with honor and wisdom. If you wish to do one thing to avenge this cowardly attack, let it be this: Call in every male of your village above nineteen years of age and ask him if he is the guilty one. When all have been questioned by you, oh King, you will know that the guilty man is a coward, a thief, a murderer, and last of all, a man who lies to his King. He will in time make himself known. Deal with him then as you will."

All had been spoken between Likum and the King. As they turned to leave the old man heard the King say to the men, "Those who will repair this home, I will honor." Likum led the way through the winding trail toward his house and the village. When the fork in the path was reached, Likum turned off and walked a few feet and stopped to watch the others pass by. He was startled when he did. As the men passed by they still wore their lava lava, but the King did not.

CHAPTER 33

Old Likum had built a fire and prepared to heat water when the outrigger touched onto the shore. He hurried down and secured the craft at the bow and stern. The men lifted Illiune and carried him to the hut and at Likum's direction they laid him down on the mat. As they were leaving the old man walked out with them and spoke a word or two. He then thanked them for Illiune and they were gone. The old man returned to the wounded boy and sat down beside him. "How are you, my friend?" he asked. "I am but tired, old man. There is no pain in the wound. Could you not see the home of my father? It was destroyed. That caused the pain I endured and could do nothing." Likum went out and returned with water. "Drink this. You will have fever soon." While Illiune lay quietly on the mat the old man took a woven basket down to the outrigger and returned with more seaweed. He then took a cloth and poured heated water over it and began washing the face of Illiune. When he had washed his head and hands, he removed the lava lava and cleansed his body of dried blood. When he was releasing the blue cloth from Illiune's waist he found the remaining pearls tucked into a fold of material. The old man said, "I will put these beads away for safe keeping." He carried the blood-soaked lava lava to the stream and dropped it in a pool of water to soak. Coming back, he covered Illiune with a clean material. When he finished the bathing he placed some seaweed behind his head and neck. He laid some on Illiune's chest and then put his hands on the weed and covered them. When he was satisfied he said, "I have heard of this magic weed. Never have I touched it. Because I believe the old tales are true you will rest until tomorrow." As Illiune felt the sensations from the sea medicine, he remembered how the Serepein slept on her mat of seaweed. He smiled as he drifted into slumber.

They came early, long before the sky was turning gold. The man said, "Here is what you ordered, old man. The King has sent this young woman to help you care for the sick one. She is very able and has worked in large houses for the sick. Perhaps you will need rest too, old man." Likum put out his hand and gave the man a large silver coin. "That is for the food. We will see if the girl can help. Tell your King we are grateful." Likum could say nothing more to the man. When he turned to the girl he looked at her for a moment and then with a smile he spoke. "We will see if you work as well as you decorate a banana tree." She looked at him with dancing eyes and a blush etched her cheeks. "I will do all I can, old man." Likum knew she would.

The girl was capable. She made broth of chicken and rice. Likum could do nothing, but she would say, "Oh, please old man, I enjoy doing this." And when Likum watched, he believed her. It was nearly mid-day when Illiune awoke. The moment he moved, the girl was at his side cooling his brow with a clean wet cloth. When his eyes first opened he looked into a lovely olive-colored face with dark flashing eyes and a ready smile. Because of his dream, and still half asleep, he reached up and pulled her down and kissed her. In her surprise she uttered, "Soh! Soh!", (No! No!) and drew away quickly. It was then that Illiune became wide-awake, and raising up quickly, stared unbelieving at the girl beside him. The physical action and changing emotions within him caused Illiune to look feverish. He was sure he was kissing his Serepein and he was flooded with happiness. Now he realized he had kissed this strange girl he did not know. As the realization settled upon him, Illiune mumbled awkwardly, "Mah Kengie." (I'm sorry). She looked at him with startled eyes and then a dimple built a smile on her face and she answered in an amused voice, "Lip-ilipil," (It doesn't matter).

Illiune lay quietly puzzled because of the girl's presence and in time he asked, "Do you know where the old man has gone?" She continued smiling and answered, "Yes, he is sleeping. I am here to take care of you while the old man rests. My name is Merrianna. I was sent here by the King because I am a good nurse." She laughed low and then continued. "When I work in large sick house of white man, they call me nurse. You are hungry now. I make good broth for you." Without waiting for an answer she began feeding him by holding his head up with an arm behind his head and tilting the cup to his lips. It was good and Illiune, still feeling awkward in the presence of this pretty girl, murmured, "Yo, Inenen yo," (Good, very good).

Already Illiune was faced with another problem. He wanted to be kind to this girl and yet he did not trust himself to be kind to her. "Why did the King do this to me?" he asked himself. When he glanced at her from time to time and remembered her as being the one behind the tree he wondered if she might have suggested to the King that she would nurse him. "Do you hide behind banana trees often, Merrianna?" he asked. She only smiled and turned her head slightly and looked at him with her large flashing eyes. Illiune began to worry. He had finished the soup and when she asked if she should change his bandage, he told her it felt all right and she should rest now. The longer she sat near him, the more he wished the old man would return. He felt embarrassed at her patient ability and personal attention. He could not help but see her arms and breasts as she was feeding him and sitting so close. She is like the Serepein," he thought, "but she does not have the beautiful silver lace on her breasts and arms." She wore a hybiscus in her hair and he could smell the coconut oil in the black tresses as she fussed over him. An odd thought entertained Illiune's mind as he watched the girl rise up and walk outside and then reenter. She would make a wonderful wife, but she is human. For a moment the idea struck him as unfair, but he had known few humans who possessed the qualities he had learned to admire.

Likum came in and smiled down at the young man. "You did not miss me, my friend. My helper tells me you were having a wonderful visit. She also tells me that you are violent when you awake." The old man continued smiling as he sat down. "I have allowed her to go for a walk. She will be back in one hour. During that time we will dress the wound with clean coverings." Old Likum had already talked more than usual and he spoke not again as he completed the work. When done, he laid a hand on Illiune's brow and said, "You have no fever yet, but it will come. Let us hope it does not become too strong." Likum sat back and waited. He knew Illiune wanted to talk about the girl. In time Illiune asked, "Is there no way we can have the girl return to the village? I am afraid of women her age. You should know that, old friend. I cannot speak with them and I do not understand them. It is not fair that she becomes attached to me because I am leaving soon. She is much too lovely to be hurt. Surely there is someone else who cares for her." The old man sat very still. He considered well the honest words of the nervous and wounded young man. Finally, he answered. "Have you forgotten what I told you before, my friend? Remember when she was behind the tree? She is desired by one of the village now. His name is Dagus!" With the word, Illiune sat up in shock. "No! do not say that old man! She is far too lovely and capable for an animal like him. I cannot love her to marry her, but he will not have her. If he as much as touches her, he will never touch again!" The sudden rage that filled Illiune left him weak and fevered. He lay back slowly with the old man's help and his breathing became uneven and rasping. The old man ached beside him with anguish. When Merrianna came in she found them thus and she came over and kneeled beside Likum. She was shaking, with more than fear for Illiune, and the old man could see the tears on her cheeks. Her breathing was uneven and though she tried to control herself, Likum heard the muffled sobs within her breast. He rose up and eased out and around the hut and from beneath a papaya tree he watched. Dagus was crouched in the edge of the foliage where the trail entered the forest. The distance was close enough that the old man could see the lust in the eyes of the pocked-faced coward.

CHAPTER 34

*T*he old man eased back into the hut and walked over to the frightened girl and whispered softly, "Let us go outside to talk." Likum led the trembling girl out of hearing distance from Illiune and then asked, "Did that fellow touch you, Merrianna?" She tried to look at the old man and then with tear-filled eyes she fell upon his chest and burst into uncontrollable sobs. Old Likum let her cry and when she was through, he said kindly, "You need not fear now. You will stay here at Old Likum's humble house. That fellow will not trouble you again. My friend here is sick and is now with fever. You must help me with him. We both must have our rest. If he speaks strange words while fevered, you must not be offended or too deeply hurt. He is a good man who has just returned from an unusual journey." Likum was well beyond the age of marriage or courtship, but when he saw the scratches and bruises on the breast and neck of the girl, he felt a hot rage of fire burn within him.

When the man came from the King to see the progress of Illiune, he was met by Likum outside the hut. Speaking low he told him that Illiune had slept well, but was now in fever. "Now hear well, my friend. The one who wounded Illiune has also wounded the girl who was sent to nurse him. Neither of us dare to leave the hut in the daylight. At night, who knows? Go to the King and tell him this man of his village who hides to knife people and take advantage of girls, is lurking in the forest beside my hut. Tell the King we need his wisdom and power to rid ourselves of this animal." With the message given, Likum held his hand out. In it was a large pearl. The man glanced at the pearl and then raised his eyes to look at the old man. "I do not take pay to help my friends." He spun around and disappeared in the forest. Within seconds Likum breathed easier.

Little time had passed when the King stepped out of the forest followed by twenty strong men and two women who carried large baskets on their heads. The men were not dressed for visiting, but carried spears, and at their side were machetes. When the King was ten paces from the door he stopped the line of followers and spoke to Likum. "You should have told me the name of the coward who wounded Illiune and now has ravaged the girl. It is not my desire to force the name, but if I am to help you, it must be so." Likum came forward and bowed to the King. "If I were a few days younger I would not have called you. You have seen my friend, now you will hear from the girl." Turning, he stepped into the hut and led the girl out to the King. "See the marks the animal makes on the virgins of your village. She would choose death rather than face him again. She will stay in my hut so long as she desires. I say this in truth: She will be as my own daughter until the day she finds a husband. The man you are seeking is Dagus, the village bully. He is the animal."

The King turned and motioned to the women with the burdens. They came up and taking the girl by the hand they led her into the hut. Calling to his men with a motion of his hand the King spoke to them briefly. "The man we seek is Dagus, the trader's friend. To he who finds him will go much honor. I would have him alive if you can, but take no chances. He is a coward and a liar and an animal with girls of our village. Today it was the Queen's sister. Tomorrow, who knows?" No other instructions were given by the King, but Likum knew that the days of Dagus were few, and he felt no pity. The fire of rage still burned within his withered old breast.

Likum entered the hut to find Merrianna sitting back against the wall as if she were trying to hide herself. The two women sat quietly, waiting. The old man knew why they were here. They would care for Merrianna until she was over the shock of her tragedy. One woman would be with her always. They would take turns sleeping, but at no time would Merrianna be out of speaking distance. Likum felt as if he were to blame. If he had told the King who stabbed Illiune, the girl would not have suffered. He pictured her as she was, lovely, eager, and capable. Now she was marked and ashamed and sick. Few girls in her condition had a desire to live. Likum realized that. He made a somber vow that he would do his best to give her new hope.

Likum walked slowly from his hut into the dusk of evening. He knew not what to do, and the anxiety in his heart for both Illiune and Merrianna caused him to feel the need of being alone to think. He pondered how quickly moods of life can change. For a short time that day he reveled in the companionship of Merrianna and Illiune. Her purposeful care of the sick one brought a joy to the old man's heart. He heard the lament of Illiune, because of her attention, with a twinkle in his eye. Illiune would recover in time because of the seaweed. If only the great spirits could find a magic cure for Merrianna.

Likum's contemplating walk was suddenly interrupted by a movement near him. He stopped quickly, alarmed. As he did, he heard a reassuring voice say, "It is I old man. Be not worried or afraid. You are closely guarded tonight. Until Dagus is found and destroyed you will never be alone. It is the wish of the King that you need not fear." Likum thanked the villager and turned back toward his hut. He did not enter, but stepped only to the doorway and beckoned to one of the women. She rose quietly and followed him a few paces from the hut. "There are many guards around us. We need not fear an enemy. Could it be arranged that I speak with the girl here in your presence?" The woman turned and disappeared. In a few moments she came out followed by the pale faced girl. Likum could see by her eyes that she was still crying, but no tears were left to fall. "Merrianna, I have something you must know. The wounded man knows nothing of what has happened. He shall never know. If you can find any strength to aid in his recovery, we need you. We are surrounded by guards on orders of the King. You will never suffer again. Tonight you and I must take turns caring for him with his fever. I shall sleep outside when I sleep. You must stay near him when I am gone. You will roll out your mat where I have mine now." As he finished speaking he turned and entered the hut and rolled up his mat and carried it outside. It was Likum's plan to get her mind off her tragedy as quickly as possible. He knew she would care for Illiune well even though she had nothing more to smile for. Likum entered one more time and knelt beside Illiune. He was still with fever, but his breathing was more even. Motioning to the girl he said softly, "You will be first to care for him. When sleep calls you, step out and say, "Come now." She looked at him, and reached out and touched his old wrinkled hand and, though he knew her heart was breaking, she forced a smile. Likum's heart leaped, as he turned and stepped into the night.

CHAPTER 35

Merrianna did as Likum suggested and rolled out her mat, but she knew she would not lie down to sleep. She was a good nurse. She had trained in a hospital for three years. When she came in the large ship to visit her sister, the King's wife, she decided to stay for a year and then return to her home island. Her training had proved valuable to the King. She could work well with numbers as well as patients. During the time she had been here, many young men saw her as one who they would like to win for a wife, but she was the Queen's sister, and they dared not pursue her. She could marry only one of royal blood. She was older than Illiune, but she knew not his age. He appeared older than his years when he returned from his experience with the dolphins. Because of his ability to win people and the King, Merrianna was attracted to him and she tried not to conceal her feelings. She found some comfort in considering these truths, but it failed to warm her heart as she sat quietly by the patient. Occasionally she would rinse a cloth in cool water and wipe his face or give him water to drink. She caught herself speaking softly to him one time as she applied the cloth. Because she spoke she felt both ashamed and relieved. In time she was thinking it was good that Illiune did not know about her grief.

As the girl continued sitting and watching, the moon lighted the inside of the hut with a flourescent glow. She could see his features and the tiny beads of perspiration that covered his skin. Once as she cooled his face her hand touched the seaweed near his head. She gathered some in her hand and as she held it she felt a steady, strange vibration. Merrianna held it for a few moments and then placed it back near his head. Suddenly she caught herself saying softly, "It is a strange medicine that cures a strange man." When she spoke she smiled, and for an instant she was herself again.

Likum was wakened by the crowing rooster at the first sign of dawn. The girl was sitting patiently beside Illiune and as Likum entered she made a sign for silence, followed by a half smile. The old man knelt down near Merrianna and she took his hand and placed it on Illiune's forehead. His fever was gone. He realized she had sat there the night through and he could not be unhappy with her. Likum needed the rest and she would have slept, but little. "It will be my turn tonight", he mused. "She will need sleep then."

Breakfast consisted of rice and fish with fruit. The two women had brought food prepared. The fruit grew thick around Likum's hut. Illiune sat up to eat and the girl gave him a leaf with food piled high. After the fever he would be hungry. There was little conversation during breakfast. After eating the women and Merrianna took the food and placed it in a pit near the fire and covered it well with leaves. The leaves, which served as dishes, they carried down to the water to dispose of. They were gone for some time and Likum spoke to Illiune. "You are much better today. The fever has left you. I must put new seaweed on the wound. I have been a lazy man. The girl cared for you all night. She would not wake me. She has been trained to care to the sick." Illiune said not a word as the old man removed the weed and looked at the pressure bandage. "It is time we removed the pad, Illiune. We will try to make it easy." Likum put a kettle of water on the fire and fed it more sticks. "We must use hot water, as hot as you can endure," By the time the water was steaming, the women had returned. Likum watched them approach the hut and stepped out to intercept them.

"The wound needs a new dressing. You may wait here until I am through. The young man is quite shy." The women smiled and began walking toward the little stream. Likum turned into the hut. He took a clean cloth from a shelf on the wall and turned away from Illiune as he poured the hot water on it. When the old man turned to treat Illiune, Merrianna was kneeling beside the wounded man and reached out her hand for the dampened cloth. There was nothing the old man could do. He handed it to her and as he did he thought, "How strange, never before has anyone taken over duties in my home." Old Likum turned to hide a smile of happiness. Merrianna was showing signs of improvement also. He watched as she applied the cloth until it began to cool. She then handed it to the old man for hot water. The compress released after about an hour of soaking. She washed the wound carefully and motioned for Likum to come and see. The edges of the cut were white around the ragged red flesh. There was no swelling or fever in the wound. "I have seen many wounds, but never one so deep as this without much swelling or infection. Surely the seaweed is a magic medicine. If all injured people could use it, much suffering would be relieved. Do you know where it is found old man? Likum heard her words in amazement. One who experienced such an ordeal as she should not be thinking of helping others so soon. He turned to Merrianna and began speaking. "I will tell you what I know. This is a sea plant that grows in water very deep and no man has ever found. No one believes me when I speak of strange people who are part human and part dolphin, but they can find this magic weed. Come with me to the outrigger for more and I will tell you of the old people, our ancestors."

Illiune heard the old man speaking to Merrianna and although he did not think she would believe his tales, he was pleased that the old man had found someone he could speak to—someone who would listen. "It is mwow", (good). He smiled for the old man. Illiune thought Merrianna a strange one. "She is so bold", he said to himself. He would have said more, but Likum and the girl returned with the remaining weed and kneeled beside Illiune. "The old man tells me we should apply the weed on the wound with no pad. I believe all he tells me and that I will do. A foreign doctor would not agree, but of course they do not have the magic medicine." She wrapped the leg with care as Likum held it up from the mat. Merrianna looked directly at Illiune and surprised him with a statement. "Likum told me of your mother and how it is that you have such beautiful hands. I am pleased he told me. It will be easier to know that I cannot have you for a husband. I am too brave with my speech, but I am honored to help someone who is to be a King of our people of old." Merrianna was smiling at Illiune and as he glanced at the old man he could see a twinkle in his eye.

Likum was aware that the two women who were sent by the King were obeying instructions. No matter what the girl was doing or where she went, one of the watchers was on duty. He was glad for the girl's sake they did not speak too much nor make themselves conspicuous. "They do their work well", he mused. They might not hear what was being said, but they were watching. Illiune sat up for a time. He felt a little light in the head when he first lifted himself, but the wound did not pain. He enjoyed the sweet scented breeze that moved down the ridge and out over the lagoon. It was a cool, refreshing breeze and reminded Illiune of the Magic Island.

CHAPTER 36

The King came down the trail as the sun hid behind the higher palms. Likum met him at the door and bid him enter. He glanced around the small room and seemed satisfied that Merrianna and one of her caretakers were sitting quietly. He turned then and spoke to Illiune. "How is the wound today, Illiune? I see you are sitting up. This tells me there cannot be much pain. Am I speaking truth, young man?" Illiune's words were few. "It is much better, oh King. I thank you for your interest. Certainly there are others more important than I that you could visit." The King smiled at Illiune. "We will have the feast tomorrow. It is in your honor, Illiune. Will I see you, friend?" From behind the King there came the voice of Likum. "He will be there, oh King. The magic weed works well." The King turned and walked out, followed by Likum. Words were exchanged and then the King moved up the path while Likum reentered the hut.

When the sun had set and the enjoyable time of evening arrived, Illiune spoke aloud. "If it is not against your wishes, my kind helpers, I would walk a little. I will be careful to not overdue. Would you help me to rise?" The old man nodded to Merrianna and they took hold of Illiune's arms and lifted as he struggled to a standing position. A dizziness hovered over him for a moment and he held tightly to his helpers until his head cleared. 'I am not so able yet, friends. I thank you for your care." After standing a short time he tried walking. There was little pain, but the leg was stiff and he moved only a few feet, even though supported by Merrianna and Likum. At Likum's suggestion Illiune stood still and the old man went into the hut and brought out Illiune's mat. "Perhaps since your fever is gone you might like to sleep out tonight, Illiune." Likum had in mind that the girl should sleep, if possible. "I will need your help tomorrow, Merrianna. Together we will take the wounded man to the great feast. Perhaps you will need rest." With that spoken, Likum came close and helped the girl in placing Illiune on the mat. They could see that standing and walking had tired him. Before the girl had turned to go, Illiune spoke to her. "You have been more than kind, Merrianna. I will see you are rewarded for your service. You will be returning to the village soon. It is best, but I tell you now. I will not forget you." As he finished speaking he reached out and touched her hand. She let him speak through and then with tears she could not withhold, she leaned down quickly and kissed his brow and then rose up and fled into the hut.

Likum visited long with Illiune that night. He told him all he knew about the tales of the ancestors and the dolphin people. Illiune listened, fascinated, but believing, because some of what the old man related, Illiune had experienced. Likum told of old days when there was a sea people who spent some of their life in the sea and some on land. "In older days they had built a beautiful palace on a low island to the south. The long approaches to the palace were waterways, which could only be traversed when the tide was high. When they were living in the sea they were as dolphins. When they lived on land they were people, like you and I. They were different from people who live in our village now only because of their hands and feet. The dolphin people had hands and feet that resembled fins on fish. They were like yours, Illiune. Your hands are like they are because your mother was a dolphin lady. Your father found her far to the south of our village. He learned to love her and she him. In time he brought her to this village, but she was not accepted by these people. This is why your father built your home where it now is. He wanted your mother to live without persecution and rejection. You were born soon after they came here, but your mother passed on within a month of your birth. Now you are the remaining hope of the dolphin people. They, the ancestors, spoke of destiny. What your destiny will be, only time will tell."

Likum stopped speaking and remained quiet for a time. He was waiting for the question he knew Illiune would ask. "How did the ancestors change from dolphins to people, old friend?" Likum answered; "I will tell you now Illiune. You must listen well. When the dolphins changed to people it was because of magic that only the spirits know. If you can believe you will understand. What I tell you now is why people call me "Old Liar". As a butterfly comes from a caterpillar, so did these people come from dolphins. When it was time to change they would roll themselves in a strange blue clay that would completely cover them. They then would spend some time in the clay cover and come out a man or woman. When the time came for them to turn from a man or woman to a dolphin they wrapped themselves in a complete covering of the magic seaweed. In time they would become dolphins." When Likum told of the magic weed Illiune held his hands up and could see what the old man had said was true. "Was it possible to be both dolphin and human at the same time, old man?" The question was asked almost in a whisper. Likum laughed low and replied. "Have you not heard of mermaids? Although I have not seen one I have heard many tales concerning them. Some have said it is because something happened to disturb their sleep within the cocoon." The statement of the old man frustrated Illiune more. His heart seemed to stop beating when he realized that the Serepein might stay as she was, a mermaid. Because of his weakened condition he spoke to Likum saying, "Please, old man, let us talk no more tonight."

CHAPTER 37

*I*lliune slept little. What Likum had told him filled him with despair and dread. He knew nothing of the Serepein except that she was beautiful and he loved her. Secretly, he had dreamed of her being a complete woman. Now he wondered if such a dream could ever come to be. He understood little of the change of the old people, but he realized that if the butterfly were not complete when it emerged from the cocoon, it did not live. The change had to be entire. This gave him some hope because the Serepein was alive and happy and graceful, and yet, she was only half changed. If her change were completed, what would she be? Was she changing into a human or dolphin? He then recalled how he had wrapped her in the magic weed and it healed her upper body and in place of the ulcerous sores there appeared the ivory skin laced with blue, gold and silver. The plant had healed her lower body also, but made no change. He wondered about it. Was it possible that she was changing into a human when something happened? Perhaps something like a typhoon which stopped the metamorphosis? Suddenly, Illiune raised himself to a sitting position and said aloud, "Yes! It is so!" Likum awoke and put his hand out and touched Illiune and asked, "What is it young man?" Illiune realized that he had spoken aloud and he murmured awkwardly, "Nothing, old man. I was only dreaming." Lying back on the mat Illiune's heart beat strangely and he placed his hand over the shiny shell. He remembered the sticky, blue clay he had removed from her lower body. It had been partially removed by something before she became covered with the slimy mud of the odious hole. If he could find the Serepein he would cover her with the clay. A feeling of excitement flooded him momentarily…and then he realized he did not know where the blue clay was found.

A tropical rain ushered in the morning and when it began to fall Likum arose from his mat and laid it over Illiune from the chest down. The old man did not mind the warm rain, but it sometimes could be irritating to one lying exposed. Illiune lay quiet and let the rain wash his face. When the clouds passed on he moved the old man's mat and raised himself up to a standing position. His leg was much better. While standing upright he could see Likum down at the edge of the water looking at the outrigger. Illiune limped slowly down to where the old man was standing and said, "Menseng mwow", (Good morning). Without looking around the old man answered, "You are much better this morning. It is good. After we eat we will leave for the village in the outrigger. This is a strange craft, Illiune. This type of boat has not been built for many years."

"Come, we will bathe at the pool since you are able to walk." Likum led the way and Illiune limped behind. The pool was warm and when they sat down the water was nearly chest deep. Illiune enjoyed the bath. It refreshed him and for the first time in several days he was famished. "I will need my lava lava, old man. I cannot go to a feast as I am." Likum remembered he had placed it in the pool to soak, but it was not there now. He waded out of the pond and went over to the hut and spoke. "Has anyone taken the blue cloth from the pool? The young man needs his clothing." In a moment one of the women came out and handed the lava lava to Likum. He in turn went back to the pool and gave it to Illiune. He looked at it closely and then spoke to Likum. "Someone has spent much time on this cloth. It is much better now than when I found it. When the women return to their village, old man, you will see that they are rewarded for their work." Likum's answer was brief. "If they will have it, it shall be so." The two men went to the hut for breakfast.

The tide was full at mid-morning and Likum suggested that the women go to the feast in the outrigger. They were told they could return the same way or take the trail through the forest. Likum did not know if the guards were still on duty and he worried for the girl. After the women had gone to the outrigger Illiune spoke to the old man. "We will take the hidden beads, my friend. Something tells me it is best." Likum went over to the wall and returned and handed them to Illiune who rolled them into his lava lava. Moving down to the water, Likum walked out and climbed into the bow of the outrigger. The women then stepped in and Illiune lifted the looped rope from the stake. The men each took a paddle and they passed quietly and slowly out of the slough and into the lagoon. Illiune could not put much pressure on his paddle because of his leg. Likum understood, and the journey to the village took longer than usual.

When the outrigger eased up on the sand near the center of the village, the King was waiting. "It is good to see you, my friends. I would have the honor of your company if you can walk with me. If the pain in the wound is too severe, men will carry you. They would be happy to give aid." Illiune smiled and spoke to the King, "We will walk with you, if you are not too swift. It is best to go slow." Likum stepped out of the outrigger and the three women followed, and moved aside while Illiune climbed out also. Illiune then motioned to Likum and Merrianna to walk one on each side and then nodded to the King, who turned and moved slowly through the crowd of villagers who had come to welcome them. When they arrived at the feasting place the King addressed the people. "My friends, I would speak a word with you. This feast is in honor of the young man who stands before you, wounded, but alive. When he left our village many weeks ago it was without dignity, because we would not allow him the respect we should have. We are all guilty of this. I was as guilty as anyone. This man does not want riches or place. What he had he has given away. To me he has given wisdom to be a fair judge of my people. To you he has given love for your fellow man, which you did not have before. This man had proved to us that love and respect are greater then greed or riches. Because we have one among us who would kill, and ravage, and lie, this young man has been wounded. He will recover because of a magic that he has power to understand. It is power and knowledge that Likum has told us about for many years, and we laughed at him and called him "Liar." He will now be a man of high place among us because of his awareness of the spirits. Now, let us enjoy the feast. Illiune and his friends will lead us."

There was much food for all. Yams, taro and breadfruit made up many dishes, boiled alone or in coconut milk. Pork, chicken, dog and fish were the meats prepared in special ways. Many fruits were provided also. There were different kinds of bananas, both cooked and raw. Papaya, mango, pineapple and coconut were piled high in baskets. "The people seem happy", Illiune thought. "It is strange how many traits humans have. Some are greedy and cruel. Some are generous and kind. They could be enjoyable to be with, but they have changing moods. Perhaps if they could not speak they would be happier." Illiune never considered people without comparing them with dolphins, after his experience with his friends of the sea. He remembered his visits with Likum. He could not imagine a free, friendly creature like dolphin would want to become a human. When he pondered the idea a strange feeling caused him to try to think of something else. He wanted the Serepein to be a woman.

Illiune, Merrianna and Likum ate together. They did not need to stay with him at all times, but Illiune pretended pain because he had an odd feeling that there might be danger. Even though it seemed unfair, he expected the unknown because he was with people. When all had eaten, the King commanded his people to follow him in honoring Illiune. The young man was embarrassed, but he could not change an order of the King. They walked by and bowed with friendly smiles and words of greeting. Illiune acknowledged the greetings and felt their intentions were sincere. Before half the villagers had passed by, he almost felt guilty of misjudging these, his people. Even the words of the trader seemed normal, as he extended his greeting. The last in line was his grandmother who stopped and addressed Illiune in angry tones. "You are liar! Dagus tell me truth. My boy Eliakim is dead. You lie to me. You tell me he is alive and give me one pearl. You steal also. You take coral and pearls from my son and say he is alive. You come home big man. Why you give Old Likum riches? They are mine from my son. Now you steal Dagus' woman for yourself. You say Dagus hurt you. Dagus will kill you! If you have more pearls he will have them. He is better man than you. You not my grandson. Dagus my grandson. He has hands!" Before she had finished she was nearly screaming with greed and rage and Illiune was sick at heart and shamed. She leaned close at the last statement and her breath reeked of strong drink. The people of the village were standing close around while his grandmother ranted her fury. He saw also a smile on the face of the trader.

For the first time since he had returned Illiune felt like hanging his head in shame and leaving the village forever. He put his hand on the shiny shell and squeezed until he felt it might break. Then, he lifted his head and taking both Likum and Merrianna by the hand he walked tall and straight to the outrigger. When Merrianna was seated, Illiune turned and helped the two women. Without a look back toward the village, he and Likum moved the boat out and homeward. All in the village and those in the craft realized that for this man of honor the day of feasting was a day of sorrow.

CHAPTER 38

There remained a strained silence as they glided along the lagoon and into the inlet leading to Likum's hut. Illiune's shame for his grandmother was not what hurt so deeply. He knew she had always been greedy and that she had never loved him. It was because of his hands and feet. She endured him because of this father, the son of his grandmother. She had called him "Likum!" (Liar). He had told her Eliakim was alive. He could accept the name, but she implied before all the people that he had stolen the riches from his father. Only Illiune could know that it was not true. The others would only know in time.

Many things occurred to Illiune that day. Dagus was still alive and intended to kill him. Merrianna was spoken of as Dagus' woman. He was sick at heart and nothing would change his feelings. He would leave this cruel place of piercing knives and words as soon as he could prepare for a voyage. When the outrigger touched the shore, Likum stepped out and secured one end and then turned the boat sideways to the sand and tied the other end. Illiune stepped out and helped the women to shore and then turned to Merrianna. He could not help, but see the strained look and tears in her eyes. Lifting her by the hand he helped her to shore also, but before he released her he whispered, "Awi", (wait). He motioned for the others to go toward the hut and then walked over to the girl and spoke to her. "Merrianna, you heard my grandmother. Do you realize that Dagus has not been found?" She nodded as tears again appeared. "You also heard that he intends to take my life?" She nodded again. "There is one more question for you, Merrianna. Have you pledged yourself to Dagus?" The girl gasped and jumped away as if he had cut her with a knife. "No! No! Never!" she cried and burst into uncontrollable tears. Her reactions not only stunned Illiune, but hurt him that he had asked. Awkwardly he tried to apologize that he had spoken thus, but he had to know. Illiune knew nothing of her suffering at the hands of the animal. In time she regained control of her emotions enough that he was able to speak to her again. "Do not worry, Merrianna, you need not fear anyone as long as I am here. No one would come here to harm you. Our King will keep guards around us until Dagus has been destroyed." There was a strong desire in the breast of Illiune to put his arms around her and hold her until all the fear had ebbed away, but he was afraid; afraid she might misunderstand and afraid that he might forget his vow. He only stepped over and took her hand and together they walked up the path toward the understanding friends at the hut.

They had moved only from the water to where they could observe the hut when they could tell something was wrong. Likum and the two women were standing unmoving, looking into the interior. When the two came up to the hut the women stepped aside and allowed them to look in. They too, stood stunned, unable to speak. Old Likum's house had been torn apart inch by inch. The floor had been dug up and the walls were slashed into ribbons. In time Likum spoke in a broken voice. "I too have been visited by an animal. He knew the guards were at the feast." Looking with grief at what remained of his old friend's home, Illiune knew it was the wealth he had brought to the village that caused the pain and bloodshed. It was Illiune's duty to rebuild Likum's home. Until it was done he would find another place for them to live, and he remembered his father's home nearby.

When Merrianna was safe with her watchers, Likum and Illiune walked together. They spoke little, but when Illiune appeared back at the hut he was carrying a spear, and at his side was a knife. No comment was made, but all knew. No man would come here to kill or hurt without paying a price. Illiune would be on guard tonight. The village men would come back to guard, but they would come much later.

There was nothing left of any articles worth salvaging. The destroyer had done his work well. Illiune spoke to the others. "Come, we will return to the outrigger and go around to the home of my father. There we will be safe and the hut is much larger. Tomorrow I will tell the King where we have gone. He would have sent men to repair the damage by now." They could say nothing and walked back to the boat and were seated.

The peaceful, sweet scented environment that surrounded them on the short journey to the next inlet contrasted sharply with the mood of the travelers. They watched fearfully as they moved from one small opening in the waterway to the next. While paddling along, Illiune remembered that he had asked Likum to take the pearls because of some premonition. He recalled painfully the words of his grandmother as she said, "Dagus will have your pearls. He is better man than you. He has hands!" Thinking about her raving gave Illiune some clues. Dagus had visited with his grandmother. Perhaps he was hiding at her home. Illiune did not fear Dagus, but he was dangerous. If they should meet only one would remain alive. Many troubling thoughts filtered through the mind of Illiune. They caused him to renew his desire to leave the village as soon as possible. This also presented a new problem for Illiune. He could not leave Likum or Merrianna. Before he could extend his plans the outrigger nudged the white sand where the fresh tropical stream flowed into the lagoon.

Illiune asked them to wait as he took his spear and walked up to the hut. Where it faced the lagoon it was open to the sea. He saw no one in the hut and then walked out back where the fence hid the hut from the land. Again he saw no one, nor fresh tracks. Someone had been there and the hut looked clean and neat. He could see where new mats had been woven into the walls to replace the torn ones. There were shining pots near the fire hole and several woven sleeping mats tied to the ceiling braces. The neatness of the hut reassured Illiune and he returned to the outrigger and said, "Come".

Merrianna walked up to the hut with Illiune. She spoke to him huskily and although he knew she was still crying within, her statement was made in concern for him. "You must rest awhile, Illiune. If you do not lie down now, the fever will return and we have but little magic weed." Turning from him she went into the hut and returned with a mat. This she unrolled on a flat area of coral sand. There was no purpose in resisting and as he let himself down he spoke to the girl. "You are very kind and helpful, Merrianna. I worry for you. If you will not be offended there is something I would tell you. My mother was a beautiful woman, if I can believe my father and Likum. She was taller than most and her skin was lighter as is yours. I do not remember her, but I dream about her often. Merrianna, the one I see in my dreams has a face like you." She looked at him and turned and walked into the work of the hut in tears.

CHAPTER 39

L ikum came over and seated himself by Illiune. He sat quietly looking out toward the reef, beyond the placid lagoon. Warm, spicy air drifted down the flowered slope and past them to the sea. Illiune knew this place. His home for seventeen years was as close to being paradise as one could find in a natural setting. Tropical growth of the surrounding area yielded many fruits. One could see bread-fruit and mango trees. Pineapple plants were set in even rows where Eliakim had placed them. Papaya and sugarcane were visible. Taro grew in a low area and banana plants leaned out from under the coconut palms.

"We must watch well tonight, friend." Likum said softly. "Animals become more vicious as they become more desperate. Do we have much rope, Illiune?" In answer to the question, Illiune replied, "Why do you need rope old man? Would you tie our spirits in? The spirit I have within is bitter. Yes, there is much rope in the outrigger." Likum rose and in a short time returned and tied off the front and side openings to the hut. He placed several layers of rope, stretched tight. The only place where one might enter was through the door opening to the trail leading to the village. When he was finished the moon was casting its silver glow over the small refuge. Once again Likum came and spoke to Illiune. "You will be more safe in the hut tonight, my friend. There is much room there for all to sleep. The women have offered to guard first. It is our desire that you rest. We will have need of you later, perhaps tomorrow." Likum helped Illiune to his feet and rolled the mat. They walked around to the open entrance to the hut and the old man handed the mat to Illiune and whispered, "I will watch a short while."

Illiune entered the hut and spoke low. "It is only Illiune. Do not worry." He was straining his eyes to see a place on the floor to roll out his mat when it was taken from him. Merrianna's voice was heard. "You must lie here quietly all night. Do you think we want to carry you? You are far too heavy. The old man and helpless women will guard tonight." With a flip of her arm, Merrianna rolled out the mat and Illiune let himself down to rest. He could feel a slight throbbing in his leg and it worried him. Unless his wound was completely healed he could not leave to travel south. The night was warm. Looking out from the hut Illiune watched the moonlight painting a silver tint on the palm trees. Far out beyond the stars were changing hues of brilliant fire. He had bitterness within that made him think he would not sleep, but the sweet warm air and distant trickle of the stream gently dropped his brow and lowered the coverings of his eyes.

Soft rain was falling when Illiune awoke to the sound of fire burning. When he opened his eyes he was surprised how late it was. Far out to the east was a golden blanket that the sun had cast upon the water of the tropical sea. He was surprised too, that he was the only one in the hut. The sleeping mats were neatly rolled and returned to their storage. Before he could rise, a voice sounded reassuringly, "Good morning, Illiune. I will dress your wound for the last time. You had no fever during the night. It is good. We have only enough magic medicine for this last covering." The voice stirred Illiune for some unknown reason. It was happy and musical, the way it was the first time he heard her speak. Looking around, he saw her standing beside Likum who had a pot of hot water in one hand and a clean cloth in the other. Merrianna held a leaf on which there laid a small heap of seaweed.

They removed the old dressing and washed the injured area with care. Illiune watched their eyes to know. Merrianna seemed concerned when the washing was done. "We will let the air and sun dry the wound before we replace the dressing. You will lie here quietly and unmoving while we go out for fruit." Her words caused an inward frown on Illiune's features. "How strange women are", he mused. "Does she think I am a little boy?" He was unnerved because she was giving him orders and he had noticed the old man's expression of knowing because of the twinkle in his eye. There was much Illiune did not understand. Merrianna was worried about the wounded area and wanted to speak to Likum in private, "His leg looks very strange, old man. I have never seen any wound like that. There is no fever or infection, but the skin is rough, like that of a shark. Perhaps we should put oil on it before the seaweed is applied. What do you think, old man?" Likum did not answer immediately. He stood quiet, pondering. He then reached out and touched Merrianna's hand as if to say, "You wait here a moment", and he went in and knelt beside Illiune. "Will you tell me if you have used the magic weed on your skin before, Illiune? It is important that I know. Did you use anything with the plant? Did you place oil on the wound beneath the seaweed? What happens when the wound is completely healed?" Illiune heard the old man's questions and replied. "Merrianna is a nurse, Likum. Tell her to come in."

When they were both sitting beside Illiune he smiled at them and said, "I must be very ill if you cannot discuss my condition aloud. Should I not know? To whom does the leg belong? The wound feels well this morning, but I know it is not sealed. Because of that it will need one more dressing. I do not understand all the secrets of the magic plant. Now please listen well and I will tell you of some of the mysteries which have been revealed to me." Before he began speaking he raised himself into a sitting position and leaned back against the wall.

"I have used the magic weed to dress wounds on my leg where the shark had hold of me. The cuts were very deep and inflamed. There was an oozing of blood and water, and it throbbed constantly. The magic weed was brought by dolphins. They kept a good supply so the wound was covered until it healed. Now you see where the wound was. It is like the scales of a fish, but the leg is healed and it serves me well. Now you worry because my wound is rough. My lower leg was also like this before the last dressing was applied. Do you see my hands? They also have shiny scales where the magic weed was pressed while applying the dressing to my leg. I have learned to think my hands and leg are marks of beauty. I cannot tell you why. As soon as the King knows where we are, I will ask him to place guards around this hut also. We will then go out on the sea in my outrigger and you will see mysteries you will not believe. All I ask is that you tell no one. When I have gone, which I must, then you will tell the King the secrets. This is all I can tell you now. Please put the last dressing on. There is much to do."

When Illiune had finished speaking, there was not a sound among the three, only quiet breathing. In time they moved to dress the wound and Merrianna said softly one more time. "A strange medicine for a strange man." The shrill whistle broke the trance of those in the hut, and Likum raised quickly to his feet and grabbing his spear he stepped out the door. He had just disappeared when Merrianna said, "Someone comes. It was the signal from one of the women on watch." With the coming of a visitor Illiune rose and dropping his hand to his knife, he followed Likum out the door. He could see the old man, spear in hand, crouching behind a taro plant where the trail crossed a swampy area of the stream. It was perhaps five minutes later that a man emerged from the foliage and stepped out into the bright sunlight of the clearing. He carried a machete at his side and in one hand a spear, as one of the King's men. Likum addressed the man from his place of hiding. "We are expecting visitors. If you come in peace, come to the stream and lay your weapons aside." The man obeyed without question, and Likum stepped out and walked unafraid to greet the man. "We cannot be too careful, friend. Please excuse our rude welcome. Now come, let us talk." The man sat down near Likum and the old man called for Illiune to come also. Likum asked, "How is it that you are here, friend?" The man spoke readily. "The King has sent all his trustworthy men in search of you. He is very impatient that Dagus has not been found and he fears for your safety. When we find you the King would offer you protection in two ways. You may come to the village or he will send a double guard. What would you that I tell the King?"

Both Likum and Illiune waited, pondering. In time Illiune answered. "Speak this to the King: He heard the accusations concerning my father yesterday. By now he knows that the evil man has destroyed the home of Likum. For these reasons we would desire that he send the guard to keep this, my home, safe. Tell him also we will see him this afternoon at the beach. We will wait here until we see the friendly guards. We thank you for coming, friend." The man stood up and bowed and turned to gather his weapons, and then hurried up the trail on the run. After he had gone Illiune and Likum walked back to the hut. When there, Illiune called Likum and Merrianna aside. "When the guards arrive we will have the watching women here. We will leave as soon as possible and take the women to the shore at the village. I know the women are here to help watch and safeguard Merrianna while she acts as my nurse. I am well now. I will not need a nurse longer. The women will be free to return to their homes and I will pay them for their work. I would like for you and Merrianna to go with me to the open water. When we return she may also go home and I will pay her a double portion."

After Illiune left Likum and the girl, he considered all he had told them, and he half-smiled and murmured to himself. "I talk much." He then went down to the outrigger and bailed out the rainwater.

When he was nearly finished, the voice of Likum interrupted him. "We would speak with you Illiune. It is of importance." Looking up he saw the old man with Merrianna. Illiune was aware of Likum's urgency and he waded ashore and sat down. "Speak friends," he offered. There was not much time. The guards would come soon. 'There is something we would have you know Illiune. Merrianna will not return to the village. The King and I have agreed that she remain here as my daughter for as long as she wishes. She does not feel accepted in the village. We will bring the watching women to the outrigger as soon as the guards appear." The two then turned and moved toward the hut. Illiune was surprised by Likum's words. He wondered why Merrianna disliked being with the people in the village. Thinking of the suffering he had endured, he guessed it was because of her beauty or height. Perhaps it was because of her lighter skin. Some day he might ask Likum, but not now. Hearing voices, he looked up to see his friends coming toward the beach. He walked up to them and as he passed Likum he murmured, "See that they are seated and ready, old man. I will be there soon." Illiune went up and into the hut. When he was out of sight from the others he took two pearls from his lava lava and returned to the outrigger. Stepping in, he picked up a paddle and pushed out. He and Likum then propelled the craft out and away, toward the village.

CHAPTER 40

*B*efore the sun signaled mid-day, their outrigger touched on the shore amid the greetings of villagers. Illiune helped the two women out and said, "You have been very kind to leave your home and come to the aid of a wounded man. I have here something for you as payment for your work. You may go to the King and he will visit the trader with you. Do not go to the trader without the King." With the words spoken he gave each woman a pearl. Their eyes lit up and a smile spread over their faces. They would work for this strange man again. Illiune turned from the crowd and stepped into the boat. Before long they were passing through the channel that led out to the sea of mysteries. Illiune turned the outrigger south and east and continued paddling. The fresh sea air and open expanse of water thrilled him. He secretly wished he was on his way to the Island of Magic, but that would have to wait. While he was paddling he spoke to Likum and Merrianna. "I have asked you to come with me so you might know how it is I had coral and pearls and magic weed. If I told you only, you would not believe. Now you will see my secret friends." He turned and laid his paddle aside and lowered himself into the sea until only his head and shoulders remained above the water. He held the shell high and when the outrigger came to a stop, he put the shell to his lips and blew a long, shrill blast. He waited a few minutes and then blew again. Illiune then grasped the side of the outrigger and hoisted himself aboard.

They came leaping and whistling and within a short while the dolphins were foaming the water around the boat. Illiune smiled and let himself down into the water with his friends. He dove and they followed, spinning around him in tight circles, so close they nearly touched him. Illiune continued his playful antics for half an hour or more, completely forgetting Likum and Merrianna. When he surfaced, the dolphins would leap high in the air playfully, waiting for Illiune to dive again. Because of his leg, he motioned to a dolphin, which came up close and Illiune laid his arm over its back and the willing creature carried him around the outrigger in slow circles. The other dolphins continued their playing. Some would rise out and speed along the surface of the water with only their powerful tail in the waves.

Illiune slipped off the dolphin and after patting its head he swam to the outrigger. When he had seated himself on the boat he removed the seaweed from his leg and held it out to the dolphins. One came in close enough to touch the plant with its nose and whistled a cry and the water foamed, and they were gone. All was quiet while the three waited. Likum and Merrianna were speechless and Illiune was smiling expectantly. When the dolphins returned they brought much seaweed. It was fresh and strong and as Illiune took it from them he could feel the strange vibrations. As each dolphin came in, he patted its head and dropped the seaweed in the boat. There was more than enough in a short time and Illiune called them to the boat and pretended he was eating. They rolled away and when they returned they dropped fish into the outrigger. A few were sufficient and Illiune stopped them again. When he informed them he had enough, they would open their mouth and allow whatever they had to fall back into the sea.

In time Illiune reached into his lava lava and removed a pearl. He held it out and one of the dolphins came up and took it gently in its beak and held it for a time. It then returned it to Illiune and with a different cry the dolphins returned to the depth of the sea to hunt. Again they returned and each carried a pearl oyster that it dropped into the outrigger. Illiune again stopped them and when Merrianna looked at the number of shells, she guessed there were fifty. By this time Illiune had rested and he slipped back into the water with the dolphins. He swam slowly toward shore and when he came to an area where he found black coral before, he dove. The dolphins followed and when Illiune reached a depth of eighty feet he could go no deeper. Turning toward shore he swam along the bottom and located a small, black coral that he broke off and brought to the surface. The dive had winded him and he felt the weakness in his leg. Looking out to the outrigger he motioned for Likum to come in. When the boat was in reach, Illiune dropped the coral in and lifted himself once more into the outrigger. His plan worked well. By the time he had caught his breath, his friends of the sea were waiting with coral of different sizes and color, black, pink and red. When Illiune had collected six of each type of coral he spoke to the dolphins. "No more, my friends. This is more than enough. Our visit has been a happy one. I will return soon and go with you to the secret pool!" With those words Illiune raised his hand to the many dolphins who were looking at him silently and intently with a happy smile on the face of each. Illiune sat down and raised his paddle and began the return to the village.

Dolphins followed for a time. They jumped, whistled and cavorted in and around the lashings and poles of the outrigger, but never once did they touch it. Illiune then spoke to Likum and Merrianna. "Have you ever seen anything so graceful and beautiful? I have, but only one. This is one of the secrets of the sea. You have seen and you know this wealth is not of my doing." Turning around to the dolphins he spoke one more time. "It is time to return, friends." The dolphins whistled and disappeared in the sea.

Likum and Merrianna sat speechless. A great mystery had unfolded before them and they found it almost impossible to believe. Merrianna did not understand what Likum meant when he said, "It is a mystery of old that happened today. One of our own is one with the dolphins." Silence reigned until the outrigger touched the shore at the edge of the village. The onlookers crowded around as the craft rested on the beach, but when Illiune stepped ashore they faded back. "Likum will go to the house of the King. He tell will him we have returned with more coral." Illiune spoke so all could hear and as Likum waded to shore, a path opened to the house of the King. When the King came, all was quiet. They were waiting for him to speak, but he was astonished and for a time he could say nothing.

After the King had looked long and wondering at the great wealth of the coral, he spoke to Illiune. "Never has this village seen such riches. Truly you are a mysterious man. What is it that you would have me do?" Illiune answered the King as the villagers listened. "First you may choose a King's gift. The rest will be sold and the money equally divided. Half shall be put in keeping for Merrianna. She may draw from it as does Likum and grandmother. The remaining half will be given equally to the villagers today, if the King will agree. The pearl shells are to be opened by the young men of the village from twelve to eighteen years of age. We do not have divers today among our people. The young men are lazy and have no pride. When they see the riches they could have by learning to dive perhaps they will learn to become strong swimmers." Illiune ceased speaking and there was silence. The villagers could hardly believe what they had heard. In time, the King broke the spell. "You are a strange one, Illiune. Never have I known so generous a man. All the people of the village remember our cruel treatment of Eliakim's son with shame. I, the King, am asking you to forgive us. Now, is there nothing you desire of these riches?" Eliakim's son spoke once more. "I accept and honor your apologies for my past treatment. For many years I suffered. I do not suffer now. I am proud of my malformaties. To me they are beautiful. Of the riches, I desire none. I am poor among you and will remain that way. Now let us take the coral to the trader."

Many willing hands helped carry the wealth to the hut of the trader. He seemed anxious to trade and the King did the dealing. The trader again paid a high price for the coral, but he was willing. After they finished the trader spoke to Illiune. "I am interested in that strange shell you carry, friend. Would you sell it? Illiune was surprised by the request. He had worn the shell continuously since his return and no one seemed to regard it before, "What would you pay for this shell?" asked Illiune. He had no intention of parting with it, but he suddenly became curious. "I will give you two hundred dollars for it," the trader replied. "I do not think it would be of much value to the buyers on the ship," answered Illiune, "Surely you would lose money and I do not care to sell it." They greedy eyes of the trader began shifting and he blurted, "I will give you five hundred." When Illiune turned to leave he held the shell in his hand and the voice of the trader caused a hush to envelop the scene. "I will pay two thousand!" Illiune walked on. The danger was greater than ever. The trader had somehow discovered the secret of the shell!

Before leaving the village, Illiune addressed the King. "I have a request of you, sir. Something tells me the danger to my friends and I has increased ten fold. It is not because of me, I worry, but the old man is valuable to your people and the young lady has a life yet to live. Could the King give us continued guarding until the danger is over? Also, because of my friends, I would have two of your men travel with us on the outrigger." The King looked long at Illiune. He seemed deeply concerned. "Why do you say the danger has increased so, my friend? Yet I know it is of no use to ask. You may be a poor man, but you are proud. It is good for a man to have pride. You could wear clothing of a great King, but you do not. With you, clothing does not matter. You have all the virtues that make a great King and yet you wear only a strange shell and a faded lava lava. I will say again, you are a mysterious man. You shall have more than enough guards and your boat will be supplied." With that statement the King motioned and it was so. The villagers opened a path to the water and two strong, willing men waited at the outrigger. Illiune instructed them to place the pearl shells on the bank where the younger boys could open them. He then asked Likum and Merrianna to accompany him to the hut of the King. When in audience once more with the King, Illiune spoke. "When one of us tells you the danger is over, you may call back your men. You are a good King. If the trader leaves your village you will do much better by trading directly with the buyers on the ship. We will go now."

The journey back to the home of Eliakim was uneventful. The two guards paddled and Illiune rested. Had he not been so concerned with the trader's desire for the shell, he might have enjoyed the trip. However, it was not so! Since he had returned to the world of men he had experienced much pain, worry, discouragement and danger. Approaching the shore, Illiune looked up. Beyond the hut he could see guards obeying the King's orders. They would be safe for now, but Illiune knew that in men, greed never dies, it only grows. After they disembarked Illiune spoke to the two men. "Thank you for being with us. Sometimes there is danger in the lagoon. You are free to go now." They waited until Illiune was finished and then replied, "We will be on guard near the water. We are good swimmers. No one will come near you from the lagoon." There was no need for more words.

Merrianna and Likum were busy preparing the evening meal when Illiune reached the hut. At the first opportunity he motioned Likum out of hearing distance from Merrianna. When they were alone Illiune asked, "Did you hear the offer for the shell, old man?" Likum nodded. "What does it mean, Illiune? Do you think someone was watching you call the dolphins? If they did, would they believe it? Merrianna and I were there, and yet we could barely believe." Again Illiune spoke. "The King has promised a double guard. They will protect us. Tomorrow we will visit the village one more time.

There are articles I would have for travel. This is only for your ears, old man."

Tropical islands are enchanting early in the morning or late evening. The closing of this day was beautiful beyond description. With the sweet flowered breeze filtering easily seaward, the three in the hut enjoyed a sense of relaxation they had not felt for many days. There was a happy mood during eating time. The fish were excellent and the three were satisfied when they had finished. With guards surrounding them they rolled out their mats to sleep. Illiune casually remarked that he would be going to the village the next day. Then, as if an afterthought he asked if they would like to go. It was settled before he finished speaking. Tomorrow he would buy his supplies for the return trip to the Island of Magic.

CHAPTER 41

$\mathcal{M}$orning came with a refreshing shower before the sun had shown above the sea. The three in the hut had eaten breakfast and were walking down the path to the outrigger. Illiune helped Merrianna in and before he could untie the boat the King's men appeared and picked up the paddles and motioned for the old man and Illiune to be seated. They pushed out, climbed in, and turned the outrigger toward the village.

Even though it was still early when they arrived, they were greeted by a friendly crowd. For the first time he saw several young men about his age. They too were smiling and it pleased Illiune. Before they left the outrigger, one of the men in the boat spoke to Illiune. "You will not worry for your boat. One of us will be with it until you return." Illiune smiled at the man and taking Merrianna's hand walked with Likum toward the house of the King. He had been told of their coming, and greeting them, asked if he could be of help. Illiune explained their intentions and asked the King if he would accompany them. He was willing and they walked with the crowd to the store.

Illiune first went over where the machetes were hanging and picked out one. He also bought a knife, long and pointed and a stone to sharpen them on. His next article was a box of imported matches that were coated to stay dry in the wet climate. He would have a fire to cook on his trip south. After these purchases he went over to the counter where cloth material of many colors was placed. He looked long at the rolls and after looking more closely, he took it to the man and ask him to cut off a piece large enough for a lava lava. While waiting he saw a small piece of pure white cloth with a bright hybiscus sewn on it. Illiune lifted it and turned it and remembered the hybiscus in the Serepein's hair. It was large enough to make a lava lava for her, and Illiune placed it on the counter with the one the man had cut. As he did he noticed a look exchanged between Likum and Merrianna, and he said quickly, "The small one I wish to tie to my mast." His friends only smiled. It was a weak excuse and he felt guilty for saying it. To the goods he added several bars of sweet-scented soap and a large bottle of perfumed hair oil. Taking his goods to the front counter, he asked the man to tell him the cost. When the price was given he paid with a pearl and the man was satisfied.

Before leaving he spoke to Merrianna. "If there is anything you would have you may buy it now. We may not return for a time." Likum and the girl moved off into the store and Illiune began picking up his supplies. There were many to help him and the goods were placed and tied to the carrying poles of the outrigger. Illiune returned to the store and found his friends still shopping. "Today is my birthday, Merrianna, so we will celebrate. You may buy whatever you wish and Likum and I will pay for it. You have served us well." She only smiled, and he knew she would buy little.

The King walked with them to the outrigger and the two men were there to take them to the house of Eliakim. They arrived at the hut before mid-day and Illiune wasted no time in preparing to leave. When all he needed was stored on the outrigger, he went up to the hut to say goodbye to Likum and Merrianna. It was difficult, and they understood. He took the remaining pearls from his lava lava and gave them to Likum. "It is not wise to keep them, old man. Perhaps when the guards are near, you would give one to each who has helped in protecting us. I will go now. I cannot remain longer. You will be much safer with me gone. It is I they want, or the shell, you will see." Illiune did not look again at either of his friends. He only reached out and touched each one on the hand, and then turned and walked to his outrigger. He untied it, stepped in and moved away.

No other outrigger was visible to Illiune when he turned toward the channel that separated the lagoon from the open sea. He passed through the passage and turned south and east. There was little breeze as yet, and he continued to paddle. For some reason Illiune decided he would call the dolphins. They would be company for the journey. Laying his paddle down, he hung his legs over the edge of the outrigger where they were knee-deep in the water. Raising the shell he blew a piercing cry and after a few moments he whistled once again. By the time he was again seated, he could see his friends coming from far out to sea. While watching them approach he decided to put up his sail. He picked up the mast and untied the cords. Dropping the mast into the slot in the forepart of the outrigger, Illiune let out the lower pole and an easy breeze filled the pandanus sail. He had just secured the rope to the outrigger when he heard a grunting snarl. He whirled to see Dagus leap aboard his outrigger with an evil smile in his eyes and knife gleaming in his hand. Illiune saw no more as blackness closed over him.

Where he fell he wedged into the narrow hull of the boat. The trader was standing over him and reaching down, grabbed the shell and ripped it up and over Illiune's head. It was then the dolphins struck. The first came flashing from the waves and its beak buried itself in the stomach of Dagus. The man screamed once in terror and pain and was then lost in a sea of foaming dolphins. The trader fared no better. He too, was caught in the midsection and went flying backward into the hoard of avengers. How long the dolphins kept up their merciless actions is not known, but when they returned to Illiune's outrigger, the mutilated bodies of the would-be murderers were being circled by sharks. All this was unseen by Illiune…for he lay unconscious, wedged under a cross-piece where the trader's blow had dropped him.

PART IV

THE CALL

CHAPTER 42

$\mathcal{E}$ liakim's first task was that of selecting a main mast and swing pole. There were many to choose from in the stand of bamboo and he was soon busy with his knife cutting a groove in the base of each. He then reached up as high as possible and snapped the poles off. He cut the tops by grooving and breaking them between two standing trees. Finding pandanus and preparing it for weaving was more trying. After locating the downed tree, he busied himself cutting the long leaves from the fronds and laying them out in the sun to dry. His first day back on the island was spent in these basic tasks. When night drew the darkness over the island, Eliakim had eaten and was lying in his bed of bamboo leaves. A warm breeze rustled the foliage of the growth surrounding the pool. The air was sweet and spiced with flowers. All this and his weariness soon caused him to sleep.

Early morning found him up and checking the pandanus leaves. As soon as they were dry enough to work, he would pound them to make them soft. If they were not softened they would break in weaving. There was not much time and Eliakim was anxious to continue his search. He had to eat well to keep strong. With this in mind he moved out through the dense growth to the reef to find fish. This took perhaps an hour from the time he stepped out on the coral. The tide was quite low and Eliakim had difficulty locating fish. When he did find some they were in a pool of deep water and he had to spend considerable time catching them. With two he turned toward his work. He determined to make a sharp spear for his next trip. Fishing would be easier.

Eliakim circled the island while making his way back to the pool. Wading along the shore, he came to an area where a thick stand of grass was growing. The typhoon had torn several large bunches out of the ground, roots and all and they were lying in the sun on the sand. He broke off a handful of the course grass from a dry bunch and found it pliable enough to weave. Eliakim decided to make a better covering for himself. Since the day he was thrown into the sea, he had worn only the ragged remains of his lava lava. Several times he had thought of weaving a new one, but it did not seem important because if his desire to find his son. Now he had time. It would be at least one more day before the pandanus would be dry enough to work. Eliakim busied himself gathering the dried grass. He then began weaving his lava lava. While working on the covering he thought it strange to be doing work usually done by women. He had not woven anything for many years. He had helped his wife weave, but that was long ago. The sail for his lost outrigger had been woven by his mother. She was a good weaver. When she wove for him she would say, "That is worth so many fish." or "Maybe now you give me two-tree dollar?" Eliakim smiled to himself when he thought of her sly way of getting what she wanted, but for his son's sake, he always tried to please her. He did not mind her playing games with other women, but when he realized she was spending money secretly for the strange drink of the foreigners, Eliakim was quite angry with her. Because he could not prevent her from drinking, he took Illiune home and had not allowed the boy to stay with his grandmother again. From that time on he would take Illiune for a visit and they would go home together. This was the beginning of the boy's education as a fisherman and diver and the beginning of a new companionship for Eliakim and his son. They became nearly inseparable.

Before the sun was overhead, the woven material was sufficient in size for his lava lava. He could not roll it in at the top and side like cloth, but by overlapping and trying it at the waist with a woven reed belt, he was satisfied. With the new covering Eliakim continued his way around the island until he came to the inlet of the bamboo pool. Because of difficulty in walking in the blue clay, he worked his way into the head of the pool by circling through the jungle growth. Eliakim could not stop to rest, even though there was little remaining to do. The idea of waiting for the leaves to dry caused him anxiety. Several times he made his way to the drying pandanus, knowing it was too green. Later in the afternoon, he took the pole that had been cut for the mast and fitted it to the raft. He then attached the swing pole to it by tying it with cords. Eliakim found that working was good medicine for anxiety. When he finished installing the mast and pole, the sun had dropped below the horizon to the west. He went into the island and returned with fruit and water. After eating he lay down on his bamboo bed and let the whispering wind carry his weariness away.

Rising very early, Eliakim threaded his way through the dark vegetation of the island to the pandanus leaves. As he knelt and touched them he could tell they were not dry enough to make a smooth sail, but could not wait longer. Gathering a load of leaves in his arms he carried them back to the pool. He stopped long enough to eat fruit and then returned for more pandanus. Weaving them was not an easy task, as they were not split in the usual small strips. Sometimes he would rip them lengthwise, but often he used them as they were. Before he was half finished, his hands were bleeding where they had been torn by the rough, sharp edges of the pandanus. In the late afternoon he left his weaving and taking a stick of sharpened mangrove, went out on the reef. His luck was better and he soon had two large fish. He carried them back to his work area and ate one. The other he put on the raft. Eating gave him renewed energy and by the time the evening shadows were closing in, Eliakim had fitted the sail to the poles. He knew it was poorly made, but it would aid him in his journey. Tomorrow he would move north.

CHAPTER 43

$\mathcal{E}$liakim set out from the island of the bamboo pool with the first sight of dawn. The tide was low and the water north of the island was quite shallow. Using his pole he traveled rapidly for the first mile and then a southern breeze came and held steady. Eliakim smiled at his good fortune and put his new sail to work. He continued to move easily and used the paddle as a rudder. The wind ceased blowing in the late afternoon and he proceeded with his paddle. When the darkness of night prohibited his travel, Eliakim turned in to the reef and slept on the raft. With the coming of dawn he set out again.

On the afternoon of his fourth day, the great, high rock, peculiar to the entrance of his village, stood out against the horizon. With his journey nearly over he found renewed energy. The wind was favorable for use of the sail, but he took up his pole and increased his speed. The sun was lowering in the western sky when Eliakim drew near to the channel that led into his village from the open sea. Before turning his raft shoreward, he decided to take in the sail. When it was wrapped securely he glanced out beyond the reef and was surprised to see an outrigger heading directly east, away from the village and into the open sea. He thought it strange, as most people would be coming in at night or moving parallel to the reef. Looking more closely at the boat he could see it had a load tied to the carrier, but could see no one in the outrigger. He strained his eyes until they blurred. There was no person to be seen. Before the sun dropped behind the island, Eliakim studied the sail. He had seen it before. It was the one he had seen leaving the reef below the island of refuge! Disbelief flooded over Eliakim. The outrigger was moving east with the sail set straight out and a south wind blowing. The more he considered the strangeness of it all, the more he doubted his reasoning. Had Eliakim an outrigger, he would have gone out through the channel and pursued the craft, but could not with a slow raft. In curiosity he turned his raft toward the reef and as he approached he could see a disturbance in the water just over the crest of the coral. When his raft grated on the reef, Eliakim stepped off and walked up on the barrier. He could see more than a disturbance in the water from there. Sharks were boiling the red colored waves as they tore at what Eliakim thought was a torso of a man. Once or twice it was lifted partially out of the water as the sharks set their teeth and twisted violently. He had watched for only a few minutes, and was sure it was a human body! Sickened by the sight and knowing there was nothing he could do, Eliakim turned and looked away up the reef. Not more than twenty feet from where he stood he saw another body lying on the coral. He walked toward it hesitantly, not wanting to realize what he saw was true. Stopping about five feet from the bloody, shark-torn body, he saw the face and then sucked in his breath in shock. The body was that of Dagus, his nephew, the son of his sister!

Eliakim could only stare and wonder. How the body had been thrown up on the reef he could not understand. The coral on which it lay was dry. He could see many bulges on the body, as if it had been terribly beaten. One other unusual thing about the body was that it had no hands. Eliakim could not carry it to the village and tell the King. With that in mind he hurried to his raft and with trembling hands pushed out toward the white sand beach across the lagoon.

A crowd of people had gathered on the shore as Eliakim approached. Some older ones turned and fled when they recognized him, but the younger stood waiting. As he stepped off the raft Eliakim spoke to a boy standing near. "Go tell the King that Dagus has been drowned and his body is on the point of the reef near the channel. Tell him also another man was being eaten by sharks outside the reef. Tell him Eliakim has returned and is going to his mother's hut." As the boy hurried to obey, Eliakim moved briskly off toward the home of his mother.

Eliakim did not think it strange because no one spoke to him as he passed through the village. He was used to their unfriendliness. It was because of his wife of long ago and the fin-like hands of his boy. Perhaps too, because he was a friend of "Old Liar". By the time he was in sight of his mother's hut the evening shadows were heavy in the darkening forest. Eliakim could see her sitting tired with heaviness in her cookhouse. He walked up quite near and said, "Kahselelia no no", (greetings mother). She looked up and as her eyes focused on Eliakim, she screamed with horror and confused babbling. "No! No! I did not mean it! I was only playing joke! Illiune is good boy! Dagus made me say it!" The more she babbled the more horrified she became. Staggering to her feet she took one step in flight and fell heavily to the ground. Eliakim could not understand her actions. He moved toward her and saw the empty bottled on the floor of the hut. He knew then, and when he knelt beside her on the ground, she still clutched a half-empty bottle in her hand. Eliakim put his hand on her shoulder and shook her gently. "No, no, (mother) it is I, Eliakim," but there was no response. She would sleep until late the next day. Raising himself slowly he turned toward the trail leading to Laud Likum's.

The shadowed trail was easy to follow as he hurried, nearly running, toward the home of the old man. Breaking out from the tropical growth into the open, he was aware of a man with a spear standing off to one side. He spoke to the guard saying, "It is I, Eliakim. Is the old man home?" The terrified guard blurted, "The old one is not at his home. He is at the home of Eliakim." Without another word the man turned and ran into the dense growth to safety. Eliakim did not wait to wonder. Moving out at a run, he crossed the opening and entered the darker area of the tropical cover. Why Old Likum was at his hut seemed strange, but Eliakim was so anxious to see his friend that he did not care to question now. Before he stepped out into the opening above his home, Eliakim stopped running to catch his breath. He was aware of the contrast of darkness beneath the forest and the brightness of the open area into which he moved. When his eyes adjusted he was stunned. There behind his hut was a tall, graceful woman hanging clothes to dry. Eliakim shook his head and looked again and though he knew it could not be, it was, and he tried to cry out, "Rosa!", but it came only as a whisper. Again he called, "Rosa!", and she turned, he saw that it was not and his heart seemed to drop into darkness. Eliakim could only stand and wonder and felt the tears of instant joy slipping down and away and could do nothing. The girl disappeared into the hut. In a moment Likum came out and looked up at the tall man in the grass lava lava. Both were nearly speechless. When Elaikim saw the girl step out again behind his old friend, he found the courage to walk toward the hut.

Reaching the place where the trail crossed the small stream, Eliakim stopped and said, "Kahselelia." The old man stood as if rooted in disbelief for a time and then blurted out, "Eliakim! Is it really you, or your spirit?" Stepping across the stream Eliakim answered. "It is I, old man. Perhaps we can speak?" Likum understood his meaning and turned and said, "This is my daughter, Merrianna. She will hear what I hear, if I do not offend you, Eliakim." There was nothing he could answer to Likum's statement and when he looked at the smiling girl, Eliakim's heart leaped with anguish. She looked enough like his former wife to be her twin. Eliakim was embarrassed that he looked so long. She only smiled and seemed to understand. When Eliakim spoke again it was a question that he managed to make audible only with much effort. "Have you seen or

heard of my boy, old man?" Almost before he asked, Eliakim dreaded
what he would hear. "Your son, Illiune, has been here several days,
Eliakim, but he is not your boy." The answer Likum gave Eliakim was
one of contradiction. "My son was here, but he is not my boy?" The
words puzzled Eliakim and he spoke quickly. "Do not be a joker, old
friend. Have you seen my son? Is he alive? Is he well?" Merrianna
interrupted before more could be said. "Illiune is safe and well and
was here until today." With that assurance Eliakim was overjoyed
and he felt as though his heart would burst with happiness. It was
than that he recalled the tragedy on the reef and his whole being
became cold with dread. He was stunned with anxious grief and he
questioned the two. "How did he leave? Was he in an outrigger? Was
he with Dagus?" All these questions burst forth from Eliakim and he
noticed the startled look of fear that touched upon the face of Merrianna when Likum answered. "Let us sit and ease our hearts. One
thinks more clearly when resting."

When they had seated themselves Old Likum began. "Illiune was
here. He came with great riches of coral and pearls. They meant
nothing to him. They were given to him by the mysteries of the sea
and his friends, the dolphins. Because of his great wealth, "Dagus,
his cousin, tried to rob him. That is why I am here. Dagus first tore
up this, your home, and then mine, searching for riches. Dagus and
Illiune could not have gone together. If Illiune were to find Dagus,
Dagus would be no more. Illiune left us only today with a strange
outrigger. He was returning somewhere because of the call of the
spirits. I say he is not your boy because he is now a man. He is by far
the greatest man this village has ever seen or known. He is much like
you in many ways. In strength he is like you, but taller. He is more
handsome than any of our village. He is like a King. People who at
one time looked down on him and mocked him, now follow him
with respect and awe. Even our King has honor because of Illiune.
Whatever he does seems to right a wrong or give comfort or peace to
those in need." The shadows were closing around the hut when

Eliakim spoke hurriedly. "Dagus is dead! I found his body on the reef. The sharks were feeding on another body in the water. There was an outrigger moving out to the sea, strangely, with goods aboard and sail set, but no one aboard that I could see. Tell me, did Illiune's outrigger have a patched sail?" The question came out quickly, but was left unanswered. "We have never seen his sail open, Eliakim. I cannot believe there was no one aboard if it were Illiune's outrigger. Perhaps he was playing with his dolphin friends." The answer from the old man made no sense to Eliakim. What did he mean, dolphin friends? For a time there was quiet and then Eliakim said, 'I sent word to the King of Dagus' body on the reef. Perhaps we can find out more in the village." They rose and started up the trail. Likum led and behind him followed Merrianna and Eliakim.

CHAPTER 44

$\mathcal{R}$umors of Eliakim's return spread rapidly through the village. At first many people were sure it was his spirit. They felt the dead father of Illiune came to persecute them because one of them had injured his son. Others believed Eliakim was alive in the flesh and had returned from a long journey. Whatever their reasons, all had gathered in the village to hear what the King would say.

When the boy related Eliakim's message to the King, his action was immediate. He sent two outriggers with four men each, to inspect the reef and sea in the area of the channel. During the time they were gone he anxiously awaited their return. The men in the outriggers were dependable and thorough. If they found the body of Dagus, the King would know that Eliakim was actually alive. The King would prepare another feast in Eliakim's honor. Perhaps Eliakim had returned with riches too. If not, he would be worthy of great respect because he was Illiune's father. When the men came back from the search, the King would speak to the people.

Upon the return of the outriggers a messenger notified the King. As he made his way to the shore the people opened a path for him and bowed. He arrived at the beach as the outriggers touched the shore and the leader of the men stepped out and reported to the King. "We have found the body of Dagus. It was lying on the reef. He has been broken in many places. We also found these floating in the water outside the reef." With the last statement he held up a torn shirt and pants. All who saw them knew who had worn them. They were the clothes of the trader. The man waited a response from the King.

The King motioned and some men walked out and lifted the body of Dagus and carried it up and placed it on the ground. Another man took the clothes of the trader and dropped them beside the body. The King instructed the people to form a line and walk past the remains of the two evil men. It was done, and except for the wailing of the mother of Dagus, no one made a sound or revealed any sorrow. Many who viewed the body of Dagus recalled the drunken screams of his grandmother when she was condemning Illiune. "You have no hands! Dagus has hands!" The King also recalled the words of Illiune when he spoke to the trader. "If you are not honest, you will be eaten by sharks." The people were waiting for a word from their King when a murmur of voices began and increased as another path opened from the outer edge of the group and extended to the center, where the King stood beside the remains of Dagus. Looking up, the king saw three figures approaching, and although he could not identify them because of the dusk, he could see the people bowing courteously as they passed.

Silence again reigned over the gathering as Likum, Merrianna and Eliakim stopped beside the body. The girl looked only once, hurriedly, and then held tightly to the hand of Likum, and Eliakim wondered why she revealed so much emotion. Perhaps she was more than a friend of Dagus. His thoughts were interrupted by the voice of the King. "Welcome to your village, Eliakim. It is solemn time for us, but also a time for relief. The body you see here, the same as it was on the reef, is that of Dagus, the son of your sister. He has done evil among his people. For many days he has been hunted by our men. They had orders to kill him if he refused to come peacefully. Likum will tell you later of his doing. The clothing beside Dagus is that of the foreigner, a trader, who lived here for a short while. He was also evil." The reference to the dead men was finished and the King changed the subject. "Your son, Illiune, returned to our village some time back. He has changed much. Likum will also tell you of his kindness. Our people wish to make apologies for our mistreatment of you and your son. We were bad people to act so. Because of the mystery of power which you, Likum and Illiune only seem to understand, we have been humbled and made to realize that man does not think good in himself. The nature of men reveals selfishness. Illiune came back with riches beyond belief and we desired them for ourselves. He has shown us that riches can be used to make men better. Likum will tell you more. If I may, I will visit you tomorrow. My men will light your way back to your home. Pwong mwow," (Good night).

The King led them back as far as his house and several men with torches accompanied them to the home of Eliakim. Eliakim was walking close to Merrianna, helping her by holding her hand and leading. She did not resist his help and as they neared the hut she gasped once and fell quietly and motionless on the path. Likum turned, but Eliakim was beside her. He lifted her tenderly and carried her on to the safety of the hut. He held Merrianna in the light of the torches as Likum rolled out a mat to place her on. As Eliakim laid her down he whispered to the old man. "We will need water quickly, Likum. She is not breathing well." By the time Likum reached the door he was met by a man with a container of fresh, cool water. "Thank you, friend," he said and turned and placed the water beside the girl. "A cloth also, old man," whispered Eliakim and when he had a cloth, he wet it and put it on Merrianna's face. Eliakim held the cloth and turned and questioned Likum. "Was she in love with Dagus, old man? I have never seen anyone act like this before. She seemed shocked but relieved and yet she swoons." Old Likum whispered an answer. "No! She only feared Dagus. He threatened her constantly and bruised her. She hated and feared him. Not one day has passed since Dagus stabbed Illiune, has this girl been free from danger. Even the many guards placed around us by the King has not released the girl from fear. The realization that she is in danger no longer caused her to faint. If she awakes…" Likum did not finish.

Neither Likum nor Eliakim was aware of the men around them. How long they knelt beside the girl they did not know. She had moved a little and they noticed a change in heartbeat, when a light appeared inside the hut and a woman dropped to her knees beside Merrianna and laid a hand on her face. "I will care for her now, if I may. She will need food also. We have brought something from the village. She will be awake in a small time, but she needs much rest." Eliakim turned and saw another woman building a fire. With a motion of his head he signaled Likum and then stepped out into the night.

CHAPTER 45

The two men sat in silence looking out on the moonlit water of the lagoon. There was much each wanted to ask, but neither would speak until they knew Merrianna was better. Eliakim did not know the girl, but because of his old friend, she was worthy of respect. He remembered speaking to her when he first saw her. Except for her hands and feet she was as Rosa, his wife. Her smile and figure and walk caused Eliakim to secretly look at her. Since that day his wife left him, many years ago, Eliakim had never thought of another woman who might take her place. Those thoughts caused a strange feeling of guilt and uneasiness to crowd upon Eliakim and he determined to begin conversation with the old man, in order to free his mind from the girl. Before he began a woman's voice called to them. "She is awake now. You may visit her for a moment." Both men moved into the hut and knelt beside the girl. She looked up and tried to smile, but they could see she was weak. She managed only to say, "I am sorry." As she spoke she moved her hand and laid it on Eliakim's. He was stirred by her action and as he looked into her eyes he answered, "Lipilipil", (It doesn't matter). There came a voice from above. "You must let her rest now, please. We will give her food. You may see her in the morning." As they rose to comply, Eliakim felt her cling to his hand and before releasing her hand, he smiled and murmured, "Pwong Mwow, Serepein," (Good night, little girl), and walked out into a friendly darkness.

Soon after lying down, Eliakim informed the old man. "I must leave tomorrow to find Illiune. I fear for him more now because of the death on the reef. There was an outrigger sailing east with full sail, but no wind favorable and no man to steer. You may not understand, Likum, but it moved in a straight line, as if someone were guiding." Eliakim waited while the old man prepared his answer. "Ke pahn kohla ia?", (Where are you going to go?). Illiune told us he was returning to seek the answer to a mystery that only the Spirits could reveal. If you have been searching for him for many weeks and have not found him, how could you know where to look?" Eliakim considered the truth to the old man's words. He was usually wise and Eliakim replied, "You speak with wisdom old man, but I must search for my son. I ask for the use of your outrigger. It is strong and fast. I will travel east for four days and then south. I will find the strange outrigger if no one is aboard. It cannot continue as it was."

There was heard only the whispering of the flowered breeze as it swept down from the ridges and seaward across the lagoon. Likum would reply to Eliakim's statements in time. Turning his head toward the forest above his hut, Eliakim could see the torches burning as the men waited to be called in by the King. Neither Likum nor Eliakim felt a need for sleep. The day had been filled with happenings, strange and sobering and both were concerned about Merrianna. The voice of Likum disturbed the stillness and his words were heavy with concern. "I will not ask you not to go in search again. It is only that I would go with you, but I will not leave Merrianna, for reasons I cannot explain. Illiune would not have us stay here knowing you are alive and well. He is under the protection of the Spirits of mystery. I have no fear that he is lost. We have seen great magic performed by your son, and it was not because of his power. All I ask is that you have patience until tomorrow. If she is able to travel, three have more eyes than one.

Likum's words comforted Eliakim. He would welcome company on the search and three would be more able than one. Thinking of Merrianna caused Eliakim to feel restless and uncomfortable. She had won the heart of Likum and perhaps Illiune. If she had he could understand. Many questions filtered through his mind, questions that might never be answered. Before sleep called Eliakim, he was again comparing his lost wife with Merrianna and although he experienced again the uneasiness, he felt himself caught in a strange web of desire. The more he pondered, the more he knew. Merrianna had won his heart also.

Dawn came with a cool wind moving the many trees. During the night a warm rain had fallen. When Eliakim rose to greet the day, the fire was burning in the pit and the odor of fish was strong in cooking. He went out from the hut and worked his way toward the patch of pineapple and scattered sugar cane. The bananas and papaya grew near the edge of the thick forest. After selecting the fruit he wanted, he returned to the hut along the path that led down and across the small stream. Before entering, he spoke through the woven fence. "Ho! Likum, are you awake old man?" The words brought a reply from the hut, but not from Likum. Immediately following, one of the women stepped out and offered with a smile. "Menseng mwow, Eliakim, pedilong", (Good morning, Eliakim, come in). He followed the woman and as he entered the hut he was greeted by Merrianna. She was sitting on a mat and she smiled up shyly as she held her hands out for the papaya. Taking it from him, she spoke in a musical voice. "I have rested well. Now it is time to be useful." Eliakim found it difficult to keep his eyes from her and because it was so, he motioned for one of the women to accompany him outside the hut. "How is Merrianna this morning? Is she as well as she looks, or is she pretending? It is important that I know." The woman thought for a moment and then answered low. "I know you have had a wife and understand the mysterious affliction of women. Merrianna is that way now, but by tomorrow she will be as strong as ever. The woman is weaker at that time and the sight of the evil man's body caused her to lose too much blood. Yes, she will be well by tomorrow."

CHAPTER 46

*B*reakfast of rice and fish and fruit was brought to Likum and Eliakim by one of the women. They ate in silence and when finished Likum spoke to his friend. 'The King and his men will be here this morning. What will you tell him? He will honor whatever you say. It is not necessary that you worry about your mother. Illiune has made ample provision for her. She is rich and the King will see that she never has need. Both Merrianna and I are also rich because of Illiune's generosity, but we would rather travel with you. We have talked about this. She is different from other young women because she is of royal blood and cannot marry a man of our village. It is custom that she must marry one in the lineage of a King. I tell you this, but you must hear it from her. See, the King comes now."

Stopping within speaking distance of the hut, the King halted his men and waited to be welcomed in. Eliakim came out and bowed to the King saying, "Kahselelia, mein ko", (Greetings to you all). Returning the greeting, the King asked, "How is Merrianna this morning?" Before Eliakim could answer, Merrianna moved out from behind the woven fence and bowed gracefully to the King. With a sincere smile and a musical voice she informed the King. "Thank you for your interest, sir. I am much better today. Tomorrow I will be as new." Likum edged out from the hut and coming forward, addressed the King. 'We are greatful for your kindness, oh King. Because of

Merrianna's sickness we have not had time to visit. We will make plans today. Eliakim would search more for his son, Illiune. The incident on the reef has spurred his desire to continue. With your permission, we would visit with you this afternoon. It is our plan to go to the village. We have business which we would have you oversee for us." Because of the finality of his statement, neither Eliakim nor Merrianna had more to say. The King answered firmly, "I will be honored to help you. It is the duty of a King." No more was said. The King turned and as he moved up the path, he held his head high and his men stepped in behind him.

Watching the group disappear into the tropical growth, Eliakim mused audibly. "There has been a great change in our King. His men respect him now. Is it possible he would actually be honored to help us?" Likum responded to his wondering. "He will help us. It will earn him more respect. Because of Illiune all the people honor him and he is a wise King. He is also a good King because Illiune said he was good. I cannot explain more. It is magic!"

When Likum finshed speaking, Eliakim asked them to sit for a visit. "I would speak to you for your ears only. Illiune is my son and I will go find him. I have made a vow before the Spirits of our ancestors. I will not rest until I find him alive, or proof that he is lost. Likum would go with me if you, Merrianna, will go also. If you wish not to go, Likum will stay with you. I must hear from you of your desire." Merrianna did not hesitate in answer. "Likum and I will go with you. I have no heart in this village. I have dreams also. If you would allow me to burden you, I will be happy to go." She let out her words with care as she gazed out to sea across the lagoon. When she had ended, she looked around to Eliakim with wonder in her eyes. Eliakim rose and held his hand out to Merrianna and helped her to her feet. Turning then to the hut, he walked with her hand in his and entered his home. To the women there he asked a question. "Speak plain talk to me. Is Merrianna well enough to walk the path to Old Likum's home? Is she well enough that she will not need you more?"

The women exchanged glances and then looked at Merrianna before one replied, "It is her choice. We would stay one more day if she is weary when you return. She is young and strong, but do not cause her to become too tired." The woman ceased speaking and Eliakim nodded. "Thank you. You have been good to come. We will be back before long shadows. We will see you then. Tomorrow we will arrange that you return to your homes." Eliakim turned and still holding Merrianna's hand, led her out to the fresh water pool, where Likum was waiting.

"Come, we will go to your home and ready the outrigger. We will go in to the village for supplies and speak with the King." Likum questioned him not. Eliakim's mind was set and they would do as he stated. The three moved up the path and as they stepped into the thick, shadowed growth, Merrianna gripped Elaikim's hand more securely. He wondered why she feared the forest. There was nothing that would injure anyone and everywhere one looked were scented flowers and fruit-laden trees. In time they emerged from the green forest and were able to look down on the old man's hut. When they neared the home of Likum, Eliakim stopped with Merrianna and allowed Likum to enter first. This he did and then came out and said, "Pedilong", (Come in). There had been much work done here also. No sign of destruction could be seen and Likum was pleased. Eliakim allowed his eyes to circle the room and then said, "I can see that Merrianna has made a new place out of your old hut, Likum. Now I can see why you value her so." There was no answer to his statement, but he could see a twinkle in the eyes and a smile on each face.

Eliakim moved down to the water and looked over Likum's out-rigger. Even thought he used it seldom, it was in good repair. It was an excellent boat and Eliakim smiled when considering how much better it would be than the old, slow, cumbersome raft he had traveled on the past weeks. He waded out and untied the line from an overhanging palm and brought the outrigger up sideways to the shore with the main hull near the bank. With a half coconut shell he bailed out the water. When finished, he returned to the two in the hut and said, "The outrigger is ready. When you feel prepared to leave, we will go." With that, he went up the path and began gathering fruit. When he returned, Likum was at the shore and Merrianna was waiting in the hut. He placed the fruit on the table and turned to Merrianna. "Do you feel strong enough to go with us? I will not leave you here alone." She smiled and answered quickly, "I will go", and held out her hand and they went down to the waiting boat.

CHAPTER 47

With both Likum and Eliakim paddling, they moved rapidly out of the waterway leading from Likum's hut to the lagoon. The air was warm and fresh with the morning rain and perfumed with many flowers. The lagoon was calm with a full tide. Before the outrigger turned into the beach a crowd had gathered and the three in the boat could tell they were expected. Eliakim edged the craft onto the sand near his raft. He stepped out and pulled the outrigger higher on the beach. As he glanced at the crowd he noticed a man standing near his raft. He spoke to the man in question. "Is there something about the raft that intrigues you, friend? Perhaps it is because it is so crude." The man moved a few steps toward Eliakim and bowed low. "The King has said no one is to touch the raft or anything on it. It has been under a constant watch." Eliakim returned the bow and replied, "Thank you, you are a good man."

Eliakim stepped to the outrigger and held out his hand to Merrianna. She smiled and lowered her feet into the clear, warm water and waded ashore with him. As they moved up toward the curious villagers, they parted and a path was made. They walked on to the home of the King, who, with his wife, was waiting for them. After greetings, Eliakim addressed the King. "We would sit and talk. What we say is for the ears of the King and Queen only." The King motioned to his wife and she turned and entered the hut. In a short while she returned with containers of water to which she had added juice from pineapples and limes. The three sat in the shade of a breadfruit tree and the King and Queen sat facing them. The King said, "We will hear you and forget. Speak." Old Likum answered for the three. "We will purchase supplies for a trip. Eliakim has vowed he will not rest until he has found his son. He has not seen him since the great wind visited our island. They were separated at that time by the Spirits of the sea. Because the vow was made, he must go. I would go with him. A mysterious voice tells me it is necessary. Now, we wish to ask you this: Would you allow Merrianna, the sister of the Queen, to go with us? She will be safe and respected. I am old, but I see well. She will, with your consent, become the wife of Eliakim. He is yet young and strong and we know he is the father of a King."

When the words of Likum entered the ears of Eliakim and Merrianna, they were stunned. Did the old man speak true? When Elaikim could look at Merrianna, she returned the look, shyly and her eyes answered the question. The depths of Eliakim was flooded with happiness and he reached over and put his hand on Merrianna's. The King was silent for some time and then he said only a few words. "That question is one the Queen must answer. They are sisters. As for me, I say this: Merrianna could not find a better man for a husband than Eliakim. I have known him for many years. It is with shame I say this because I allowed my people to be unkind to his son and his son's mother. I would honor him as a brother-in-law." The King had said much. It is not an easy thing for a man of high place to admit being wrong. The Queen raised her head and looked at her lovely sister. There were tears on her cheeks and she spoke with difficulty. "If you will have this man for your husband, I will not say no. You are not growing younger every day. I only ask that you come and visit us occasionally, for you and I are sisters of the same blood. Before Illiune returned I would not have allowed you to marry his father. Everyone was aware of the strange tales that Likum spoke. Eliakim was the only one who believed. Now it is different. We know the powers of the Spirits of our ancestors have visited our village and made wrong right and brought respect and honor to the King and I. This we have now, but did not deserve. I ask one thing more. I would have her spend this last night with me here, and we will see you on your journey at tomorrow's dawn." The Queen smiled and the visit was over.

The three arose and turned toward the store. Eliakim spoke to Merrianna. "Whatever you would have, you may purchase. Likum, you also may buy what you will have. See, here is something to pay for all." With the statement he handed the old man a large pearl. Likum rolled it slowly in his hand and then held it up to the light.

"It seems that it is not only your son who has a key to the vast treasures of the sea. Do you know the value of this pearl? Where did you find it Eliakim?" Eliakim answered the old man, but his answer only invited more questions. "I know not the value among traders. It is a rare pearl. I found it on a coral mound near the Island of the Dead." When he spoke thus, Merrianna gasped and her eyes became wide with wonder. She did not speak, but Eliakim stood close and reassured her. The old man stated with wisdom, "This pearl is from water very deep, only the old divers could have gone deep enough. There is only one I know who could have found it. His name is Illiune. The pearl is worth more than five hundred dollars where men trade for pearls."

The three moved on with a throng of people until they came to the store. Eliakim purchased a machete and sharpening stone. He also looked for a knife with good steel. After placing them on the counter, he asked for a box of wax-coated matches. He also picked out a container of perfumed coconut oil which women combed into their hair. Before he was through he added three boiling pots of different sizes. Eliakim went then to the place where cloth was sold. After looking for a time he selected a roll of material, blue in color, with bright orange flowers. He carried it also to the counter and placed it with his earlier selections. He would buy two things more.

He went back and picked out three sleeping mats of the best quality and several bars of perfumed soap, which came on the ship. Eliakim was through shopping and asked the man to tell him the cost of his purchases. There were many willing hands waiting to carry his goods to the outrigger. When he thought of the items Merrianna and Likum would buy, he walked away from the counter and returned with a large coil of rope. Vines had not always been easy to find.

Merrianna took more time in buying. She knew what a woman would need for managing a home and had much money of her own with which to buy. Cooking spoons and knives she laid out with several rolls of different kinds of cloth, some for cooking and cleaning and some for clothing. To this she added rice and salt and spices. By the time all the gods were gathered, and Likum, too, had what he wanted, the pile was not exceptionally heavy, but it was large. The storekeeper suggested they leave all their goods and they would be loaded and ready in the morning. They agreed, the bill was figured and Eliakim offered the pearl in trade. The store man looked at the pearl and said, "I cannot accept the pearl. The King must tell us the value and I will return what is right." Eliakim glanced at the man as if he did not believe what he heard, but Likum added, "It is the law now. The King must oversee all business which involves trade items." Elaikim bowed to the man and the three passed out through the many people to the hut of the King.

After greetings, Likum began. "Would you price a pearl for trade at the store? The man would not deal without your advice. I would wait here for your return." The King stood up and held out his hand for the pearl, which Eliakim put in his hand. He rolled it slowly and held it to the light. He then said, "Likum knows better than I the fair price of this pearl. It seems unusually large and of excellent color. I will tell the man it is worth three hundred and fifty dollars in trade. What do you say Likum?" The old man replied honestly, "The King knows the value of pearls. It would be a fair price." The King then turned toward the shore and walked away with Merrianna and

Eliakim. They made the exchange and much money was returned to Eliakim. He turned to the King and asked, "If you will agree, I shall pay the women who came to care for Merrianna. Would you have their husbands wait for us at the outrigger?" The King answered, "It will be." They then made their way to the hut of the King.

Likum waited until the three came back and then suggested to Eliakim, "Your raft must be made secure before we leave or you should give it to someone. If you have anything on it of value, we should have it on my outrigger. Perhaps you will take care of it while I have a word with the King." Eliakim bowed to the old man and he and Merrianna threaded their way to the water through the many people.

Likum lifted a small woven sack from his lava lava and handed it to the King. "I have never had a son or daughter. Eliakim has been as a son to me for many years. Merrianna has been as my daughter for only a few days. Tomorrow I would that there is a wedding for them here. In this sack there should be payment for all costs. Whatever is left, you may use as you like. It will make the heart of this old man happy." The King heard Likum out and then opened the pouch and tipped it up and the pearls rolled out into his hand. Likum heard a slight intake of breath and saw the surprised look on the King's face. "Because of what you have been subjected to by our people, I apologize. If it would please you, a wedding will take place. Many years we heard you speak the truth and we would not listen. When this strange truth was revealed to us by Illiune, it caused us not only to believe, but has given us a new purpose in life. Yes, we shall do our best to prepare a wedding fit for a Queen 's sister and the father of a King. I would not use your money for the wedding, but I know you wish it so. All will be done. It is an honor." The King exchanged bows with Likum and the old man turned and walked down to the waiting outrigger. Eliakim was talking with a man near the raft as Likum drew near. He had not yet stepped onto the sand when he saw a blue color on the raft that caught his attention.

Excitement stirred Likum and he could not help, but walk over to the raft and reach down to rub his hands over the smooth, hard, blue clay. He did not speak, but only looked, until he was sure it was the mysterious clay, which formed cocoons. He had seen it only once, many, many years before. He would speak to Eliakim as soon as they were alone. In time Likum waded over to the outrigger and stepped into the back and waited. After Eliakim finished speaking to the man, he and Merrianna walked up toward the King's house. The man near the raft pushed the craft out and with the pole he propelled it along the shore. Eliakim had done as Likum suggested. While he sat contemplating, he saw a small pile of the magic seaweed in the bow of the outrigger. Likum smiled secretly. In the last few moments he had seen two of the miracle medicines of the ancestors.

CHAPTER 48

The two men, husbands of the women at Eliakim's house, came down to the outrigger. "We are the men who will go with you. Our women are at the home of Eliakim." Eliakim turned to Merrianna and said, "Tomorrow we shall be here early. The night will be long." He turned and the four men moved out and along the shore of the busy village.

Shadows were many when they nudged into the sand near Eliakim's hut. The women were surprised at Merrianna's absence, but Likum informed them she was well and stayed at the home of the Queen for the night. When the outrigger was secured, Eliakim went up to the hut and spoke to the women. "You have been good to come and care for Merrianna. You may return to your homes tonight. Please take this as a gift from Merrianna. It would please her." He handed each an equal amount of money. The eyes of the women danced with joy and their lips formed a (Thank you). The four villagers then chatted up the path toward the village.

Much was the visiting that night between Likum and Eliakim. They had little opportunity before to feel free in conversing. Eliakim was the first to break the silence of the evening. 'I am grateful to you old man for your words which will make Merrianna my wife. I did not know that my heart was so plainly seen. Although I had my son these past years, they have been long and lonely. From the moment I saw her, I loved Merrianna. Please do not ask me how or why. It is something I cannot explain. I will treat her well, old man." Eliakim had opened his heart to Likum. The old man only smiled and answered. "If she were truly my daughter, I could not have hoped to have a better son-in-law. When she came I knew she would somehow remain. Illiune attracted her for a short while, but Merrianna soon realized that he would never love her as a wife. There is some mystery about your son. It would have been impossible to keep him here. He was compelled by the Spirits. To stay, his going would have been as impossible as stopping the waters from moving. A voice tells me we will understand his strange calling some day. It cannot be long, for I am growing old. Now let us speak of something other."

"The blue clay on your raft, where did you find it, Eliakim? Was there much there? Do you know of its power? Speak, For I must know." Eliakim was startled by the old man's questions. "Is it that strange old man? Where I found it, there is more, much more. It is unusual clay. When it is on your hands or feet, it is nearly impossible to wash off. I know not of its power, but it makes excellent sealing paste. When the sun dries it, it is like stone. I found it in a small pool on an island where I became well from my many wounds from the sharp coral. Some day I will take you there. It is not difficult to find." When he had finished, Eliakim waited for a response from the old man. He could not at first believe what he would hear. "The clay you found is that which was used by the old people, our ancestors, when they changed from dolphins to people. They rolled in the clay until they were completely enclosed in a cocoon. How they breathed or fed is one of the mysteries. It is common for insects to come out of cocoons. Think of the butterfly. If it is possible for them, it could be possible for dolphin people. Your wife, Rosa, was one who changed into a woman. She could not speak. Remember her hands and feet? When people emerge from cocoons they retain some traits and features of the dolphins. She was always kind and happy and smiling, was she not? So are the dolphins. They love life for the joy of loving.

They are helpful in all ways and yet they never possess the evil traits of people. In the old days people, our people, were more like dolphins. They could become dolphins, too. They changed by wrapping themselves in a thick covering of the magic seaweed that you have placed in the outrigger. Do you know where it came from, Eliakim? It has never been found by people of our time. Today it can only be gathered by dolphins or dolphin people."

Eliakim sat long in thought. He knew the old man spoke true. Yes, he remembered his wife and her features. He also recalled her constant joy of life and smiling face. Likum knew the secrets of her being and had never told Eliakim all. That was the mysterious understanding Likum shared with Rosa, his wife. This, then, must be the reason for Illiune's change in appearance and drive. He was beginning to understand that the powers driving Illiune were those of the ancient sea people. Illiune had been subject to the calling of the ancestors. He was answering that call. Elaikim considered all this with a certain dread or loneliness. Even if his son were alive, he had lost him. However, as he thought long, he felt a warm relief filling him with a strange joy. Illiune had to be alive! The Spirits could not work within him if he were dead. And, because he was alive, Illiune was still his son. When he marveled long he again conversed with Likum. "I know now, as you, that Illiune is alive. Had I not vowed that I would search until I found him, I would not go. As I have vowed, so must I do. We will leave as planned in the morning."

Rain, soft and pure, washed the island during the night. A more perfect morning could not have been. The two men prepared themselves special. It was a special day. Eliakim shortened his hair and removed the scattered hairs from his face. He bathed well and put on a clean lava lava. By the time he was ready, Likum had prepared himself and was seated in the outrigger. They moved out from the shore silently, as if afraid of waking the dawn. When they approached the village they could not believe what they saw. A sea of faces was awaiting them. The people were dressed in their brightest colors. Many women wore flowers in their hair and several men wore mar mars on their heads. They were met by the man from the store who said, "First you will come with me to the store. It is the wish of the Queen's sister." Likum motioned him on and Eliakim followed the man. When they entered the store, the owner handed Eliakim a bright yellow lava lava on which there was a brilliant red hybiscus embroidered with shiny thread.

The owner of the store smiled and said, "One of royal lineage must wear a royal lava lava. You will not worry about your goods. When you are to leave, they will be ready on your outrigger." Eliakim knew it would be so. Even he, Illiune's father, was beginning to experience the goodness of people, because of Illiune's influence. With the store owner, Eliakim returned to the outrigger and Likum. They then passed through a path of happy people to the house of the King. They greeted the King and he in turn bowed and said, "Greetings to you." As he moved his hand toward them, the man from the store stepped back into the crowd. Likum and Eliakim stood with the King amid a great throng of excited and expectant people. The King spoke to the two. "Would you look toward the water and see all those who have come to see the marriage and embarking. It is truly a wonderful thing to see people filled with love." As they looked they heard a murmur of awe from the crowd. The King spoke again. "Eliakim, you will now take your wife from the Queen." When Eliakim turned to obey he could not believe how lovely his Merrianna could be. She was also wearing a lava lava of the same yellow cloth. She wore a yellow mar mar on her head and a red hybiscus in her hair. She wore many fresh flower leis and a smile of intense happiness. He took her hand and turned to face the people. As their happy faces greeted the married couple, the King addressed the throng. "Today Eliakim has become the husband of Merrianna, the sister of the Queen. They deserve honor among you, their people. Now we will follow them to the feast."

As honored guests, the married couple led the others along the line of food of many dishes. The people had worked all through the night in preparing. The village was a joyful place during the breakfast feast. When all had eaten well, the King gave a command and the people formed a line and walked by the newly wedded couple to wish them happiness. Eliakim's mother came also. She was sad, but she was sober. The tears in her eyes were real when she spoke to her son. "I wish you well, my son. I have not been a good mother, but hear this: I will never touch strong drink again. When you return, my house will be open." With a sobbing cry she turned and squeezed into the crowd. Eliakim's heart reached out for her, but there was nothing he could do. He purposed he would visit her first if they returned to the village.

When the last person had walked by, Eliakim and Merrianna faced the water and a flower-covered path lay before them. They walked slowly, smiling, over the carpet of blossoms and when they reached the shore, their outrigger was loaded with food and water and the goods from the store were tied on and bedecked with flowers. No one in the village had ever seen such a wedding. "And it costs so little," Eliakim mused. "There will be more weddings like this. These people enjoy happiness." When they had seated themselves in the outrigger, several men pushed them slowly out into the calm water of the lagoon. As they lifted their paddles to the crowd, a happy song burst forth from the throats of the villagers. The melodies could be heard until their outrigger passed through the channel, and on out to sea.

CHAPTER 49

*L*apping waves softly brushed the sides of the outrigger in which Illiune lay. He began to hear and feel reality in the early dawn. His head throbbed and when he attempted to open his eyes he could not see. Fear gripped him momentarily, but when Illiune realized that the darkness might be the night, he partially relaxed. The young man could not tell where he was or remember where he had been. Sometime later, as the dawn yielded more light, he raised his head and tried to look out, but still could not see clearly. Shaking his head only increased the throbbing and because of the pain, he again slipped into unconsciousness. When he awoke later, the sun's rays were reaching skyward. Illiune worked his arms up near his shoulders and pushed. The pain in his head caused brilliant flashes of multicolored lights, but the young man steadied himself and his vision cleared somewhat. He was puzzled by the redness of the surroundings and because of the throb in his head, put his hand up and felt the lump on his skull. He did not remember falling. He could not remember anything. When removing his hand it felt sticky and he then knew why his eyes were blurred. They were covered with blood from a wound on his head.

Illiune sat up slowly. Realizing he was in the outrigger, he reached down and lifted water to wash his eyes. In time he could see dimly and wondered how the sail became set. There was no land in sight.

He determined he was moving east because of the rising sun at the bow. Looking behind he could see the wake of his outrigger, but there was little breeze. He was puzzled and wondered if the dolphins could help. He reached down for his shell and there was nothing. He looked down and felt again. There was no shell. There was not even a rope! Turning, he looked behind him in the outrigger. Perhaps the shell dropped into the boat when he fell but though he looked and felt many times, it was of no use. The shell was gone! A terrible loss gripped Illiune. He heard himself saying, "Soh, Soh", (No, No). But it was true! He struggled within himself to remember and he saw in a blurred vision the leering face of Dagus as he lunged toward Illiune with the knife clutched in his hand. The thought of the shell being in the hand of Dagus nearly caused Illiune to cry out, but he did not. He only bowed his head and in pain and despair he wept sad, bitter tears.

The playful song of the dolphins woke Illiune. When he looked out they were watching him as he moved they whistled softly to him. In exhilaration he reached out and let his hands slide along their backs. They seemed to form a line and swam by to be touched by him. Without knowing he spoke to them. "So, you have come to help me again. There have never been friends like you. You must help me to know where I am and how I may return to the Island of Magic. I have lost my shell. Could you help me find the Serepein without it?" All this did Illiune speak to his friends as he wondered. The dolphins swan steadily eastward as the outrigger led the way. Illiune decided to continue east one more day and if no land were found he would travel south. By the time the sun was setting in the west he had eaten fruit and drank water. Remembering the healing seaweed the dolphins had brought, he placed some on his wound and tied it with a strip of cloth. While sitting in the outrigger, he noticed that the white cloth with the red hybiscus was missing. It had been on top of the goods. This added to the worries of Illiune, but he could not think clearly. Before darkness closed in, he was lying in the bottom of the outrigger with his head pillowed on the magic weed. He slept soundly all the night.

Morning brought a brilliant sunrise, followed by a soft, warm rain. Illiune felt much better than he had the day before. His head did not ache and his eyes were clear. He ate fish that morning. It was brought by the dolphins. While eating the white meat, he wondered if anyone had ever been treated so kindly by his friends in the sea. It was a mystery and he could not fully understand it. With the playful dolphins surrounding him, the day passed rapidly and because he could see no sight of land, Illiune turned the outrigger south and adjusted the sail. The craft turned gracefully and continued its speed. Illiune ate fruit again in the evening and before the sun had dropped away below the sea, he was asleep. Illiune awoke during the warm moonlit night and saw millions of stars winking brightly. Occasionally he could see a phosphorous glow in the water where a fish darted by or was spooked by the outrigger. There was a slight breeze from the north that helped propel him along. He marveled again that the outrigger continued in a straight course without a rudder. "It surely must have been built by experts," he mused. When the night became lost in the morning's dawn, Illiune was still awake, waiting to see the first ray of the rising sun.

The outrigger sailed south all day. Illiune ate, drank and watched, but he saw nothing except the dolphins and the endless sea. The dolphins kept him occupied so that he did not become wrought with anxiety. As long as they accompanied him, he had nothing to fear. His confidence in the dolphins was complete. They would care for him. When he considered his experience with Dagus he was satisfied that his sea friends were more honest and helpful than his own people. Many were often good and kind, but their moods sometimes changed and they were evil or greedy. Illiune had no desire to return to his village. If he could find the Serepein, he would have happiness. In thinking of her, he wondered about the magic Old Likum had told him of. Could it be possible that he could find some magic clay and cover her? He would feed her and care for her as he had done before. To think of her becoming a human, beautiful and young was almost too wonderful to comprehend. Illiune smiled to himself and dreamed on.

All night he moved south and in the morning the sea was still landless. After eating fruit and fish, Illiune spoke to the dolphins. "I cannot seem to find land, friends. Is it possible you could help me? I would go to the channel that leads to the Island of Magic." The dolphins heard Illiune's plea and he could feel the outrigger changing course. When the turning was complete, he was moving directly west at the same constant speed. They continued on this course and as day turned to evening, Illiune became overcome with sleep and again he dreamed of the dolphin girl. Upon awaking the sun was no longer in the sky, but he could see a reef-line in the distance. As he neared the white breakers a wrecked freighter on the reef to the north convinced him that he was headed almost directly toward the channel. He was so absorbed in watching for the narrow opening in the reef, he did not see the outrigger moving swiftly toward him from the north.

In time Illiune sighted the small entrance and it seemed to lie in direct line with his course. Assured that he would soon be in the quiet, friendly waters, he let his eyes move northward. In disbelief and instant desperation he grabbed up his paddle and stroked madly at the water. An outrigger was bearing down upon him not a quarter mile away! Illiune paddled furiously toward the channel. He felt it would be his best chance of survival. Driving forward, he was sure that the strange outrigger was guided by Dagus. Fleeting thought caused Illiune to sense a strong desire; a desire to destroy that which was seeking to destroy him. In doing so he would take back the shell that had been stolen. Never in his young life had he experienced such a feeling. The thought, once planted, seem to grow, but in Illiune it calmed him and his fear and panic were replaced by a determination which increased his ability to plan.

As his outrigger entered and passed through the channel, Illiune hauled in the sail and with his paddle he swung the craft sharply and beached it behind the higher coral in the inside of the reef. He then took his knife and stepped into the water and ducked low, waiting for the evil Dagus. The timing was nearly perfect and in the deep dusk of late evening Illiune crouched as a lion waiting for its prey. The bow of the outrigger appeared and as he saw the outline of the passenger in the front he felt an uncontrollable rage. Dagus had stolen Merrianna! Illiune's muscles quivered with anticipation and as the next form appeared he could see Old Likum, sitting helpless, fearing that at any movement he would feel the knife of Dagus in his back. For a few seconds only, did Illiune take in this believable picture and his purpose to destroy Dagus increased. His leg muscles knotted with anxiousness as the form in the back of the outrigger took shape. Illiune crouched more and readied his knife for the thrust and as the stern of the boat passed in front of him, he saw the form appear within his vision. His whole being became one of a destroyer as his intent climaxed! He reared up, but as he did the form in the outrigger seemed to strike the knife from his hand and he dropped haltingly back into the water mumbling, "Soh, soh," (No, no). His body shook from fright and shock from what he had nearly done. The sudden change of feeling was almost unbearable. A sickness gripped him momentarily and he felt faint. He staggered backward onto the sand and was conscious of several voices speaking to him and then the warm steady embrace of a father who had found his long lost son.

CHAPTER 50

*M*errianna and Likum moved away as the father and son were reunited. Many were the words that could not be spoken. Tears of emotion were shed unashamed. The father was nearly overcome with happiness and Illiune was sick with what he had almost done. Every muscle in the young man was drained of strength and he would never forget how close he had come to driving the knife into his father's heart. Before the two could speak with calm and controlled voices the darkness had covered them with the shroud of night. The moon appeared and in time Likum and Merrianna returned to the high sand where the father and son were sitting. Illiune spoke to them plainly. "Please excuse my weak emotions friends. It is not every day that a son finds his lost father." There was no need for reply. The old man's wrinkled smile could be seen in the glow of the lunar light and he grasped the hand of Illiune and then released it and stepped back. Merrianna came forward and kissed him on the cheek. Although the light was little, Illiune saw in Merrianna's eyes a different look. She had happy features, like those he saw behind the banana plant and during the first few hours when she was caring for him in Old Likum's hut. His wondering ceased when Eliakim spoke.

"Please do not be offended in what I say, Illiune. Merrianna and I were married before we left the village. The many long and lonely days are gone forever. I will love her always. We do not intend to return to the village to live, but we will go back to visit. Likum would not stay at the village when he knew I was continuing my search for you. Finding you has made a father's sad heart happy. Do you approve of our marriage, Illiune?" The last sentence was not uttered easily. He would have asked the question sooner, but could not. He waited for his son's response. Illiune was still in shock from the near tragedy of a short while before. His answer was long in coming, but when it came it was spoken honestly. "I am not unhappy because of your marriage. I, too, realize you and I need more than each other in order that our life is complete. There has been a mysterious calling which makes me know our lives must endure separation and change. You are my father and I am your son. That will always be. I can think of no one I would rather have you marry. Had it not been for the calling I spoke of, I would have been happy to have her for a wife. As it now is, I am twice happy, I have found both my father and his wife."

Eliakim smiled at his son and touched his arm as he said, "You speak as a man Illiune. I know you speak true. We will honor whatever it is that your calling requires. Until then, let us have joy in what days we may have together." There was little sleep that night. The father and son told their experiences concerning the ordeal in the sea and finding safety on the reef. Illiune spoke freely of the sharks and dolphins, but he did not mention the dolphin girl. There were times when his association with the Serepein of the sea seemed almost unbelievable to him. How could another believe it? His affection for his Serepein had never altered. If any change occurred it was a strengthening of his desire to be with her once more. After speaking with Likum, Illiune had determined to find her and if she had not changed, he would search for the source of the strange, blue clay. The more he thought of the possibility of her changing into a woman, the more enchanting his dreams became. In the early dawn both he and his father at last were sleeping. When the golden rays of the sun lifted above the peaceful sea, they saw and smiled down on them.

It was the soft touch of the sun's glow, which woke Likum. His stirring aroused the others and the faces of all wore smiles of happiness, as they looked out toward the glorious morning. The tide was partially out and Eliakim went over to Likum's outrigger and lifted out a fishing spear. Merrianna smiled a question to him and as he waited, she joined him and the two walked north on the reef. Old Likum spoke to Illiune as they watched the two walk hand in hand. "They are both as my own children. Nothing has made me happier for many years. Merrianna is so much like your mother. Your father was sure it was she, returned, when he first saw her. I could see they loved each other. It is strange, but true. So much has happened these last few days, this old man's mind can hardly comprehend. Could you believe the people of the village have a joy in life that they never had before? The King and Queen have much honor. They are good to their people and enjoy serving them. The trader is gone…" Illiune interrupted the old man. "What is that, friend? Why has the trader gone?" Old Likum nodded his head and told Illiune about the incident on the reef and what was found there. When he finished speaking, Illiune asked one more question. "Did anyone find my shell, old man?"

"About the shell I have heard nothing, but all seemed so strange. The body of Dagus was so beaten it looked as if every bone was crushed. Yes, it was strange. His hands were missing, as if bitten off by sharks. No one knew how his body was thrown up on the reef. As for the trader, your father saw the sharks tearing him to pieces." Illiune did not reply. Silence settled over them and the lapping waves washed the shore as he recalled the words of his grandmother. "Dagus has hands!" he remembered also what he had spoken to the King concerning the trader. "If he is not honest, he should be beaten and thrown to the sharks." As Illiune thought of the fulfillment of his words, he was aware of the power of destiny, to which he was subject.

Eliakim and Merrianna returned with fish and, as they approached, Old Likum spoke up. "She brings you luck Eliakim. I see now why you value her." As he looked at them, the eyes of the old man twinkled. They ate fruit and fish for breakfast. They also drank water from coconuts. After eating, Illiune informed them of his thoughts. "It must have been Dagus and the trader who attacked me as I was putting up the sail. I did not see but one. It was Dagus. I felt the lurch of the outrigger and when I turned, he was coming at me with his knife. That is all I remember. When I awoke the next day, I was far out to sea. My only wound was the cut on my head. The sea-weed has made it well. I have lost my shell. It was given to me for two reasons. One was to call the dolphins, as Likum and Merrianna know. The other reason I can not tell. One thing I know. I would have it back above all else." There was silence again. The three could see the loss of the shell was causing Illiune much sorrow. Likum knew the trader valued the shell. He had heard Illiune refuse two thousand dollars for it. He was sure the shell was the reason for the attack on Illiune. Likum finally broke the silence. "We do not know where the shell is, but you should not burden yourself with grief. If the shell is to be found, it will be. Let us trust the plan of the Spirits. What they purpose cannot be changed by man, no matter how evil. Let us say no more. We must act for today."

CHAPTER 51

Likum spoke wisely. There was no reason to sit idle. Because he suggested they act, Eliakim ask, "What would you do old friend? Is there some place you would like to go?" The old man looked at the three and then answered Eliakim. 'You said you could find the place of the blue clay. Is it far? I would go there." At the words of the old man, Illiune jumped to his feet and ask, "What is that old man? Does father know the place of the blue clay?" Likum looked at the young man, and before he could reply, Eliakim answered him. "Yes, Illiune, I know the place of the blue clay. I spent many nights there building my raft to search for you. I also spent many hours washing the sticky clay from my hands and feet." He smiled with his last sentence. Speaking in a lower tone, Eliakim pointed to his son's hands and continued. "Speaking of hands and feet, Illiune, I see there has been a change in the skin of your hands and feet. I do not understand how it has happened so rapidly, but surely it is because of the Spirits of Destiny. Your hands are now exactly as were those of your mother." Silence pervaded for a time and Likum added to the mystery when he said, "Only those of royal blood have scales of many colors. Yes, it is a secret of the Spirits." In time Eliakim returned the group to reality by pointing to what resembled a blue cloud on the line of reef far to the north. "The pool of blue clay is behind that small island. If two can use paddles with our sails we could be there by the time the sun is low." The statement seemed to stimulate the four and they hurried to the outriggers and moved north. Gliding out from the reef they were favored with a brisk south wind. They set their sails and their speed increased. The weather and wind combined to make the journey pleasant. Rain clouds shielded them from the sun nearly all day. Occasionally a light drizzle fell and cooled them as they paddled. Even before the sun touched the western sea, they were moving into the channel leading to the bamboo pool. The bright blue of the water fascinated Illiune and the old man. Likum had known about the blue clay for more than seventy years, but had no idea where it could be found. Why he had never searched here he did not know. He was sure it was in deep water, hidden from all men. They were still wondering about the clay when they entered the pool. Eliakim and Merrianna had already disembarked and were walking back into the maze of green to get fresh fruit and cool water.

Likum stood in the front of the outrigger as it glided easily to shore. He then stepped out and pulled the bow up onto the bank. Illiune seemed transfixed as he sat motionless, tall and broad in the stern. The secret dreams he envisioned were not known to anyone, but himself, and perhaps the Serepein. At length he stood up and looked down into the clear blue water. The old man watched Illiune. He saw him lean out and slip into the pool and because of the clarity of the water, he could see the young man swim slowly around the bottom. The old man's chest nearly ached for Illiune as he tried to imagine holding his breath as the young man was doing. He could not in several breaths, equal Illiune. In time Illiune surfaced, refreshed his lungs and dove again. There was not an inch of pool he did not investigate. When he surfaced the second time he seemed bewildered or disappointed. He swam back to the outrigger and lifted himself onto the stern. He again searched the pool intently and suddenly he slipped into the water and Likum could see him deep in the pool's center, moving his hands and arms over the clay in the central depths. As the old man watched, fascinated, he saw Illiune wrap his arms around a mound of that strange blue clay and as he did it moved in his arms as if it were a lump separate from the rest. Illiune returned to the surface and his features had changed from disappointment to a secret glow.

By the time Illiune had waded ashore and washed the clay from his hands and feet, Eliakim and Merrianna had returned, carrying fresh fruits and coconuts. They ate leisurely and visited about the island and the blue clay. Illiune had little to say, but when they had finished eating he addressed his father. "Would you tell me how and where you found my mother? You have never told me all before. Only Likum knows. I would know, now, tonight." Eliakim knew this was not the voice of a small boy. It was the plea of a young man and he had a right to know. Eliakim put his hand over that of Merrianna's and began. "I have never told you all before because of the grief it brought me. It is not that way now. I will speak plain. I found your mother off there to the west. In the morning you will see the large island in the distance. I was a young man then and full of adventure. I was searching for better fishing grounds when I came upon this strange island Likum had told me about many years before. I would not have believed his tales either but when I saw I believed. That island is the old home of our ancestors. There they built a beautiful palace of long black stones. Where the stones came from or how they were moved there, no one knows. There are many canals built of those stones. The canals lead into the palace and one can go in only when the tide is full. I was searching in this great palace when I saw a beautiful girl standing on a ledge near a pool of water. I remember her as if it were only yesterday. She was tall and slim, like Merrianna, but her skin was more the color of ivory. Her hands and feet shown bright in the sun because they had many tiny scales on them. Her hair was wavy and black like shiny, black coral. When I saw her I was amazed at her beauty and thought I must have been dreaming. I called out to her and she looked at me for only a moment and then fled away into the palace.

I searched for her for hours, but could not find her. She had been swimming in the pool because she left wet prints for a short way and then they disappeared. When I gave up searching I returned to my outrigger and spent the night. The next day I saw her again. She seemed lovelier than before. After many days of seeking and watching, I was able to speak to her and she did not steal away. I tried to talk to with her, but she could not utter one word. The only sound she made was a low treble. In time we fell in love. I cannot say how or why, but it was so. I named her, Rosa, because she was beautiful, like a flower. Likum told me many times it was the work of the Spirits and I was being honored by fulfilling a strange mystery. I doubted it then, but now I believe. All he has said has been true or come to pass. The rest about your mother, I think you know. She lived only a short time after you were born. I loved your mother with an intense love and she loved me also. Until I saw Merrianna, I vowed I would never marry again. Now it is past. I can speak of it as if it were a dream. That is all. Tomorrow we will go to the palace and I will show you where your mother stood the day I found her."

CHAPTER 52

Sleep came to all sooner that night. They were weary, but happy with the events of the day. The air was warm and gentle with a light breeze filtering through the bamboo at the edge of the pool. There were dreams dreamed during the night but Illiune's dream woke him in the early dawn and he caught himself crying out, "Please come Serepein !" Surprise startled the young man, and he looked around to see if anyone had heard him. If they did, they gave no sign and he tried to return to his dream, but like his mother, it fled into the palace.

Illiune arose and walked around the island to the reef and went in search of fish. Before the others were awake, he was back and had a fire burning and the fish wrapped in leaves for baking. It was a merry group which breakfasted that morning. They were prepared to leave for the Island of the Palace before the sun had risen. Again they were two to the outrigger and the breeze favored them as the island lay west of the reef and the morning wind was brisk and steady. The Island of the Palace was nearly five miles from the blue clay pool and during the long trip, not a sign of any other person did they see.

It was past mid-day when the leading outrigger approached the canal entrance to the Palace. As Eliakim lowered sail, Illiune also lowered his and they continued on with paddles. The passage had not been cleaned for many years, but because the tide was full, they managed to work their way into the center of the Palace. When Elaikim signaled to stop, they tied their outriggers and followed him up into the vine-covered ruins of the once beautiful place. They walked along a street and up a long rise of steps until they were standing high overlooking the canals below. Eliakim spoke to them as he pointed toward an area resembling a park with a pool, all built with the same strange, long, black rocks. "That is where I stood that day." They looked down and because no one was seen, they searched the many streets of stone and water with their eyes. Illiune hoped the Serepein might be even as his mother, but she was not there. The three with him watched as he continued to search out the Palace from where they stood. When convinced no one was to be seen he spoke to the others. "I would go search out the Palace. I will return to the outriggers before the shadows."

Because of what his father had told him, Illiune hurried to search. At every turn and corner and street, he thought he might find his dolphin girl, now a lovely lady, but he did not. He made his way to the place his father had pointed out and searched intently for some sign of hope. There was none. With an ache in his heart he turned and began to retrace his steps to the outriggers. He had not gone far when he heard the cry of a woman and halting to listen, he heard the cry again. He turned and hurried back to the high wall where he had left the three. When directly below the ledge, he looked up and saw Merrianna pointing downward. She seemed frightened and as Illiune turned his head to where she was pointing he saw Old Likum lying on the stone blocks, half hidden by the foliage. Illiune hurried over and knelt beside the old man. He was breathing slow with a rattle in his chest. There was blood, fresh and red and Illiune knew he had been cut when he fell. Before Illiune had time to roll Likum or straightn his body, Eliakim and Merrianna were bending over him. Merrianna felt of his wrist and looked into his eyes. She spoke quickly to the men. "Go now and bring the magic weed. The old man is very weak. If it cannot help, we will lose him." The two men hurried off and were soon back with weed. "I will need cloth also. He has a deep cut on his head. It will require a pressure bandage. His hand, too, has a ragged wound."

Merrianna's training was of great help. She felt along the old man's sides and spoke again. "He has broken ribs. He will be sick many days." They worked steadily with the magic weed and in time the old man was breathing easier. The blood had stopped oozing from his head, but the hand was still showing bright red blood. "He has severed an artery", Merrianna stated. "Let us hope it will seal quickly." There was little to say as they looked down upon the old friend. All owed him much, which they could never repay. "He was much like a dolphin," Illiune stated low. "I have never known him to be angry. His whole life has been spent in trying to help his people and tell them of the old way. Because he has, he has known nothing, but scorn and mocking. It has been only the past few days that he has been heard. Yes, he was very much like the dolphins." Eliakim nodded his head in agreement and Merrianna said nothing. The tears on her cheeks revealed her feelings.

All night was spent in caring for the old man. Even though arrangements had been made for sleep, it would not come. When dawn came, it seemed hesitant and Eliakim looked up and then warned the others. "A squall is coming and it may be strong. We must find a place to shelter the old man from the cold rain. He and Illiune turned to search and in a few moments Eliakim called, "This place will do," and he came back to the old man. As he and Illiune lifted Likum, Merrianna whispered instructions. In time they had placed the old man in a room of the Palace, overlooking the outriggers below. The room was quite large and well covered with stone and tropical growth. At Merrianna's suggestion the father and son brought in several armfuls of dry leaves and Merrianna made a bed for the old man and he was placed thereon. The work was finished when the squall lashed the Palace as if to drive out the intruders. The black clouds hovered over the walled city, but in all its savagery, no rain fell on the four in the Palace room.

By mid-day the storm had passed and the sun and sky turned the ancient city into a glistening sanctuary. As the three were watching the transformation there was a low moan from Likum. All turned with one motion and moved to the side of the old man. Merrianna felt his pulse and smiled up at the two. "Your magic weed must surely possess great healing powers. Already his heart is steady. We will need more medicine if possible. It seems to be stronger when it is fresh." Eliakim looked at the old man and then turned to his son. "We will bring food here to Merrianna and the old man. We then will go for magic weed if you know where to find it." Illiune did not want to discourage them and when he spoke he said only, "We will go." The two men went down to the outriggers returning with green coconuts, fruit and a roll of cloth. They also left a machete with her and then Elaikim touched her hand and said, "Take care. We will return shortly." The two men turned and hurried to the outriggers. They lifted the woven covering from Likum's carrier and placed the goods from Illiune's craft onto the old man's boat and then covered all with the mat.

Stepping into the outrigger they lifted their paddles and moved out of the canal toward the lagoon. The journey out was difficult because of the half-tide, but by wading at times the two were soon in open water and traveled directly for the channel in the reef. The craft was fast and the two men strong and they passed out into the open sea in an hour. Only then did Illiune speak, "I do not know if I can call the dolphins without the shell. Let us hope that they will know this outrigger. They were the ones who brought it to me." The two held their paddles still as they looked out and around but they saw nothing, only the constant sky and water. After an hour of waiting, Illiune picked up a handful of the magic weed and held it under the surface of the water. He could feel the tiny vibrations in the mass even though it was quite old. However, being old did not destroy its value, as within minutes the water around them became alive with smiling, whistling dolphins. Illiune could not help himself, but dropping the seaweed into the outrigger, he turned and slipped over the edge of the boat and dove deep with his happy friends.

Eliakim watched and marveled at the unbelievable companionship of the dolphins and his son. The old tales of Likum returned to him as he watched a mystery of the sea. Because of the urgency of their journey, Illiune soon returned to the outrigger and reaching down he picked up the handful of seaweed and held it out to his friends. Their understanding seemed to be perfect and with squeals of anticipation they disappeared from view. Eliakim was spellbound. He was beholding a miracle of mystery. He could remember Old Likum's words, "You are part of the calling of the Spirits," and he felt suddenly very small and weak. The dolphins returned with much healing grass from the sea, and Illiune, in time, spoke only once. "It is enough friends. You will never be repaid, but I will return soon and tell you how you have helped." The dolphins whistled joyfully again and Illiune listened to their voices intently. "I have never heard such joy in their voices. They seem almost to burst with happiness." As he lifted his paddle to begin the journey back to the Palace, he heard a strange whistle and turned to look. There, within twenty feet of the outrigger, were two dolphins. They were raised about half way out of the water and between them was the white cloth with the brilliant red hybiscus. Illiune could say nothing, only look. In time he reached his hand out for the cloth and the dolphins smiled and disappeared. He knew he would not see them again that day.

CHAPTER 53

The father and son spoke little on the return to the palace. They were again favored by the wind and tide and it seemed, but a short time and they were winding up the canal to their place of departure. Tying the outrigger beside that of Likum's, they took up the mat and placed nearly all of magic weed on it and carried it up the Palace steps to the room where Merrianna was waiting. When she saw them approaching she rushed out and walked beside Eliakim as they carried their burden to the side of Old Likum. Merrianna dropped to the old man's side and removed the sea medicine from his head and replaced it with the fresh weed. As she did she could feel its vibrations and heat. She also put fresh weed around his side and chest where his ribs had fractured. When she began to change the magic weed on the hand, she uttered a whispered, "Oh!" and then turned and motioned for the two to look. As they watched she lifted the old man's hand and they could see the ragged edges of skin lying between his fingers. They could also see a rough sandpapered-like condition of the skin wherever the magic weed had touched. They did not need to speak to know. The old man had known of the dolphin people because he, too, was one of them. Eliakim whispered, 'I know now why he did not want the doctor to operate on Illiune when he was a baby. He was right. One cannot change the destiny of the Spirits." Old Likum had his hands and feet changed by someone, but it could not change what he knew. The attempt to hide reality only made him weak as a swimmer and an outcast among people. Those who looked down upon the kind old friend realized again that the powers of the Spirits cannot be changed by man.

The warming sun had dried the leaves lying on the stones after the squall and the two men gathered enough to make beds for all. They wished now they had taken time to gather fish. The old man needed meat. Illiune told them he would find fish in the morning and with that resolved they laid down on the beds of leaves, but again sleep was long in coming. During the night, Likum mumbled several times and when the men looked up, they could see Merrianna at his side with water or comfort and they both again knew it was good to have her.

When the sun touched the Palace with its fingers of gold, Illiune was walking up the steps leading to the room. He had fish, small, but many. He carried them on a bamboo limb. Eliakim saw him coming and set out for the outrigger to get a boiling pot and matches. Illiune laid the fish outside the room and saw Merrianna and Old Likum sleeping. "It is good they sleep." He said aloud. He prepared the fish and gathered fuel for a fire. The two men had food ready when Merrianna awoke and her smile made them feel warm and assured. "You make good women to prepare food," she said. "Now I will feed our old friend." Likum ate well that morning, but he could not sit up. He was helped by Eliakim and Illiune. When leaning back against the wall he seemed his old self again. "How long have I been sleeping, friends?" he asked. "Why am I so weak and in this strange place?" Merrianna spoke to Likum softly. "You fell and injured your head and hand old man. You have been sleeping for some time. The magic weed works well on you, too. Let us hope we can remove it in a little time. Illiune tells me that you might change into a dolphin, but we know he is teasing us." She watched the old man's face and eyes and could tell by the look that he realized they knew his secret. They laid him down upon the bed and wondered. "Do you think he would like to become a dolphin?" Merrianna asked. "It could be done. I am sure. He has told me." Eliakim spoke. "If he is not well in time, the magic weed will do its final work. We must watch with care. I have never heard of a creature that was half-human in the lower body with a dolphin's head. We will obey the Spirits."

The three watched the old man carefully, but they could see no change. In the morning Merrianna removed the dressing from the head and the wound was closed and there was little swelling. When she removed the magic weed from his chest and side, the soreness seemed to be gone, but the skin looked and felt like sandpaper. Illiune touched the old man's skin and spoke to them. "It is good he is well. Do you see the rough skin? If we cover him with the magic weed again, he will have scales where it is now dry and coarse. That is how my leg looked also, but my wounds were infected because of the deep cuts of the shark's teeth and neglect. I was frightened at first, but now I have no fear. On some it is a mark of beauty." Those listening wondered at his last statement, but they did not question. When the covering was removed from his hand they knew Illiune spoke true. Where the skin had been rough before, there were now scales, fine and shiny, gold and blue and silver. They smiled at the old man and he returned the smile and said. "Illiune and I have something in common." They all knew he meant more than the shiny hand.

The old man rested again that day and by evening he could walk alone after they helped him to his feet. Because of his condition they pondered their next journey. No decision was made until that evening. They had eaten and with the fire burning bright they spoke of continuing. Merrianna had no special choice. She made it known to all that wherever Eliakim would go, she would go also. The old man spoke. "We went to the island to see the blue clay because it was my request. We came to the Palace because of Illiune's desire. Now it is your choice Eliakim." The words Likum spoke were fair. Silence settled over them for a time and then Eliakim let his heart be known. "I am ready to make a new home for Merrianna and myself. You both, as a son and a father, are welcome. I would make our home on the island of the blue clay. The island was kind to me when I was near death. If an accident or sickness comes to one of us, it is but a three day journey to the village. Illiune has told me we may face separation for a time and I understand. But, as a father, I would know where he chooses to make his home, that I might see him. I would also that you are not too far from us old man. What do you say?" Eliakim finished speaking and there was little sound except the distant roar of the water on the reef.

CHAPTER 54

$\mathcal{T}$he surrounding darkness, in time, carried the voice of Likum. "I would see more before we separate, if you would honor an old man. I have heard of the Island of the Dead Kings with its weird cryings. One time long ago, I was on the island, but I was very young and stayed only a short while. There is magic on the island and I would like to visit it one more time. Since Illiune has told me of the days he spent there, I am more anxious to go. If you would go with me I will be satisfied. Afterward, I will help you build your house and then I will return to mine. I have respect and place there now and life will be better. Often I will come to see you. Your home, too, needs care Eliakim. What you would have done with it?"

Eliakim had occasionally thought of his home, but when the old man openly asked, he answered. "Speak to the King about it. If he knows of any poor young people who would live there and care for it, they are welcome. It would be good if that home could ring again with happy voices." Except for Illiune, all had spoken their wishes. In time he began. "You have been kind to me in all ways. I cannot now say where my home will be. You have seen strange and mysterious happenings that have not been of my doing, but of the power of Destiny. I know not where it will lead. I would that we all go to the Island of which Likum speaks. After that we may separate. I would have us together until then." The discussion was over and no one questioned what they would do. Illiune had spoken.

Because of the weakness of the old man, they did not leave early. They waited until the tide was full and then moved out of the foliage-covered canal to the lagoon. Far to the south lay a blue mist and though it seemed strange to the three, Illiune said, "See! That is the island which we shall visit." By late afternoon they could see the bowing tops of the coconut palms above the foggy mist surrounding the island. The mist added to the mystery of the place. Eliakim remembered seeing the island appear from fog and dissolve in the sunlight. He would follow Illiune to the island, but had determined beforehand that neither he nor Merrianna would walk on that forbidden ground. Had it not been for the miracles the boy had shown them, he would have pleaded with Illiune to keep away from the island also.

Shadows were long when the two outriggers approached the white sands of the shore. Because of the lack of light, Illiune suggested they turn out toward the reef and spend the night in the shelter of the square nut trees. This they did. When they touched onto the coral sand, Eliakim pulled the outriggers up and Illiune helped his father lift Likum out of the boat and stood him on the reef. In time the old man was able to walk by himself, but the three with him knew he was still a very sick old man. The sky was clear and before they had finished eating, the stars were glowing brightly in the tropical heavens. The breeze from off the island was warm and sweet. When Likum had been stretched out on the soft coral sand he dropped into sleep immediately. Merrianna and Eliakim were soon sleeping also, but Illiune lay awake pondering what the next day might bring. There seemed to be an unexplainable premonition of fulfillment crowding into his soul. He did not understand the reason for the feeling. He had lost his shell. It was his hope for reuniting with the dolphin girl. He remembered the clay pool and what he had found in the central depths. He had told no one, but thinking of it now added to the warm glow of anticipation. His visions of the dolphin girl, beautiful and complete, crowded in around him and Illiune, too, was soon in the land of dreams.

The morning sun came up to greet Illiune as he walked back toward the nut trees where the others were talking of rising. He carried two large fish. When they had eaten, Eliakim told them he had spent one night under those very trees. He told them also of finding a hybiscus flower, which had been tied with a blue thread. There was no response to the statement, but Illiune, for an instant, felt a hot flash caress him. His secret was being exposed. Eliakim also showed them the high coral growth on which he found the large pearl. When he spoke of it, all three looked to Illiune, but he seemed not to understand. Finally, Eliakim told them of the mat of magic weed he had found where the outriggers rested on the sand. He was about to continue when they heard the whistle of a dolphin and when they looked out they saw a silk cloth with a bright red hybiscus, being held by two partially upright dolphins. Eliakim had seem it before in the possession of the dolphins, but Marianna and Likum smiled at each other and the old man spoke with a twinkle in his eye, "So that is the mast on which the flag is flying!" Illiune again felt a hot flash engulf him momentarily.

He knew there was no use to ask the dolphins to bring his cloth to him. He turned his back on the dolphins, but turning did not silence their joyous whistles. He realized they were teasing him, but he did not appreciate teasing at the time. Illiune spoke aloud to the three. "I will go to the island. If there is no danger there I will return and we will all go together. It is early and we have much time. Perhaps my friends, the dolphins, will keep you entertained." Illiune then walked down the reef to the long coral spit leading into the island. As he made his way toward the beach he wondered at his uneasiness caused by the knowledge of the three and the teasing dolphins. One needed to be alone at times. Already he was feeling better.

Nothing seemed to have changed as he approached the white sand beach below his tree house. He looked for some sign of recent visitors, but there was none. He climbed up into the curve of the great square nut tree and smiled when he thought of the drive he had experienced in building the shelter. "It was because of man's custom," he mused, and smiled again as he let himself down and walked around to the hidden entrance of the secret pool. He was trying to hide his anticipation and anxiousness, but it was impossible. He raised the mangrove foliage and was about to step over the ledge when he saw strange blue marks on the top of the wall. Raising the limbs still higher and away, Illiune saw that the marks were made by the blue clay of the bamboo pool. Taking out his knife he scraped at the strange material. It was hard like the rock itself. How long it had been there, he could not tell, but it had been placed there after Illiune left the island.

His emotions caused an ache in his heart and his anticipation increased. Illiune stepped into the water of the secret pool and let his eyes inspect the interior. There were many rays of light entering the secret sanctuary and he could easily see all as he left it. Trickling water caught his attention and he waded over to the ledge and climbed up on the rock. He then moved to the fresh water pool and leaned over and drank. It was sweet, fresh, and cool. Illiune turned and walking to the edge of the rock ledge, he stepped down into the warm water. The ache in his heart increased because the Serepein was not there and he waded over to the place where he had laid the magic weed mat for her to sleep on. The mangrove limbs with foliage were still there. He had placed them on the ledge to keep the sick "Dolphin-girl" from rolling off into the water. He would not touch the limbs. He intended not to touch anything more and turned to leave. Illiune, the man, could not keep the tears from flowing. For days and weeks he had dreamed ahead to this moment, when he would return to his island and find the Serepein in the secret pool. Only those who have experienced such happenings could understand. Even though he determined not to falter, he could not contain himself. In weakness and in love he stumbled back to where his dolphin girl had lain so many nights. Dropping to his knees and weeping helplessly, he allowed his hands to explore the mat on which she had slept.

His breaking heart could not hear the voices of his hands as they tried to quiet him. He continued in the kneeling position until he could cry no more. When he rose to face reality he felt something clutched in his hands. Holding them up he saw, but could not believe. With a joyous cry he waded quickly to the wall and raised the mangrove covering and the brilliant sun revealed the shell shining blue, gold, and silver in his hands! Illiune's whole being flushed with happiness. The change of emotions was so abrupt he could not rid himself of the aching within. He knew he must calm himself. He would not be able to face the others in his present condition. Leaving the pool he turned and walked back into the green of the tropical forest, clutching the shell…his link with Destiny.

Several hours passed and those on the reef became alarmed that Illiune did not return. They had made plans to go in to search when they saw him walk out of the tropical growth and wade across the channel toward them. They could see he was holding something close, long before he stepped out beside them on the reef. When he was with them again, he smiled and said, "We shall see what mysterious revelations still hold. See, the shell was in the secret pool of Paradise Island. Only the dolphins or one of their kind could have put it there. I must call and thank them for it."

The tide was full when Illiune waded out into the pool on the seaside of the reef. It was here he had held his dolphin girl to him that last day. He remembered how she turned and trebled into the deep. Those on the reef breathed deep and watched in question. Illiune put the shell to his lips and blew a shrill blast. Within moments the water around him, as far out as one could see, became alive with smiling dolphins. The three watching, found it difficult to believe. They watched as Illiune dipped the shell into the water and as he did, the dolphins halted all their antics and looked at Illiune as if waiting for a command. There was not a sound that could be heard…and then there came a strange trebled cry from the shell.

No one moved, not even a dolphin. To those who observed, the world stood still. Silence surrounded and held them in. One more time Illiune dipped the shell and blew a long trebled cry. He watched out toward the sea, but the ripple in the water came from the lagoon behind Illiune's friends. They turned and looked and saw in astonishment! From the waters emerged a woman beautiful to behold. She wore a white silk lava lava with a brilliant red hybiscus. She was smiling and held her fingers to her lips as if to say, "Rong etcha", (Just listen). None had ever seen one so graceful, with ivory smooth skin and black, flashing, laughing eyes. They could see the belt of glistening gold around her waist. Above the golden belt, shimmering silver extended upward, forming a lacework over her breasts. Below her golden belt, the lustrous gleam became a shining blue that outlined the silk. Glossy black hair hung in waves and touched at her hips. Not a word was uttered by any. One more time Illiune dipped the shell and pierced the air with a trebled cry. The answer was instantaneous and as he whirled around he saw and knew! They had eyes for only each other as they moved, with arms outstretched and the three watching, saw a wonder of the universe portrayed by love.

THE END

0-595-23171-3